"YOU'LL F[...]
BARBARIAN!"

"Oh, but I will, demoiselle. Lacking any other source of profit, I fully intend to take my reward from your person." He stalked closer, watching her eyes widen. "Now, what do you have, demoiselle, that would be worth your virtue, your health, and perhaps your very life?"

His eyes fell to her necklace and he was about to name it when she turned to face him with a look of disdain so potent that he felt it like a physical slap. And instead, he demanded something he sensed would cost her far more than a scrap of gold.

"A kiss," he demanded. "I believe I will have a kiss of you."

"Barbarian," she snapped.

"Yes, a vile, bloodthirsty barbarian," he growled. "Count yourself fortunate that I have already had my supper this night." He covered her lips with his and there was no escaping his possession.

Other Avon Books by
Betina Krahn

BEHIND CLOSED DOORS
CAUGHT IN THE ACT
MY WARRIOR'S HEART

BETINA KRAHN

THE PRINCESS AND THE BARBARIAN

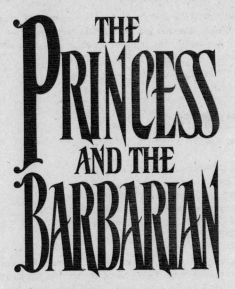

AVON BOOKS  NEW YORK

THE PRINCESS AND THE BARBARIAN is an original publication
of Avon Books. This work has never before appeared in book form.
This work is a novel. Any similarity to actual persons or events is
purely coincidental.

AVON BOOKS
A division of
The Hearst Corporation
1350 Avenue of the Americas
New York, New York 10019

Copyright © 1993 by Betina M. Krahn
Cover art by Mitsura
Inside front cover art by Victor Gadino
Published by arrangement with the author
Library of Congress Catalog Card Number: 93-90111
ISBN: 0-380-76772-4

First Avon Books Printing: August 1993

AVON TRADEMARK REG. U.S. PAT. OFF. AND IN OTHER COUNTRIES,
MARCA REGISTRADA, HECHO EN U.S.A.

Printed in the U.S.A.

RA   10 9 8 7 6 5 4 3 2 1

For Ellen Edwards,
whose skill, dedication, and friendship
have meant so much to me.

Prologue

Smoke hung in a vile gray-green haze over the skeletal hulk of what was once the great hall of the palace of Cardiz. The polished marble walls were now blackened, the colored window glass and magnificent carved furnishings lay in splinters, and the glorious Persian weavings which covered the soaring walls were reduced to wet, stringy tatters. The battle for control of the kingdom was finished, the rebellion extinguished. In the midst of the smoke and cinders sat iron-thewed Saxxe Rouen, on a step near the main floor.

The elbows of his massive arms were propped on his sinewy knees, his broad chest heaved behind battered leather and mail, and his huge, corded hand still clutched his red-stained sword. Beneath a haze of dark stubble, his chiseled features were fiercely set, and a trickle of blood ran from a cut at the edge of his long, dark hair, down his forehead, grazing the corner of his eye. Beside him, his comrade in arms Gasquar LeBruit was sprawled on the floor wheezing with exhaustion, his metal breastplate dented and spattered with red.

"Another kingdom saved." Saxxe looked around him with a sigh of disgust. "If you can rightly call this being *saved*. Another fortnight, another kingdom. . . . In the thick of fighting I kept thinking that Zarif the Usurper's men were the ones with the crimson turbans. Damn near got me killed. Crimson was Desmond's Dread Horde . . . a fortnight ago."

"A month ago." Gasquar raised his helmeted head from the floor. "But, then . . . who keeps track?"

"I hate this." Saxxe's green-gold eyes narrowed on

the precious colored glass that now lay strewn over the floor, amidst a spreading puddle of red-stained water. "We're always slashing and hacking, and defending and upholding. What the hell does it get us?"

Gasquar shoved up on one arm and shot a bleary look at him. Saxxe got like this sometimes, especially after a particularly nasty battle. "We get a pouch full of silver. And a fortnight of the ale and the demoiselles—"

"A pouch full of silver?" Saxxe snorted, pushing to his feet. "How long has it been since anyone paid us in silver?"

Gasquar's response died on his lips, and he squinted and rubbed a callused hand through his wiry beard, trying to recall. After a long moment under Saxxe's scrutiny, he brightened. "But . . . we have had the ale. And the demoiselles."

"And a fortnight of the headache after," Saxxe growled.

"*Oui* . . . a magnificent ache in the head after." Gasquar flashed a grin filled with unabashed venery. "It is how we know we have got full worth for our coin!"

"It's a damnable waste," Saxxe declared irritably, hauling up his heavy, silver-handled broadsword and looking around for something to wipe it on.

"It is our lot in life," Gasquar countered, watching Saxxe stride purposefully across the hall. "We are warriors . . . it is what we do. And . . . *Sacre Bleu!*"—he gave his burly chest a thump—"we love it!"

Saxxe paused in the midst of cleaning his blade on a bit of ruined tapestry and frowned. He *did* sort of love it . . . the lightninglike sear of battle fire in his veins, the pumping swell of blood in his muscles, the soaring sense of invincibility . . . the potent, almost sexual feeling of taking on three opponents at once and seeing the death fear in their eyes as he took them down one by one. Sometimes it was damn well intoxicating. But then came the foul, acrid aftermath of battle; the smoky halls and smell of scorched furnishings and red rivers of gore . . . the feeling of depletion. And, increasingly, a sense of futility. Like now.

"I've had a bellyful of fighting for other people's kingdoms . . . and lands and homes and heirs," Saxxe snarled, inserting the tip of his blade into the sheath strapped across his back and sliding the sword home. He propped his great fists on his hips and swung his shaggy head around, taking in the splendor of the caliph's audience hall, which, even in ruins, was more grand than anything he had known in his wayward, wandering life.

"I want a damned kingdom of my own. I want land . . . a great holding . . . with orchards, fields, and streams. And sons . . . a raft of sons . . . a whole houseful of them. And concubines . . . a whole damned harem of them, like that fat Caliph of Shalizar had." His eyes glowed hot and golden at the thought. "All different sizes, shapes, and colors . . . a different one for every night of the year. And a soft bed to sleep in night after night. No more sleeping on the ground or in caves or in pesthole taverns between hires. . . ."

"Ahhh." Gasquar lurched to his feet and staggered closer, pausing to wipe his blade on the ruins of a nearby curtain. "You speak of beds and women . . . the battle fire is not yet gone from your blood, *mon ami*. You would quench your fiery lance in a woman's sweet well, *oui*?"

Saxxe glowered at his friend. Gasquar had a way of reducing all problems to fit the space between a woman's knees. There were times when Saxxe appreciated that simplification of life. But not now.

"Think, my friend. We have roamed the entire world in these last five . . . six . . ." He paused and scowled as he came up short of the number he intended. "Just how many years *have* passed since the Holy Crusade ended?"

Gasquar dragged his battered helmet off and gave his head a thorough scratching. "I am not certain." He tucked his helm under his arm and began to contemplate his thick, sooty fingers. "We were two years with Louis at Alexandria and Damietta . . . then a season in Thrace . . . and then the wars of the dukes of Venice and Naples. Another year, we fought the infidel Moors in Spain . . . or was that two?"

Saxxe snorted disgust. "It seemed forever." He scowled, trying to remember, and found that the nature and durations of the conflicts ran together alarmingly in his mind. "Well . . . I had sixteen years when I rode off on the Crusade and now I have . . ." He lifted a sinewy fist and punched out his fingers one by one, his eyes widening. He tried again with both hands, and found himself staring at his callused palms in disbelief. "First I cannot remember how many years I have fought, and now I cannot even recall how old I am!"

"You and I"—Gasquar shrugged—"we have never been quick at the numbers, *mon ami*."

Saxxe paced away, his bronzed features growing redder and hotter. "Damn and double damn! Years—bloody *years* in the mercenary trade—and naught to show for it but a mess of scars!" he bellowed. He wheeled on Gasquar with burning eyes. " 'Prithee sir, he is my only son,' they say . . . and we take up arms and fight. 'My family home, my inheritance, my lands,' they mewl . . . and we ride out to rescue and restore. And then, when we have spent our strength and shed our blood in their miserable service, they turn their bald faces upon us, whining: 'The churls have plundered my treasury, goodly knight,' and 'Surely you will take your reward in heaven, sir.' "

He stalked closer, his voice dropping to a hoarse, determined rasp. "Well, I'm through storing up rewards in the hereafter—I want my share in the *here and now*. And, come the dirk or the Devil himself, I intend to have it."

He snatched up his shield and headed for the ruined door, stepping over splintered beams and groaning soldiers without breaking stride. Gasquar jolted after him, and soon they were striding across a courtyard garden littered with broken statuary and vanquished enemies.

"A fighting man has to look out for himself . . . make his trade pay. Silver is all a self-respecting mercenary is interested in." He halted in his tracks and raised a clenched fist toward Gasquar. "From now on, we fight only for silver. From this day forward, Gasquar my friend"—his eyes burned like fired bronze—"we demand cold, hard coin in advance, before rescuing or defending or upholding anybody."

Gasquar flashed a grin and smacked his hamlike fist hard against Saxxe's in a show of solidarity.

"Cold, hard coin."

Chapter One

The city of Nantes,
on the western coast of France—1262

The sea breeze rolled in, charged with the feel of an impending storm as it glided through the narrow lanes and crowded market squares of the bustling port of Nantes. All over the city, merchants and their patrons cast eyes heavenward, expecting storm clouds, and shook their heads in confusion at the clear sky. When the bells of eventide finally tolled the hours of Vespers, the merchants and tradesmen forgot their customary last calls and eagerly closed down their shops to seek the comfort of their hearths. As the sun's last rays withdrew from the streets, an unsettled sense of expectation hovered over the city.

Crown Princess Thera of Aric and her companion, Countess Lillith Montaigne, shared that sense of expectation as they sat huddled behind a carved wooden screen overlooking the inner court of one of the city's leading nobles. In the stone-paved yard below, household servants bustled back and forth laying three trestle tables with fine linen and silver wine cups . . . anticipating, as did Thera and her companion, their master and his party of noble guests.

The evening breeze wafted through the vine-covered trellises ringing the court, providing welcome relief to the two women in their hiding place upon the wooden gallery. But with each slacking of the breeze, heat and foody smells billowed from the nearby kitchen doors, engulfing Thera and Lillith in aromas of sage-stuffed capon and garlic-rubbed lamb. Overwarmed and aching with anxiety, Thera released a taut sigh and fanned herself with the edge of her mantle.

"Let me take your cloak, Princess," Countess Lillith said in a whisper, reaching for Thera's outer garment.

"Nay, I would leave it on." Thera clutched the top of the heavy woolen garment together at her throat and cast a forbidding look at her companion. A fine sheen of moisture covered her fair features, damp tendrils of burnished hair clung to her temples, and her vivid blue eyes glowed with a heat that had little to do with their uncomfortable circumstance.

"You'll roast like a guinea fowl, trussed up like that," Lillith insisted, wresting control of the garment and dragging it from Thera's shoulders, baring the pristine white of her fitted silk gown. "Faith—just look what the hood has done to your hair. You should have let me do you up proper plaits . . . or worn a crispinet." She wriggled closer on her stool and began to retuck wisps of hair into the long, single plait that began halfway down Thera's back.

"Don't fuss, Lillith," Thera said, brushing away her hands. "It doesn't matter how *I* look. No one shall see me but you."

Lillith sat back and scowled at her mistress. This was not the princess she knew. Her usual princess would not suffer the slightest disarrangement or the merest smudge on her garments, nor be seen in public with so much as a hair out of place on her head.

"But, perchance, if you are taken with the duc's manner and appearance . . ."

Thera pinned the plump, dark-eyed countess with visual daggers. "In that highly unlikely event, I shall slip away, back to our good host's house, and send Henri tomorrow with an inquiry on the possibility of"—her mouth puckered as if the words were distasteful—"marriage negotiations." The decision was made, and the subject, her royal annoyance proclaimed, was closed. She applied her eyes once more to the decorative holes in the screen, watching the movement below.

Lillith sighed and searched Thera's striking features in profile . . . her delicately arched brows and carved cheekbones, her straight, perfect nose, and her slightly squared jaw. She was the very picture of regal poise and determination. Or of royal stubbornness run amuck . . . depending upon one's view.

Crown Princess Thera Aric had been raised from the age of two years by her widowed mother and a covey of doting noble ladies, with the assistance and advice of a solicitous Council of Elders. Tutors were culled from the burgeoning universities at Paris, Orléans, and Oxford to instruct her in both the *trivium*—grammar, rhetoric, and logic—and the *quadrivium*—arithmetic, geometry, astronomy, and music—of the seven liberal arts. For strength and health, she was taught to ride and to swim, and for entertainment she had a menagerie of pets, a host of attentive adults, and a palace full of gardens and architectural wonders. Then, when she reached a suitable age, children of the kingdom had been selected to come to the palace to share her tutors and experiences . . . to ensure that she would know and love her people.

Every part of her life had been planned and guided with flawless precision. She had grown into a strikingly beautiful young woman with a wondrously keen mind, a deep affection for her people, and a strong sense of her royal duty. In truth, her extensive education had prepared her admirably for every aspect of her royal life . . . except the fact that she would someday have to marry and share her kingdom with a man.

"Perhaps the Duc de Beure will be tall . . . with hair the color of new-spun silk . . . and a face that would make the angels sigh," Lillith mused, watching Thera from the corner of her eye.

"Or perhaps he will be short, bald as a melon, and smell like overripe curds," Thera countered testily. Lillith frowned and tilted her nose, undaunted.

"Chancellor Cedric says Normans are wondrously fine bowmen . . . that they can nick the spots off a hound at forty paces."

"I shall remember that," Thera said, "in the event I should ever have a hound that needs a few spots nicked off. However, in point of fact"—she leaned closer—"Norman yeomen are the ones handy with a bow. Norman *lords* are always bladesmen ... huge, galumphing, radish-faced fellows who use their chins for whetstones and would rather sleep with their broadswords than their wives." The very thought of having to wed such a creature sent a shudder through her.

"Well, he will surely love to ride," Lillith asserted stubbornly. "Norman lords are unsurpassed as horsemen ... true masters of the arts of breeding and training horseflesh. And Elder Mattias says we could use new blood in Mercia's stables."

"There is nothing whatsoever lacking in Mercia's stables," Thera declared, her voice rising, so that Lillith's eyes widened and she put a finger to her lips. Thera glowered, but lowered her voice. "I know full well what Elder Mattias wants ... he wants horse races again." She turned back to the screen and leaned closer to it. "And what a huge waste of time and effort that would be. Where's the point in breeding faster horses, when even our slowest mounts can cover our entire kingdom border to border in less than an hour?"

"One and three-quarters," Lillith muttered under her breath.

"What?" Thera turned back with a scowl.

Lillith gave a start. "Letters. I said Elder Margarete insists he will be a man of letters ... able to speak a number of languages. She says Norman nobles educate their sons in fine estate."

"Fine only if you consider warfare, wine-bibbing, and oppressive taxation a proper curriculum," Thera said disgustedly. "Just imagine what sort of things a man who has applied himself diligently to such studies would add to the life of Mercia."

Lillith drew back her chin, annoyed by Thera's determination to dislike her potential husband, sight unseen.

"Well, we in Mercia never journey anywhere. Perhaps he will have traveled much and can tell us all about Paris and Venice and the Holy See of Rome." Her face lighted anew. "Perhaps he has even seen the Holy Lands themselves."

"Lillith"—Thera crossed her arms with an air of strained forbearance—"there are packhorses all over France who have seen the Holy Lands at one time or another. It hardly qualifies them for sainthood, either."

The countess reddened. "Elder Audra says he will have a fine head for numbers . . . will be deft at ciphering and quick on the beads. And Elder Jeanine is certain, if he has spent time in Venice, that he has learned the new Arab numerals and astronomy . . . so he can render star charts and do the computus for us—"

"*I* do the computus for us. I calculate the fall of feast days and Christ Mass and Easter," Thera declared, truly incensed now. "And if my counselors find the Duc de Beure so worthy why don't *they* bloody well marry him and leave me out of it!"

Lillith clamped her hands on her knees and blurted out: "Because they're not the heir to the throne of Mercia. They don't have to marry, according to law, in order to be crowned queen of their own realm. And you do."

There was the bitter truth of it. Thera glared down into the empty courtyard . . . seeing only her crowded and distressingly conjugal future. Married. It was the blight of her otherwise perfect life: she had to marry to be crowned queen of the kingdom she already ruled.

Since ascending to the throne two years ago, at the age of seventeen, Princess Thera had managed to delay, dissemble, and generally avoid the problem of finding a man with whom to share her throne. The Council of Elders, whose task it was to advise the princess and oversee the welfare of the kingdom, had grown increasingly distressed by the way she defied both their revered law and the sacred natural order to remain unmarried. For *order*—natural and otherwise—was what Mercians valued above all else.

In Mercia's isolated society, there was a reason and a rule for everything . . . including a rule requiring that the heir to the throne must be wedded before he or she could be crowned. Their code of law had grown out of the ways of the old Celts and embodied the old ones' recognition of the necessity of both the male and female principles in nature . . . and in the affairs of humans. The statutes set this forth in most emphatic terms: the kingdom would prosper only when governed by a king and a queen who shared both bed and power.

With the wane of each passing moon, the councillors eyed the empty thrones in the presence chamber with a bit more anxiety. Too well, they recalled the ancient prophecy warning of the woes that would befall the kingdom in the days of an unwed heir and an empty throne. For the last seventeen years, since Thera's father had died, the fates had been more than patient with Mercia and its youthful heir. The rains had been plentiful and the harvests good, the flocks flourished, and the fine cloth produced by Mercia's looms commanded good prices. Then came the unexpectedly hard winter just past, exacting a toll of their flocks and harvests, and the elders feared that Mercia's dispensation of grace had finally ended.

There the council and Thera had come to an impasse, for the same law which stipulated that Thera must marry before she could be crowned was also emphatic in granting her a choice in whom she wedded.

From the day her chancellor and the Council of Elders had requested their first official audience with her until this very moment, the shadow of her mandated marriage had loomed over her reign. The cursed phrase "for now" seemed to be an inescapable postscript to every proclamation she issued, document she signed, or opinion she expressed. It was as if her learning, her wisdom, and her hard work meant nothing unless validated by a man . . . a husband.

It galled her that a nameless, faceless man would someday stride into the palace of Mercia and, simply by virtue of his possession of a male member, claim half of the kingdom she had prepared all of her life to rule. Worse yet: with that same wretched appendage he would also lay claim to her . . . to the privatemost parts of her body, to her nights and days, to her womanly rhythms and fertility. She would have to share her throne, her table, her bed, and her very thoughts with this annoying interloper.

And what would she get in return? She glowered, thinking of it. A swaggering, snoring, sword-wielding boar who regularly mistook her for a mattress . . . a lifetime of galling deference to a man who might or might not even recognize his own written name . . . and years of watching her belly swell and suffering the recurring horrors of childbed. It was a humiliatingly unfair trade.

Her only hope, she had realized early on, was to be as slow and as selective as possible in finding a husband . . . so that she might establish her reign and authority firmly before admitting a stranger to her realm and her bed. To that end, she had decreed that she would wed no man without first setting eyes upon him. And it was to that end that she had journeyed from her isolated kingdom to the city of Nantes, to see for herself her chief matrimonial prospect . . . the Duc de Beure.

"Ever since we left Mercia you have been singing the duc's praises," Thera said, turning back to Lillith with a searching look. Her irritation had subsided, allowing the anxiety underlying it to reassert itself. Her hands curled into cold fists in her lap. "You sound as if you truly *want* me to marry."

Lillith took a fortifying breath. "Perhaps that is because I *do* want you to marry . . . for Mercia's sake . . . and your own."

Thera gave a short, defensive laugh. "What could a man possibly do for Mercia that I cannot do for it myself? I lead the council, direct the treasury, oversee the trading and commerce, consult with the head weavers, craftsmen, stewards, and bailiffs. I appoint officials, settle disputes, and study writings from other lands to improve our husbandry and trades. I know all of my subjects by name and sight. . . ."

Lillith cocked her head, noting that Thera had ignored the hint of what marriage might mean to her personally. Thera always dealt only with the public and official aspects of a union . . . never with the personal ones.

"You were married once yourself, Lillith." A canny gleam entered Thera's eye. "If wedded life is such bliss, then why are you not eager to repeat it?"

"You know full well the story of my marriage, Princess. I was young. He was old and kindly . . . and seedless. I am the Countess of Mercia now," Lillith said. "I have a duty. And until it is discharged, I am sworn to solemn vows and cannot marry. Your lot, on the other hand, lies in a very different bushel from mine. Mercia needs a queen." She leveled a faintly accusing look on Thera. "And a king."

The color in Thera's cheeks deepened. "May I remind you that on the day I am fully wedded, you will no longer be a countess."

"Faith, what good is being a countess anyway if you've nothing to count?" Lillith grumbled, clasping her hands together and tucking them between her knees. After a moment she glanced at Thera from the corner of her eye. "Sooner or later you will have to confront the prophecy. 'These seven woes,' " she began to quote, " 'one for each night the bed of the ruler goes unfilled. With trouble and contention ripe, the kingdom will be cursed . . . chaos in the land and in the seasons . . . in the hearts of men and in their reason . . . the sky will withhold its tears but women shall weap . . . the seed will wither and the wombs shall sleep—' "

"Not another word!" Thera shook a finger at the countess, then forced herself to ease. "Scarcely a day goes by that I am not harangued about that wretched prophecy. One disappointing harvest in seventeen years and the council is in an uproar. Logic alone should allow that after so many prosperous seasons we might expect a fallow year." She turned a penetrating look on Lillith.

"My solitary bed had nothing to do with lack of rain or the shortness of sheep's wool—"

A burst of noise and movement occurred in the courtyard below, and their attention flew to the screen to search the arrivals for a glimpse of the Duc de Beure. Thera spotted the host of the feast, the Earl de Burgaud, clad in a gold-embroidered tunic and flat burgher's hat, directing his guests to the pillow-strewn benches and chairs around the tables. Next, her eyes fell upon the familiar form of her host in the city, the dapper Henri Jannette, the Earl de Peloquin, a lord of her own court who now resided in Nantes and served as Mercia's agent in the world of commerce.

Thera's heart pounded as she searched the faces and forms for the one who could put an end to both her maiden state and her solitary reign. And there he was.

At first she mistook him for a partition the servants were carrying, then for a part of the wall that was moving. But a head took shape in her vision and she spotted hands at the ends of thick, upholstered arms that were flung wide in a gesture. As introductions and presentations were made, rumblelike laughter set that mass of flesh vibrating. She watched in disbelief as the corpulent figure inched its way through the other guests, behind the earl. A flurry among the servants produced two stout chairs, and the massive guest rolled onto them with a grunt that passed for approval.

She blinked as Henri took a seat on one side of the huge fellow and the earl took a seat on the other side. Her jaw slackened. Surely, there was a mistake. But the seating arrangement and Henri's startled glance in the direction of her concealment drove home the reality of it even before the earl rose and lifted his wine cup to offer a toast to his exalted guest.

The Duc de Beure. She watched with trancelike horror the stubbled bearlike jowls, the eyes bloated to slits, the hair hanging in greasy tangles, and the bulbous lips that parted to reveal a bottomless cavern of a gullet. As the serving began, the duc snatched trays from the servants' hands, and in short order had downed a whole pitcher of wine, demolished an entire capon, and started on a full joint of lamb.

Whenever his host engaged him in conversation, the duc first hauled back in his chairs and produced a rending belch, then replied in guttural huffs and grunts. Grease dripped down his chin, and fresh crumbs and droppings soon joined the remnants of past gluttonies which stained the woolen tunic covering his shelflike girth.

Thera swallowed hard, conjuring an image of this human plague of locusts gnawing its way through her kitchens and ample storehouses, then through Mercia's well-stocked granaries. For one fleet and terrifying moment, she saw him on the beautiful silk-curtained bed in her personal chambers. And she heard the web of bed ropes snap and saw the boards crack.

"He's a swine," she whispered. Tearing her eyes away to glance at Lillith, she found her companion staring at the spectacle of the duc's behavior with both hands clamped over her mouth. "Nay . . . he is a whole *herd* of swine."

He was also the only marriageable duc in all of Normandy and the provinces of the Champagne. Slowly it dawned: she was saved . . . spared! Relief flooded through her icy limbs. When Lillith turned to her with eyes as big as goose eggs above her covered mouth, Thera was seized by an unholy urge to laugh, and bit her lip to hold back her mirth as she applied her eyes to the holes in the screen again.

The duc chomped, guzzled, and dribbled . . . listing on his seat to talk with his mouth stodge-full, then pounding the table with his hamlike fist as he roared for more wine. Poor Henri's harried expression, and the way he averted his face and fanned his hand before his nose, hinted that the duc's aroma was every bit as distasteful as his feeding habits.

Repulsive . . . malodorous . . . filthy . . . crude . . . He was utterly—*perfectly*—revolting. With each loathsome trait he exhibited, Thera's spirits brightened and the corners of her mouth curled farther upward. If she had tried to conjure the worst of all possibilities in one man, she couldn't have produced a being half so blessedly and fortuitously dreadful!

"Look at him . . . as bloated as a cow dead three days," she declared, beaming.

"Well, he would not be especially difficult to please at table," Lillith offered weakly. "He appears to eat almost anything."

"Everything," Thera corrected, her perverse pleasure in his hideousness growing. "His hair is nothing but grease and nits. And his garments . . . poor Henri is suffocating from the smell."

"Hair may be washed and garments may be changed," Lillith countered, struggling to say something which did not violate either Christian charity or her vow of honesty. "I doubt he would prove a demanding husband." She slid her gaze over the duc's ponderous bulk and winced. "He appears to be more interested in food and drink than in . . . fleshly pursuits."

"For which women everywhere must surely thank God," Thera retorted, adding cannily: "However, making it through the required seven nights with him might prove something of a problem."

"The seven nights." Lillith shuddered at the thought and lapsed into raw honesty. "Sweet Mother of—You would be overcome by the stench or squashed flat first!"

"Seven nights . . . our revered law is most adamant on that point. I believe that eliminates the good duc from contention altogether," Thera intoned, unable to contain herself any longer. Her laugh bubbled forth and Lillith spun around on her stool, scowling at Thera's glowing face.

"He is a beast," Lillith declared, glimpsing both the pleasure and the relief beneath Thera's mirth. "And you are delighted."

"Nay, I am . . . devastated." Thera held her chest, try-

ing to contain her reaction, but her abrupt sense of lib-
eration, after weeks of slow-growing tension, was heady.
Tears formed in her eyes, her shoulders quaked, her
face flushed crimson, and, as the duc's boarlike bellow drifted up in the silence, a full gale of laughter
struck her.

Fearing she would give their presence away, she
clamped a hand over her mouth and pointed toward the
kitchen, just down the gallery. Lillith hissed a warning,
but Thera was already dashing for the doorway, and the
countess was left to pick up their cloaks and follow as
quickly and silently as she could.

Thera hurried through the hot, smoky kitchen, holding her spotless white silk up and out of harm's way,
and escaped into the cool, darkened shelter of a stone
passageway. There she halted and leaned against a wall
to let the last tremors of mirth wash through her. Lillith
joined her and sagged against the stone, too, panting for
breath.

"You know what this means," Lillith said, glancing
back at the arched opening, through which the noise of
the kitchen and the muffled drone of the banquet drifted.

"I do indeed," Thera said with vengeful pleasure. "It
means the council will have to range still farther away
to find me a husband, perhaps all the way to Milan
or Venice. It may be months"—her eyes glowed at the
prospect—"or even *years* before they find another suitor
of such exalted rank who has no hope of inheriting a
kingdom of his own." Satisfaction curled, catlike, around
the edges of her smile. "And until an acceptable candidate can be found, I shall just have to rule alone."

"An acceptable candidate . . . a man acceptable to *you*,"
Lillith said tartly. "Then I fear we shall be waiting a very
long time indeed." Her eyes narrowed. "A man has to
die before he is made a *saint*, you know."

Thera laughed. Only Lillith dared speak to her so. The
irreverent countess was witty, perceptive, and uncommonly well-spoken. But the quality which had earned

her the role of Thera's countess was her thorough and unstinting honesty.

"Well, that explains why saints are in such short supply. A pity. I rather had my heart set on one," Thera said, reaching for her cloak.

"What are you doing?" Lillith watched with confusion as Thera whirled her silk-lined garment onto her shoulders and fastened the silken ties.

"We are returning to Henri's house. And when we get there I intend to rid myself of this damp, sticky gown and give my skin a thorough scrubbing. I feel tainted from having witnessed that lout's excesses. Come, Lillith."

"Come? Now? Without escort?" Lillith glanced about the passage and peered back over her shoulder at the kitchen doorway. "But we were to wait here for the earl and his men, until the banquet is finished."

"Finished? They shall be banqueting half the night, and I do not intend to remain a moment longer under the same roof with that heap of Norman tallow."

"Princess!" Lillith, truly alarmed, grabbed Thera's cloak. "This is not Mercia. The earl says the streets are not always safe at night."

"It is not fully night yet. And I marked the way as we came. It isn't far." With regal finality, she lifted her hood up over her head and struck off for the stairs leading down to the street door. "Come on, Lillith . . . the light is wasting."

Lillith glanced around the dim passage and groaned, realizing there was no help to be had in dissuading her headstrong mistress. She drew her own cloak about her shoulders and hurried for the stairs as well.

Chapter Two

The narrow street was deserted when they stepped outside. Thera paused a moment, taking her bearings. Things had looked different earlier, from the back of a horse and in full daylight; now the houses loomed taller and hovered over the streets with a brooding air. The streets seemed narrower . . . crowded by the presence of the deepening shadows. But after a moment, she located the direction from which they had come.

"This way," she declared, pointing.

They hadn't taken a dozen steps when they were nearly run down by two large, bony hounds chasing something furtive and ratlike along the edge of the houses. The scramble stirred the dust in the street and with it wafted up the faint smells of moldering wood, soured kitchen water tossed into the open gutter, and animal dung. Thera covered her nose with a wince.

"By the saints," she muttered. "In France, the streets and the noblemen smell alike."

When Lillith hung back with a worried expression, Thera seized the edge of her cloak and pulled her along, keeping close to the street doors of the houses, beneath the overhanging upper stories. They followed the winding street past several narrow alleys and finally turned onto a slightly broader thoroughfare. Muffled voices occasionally floated down from the unshuttered windows far above the street, and dogs barked in the distance, but Thera began to have an odd sense that she and Lillith were alone in the city, and she found it strangely unnerving. It was as if the people had withdrawn from the streets, abandoning them to the darkness.

The farther they went in the deepening gloom, the more the house fronts and the signboards began to look alike. Thera halted at one corner after another, searching in vain for the red shop front with the three gilded pills on the signboard which marked the apothecary at the end of the rue le Carreaux. Soon the twilight was spent and they were still searching.

"We should have been there by now. It could not have been this far," Lillith whispered, searching the shadows. "We're lost!"

"We are not lost," Thera whispered back, hauling Lillith close to glare at her. "We are in Nantes." She glanced at the discomforting gloom all around them and frowned. "On a street." Her frown deepened. "At a corner. Of some sort."

The winding streets narrowed as they went on, and several huddled forms scurried past, keeping a wary distance. Thera marked the slamming of doors and the sound of bars being drawn. Then from somewhere nearby they heard the creak of leather harness and the muffled thud of hooves . . . numbers of hooves. The two perceptions formed a connection in her mind, and without fully understanding why, she began to walk faster and search the darkness with a new sense of urgency.

A male shout split the air from some distance away, uttering words unintelligible but bearing an unmistakable bark of command. A moment later the street behind them filled with horses and the dull clank of armor and the rattle of metal against wood. Thera pulled Lillith around the nearest corner and into an alley, narrowly escaping an onrushing column of riders. In the dim light, they could make out the massive size of the horses, the dark glint of metal helmets, and the patterned configurations that could only have been shields.

"Soldiers," she breathed, and she heard Lillith's intake of breath.

Henri de Peloquin was right, Thera realized; this was indeed a different world from Mercia. The stench, the soot-laden sky, the haunted feeling of the streets, and now soldiers riding through the night; it was nothing at all like her realm. A knot of anxiety began to form in the pit of her stomach. She pulled Lillith into motion again, and they darted back into the street and around another corner, opposite the direction the soldiers had gone.

Soon they came to a deserted street lined with rickety merchant stalls and shuttered shops. They gave wide berth to the open door of a tavern and the drunken forms slumped against the walls on either side. Just as they drew a breath of relief, they heard barking and baying . . . which drew ominously closer. A pack of gaunt, wild-eyed hounds appeared out of the gloom behind them, ranging through the streets on their nightly hunt, like a ravenous tide that searched out and engulfed everything that moved.

Galvanized, Thera lifted her skirts and cried out, "Dear God—Lillith, run!"

They bolted down the street just inches ahead of hunger-wasted bodies and snapping jaws. When they glimpsed light and commotion in the widening street to one side, they headed straight for it and plunged smack into the middle of it. The starving hounds followed them to the very edge of the crowd, then halted, snarling and turning on each other as they retreated from the threat of so many humans.

Thera and Lillith had little chance to savor their deliverance, for they were now caught up in a surging, jostling crowd of frantic city dwellers. On all sides they were pressed and shoved by unwashed bodies with thickly thatched heads and gaunt, frightened faces. Above their wails and panicky shouts, Thera heard crashing, thudding, and the squawk of fowl. As she struggled to keep her feet, the throng abruptly thinned and she glimpsed the reason for the townspeople's terror.

The street was littered with splintered boards and broken crockery, strewn tinware and baskets. Wooden planks and ripped awnings hung from half-demolished stalls, and chickens and geese squawked as they escaped from cages on an overturned poulterer's cart. And in the midst of that tableau of destruction were several large, dark-clad figures, laughing and uttering drunken curses as they hacked at the remaining stalls and goods with battle-axes and broadswords.

Thera froze watching those great weapons, stunned by the shaggy, dark-shrouded forms that wielded them. Never before had she seen such creatures. Their faces were covered with scraggly beards, their bodies were thick-muscled and sinewy, and their eyes seemed to burn with the Devil's own fire. They wore knee-length cloaks made of animal furs, leather cross braces over their bare chests, and boots that laced tightly from ankle to knee. Every aspect of their fierce appearance and brutal actions bespoke a feral, animalistic nature. *Barbarians*, she realized with some shock. They had to be the infamous barbarians from the east who were sometimes hired as mercenaries by western nobles.

The hapless merchants tried to protect their wares, only to find those vicious swords and axes turned on them. The weaponless townspeople did what they could: shouted curses, shook fists, and rushed at the vandals . . . only to scatter like sheep whenever one of the barbarians turned and charged them full out, swinging his blade.

In one such foray two of the barbarians joined to threaten and bully the crowd. As the townspeople fell back, a young girl tripped on the debris in the street and went sprawling, straight in the path of the murderous heathens. She was little more than a child, twelve or thirteen years, wearing long dark braids and a threadbare tunic that was too short for her developing frame. The marauders lumbered to a halt, panting, staring at the girl's frightened eyes and exposed legs, and deciding quickly on another sort of pillage. With an ugly laugh they lunged at her. Several in the frantic crowd surged forward to help her, but it was instantly clear that the barbarians would reach the girl first, and her would-be rescuers scrambled back . . . all but one.

Thera's fingers closed on one of the girl's arms the same moment the barbarians' hands clamped around her ankle and wrist. The girl twisted and flailed, turning a frantic plea to whoever was trying to help her.

"Help! Save me—for the Virgin's sake—save me!" the girl cried out as the barbarians jerked her to her feet.

The wanton destruction Thera was witnessing had prodded her sense of justice, crowding it into a combustible knot in her chest. When the barbarians charged straight at the crowd around her, that volatile tangle of pride, outrage, and duty was set ablaze. One look at the girl's terrified face was all that was needed to spur her to action. She was used to royal prerogative, to taking charge, to protecting those who could not defend themselves. It was her royal duty.

"Let her go—you brutes!" she shouted, confronting their grizzled faces and rapacious eyes as she struggled to maintain her grip on the girl. "Let her go, I say! How dare you lay hands on a citizen of this good realm—"

"Princess, nay!" Lillith cried, tugging at her cloak. "Come away. You cannot do this—"

The barbarians were stopped by her resistance in the same moment the strain of Lillith's pulling loosened the ties on her cloak. The hood slid from Thera's head and the heavy garment fell open. Those close by in the crowd murmured at the sight of her, and all motion seemed to halt as the barbarians transferred their hungry stares from their waifish victim to the one who had interfered with their pleasure. In the torchlight her burnished hair caught fire, her fair skin glowed, and her open cloak revealed a ripe, womanly form swathed in pristine white.

"Princess, ple-ease!" came Lillith's hoarse whisper from behind her.

"Let her go," Thera demanded, drawing herself up to the fullest, glaring at them with all the determination she possessed. Emboldened by their pause, she continued: "You've wreaked enough destruction here. Release her . . . slink back into the gutter from whence you came, you filthy dogs!"

They must have understood at least part of what she said. Looking to each other, they scowled and repeated the word *dogs* with a snarl. Then one added something in their guttural tongue which produced an ugly laugh in his comrade, and the pair turned menacing looks on her. She swallowed hard, refusing to quail before them.

"Very well then . . . I'm going to *count*," she declared. And as their eyes narrowed, she carried out her threat, slowly and deliberately, barking each word a bit louder. "One . . . two . . . three! *Four!*"

They suddenly loosened their hold, and the girl lurched back into Thera's arms. The princess held the child tightly for a moment, and as she released the girl to the safety of the crowd, she felt a pulsing surge of triumph. The child's release vindicated her reckless course, and with her authority established, her mind was already racing on to her next command.

She was totally unprepared for the barbarians' lunge and was caught with a breath half taken, unable to utter more than a choked cry of surprise. In a heartbeat, they had seized her arms and shoulders, and were growling threats in their base tongue that needed no interpretation. She wrestled furiously, demanding they release her, which only drew several of the other marauders from their bashing and hacking. Joining their comrades circling her wriggling, defiant form, they assessed her with eyes burning with a new kind of fire.

"Do something! Help her!" Lillith cried out to the crowd, which shrank back their faces gray with helplessness. "Worthless cowards. She helped you—" But when Lillith threw herself at one of the barbarians' backs, she was slammed to the ground by a brawny fist. She lay stunned by the impact as the barbarians dragged Thera onto their shoulders and bore her, kicking and flailing, from the street.

Across the square, just out of the range of torchlight, a force of mounted soldiers was crowded between the overhanging houses on another side street. They wore mail and iron-bound helms, and their shields bore the crest of a noble house. At their head sat Drustane Reynard, duc de Verville, astride his massive black destrier, watching his barbarian mercenaries destroy the market stalls and terrorize the citizenry. He was clothed all in black, from the plume on his helm to the tips of his leather boots. Even his eyes were black, and glowing like polished obsidian. His handsome, aristocratic mouth bent in a grim smile as stalls splintered and townspeople scattered before the agents of his will.

"This will teach the earl to deny my men access to the whores and taverns of his precious city," he said with a sidelong glance at the stony-eyed captain of his personal guard. "And to think, he might have had an exchange that was both peaceable and profitable. I tried to be reasonable. Was I not reasonable with the man, Scallion?"

"Most reasonable, *mon seigneur.*"

"All I wanted was a bit of diversion for my battle-weary troops and the chance to provision . . . a bit of pleasure combined with a bit of trade. Most inhospitable of him, sending his lackey to turn my men away at the city gates." The duc's smirk broadened to a vengeful smile. "And most unwise. Now he no longer *has* city gates."

The commotion on the far side of the square suddenly stilled, and a high-pitched scream rent the charged air . . . a young girl's scream. De Verville laughed with a cynical edge, knowing it meant that his barbarians were about to take a part of their reward. He nudged his mount forward, shoving aside some of the crowd, sorting through the human rabble for the source of that cry. Spotting several shaggy fur cloaks focused around a smaller form, he raised in his stirrups for a better look, his blood stirring in his loins at the thought of the vengeance his hirelings were about to wreak on a daughter of the earl's city.

"Ho—what is this?" he uttered softly, raising a brow at the sight of the fiery young beauty facing his fiercest mercenaries. "Where did you come from, Precious?" he whispered with sultry interest. When the captain kneed his mount forward and drew up beside him, the duc pointed to her.

With the sweep of a practiced eye, Drustane de Verville took in the burnished halo of her hair, the delicacy of her features, and the authority inherent in her stance. Even through the hazy torchlight and distracting motion, he could tell the young woman was not of common stock. Squinting, he searched her dark cloak for clues to what lay beneath, and was rewarded a moment later when her cloak opened and was dragged half from her shoulders as someone in the crowd tried to pull her away from his men. White . . . she wore white.

"A fetching demoiselle, *mon seigneur*," the captain ventured, watching the glint in his lord's eye.

"Too damned fetching for the likes of them," de Verville said with a coarse laugh, sinking back into his saddle. "I could use a prime bit of bed-sport myself this night. Perhaps you'd better *rescue* the demoiselle, Scallion, and bring her to my tent, outside the city gates." As his mercenaries hoisted the young woman onto their shoulders and she fought them, her cloak fell away, baring raised and twisted skirts and long, pale legs. A shaft of desire sank through the duc at the sight of those delectably vulnerable limbs, captive and writhing.

"Go, Scallion. *Hurry*," he commanded, giving the captain's horse a kick that set it snorting. "There will be nothing left to enjoy if they finish with her first!"

The captain signaled several of his men and together they plunged forward into the crowd, bent on rescuing the defiant young beauty. But as the barbarians raced from the square with Thera on their shoulders, the townspeople grew bolder and surged after them, shaking fists and snatching up splintered planks to wield as weapons. They crowded into the street where the mercenaries had disappeared, shoving and shouting, venting their anger and blocking the way of the duc's men.

The black-clad soldiers forced their massive war-horses forward like battering rams, and the townspeople who braved the horses' hooves were bashed aside with shields as the duc's men plowed determinedly through the crowd. But the delay had cost them precious time, and when they finally broke through and charged down the narrow street, there was not a trace to be found of the barbarians or of the duc's intended bit of bed-sport. When they returned empty-handed, the duc fixed his captain with a cold, threatening glare.

"I want her. Find her. Scour every pesthole and sewer in the city. There cannot be that many alleys available for a raping!"

A dark blur of sensation enveloped Thera as she was borne through the dank streets on the rock-hard shoulders of a brutish barbarian. Her blood had drained to her head, making coherent thought difficult, and with each step her captor took, the breath was pounded from her chest.

From time to time, her captors paused to shift her from one set of shoulders to another and to drink from an earthen jug they had stolen from one of the wrecked market stalls. As they drank, they inspected their prize, clasping and smacking her bottom through her gown and laughing as she choked out a groan and squirmed.

Her terrifying journey came to an end in a darkened alley at the rear of a noisy tavern. The barbarians dumped her onto her feet, and when her knees buckled they held her up and put the jug to her mouth to force her to drink. She jerked her head aside, refusing the soured wine, and they laughed, ripped her cloak from her shoulders, and began to paw her. The feel of their rough hands grabbing and probing her body galvanized her reeling senses. The terrifying feeling of captivity knocked her sense of royal self-possession back to duty. Fight—she had to fight them!

Outrage pumped new strength into her limbs. Suddenly she was alive with anger, twisting and grappling against their rough hands, trying desperately to free herself. But the harder she struggled, the harder they held her, and it slowly dawned. Four, five . . . there were at least six of them. Half a dozen filthy, vicious barbarians . . .

She hadn't a prayer.

She did, however, find a scream.

In a smoky tavern just yards away, ale and talk flowed freely among the crude planking tables that were bathed in the smoky light of tallow lamps. The heat of a cook hearth and of touchy male pride combined to raise both spirits and tempers among a tough contingent of patrons around those tables. And squarely in the midst of the contention sat Gasquar LeBruit.

"I say it is the Moors," he declared, his bearded jaw jutting. "You have not been truly tested in battle unless you have honed your blade against Saracen steel. They fight like the very demons of Hell itself." His eyes caught fire and his voice dropped to a dramatic rasp. "Why, in the battle of Cardiz, I cut off one swordsman's hand and he caught up his falling blade in his other hand and continued the fight." The caws and laughter his claim produced only spurred him to greater heights. "By the saints"—he lifted a callused hand—"I swear it is true. Then when I cut off his other hand, he caught his blade in his teeth and came at me again." His eyes flashed with wicked lights and the corners of his broad mouth began to curl. "By the time I was done, there was naught but an ear and a pizzle on the field of battle. And—*Sacre Bleu*—I tell you a truth—that pizzle put up a hell of a fight!" The place went up in a roar of laughter, and the proprietor shoved yet another tankard of ale into Gasquar's hand.

"Ask my friend if it is not true!" He stalked toward Saxxe, who sat at a table against the wall with a number of battle-toughened warriors who wore a motley assortment of odd garments and armament garnered from the four corners of the earth. Some of that rough brotherhood enjoyed Gasquar's tale and some dismissed it, but none disputed it, for one of the few courtesies that gathering of hard-bitten soldiers and knights for hire accorded one another was the privilege of the grand lie.

Gasquar staggered over and sank down on the bench beside Saxxe and the others, his face ruddy with pleasure. Just as he opened his mouth to say something, a scream penetrated the thick, sweat-laden air. The noise in the tavern stilled briefly, then resumed at a lower level. Saxxe drew a deep breath, closed his eyes, and downed the dregs of his tankard, willing himself to ignore that unsettling sound. Screams, especially women's screams, meant trouble. And he didn't mix in trouble of any sort unless there was a clear profit to be made from it.

"It is an odd fact of our trade," he mused, "that after a while we get quite good at reading screams. That one, for example. A woman, of course. And angry. Mad as a wet guinea hen. The sort of scream a woman makes when she's caught her husband in a bit of ballocking on the side." He flashed a wicked grin and the others chuckled as he picked up Gasquar's tankard and drew a long draught from it.

"Now, some women scream when they're shocked or surprised . . . like when they discover a rat in a rain barrel," he continued, wiping his mouth with the back of his hand. "That's a short, hard shriek of a sound. One blast and they're done." His hand lingered to smooth his thick, dark beard, then fell to the huge broadsword that lay propped against his thigh. "And then there's—"

A second scream rolled through the unshuttered window, and Saxxe's gut tightened in spite of himself. "Two screams," he observed casually, sliding his hand over his blade, tracing the bronzework on its scabbard. "In my experience, a woman seldom needs more than two . . . one to get your attention, the other to get her meaning across." The others laughed, while Saxxe cast a restless, sidelong glance at the open window.

"*Alors.*" Gasquar turned to Saxxe with an upraised finger. "Do you recall the demoiselle in Venice, *mon ami*, when we fought for the Duc de Montalba? The little dusky one with the voice so sweet?" A lusty smirk stole over his face as he turned to the others. "At the height of her passions, this sweet little flower would open her throat and scream like a panther caught in a trap. Such screams." His gaze drifted past his audience into remembered vistas. "Such loving."

"He was half deaf before we left Venice for Rome," Saxxe declared, giving Gasquar's shoulder a shove.

The drunken laughter that followed was cut short by still another cry from the same throat; this one shrill and vibrating. Saxxe's thigh muscles tightened and his belly tensed. He shifted on his seat, rubbing his palm restlessly against the pommel of his sword, then wrapping his huge fingers gingerly around the handle grip.

"Three," he said, running his other hand back through his long, shaggy hair. "And she's gone from furious to frightened. High-pitched and wavering . . . that's the sound of fear. Perhaps her old husband has decided to teach her a lesson or two."

At the fourth scream—shriller still, but somehow weaker—Saxxe shoved abruptly to his feet and cast Gasquar a taut, speaking look as he headed for the door. Gasquar lifted a rueful eyebrow and turned back to the others.

"*Dieu*—you are hopeless, Rouen," Saxxe muttered to himself, stepping into the darkened street and pausing to listen. There was a low rumble of voices, but he could not say whether it came from the open tavern door behind him or somewhere else. "Look at you. A few miserable screams and you are twitching like a lute string." He held his breath, waiting. And this time when it came again, raw and terrified, he lurched into motion and followed the sound straight down the alley beside the tavern to its source.

In the cluttered and ill-lit back street, half a dozen mercenaries were holding a struggling woman down on the filthy ground. One held her hands and two her feet, while another knelt between her legs and tore at his clothes. Two others slouched against the back wall of the tavern, emptying a wine jug down their gullets and calling guttural encouragements as they waited their turns. They were so drunk or so brazen that they did not even try to muffle the woman's cries.

Saxxe shifted from one foot to the other, clenching his jaw and feeling his wretchedly chivalrous impulses rousing at the odds the woman faced. "Six on one," he muttered, wincing. "And it would be Mongol-Slavs. Vicious, treacherous animals—their sort gives hired soldiers a bad name." He pulled his blade sling over one shoulder, resettled his twin daggers to the sides of his waist, and tightened his grip on his sword hilt. He paced two steps away, then two steps back, his muscles going taut, his nerves beginning to vibrate with a familiar tension.

"It is no concern of yours, Saxxe Rouen." He jabbed a finger at the shocking scene. "That six-on-one would become *six-on-you*!" He growled from between clamped jaws. "And God knows, there's never any profit to be made in rescuing a demoiselle in distress."

Then the barbarian fell atop the poor woman, and the cry that issued from her throat hit Saxxe like a fist slamming into his gut.

"Gasquar!" he bellowed, unsheathing his blade in a single powerful motion. "Gasquar—we fight!" he roared, charging in with his blade swinging.

The barbarians were not so drunk as Saxxe had hoped. With the advantage of surprise, he made it to the woman and delivered her abuser a hard kick in the ribs that lifted him partway off her. But those holding the woman fell back only for a moment before abandoning their prize and scrambling to their feet. The two by the wall had dropped their jug and unsheathed their weapons in a trice, meeting his attack full out. Their blood ran hot with carnal expectation and they now bent that coiled energy to the fight.

Saxxe swung and dodged and slashed, fighting to make a stand beside the woman, who seemed too hurt or too stunned to take advantage of her sudden release. Twice he felt a blade rake the leather braces on his chest, and at least twice he felt his own blade dragging through leather or flesh—he knew not which. They came at him from all sides and he pulled one of his daggers and used his feet, drawing on every bit of his agility to keep from being battered away from the woman's side or sliced open from groin to gullet. It seemed an eternity before Gasquar's familiar call rang out in the chaos.

"Ah-haaa!" Gasquar rushed down the alley with his blade drawn and his grin broadening. "I see you have managed to find us some trouble, *mon ami!*" He charged in with a bold laugh, and the odds were suddenly six to two.

The Mongol-Slavs rushed to meet Gasquar as well, and the fighting was fast and fierce and showed no signs of a quick ending. Without shields they were forced to fight two-handed: slash, thrust, and downcut, over and over, intercepting Mongol steel with one blade while striking with the other. When Saxxe finally caught sight of the woman struggling to make it to her hands and knees, he realized the rescue was already accomplished. And he knew from years of experience that nothing would be served by hacking it out to the finish with such unpredictable opponents. The risk of bloodshed was too great, and a mercenary's livelihood depended upon keeping his skin intact in order to fight another day.

Deciding, he made a sudden, powerful charge and managed to wound one of his opponents and send another sprawling into the dirt. He called to Gasquar to guard his back, and the burly warrior bolted to shield his comrade's movement, pivoting and engaging the barbarians fearlessly. Saxxe sheathed his weapons and hauled the woman up and onto his shoulder, making for the street end of the alley.

Gasquar made a valiant stand against odds of four-on-one, then as soon as Saxxe was cleanly away, he too made a fierce final charge, then wheeled and ran like the very Devil. With battle-roused fury, the Mongol-Slavs sent up a cry and rushed after them.

Chapter Three

Saxxe raced through the dark streets, his mind churning like his powerful legs. He knew that Gasquar would have taken a different turn, which would force their pursuers to divide forces in order to catch them both. But the woman on his shoulder grew heavier by the stride, he could hear the barbarians behind him, and he had no assurance that Gasquar's tactic had worked. If he stopped now, he might find himself facing the lot of them again, single-handed. His best course was to find an unbarred door and get behind it until the mongrels gave up and slunk back to whatever pesthole had spewed them forth.

He began trying doors—any door, every door—in the maze of crowded alleys, and it wasn't long before he found one that yielded. Pushing back the weathered planks, he ducked inside and slammed them shut behind him. In the dim light, he searched for a bar to brace the door and seized a warped plank that looked as if it had served the purpose before. He managed to wedge the wood between the iron and wooden brackets, then rolled the woman from his shoulder against the wall. She slid, and when he instinctively leaned in to support her with his body, she began to struggle and cry out—still blindly fighting. As voices and thudding feet approached outside, he thrust his weight full against her and clamped his hand over her mouth to prevent her from giving them away.

"Quiet—damn it—they're just outside!" he commanded in a fierce whisper, seizing one of her frantic hands and pinioning it above her head. It was all he could do to control her wriggling body and muffle her cries. "If they hear you and come after us—I'll hand you over to them, I swear it!" His threat must have penetrated her confusion, for her cries stopped and her movements slowed.

The sounds of rattling weapons and shouts came from just outside the door. Something—a fist, boot, or shoulder—banged against the door, and Saxxe watched the aged planks vibrate under the blows. After an interval, there were other, muffled, thuds which seemed farther away. Then, as abruptly as they had come, the voices receded along the street as the barbarians moved off to continue their search.

As the sounds of their pursuers faded, she began to struggle again, shoving against his ribs and trying to call out. "Be still, woman. You're safe enough," he said, his chest heaving. But his demoiselle in distress either didn't hear or wasn't convinced; she writhed and twisted frantically.

She was a fiery one, Saxxe realized. Attacked by a horde of barbarians, she had managed a number of impressive screams and still refused to surrender. He briefly considered shaking her to bring her to her senses, but decided that it went against the noble spirit of his deed.

It took a while for her to wear herself down, but she gradually stilled against him, and he could feel her bracing for whatever he intended. Saxxe closed his eyes for a moment, recovering the rest of his breath and his self-control, then pushed back enough to look down at the woman he had just rescued.

His heart gave a powerful, arrhythmic thud.

Above the hand he held clamped over her mouth, he saw large, light-colored eyes, beautifully shaped and thickly lashed, set in skin that was smooth and clear. She was young, and if the rest of her face matched what he could already see, she would prove quite a beauty. His taut, overheated body and battle-fired senses focused instantly on the womanly shape and softness pressed against him.

"Well, well," he said, still panting, his broad mouth curling up on one end. Giving in to curiosity, he removed his hand from her mouth. His gaze fastened on full, aristocratic cheekbones, then slid down a straight, delicately carved nose to a pair of seductively bowed lips that seemed to be made of ruby-red silk. She was beyond lovely, he thought with some shock; she was breathtaking. Surprise sent a hot trickle of carnal excitement through his loins, and he stiffened and ruthlessly quelled it. A demoiselle this beautiful was undoubtedly valuable to someone . . . someone who would pay well to have her back. . . .

The instant Thera looked up at the huge shadowy beast who held her pinned to the wall with his body, she felt a frisson of fear. She'd been snatched from beneath one filthy, rampaging barbarian by another smelly brute who seemed intent on squashing her witless himself!

Potent and utterly foreign feelings of helplessness, fear, and disgust roiled through her. For the first time in her life, both her circumstances and her responses to them raged out of her control. Of all that had happened to her, it was that utter loss of command, that sense of powerlessness, that terrified her most. It struck at the very core of her royal being, and her frayed and embattled defenses rose to meet it . . . striking out to reclaim what power and authority they could.

"Let me go," she demanded in a strained rasp. Saxxe looked up to find her striking eyes filled with molten anger. "Take your wretched hands off me."

"What?"

"Get off—get away from me, you brute," she ordered, jerking her face as far away as she could and pushing at his stomach with the heels of her palms.

"Brute?" he echoed.

"Release me immediately, or—" She halted, trying desperately to think of a threat that a fierce, pillaging barbarian would find intimidating. "I swear, I'll . . . I'll see you hunted down and . . . and drawn and quartered."

"Drawn and quartered? For what?" he demanded with a snort of disbelief. "Rescuing you?"

"For carrying me off and holding me prisoner."

His jaw went slack. "Carrying you off—" Instead of the tearful gratitude he might have expected, he found himself accused of the very offenses he'd just prevented . . . and by the victim he'd just rescued. He choked on the absurdity of it. "*Dieu*—of course I carried you off! If I hadn't, you would be lying naked and senseless in that alley even now . . . with a Mongol-Slav bastard in your belly."

His words hit her like a slap. *Naked. A bastard in her belly.* For one fleeting moment, she again felt their hands pawing at her, pushing her to the ground, and wrenching her legs apart. What had almost happened rose in her mind with sickening clarity. For the first time, she connected it with her own physical body— her belly, her thighs, her womanly parts—and understood the pain and physical violation she might have suffered. Then once again she recoiled from the horror of her own vulnerability and retreated into royal prerogative.

"Now, instead, I'm standing squashed and half suffocated in a hovel," she hissed, "with yet another heaving, malodorous barbarian breathing down my neck."

"Heaving . . . malodorous . . . barbarian?" Each word sounded harder and flatter. In the midst of that huge shaggy head, two large dark eyes began to burn like hearth coals, and she felt his body lean harder into hers.

She couldn't help flinching as he traced a menacing path along her collarbone to the edge of the rounded neck of her gown . . . and beneath it. Hooking the fabric of her gown and chemise on his finger, he twisted and jerked hard, pulling them up and away from her shoulder. A huge, blue-bladed dagger suddenly arched above her and came crashing down, wrenching a strangled cry from her as it tore through the cloth and sank deep into the wall behind her.

She quivered with shock as he hooked the other shoulder the same way and sent a second dagger plunging through it into the wood behind her. Then he backed away, leaving her pinned against the wall. She hadn't even realized she had been standing on her toes until she slid and landed flat on her feet . . . and felt the shoulders of her gown lift and heard the sickening rip of cloth. She gasped and wobbled back up onto her toes, reaching for the hilt of a dagger but unable to pull it out with only one hand.

The full extent of her plight dawned when she reached for the dagger with both hands and heard a huge rending sound. She flattened against the wall and found half of the shoulder of her gown cut through and the rest threatening to part at any moment. She was trapped . . . held captive by her own garments!

A sardonic chuckle brought her head up, and she found him watching her with what she sensed was a vile look of pleasure, though she could not be certain for the shadows that covered the top half of his face and the disgusting bush of hair that covered the rest.

"A little trick I learned from the Saracens . . . though I believe their particular practice involves catching a bit of flesh as well as cloth," he said in a deep rumble, folding his arms over his chest. "We *barbarians* keep our daggers double-edged and sharp for just such occasions, demoiselle." She couldn't stop the heat flooding into her face or the chill that raced through her shoulders, but she did try to recoup some of her self-possession by standing straighter and raising both arms to grab the dagger handles on each side of her. The ominous sound of tearing threads stopped her again.

"By all means, demoiselle, do continue," he said in a taunting tone, leaning back on one leg and stroking his beard with a big, sinewy hand. "I am just waiting for the rest of your gown to give way. It should prove most . . . entertaining."

There was no doubt he was smiling this time; she could see a flash of something light in the midst of his beard. The odd realization that he seemed to still have teeth distracted her momentarily from the suggestion in his words.

"You'll have a long wait, barbarian," she declared. "I'll hang here until Doomsday before I give you that satisfaction."

"Oh, I doubt it will take that long for you to decide to satisfy me, my fiery demoiselle," he said with what passed for a laugh. "Who are you? What is your name?" When she remained stubbornly silent, he turned to search out the source of light in the chamber.

Their refuge was a kitchen of sorts, and the meager illumination was provided by a single tallow lamp and a brazier of glowing coals on an upraised stone cook hearth. He took down the hanging lamp and carried it over to get a good look at her. But as the light poured over her, he stopped in his tracks.

Her fitted gown was stretched tightly over long, supple curves; high, full breasts; a virgin-narrow waist; and straight shoulders. Then his gaze traveled upward. Her eyes were startlingly blue, the color of rare, polished sapphires. Her skin had the texture of cream, and her hair was a light, burnished brown . . . the exact color of cinnamon. Without his summoning it, the memory of the smell and taste of that luxurious spice bloomed in his senses, and his mouth began to water. He scowled as he felt the gnawing of hunger in his belly and an all-too-familiar thickening in his blood, and he smothered those instinctive reactions with irritation.

He had business to conduct here. The haughty witch owed him something for her rescue, and he was determined to collect. As he edged closer, his gaze fell on something he hadn't seen before: a necklace, a delicately worked band of plate links that appeared to be real gold and was inlaid with colored stones. The lust-driven Slavs had apparently missed it. His eyes slid the short distance to her breasts again, but this time he made himself concentrate on the fabric that covered them. White was a color reserved for the wealthier classes, and the silk was the finest he had seen since his days in the merchant wars of Venice.

"Who is it that suffers the scrape of your sharp tongue and still buys you silk gowns?" he demanded. "An aging father? A rich, limp-timbered husband?" Annoyed by her continued defiance, he finally came straight out with it: "Who would pay well to have you returned, demoiselle?"

Still she would not answer, and his humor began to fade. "*Dieu*, you are a stubborn one. Whoever he is, he has not taken a strap to you often enough."

But in truth, it was not defiance that kept her from answering; she simply could not speak with a frozen throat. The lamp he held up had allowed her a thorough look at him as well. His shoulder span was a full yard across, his arms bulged like ale kegs, and his legs looked to be the size of tree trunks. Dark hair hung past his shoulders in a wild tangle and his face was covered by a wide, thick beard, both of which gave him a feral aspect. The only other parts of his face clearly visible were heavy, bristled brows that centered above a strong nose that ended in a blunted point.

His clothes—what he wore of them—were like nothing she'd ever seen before. His heavily muscled chest was bare behind a crisscrossed pair of wide leather braces that were fastened in the center by a metal boss, and his waist was banded tightly by a wide leather belt with a huge bronze buckle. On his bottom half, he wore a bloused skin garment resembling loose-fitting hose, and from the knees down his legs were covered by tall, fur-banded boots that were laced to conform to his leg. As he turned away to prowl the chamber, she watched his powerful, animallike movements and felt her knees go weak.

"Where were you when the Mongol-Slavs took you?" he asked, trying a different route to uncover the source of her obvious wealth. "In your home? The streets? A tavern perhaps? Surely you are eager to get back to your family. Or husband. Or perhaps a rich lover." Still she would not answer.

With a sidelong glance, he turned away to give the silence and her fears a chance to loosen her tongue as he investigated the jars, crocks, and bundles on the lone shelf along the far wall. He lifted lids and sniffed the contents until he was surprised by the sweet, waxy fragrance of honey. Grinning at that unexpected windfall, he dipped two fingers into the jar and transferred a huge scoop of dark honey to his mouth, holding it there, savoring the way it melted on his tongue. Licking his lips, he stole another bite, then swaggered back to his stubborn captive.

"So, you still will not give me the name of someone from whom I may claim a reward."

"You dare claim a reward for assaulting both my person and my senses . . . for destroying my garments and taunting and tormenting me?" she said, jerking her face away. "You'll get nothing from me, barbarian, but trouble."

"Oh, but I will, demoiselle. Lacking any other source of profit, I fully intend to take my reward from your person." He stalked closer, watching her eyes widen and shift back to him, though she stubbornly refused to move her head. "Now, what do you have, demoiselle, that would be worth your virtue, your health, and perhaps your very life?"

His eyes fell to her necklace, and he was about to name it when she turned her face back to him with a look of disdain so potent that he felt it like a physical slap. Instead of the necklace, he demanded something he sensed would cost her far more than a scrap of gold.

"A kiss," he demanded. "I believe I will have a kiss of you."

Her eyes widened, then narrowed furiously. "I'd sooner kiss a snake."

"Truly?" he said with a wicked grin. "Then you possess surprisingly depraved tastes in passion for a demoiselle. Your confessor must have an interesting time of it."

"Barbarian," she snapped.

"Yea. A vile, bloodthirsty barbarian," he growled quietly. "Count yourself fortunate that I have already had my supper this night."

He closed the distance between them in two long strides and intercepted her frantic hands, forcing them down to her sides. Then he pinned her squirming body more firmly to the wall with his. As his shaggy head lowered, she strained her face away, and he released one of her hands so he could seize her face and force it back.

"Now, demoiselle," he murmured hotly, "close your eyes and pretend I am a snake."

He covered her lips with his, and there was no escaping his possession. The heated smell of him assaulted her, filling her head and lungs with the vinegary tang of male sweat, the metallic air of oiled steel, and odors of horse and leather. She refused to inhale, feeling that he would somehow invade her on the very air she breathed. But he must have sensed her strategy, for his kiss went on and on, until she grew breathless. When her lips finally parted in a gasp, his slanted over them, taking advantage of the softening of her mouth to engage her lips more intimately.

The force of his mouth on hers eased, and she was surprised by the curious hard-soft quality of his lips against hers. Then he began to move his lips against hers, slowly, deliberately, in changing combinations of alignment and pressure, as if he were searching for something. And suddenly he found it . . . a certain pressure, a certain blending of contours and motion that produced a shiver in her shoulders.

Her determined resistance was eroded by wave upon wave of new sensations, things she could never have anticipated: the tickle of his beard against her face, the firm but pleasant pressure of his mouth against hers, the sensual flexing of his lips as they shifted against hers, the salty-sweet taste that somehow seeped into her mouth. She stilled and his grip on her jaw gentled to something more like a caress.

So this was a *kiss*, she thought frantically, caught totally off guard by spreading ripples of unexpected pleasure radiating through her. She had received motherly kisses of approval, respectful kisses of homage, and ceremonial kisses of state, but never in her memory had she received a personal kiss . . . a kiss that generated feeling in her. And this was indeed a personal kiss, an intimate encounter that stirred a tangle of emotions in her and somehow demanded a response.

He shifted his shoulders against her, flexing, seeming to caress her body with his as he probed the inner borders of her lips with his tongue. With a will of its own, her body began to relax against him, allowing that shocking intimacy and exploring it. Then his arms slid around her and pulled her harder against him so that their bodies molded tightly together, and her hands fluttered up his sides, hovering.

A soft moan rolled from the depths of her throat, both pleasure and distress. He parted her lips farther, invading them with long, liquid strokes of his tongue, and to her utter surprise, she tasted honey. Sweet and dusky, laden with the taste of sunshine and meadow flowers, the heavy succulence of fertility and bounty . . . he tasted of *honey*. At that disarming discovery, she yielded to his possession, opening to him, feeling his shocking oral caresses sending trickles of pleasure through her body.

Engulfed in a warm mist of newborn feeling, she felt his hands moving over her back and sides, working a curious magic under her skin. Half-formed desires were rising up in her, swirling sinuously through the most sensitive areas of her woman's body. As if he sensed it, his hands flowed to those places that had begun to ache and tingle strangely.

Whether it was the feel of his touch on her breasts or the brief separation of their bodies that had allowed his hands to slip between them, a disturbance rippled through the pleasure fog shrouding her wits. Coming slowly back to her senses, she found her fingers clenched around the leather braces that crossed his broad back and her body molded so tightly against him that her gown clung to his bare skin as she pulled away. Her lips felt thick and swollen, her heart was racing, and her body seemed sluggish and awkward. Alarmed, she peeled her hands from him and shoved back against the wall, jarring the sensual haze from her mind.

The dark heat of his eyes and the heaving of his chest mirrored her own arousal. The sense of what had happened to her, and of the humiliating way she had participated in a kiss meant to humble her, doused her like a pail of cold water.

"You've had your price, barbarian," she whispered, trying desperately to convert the heat pouring through her veins into energizing anger. "Now let me go."

He raised his hand, but as she shrank from it he grasped the hilt of one of the daggers that held her to the wall and pulled it free. With her gaze caught in his, he removed the other blade and settled the pair into the empty loops at his sides.

She jerked her garments back into place and crossed her arms over her chest, holding her gaping gown together with trembling fingers. In that moment she had a vague sense that he had claimed something more from her than just a kiss.

As she slid along the wall to the door, he followed and clamped his hand over hers on the bar. She held her breath, frantic that he might try to prevent her from going. But his other hand slid to her throat, touching her gently, raking across the nape of her neck, then releasing her with one last, brushing caress. The door creaked as it swung open and, without a look back, she clutched her gown and darted out into the darkened street.

Saxxe stood inside the opened door, letting the cool air wash his overheated body. He tore his eyes from the darkened opening and lifted the jeweled necklace he held, watching it wrap seductively around his fist . . .

the same way impressions of her soft breasts, silky lips, and cinnamon-colored tresses were wrapping around his slumbering desires.

"The Prince of Fools you are, Rouen," he muttered with a snort of disgust. "She was worth a small fortune, and you let her slip through your fingers. When will you finally learn to wring some advantage from the troubles of others?"

He gave the necklace a stroke, then tucked it into his belt, feeling a strange quiver of excitation as his fingers brushed his bare waist. His skin was wildly alive, hungry for sensual contact. And as he took a steadying breath, he felt a throbbing fullness and heat in his loins. Closing his eyes, he could still see her . . . tousled, flushed, her gown clinging to her moist skin. On his next breath came the scent of attar of roses, and in his fingertips he recalled the costly textures of silk and alabaster-smooth skin. She was the very sight, the very scent, the very feel of luxury.

His haughty demoiselle was the embodiment of the world of the nobility . . . with all its privilege, wealth, beauty, and promise of pleasure. She had roused desires in him that he had thought well buried: not just the need for physical passion, but troublesome cravings for a share of that noble estate for which he had so often spilled his lifeblood.

"Nay . . . you were right to get rid of her, Rouen. The little witch spoke the truth. She had nothing to give you except trouble. And *trouble*, my friend, is the one thing you have no difficulty finding on your own."

Every darkened doorway seemed a looming chasm to Thera as she hurried through the streets. Here and there she met people hurtling by, bearing blankets stuffed with belongings on their backs. But they seemed as eager to avoid her as she was them, and she made herself go on, searching the houses and shop fronts.

Just as her fears and fatigue threatened to overcome her, she spotted three gilded pills on a signboard overhead. In the graying light she managed to make out the red of the shop front over which it hung, and her heart gave a lurch. She began to walk, then run down the street.

Around a curve she saw a number of torches moving her way. With a caution born of her recent terrors, she ducked into a doorway and waited with her heart beating frantically for them to pass. As the torchlit forms crept stealthily by, she recognized the Earl de Peloquin's chief steward and called out to him. In a trice, she was surrounded by torches and servants and safety. Keeping a harried watch up and down the street, they trundled her quickly toward the earl's house.

Some distance away, in a modest tavern near the wrecked market square, the Duc de Verville was receiving a report from his captain that made his face darken and his fists clench. "What do you mean they lost her?"

"We found the Mongol-Slavs . . . but not the girl," the captain stated warily, watching his lord's mounting ire. "They lost her to some other soldiers in a fight . . . now she is nowhere to be found."

"Lost her in a fight? My Mongols bested in a *fight*?" The duc shoved to his feet, hurling a tankard to the damp, reed-strewn floor. "Damn their black souls . . . probably too drunk to raise either swords or pizzles. They're not worth a brewer's fart when they've got a skin of wine in them!"

"Perhaps another demoiselle," the captain offered cautiously, eyeing de Verville's tightening face and narrowing eyes. "There are any number of young girls in the market square, *mon duc*." But even as he said it, he realized it was a mistake.

"The spawnings of common brutes?" the duc said, turning a jaundiced eye on Scallion. He had no taste for the common trull or even the lowborn virgin. It was the daughters of the nobility he craved, and only the most beautiful among those. To slake his passions he chose only the choicest morsels of femininity, young girls guarded and pampered . . . demoiselles both beautiful and refined, who could satisfy his epicurean tastes for beauty as well as the driving need in his loins. In every small barony or castellany he conquered, his hard-fighting mercenaries seized and saved for him the daughters of the local knights and lords.

"I shall overlook that nauseating suggestion," he said tautly, drawing on his heavy leather gauntlets. Then he roared: "I want that demoiselle! Search house to house if you—" He halted as it occurred to him: "Someone in the crowd tonight must know about her, who she is, where she lives. Start in the square itself. And this time, I shall come along to see it is done right."

A quarter of an hour later, Drustane de Verville sat astride his mount in the wrecked market square watching his soldiers question the hapless citizens who had been trying to retrieve their damaged wares or had been dragged from their homes in the nearby streets. He ground his teeth in frustration, watching as one after another of the townspeople was shoved aside. By the time his captain approached, he was in a foul mood indeed.

"They say they know nothing of her, *seigneur*," he said, dropping a nod of salute. "I have said that we seek to rescue her from the marauders, but still they swear oaths that they have never seen her before this night."

"A likely story," the duc snarled. "They protect her."

Suddenly a pair of his soldiers dragged a trembling shopkeeper across the square by the scruff of the neck and held him up before the duc, demanding: "Tell our *seigneur* what you told us."

"I-I w-was there," the fellow mewled, "a-and I heard the one who tugged on her cloak call her 'Princess.'"

"'Princess'?" The duc scowled, rocking back in his saddle. "Princess." New interest rustled through him as he considered it. "There is no royalty in these parts. What do you know of this 'princess,' old man?"

"N-nothing, *seigneur*, I swear. I only heard the one with her beg her to come away and call her 'Princess.'" He raised gnarled hands in supplication. "Please, *seigneur*, I have children to feed."

The duc eyed the quaking townsman, reading truthfulness in the fear-widened whites of his eyes. "Reward the good fellow, Scallion, so that he will know that the Duc de Verville is a man of compassion." And as the little man scrambled away, clutching a handful of silver deniers in his fist, the duc watched with a cynical twist of a smile.

"A princess. If she truly is royalty, then I must indeed find her," he declared with renewed determination. "If she is one of the king's daughters, then she offers more than just a diverting bit of bed-sport. For to rescue a beautiful princess would be a noble act deserving of . . . a great reward." His dark eyes darted as he considered it. "Perhaps even the lady's hand in marriage."

There was no better way to become royalty than to marry it, the duc knew. And becoming royalty was the consuming goal of handsome Drustane Reynard. Born the fifth son of the impoverished Duc de Verville, in the Alps of France, he had survived the illness, injury, and obligation to serve the king in battle which had stricken down three of his brothers who stood between him and the title. And when his eldest brother, the heir to their aged father's holdings, returned from King Louis's Crusade, he contracted a mysterious wasting illness . . . which left Drustane heir to the all-but-landless title.

Years of eating scraps and wearing his brothers' cast-off rags had left the penniless young duc with a fierce hunger for wealth, power, and position. He married quickly and ruthlessly, and was soon a widower with control of his dead wife's generous dowry. He used his inheritance to hire mercenaries and secretly began to harry the mountain passes where caravans of merchants were most vulnerable.

As his wealth increased, so had his ambitions, and his boyhood dream of a kingdom of his own came to life in his heart once more. He looked about for a place to make his own, and cast his eye upon Brittany. Sparsely populated, devoid of resources, and held by a duc who seldom troubled with the far reaches of the realm . . . it would afford his mercenaries access to trading roads and sea ports and eventually to the burgeoning cities of the Champagne . . . which belonged to the king himself.

Guile carved a humorless smile deeper into his handsome, clean-shaven features. His ambitions might find a quicker path if he could seize and marry a royal princess. "Scallion!" he roared, causing his captain to stiffen in expectation. "I must have her. Scour the whole cursed city. Find her if you have to take every wretched hovel in this district apart timber by timber!"

In a richly furnished chamber on the uppermost floor of the home of the Earl de Peloquin, beeswax candles shed both golden light and a sweet scent, driving out both the gloom and the noisome smells of the city below. Thera stepped out of a huge wooden tub of warm water onto a thick Moorish carpet and into a large, thirsty sheet of linen. Lillith brushed aside the hands of the earl's maidservant, dismissing the girl, and proceeded to wrap her mistress in the cloth herself, while continuing her tale.

"Well—I was so lost and so desperate to get help that I finally got up the courage to enter a tavern. Terrible places, Princess. The stench." She shuddered. "I begged the tavernkeeper to guide me to the rue le Carreaux, and do you know—the ignoble brute—he required three silver deniers in payment! Troth, doesn't anyone do anything out of charity or nobility these days?"

"Apparently not," Thera murmured, thinking of her own encounter and the price required of her. Unwittingly, she sent her fingers to her lips and traced them.

Lillith saw that unconscious movement and the shiver that followed, and pursed the corner of her mouth. Thera's summary of the terrifying events following her abduction had been terse: she had been rescued by a soldier, who then released her. But her comment just now left Lillith with the uneasy feeling that there was more to the story. She flicked a glance at the soiled and slashed gown which even now was being reduced to cinders in the hearth, and she halted in the midst of rubbing Thera's hair between the linen.

"Are you certain you are . . . all right?"

"Of course. I'm fine now that I've rid myself of the filth of the streets," Thera insisted, pulling both the sheeting and her self-possession tighter about her as she turned on her chair to avoid the sight of her favorite gown going up in flames.

"Weren't you frightened?" Lillith finally had to ask.

Thera rubbed her shoulders, which were already reddened by Lillith's vigorous scrubbing, as if ridding herself of the lingering taint of her experience. How could she answer? How could she admit that for a time, just before and just after her rescue, she had been frozen with terror, speechless and unable to move? Such feelings might be understood or even expected of a gently reared young noblewoman who found herself in similar straits. But she was not just any young woman; she was a crown princess—the ruler of a kingdom, the guardian of her people. The fact that she had been paralyzed by fear and helplessness shamed her to her very marrow.

But as unsettling as those feelings were, there were others that troubled her as much. In the course of those two tumultuous hours, she had experienced sensations and emotions she had never known before: raw loathing, disgust, confusion, and flashes of physical pleasure. The range and depth of her feelings shocked her . . . as did her highly personal reaction to her barbaric rescuer and the wretched kiss he took from her. She stiffened and shoved that memory into the dimmest corner of her mind. It didn't do to dwell on such things now. It was over and done. Past.

"Nothing is ever gained by surrendering to hopelessness," she said with a regal sniff. "I fought . . . as I expect my father would have fought if he had been overtaken by barbarians and thieves."

"And the one who rescued you?" Lillith asked, trying to contain her burning curiosity.

"I have already said," Thera answered curtly. "He was a soldier of sorts. Quick with a blade."

"And noble of spirit," Lillith offered, watching her keenly. "To have rescued a princess in distress . . . surely such chivalry deserves a reward."

"A truly noble spirit does not seek rewards . . . except those laid up in Heaven." Thera's face reddened as she turned on Lillith with narrowed eyes. "He did not know I was a princess, of course. No one in all of Nantes, save Henri de Peloquin, knows of me or Mercia. Do you think I would be so reckless as to tell a—" She seized a brush from the open chest near her feet, thrusting it into Lillith's hands, a not-so-subtle indication of her irritation with the topic. "I demanded my freedom in no uncertain terms, and, of course, the fellow realized he was outranked and outmatched . . . and released me."

A scratching came at the door and Thera called out over Lillith's voice, admitting a servant bringing word that the earl wished to speak with her as soon as possible. It was a perfect excuse to bury herself in the task of dressing and avoid Lillith's prying.

An hour later, she left her chamber intending to join her host in his hall. But she found the dapper earl waiting on the stairs just outside her door with a harried expression. At the sight of her, obviously in glowing health, he quickly made a deep obeisance.

"Princess!" He took the hand she extended him and pressed his forehead to it in homage. "I died a thousand deaths in the time you were missing! Thanks be to Heaven that you were restored to us hale and well." But he looked as if his words gave him precious little comfort as he swept a hand toward the stairs. "You must come with me, Princess. I have something you must see."

Thera soon found herself standing with Henri and Lillith in the shadows of an arched stone gallery two stories above the street. As they watched the murky street below, a teeming knot of figures separated and began swaggering up and down, calling out drunkenly to the householders behind the barred doors that lined the street. Between their shouts could be heard the clank of metal on metal and the dull thuds of blade hilts and boots slammed against doors.

In the distance, Henri pointed to a column of smoke rising out of a sickening yellow glow which could only mean one thing: fire. As the wind changed, sounds of horses and shouting and confusion were borne toward them, and they suddenly spotted slashes of yellow flame at the end of the rue le Carreaux. They searched the darkness with their hearts in their mouths, fearing those flickering lights might be spreading flames. But sound added dimension to the shapes moving about those flames and they took form . . . men on horseback, bearing torches and shields and spears, riding recklessly through the streets.

"An armed force from the east arrived outside the city earlier in the day, Princess. They demanded access to the city, but the Earl de Burgaud refused to admit them, thinking they were naught but a band of mercenaries. But their number swelled as more and more soldiers arrived—some knights, some hired soldiers on horseback, and some foul, bestial barbarians from the east. They made camp in the fields just outside the city, along the Paris road. Then, as we banqueted tonight, word came that the city gates had been taken by force and that bands of these mounted soldiers had entered the city and were marauding the districts nearest the bay."

"Soldiers," Thera murmured, recalling what she and Lillith had seen earlier in the darkened streets. It had been the beginning of an invasion and they had walked straight out of the earl's house and into the middle of it . . . without a clue to what was happening around them. "Barbarians and mercenaries. They were wrecking a market square when . . ." When she foolishly pitted herself against a half dozen of them at once, she realized.

A chill went through her shoulders as she looked out over the predatory bands prowling the streets below and recalled the wanton fury of the destruction she had witnessed firsthand. She moved to the stone railing, shrugging off Lillith's plea that she keep to the shadows, and stared at the ugly yellow pall spreading over the sky . . . sensing the almost palpable waves of fear spreading from house to house throughout the city.

"It is a full army, Princess . . . bent on taking vengeance—and whatever else it wants from the city," Henri declared, moving to the railing beside her. "The Earl de Burgaud's brother has led most of the earl's garrison to the east to render service to the king. The city is all but defenseless."

Remembering the terrors she had experienced and seeing them now repeated on a broad scale, all over the city, Thera experienced a violent paroxysm of the very foundation of her thinking. With appalling clarity, she suddenly saw that her world and her understanding of it, despite her learning, had been little larger than Mercia itself . . . a place where order, safety, and the rule of reason were taken for granted . . . where armies, sieges, famine, and outlawry were the stuff of fireside tales. From her isolated realm, the troubles and upheaval of the burgeoning cities and great kingdoms had seemed distant and unreal.

But now she was plunged into the midst of it all . . . the diversity and disorder, the violence, dirt, and confusion. And as the underpinnings of her world were forcibly stretched, her thoughts were for her people and her home. Her mind filled with visions of their trusting faces, their simple ways and loyal hearts. This madness and mayhem must never be allowed to touch them . . . must never spread to her beloved realm. *Never.*

"Princess." Henri's voice brought her back to the present, and she found him regarding her with a look of abject misery. "I fear I can no longer guarantee your safety. I entreat you, my lady . . ." He put out a hand to touch her, then halted and drew back, abashed at his own boldness. "Depart for Mercia as quickly as possible. We may still secrete you from the city . . . if you leave before dawn, by the old High Gate."

A distant roar, the sound of a collapsing structure,

intruded. As the firelit horizon brightened briefly, Thera gave a somber nod.

"We have much to do if we are to leave before dawn," she said. Then, aching inside at the thought of what lay ahead for the city and for her loyal subject, she reached for Henri's hands and squeezed them. "And may Heaven protect you and your house, my good Henri."

Chapter Four

L oud voices drifted up through cracks in the floor of the upper room of the tavern where Saxxe Rouen and Gasquar LeBruit had spent the night. Saxxe shot up on one arm, his hand going for the long blade at his side as he slid a glance over the drink-weighted shapes of the other soldiers and knights for hire who shared those rough lodgings with him.

These were hard times for hire-soldiers, unpledged knights, and landless younger sons in France. The fifth Crusade had ended in defeat and disarray some years before, leaving a whole cadre of men bred and trained for the glory of battle without a worthy cause in which to ply their skills and gain their livelihood. Lacking both income and land, and unable to marry without one or the other, many were forced to sell their fighting prowess wherever they could to earn their living. And after years of rolling from battle to battle and conflict to conflict, a number of them had come to lodge in this wretched tavern in the bustling port of Nantes . . . waiting for the next feud between nobles or nations to break out.

Saxxe rolled onto his haunches and gave Gasquar a prod to awaken him. A jerk of his head toward the door was all that was needed; Gasquar came to his feet, snatched up his helm and sword, and followed Saxxe into the sour-smelling passage. Down a rickety set of back stairs, they found a barrel of water and a well-used gutter. Then, with their hair and beards still dripping, they reentered the tavern.

A dozen rough-clad soldiers occupied the ale room, some sprawled over tables and benches and others pillaging through the shelves behind the row of barrels topped with planking that formed a serving board. Like the city itself, the tavern had just fallen victim to invasion, and the tavernkeeper and his servants had apparently fled.

Saxxe and Gasquar helped themselves to a tankard of ale and snatched loaves of bread from the basket of day-old bread in the kitchen. As they propped themselves on a bench and made quick work of the food, they could feel the invaders eyeing them. Finally, their burly captain strode over with a tankard in his hand and planted himself before them, openly assessing their odd garments and fine weaponry—and the calluses on their hands that spoke of the frequent use of blades.

"You are fighting men, I see," he said in a graveled voice that bore the accent of the provinces of northern Spain. When Saxxe nodded curtly, the man's gaze dropped to the elaborate hilt and scabbard of Saxxe's sword. His brows rose. "Damascus steel?" When Saxxe's hand slid possessively to his blade, the bull-like Spaniard laughed, acknowledging that protective impulse. "From the looks of you, you each have dealt your share of deathblows." He scratched his grizzled chin. "Join us. We have more battles ahead and could use strong fighters. The pay is good and each man keeps a share of the spoils he takes."

A taut smile bloomed on Saxxe's face as he clamped a restraining hand on Gasquar's arm, below the tabletop, to keep him from accepting. "Nay, we have all the work we need," he said, adding "my friend." The fellow scowled, considered Saxxe's matter-of-fact tone and expression, then shrugged and turned back to his men. When Saxxe and Gasquar stepped out into the smoke-tainted air of the street a short while later, Gasquar was glowering.

"And just where is this work we have so much of, *mon ami*?" When Saxxe strode stubbornly on, he stopped and cupped his ear. "Eh? I cannot hear you. . . ."

"They're with the invaders," Saxxe said, jerking a

thumb back over his shoulder. Then he realized Gasquar had halted and turned to face him.

"So?"

"They fight with those cursed Mongol-Slavs . . . and you know how I hate Mongol-Slavs. Like ravening wolves, they plunder and pillage and raze and rape—I'll have no part of that."

"You will have no part of bread or ale or meat, either," Gasquar declared irritably, "if we do not hire into some lord's garrison soon. The coin . . . it is all but gone."

There was a cry and a rumble from nearby, and both wheeled to witness a shopkeeper trying to prevent three mercenary soldiers from ripping the shutters and hinged wares shelf from the front of his shop. Farther down the street they spotted more soldiers taking goods from other shops and shoving aside the people who tried to prevent them. And among the rooftops, they spotted the blackened ribs of several smoldering houses and stalls.

"Look around you," Saxxe said in disgust, waving at the destruction in progress. "This is their work." Turning on his heel, he started for the stable near the city gates where they had left their mounts. "They ride under no colors. They slink into cities in the dead of night, thieving and torching and terrorizing—" He halted and took a deep breath. "I have no desire to sit around in a stagnant pisshole of a tavern watching a city being ripped apart around me. I say we quit Nantes and try our luck elsewhere."

Saxxe set off with a determined stride, and Gasquar fell in beside him, unable to dispute his friend's conclusions. "Besides, it is time we moved on." Saxxe gestured toward the beleaguered city walls and beyond. "Somewhere out there is a kingdom just waiting for me." He frowned. "Or a castle." His frown deepened. "Or a landholding . . . at least a meadow, an orchard, and a stream."

"Or a prime, plump widow, plagued with full coffers and an empty bed," Gasquar added. Saxxe laughed and clapped him on the shoulder.

"Yea, a plump widow would suit me well, too . . .

provided her purse was fat enough."

Gasquar chuckled and pointed to a side street which would allow them to avoid an overturned cart and a milling crowd obstructing the street ahead. But they hadn't gone fifty yards along the narrow, deserted lane when a scuffle broke out ahead, blocking that thoroughfare, too. Growling annoyance, Gasquar turned back to seek yet another route to the stables, but Saxxe stopped dead in his tracks, staring at the scene.

"Unhand me, you wretch! Let me go, I say!"

Those words, that voice . . . a distinctive white gown and a flash of burnished hair . . . Saxxe halted and stood speechless for a moment. Then he jolted backward and snagged Gasquar's arm, dragging him into a doorway.

"*Sacre Bleu*, what has got—"

"It's her," Saxxe whispered, gesturing to the flurry of limbs and cloaks and shying horses down the street. "The demoiselle we rescued last night. They've taken her again." Something in his chest gave a lurch, then seemed to settle into place at this visual proof that the past night's unusual encounter had not been just an ale-spawned dream.

Together they watched as soldiers—black-clad soldiers in unmarked mail—struggled to subdue and bind a wriggling female form clad in a stark white gown. Saxxe's mouth quirked up at one corner as he watched his haughty demoiselle kick and claw like a cornered cat. "Look—four of them, fully armed, and still they have trouble holding her."

"*Sacre Mere*—she fights like the badger gone to ground," Gasquar said, giving a low whistle.

"Last night *six* Mongol-Slavs barely took her," Saxxe declared.

"Six?" Gasquar's thick brows rose with respect.

"I, on the other hand, managed her by myself, alone," Saxxe said, with a crass bit of male pride.

Gasquar winced as he saw her foot connect with the unprotected junction of a soldier's legs. "What did you do, *mon ami*? Surely you did not thrash her."

"I was sorely tempted." His mouth quirked up on one side. "But I kissed her instead."

"Ahhh . . . the kiss." Gasquar nodded. "A wise choice. It is the remedy for all the problems a man has with a woman, *oui*?" He studied the unusual glint in Saxxe's eye, then gestured to the demoiselle with a jerk of his head. "Perhaps you could do with another kiss, eh?"

Saxxe straightened, sobering, and tucked his thumbs into his wide belt. Another rescue? Another kiss? Another wretched dilemma, was more like it! And his life of late had become too damned full of dilemmas to suit him. He huffed quietly and shifted his weight on his feet. If he had the sense God gave a turnip, he'd turn on his heel and walk away.

But he couldn't walk away. And for some reason he couldn't tear his eyes from the sight of her elegant curves twisting and wrenching in hot defiance, either. He watched her struggle as they finally bound her hands and stuffed a cloth in her mouth, and he was flooded by tactile memories; her body taut and wriggling against his loins . . . her lips parting for him . . . her silky skin beneath his callused fingers. She had tasted like riches and ease. Inside his belt, his thumb nudged the hidden gold links of her necklace, and he felt a ripple of something curiously akin to desire.

Another kiss? His eyes narrowed at the carnal drift of his thoughts and he expelled an annoyed breath. Another pitched battle, was more likely.

Then he caught sight of the second form, a woman in a dark cloak being hoisted onto one of the horses and tied to the saddle, and his mind began to race. There was someone with his fiery demoiselle this time! It struck him forcefully: here was another chance to learn her identity and claim a fat reward. And with two women, perchance there would be twice the profit.

That golden word, *profit*, echoed enticingly through the depths of him. It would undoubtedly mean another fight to free her; this chance for profit was not without risks. But then, few opportunities were.

"What say you? Shall we do something to help your *petite chatte fâchée* and her friend?" Gasquar demanded, eyeing the second woman himself.

"They must intend to ride a bit . . . probably to their camp outside the city walls," Saxxe said tersely, delaying, trying not to let either his carnal or his chivalrous impulses sway him as he watched his wealthy demoiselle being wrestled into a saddle and tied to it. The soldiers picked up a cloak lying on the ground and secured it around her shoulders, laughing at her protests and promising that their lord would soon be taking it off her . . . along with the rest of her clothes. A heated vision of white silk being ripped from creamy skin flashed through Saxxe's inner senses, and his hands slid from his belt into determined fists at his sides.

"Our only chance is to follow and watch for the time and place to take them," he said. "Horses—we'll need our mounts."

"Leave that to me." Gasquar returned stealthily the way they had come, and when he reached the end of the lane, broke into a run for the hire-stables. Saxxe darted across the street to another low doorway and followed the soldiers, keeping to the shadows and running quietly to close the distance between them whenever he could.

The soldiers kept to the back streets, crossing every junction of thoroughfares with extreme caution, as if wary of being seen publicly with their prisoners. More than once, his demoiselle kicked her mount into nervous motion, trying to break free, but each time the soldier holding her mount's reins managed to regain control of the animal.

Gasquar was waiting at the edge of the square just inside the wrecked city gates. Saxxe spotted him above the crowd trying to leave the city, and wove his way around the edge of the square to join him. He could see that the demoiselle and her abductors had been stopped by the motley-looking group of soldiers guarding the main entrance to the beleaguered city. After a brief exchange, they passed on, between the battered stone towers that once had supported the massive city gates. In the blink of an eye, Saxxe swung up onto his horse, and he and Gasquar headed straight for the gate.

"We have just hired on with one of your captains," Saxxe declared to the suspicious men glaring up at them, blocking their way through the gates. "We were told to report to the camp outside the city."

"Which captain?" they demanded, scowling at each other.

"I do not recall a name . . . only a great Spanish belly and the smell of much garlic," Gasquar proclaimed with a bold flourish. Saxxe's sword arm tensed with expectation.

"El Boccho," one said with a flash of recognition. The others laughed and waved Saxxe and Gasquar through the gates.

Outside the city walls, the road descended a grassy slope toward a stream shrouded in trees. Beyond was the invaders' sprawling camp, which from a distance appeared surprisingly organized, like a city unto itself. If the soldiers and women reached that far, both Saxxe and Gasquar knew, their mission was forfeit.

"We will have to take them just before they enter the trees," Saxxe said, searching the woods. "No time to cross blades—just go for an arm wound and make our escape that way." He pointed to an unguarded stretch of trees to the north. "We'll have to ride like demons . . . and hope my little cat and her friend know how to keep their seat on a horse."

Gasquar grunted agreement and drew his blade from the scabbard slung across his shoulder to tuck it beneath a shaggy cloak of animal pelts thrown over the front of his saddle. Saxxe did the same with his sword, maintaining a sound grip on the hidden hilt, and together they kneed their horses to a gallop and closed in on their prey.

The ropes bit into Thera's wrists, her lungs felt raw, and her muscles ached from the violent exertion of her struggles. For the second time in two days, she was captive in the hands of pillaging barbarians. These mail-clad soldiers wore a better class of garments and recognizable armor, but they smelled no better and they certainly behaved like cursed barbarians.

If only she had been quicker to realize the danger and react, she groaned silently. They had been halfway to the old High Gate of the city, in the early gray light, when they came across a band of soldiers searching dwellings. She had stubbornly insisted on traveling with only her own small escort so as not to draw attention to herself. They should have bolted for the north gate the minute the soldiers spotted them. Instead, she had signaled her captain to comply with their order to halt, thinking that they could hand over some coin and be on their way.

"White," one of them had called out when he glimpsed her gown through the opening of her cloak. "It's her—she's the one!"

They sprang at her and Lillith, and her captain gave her a shove and yelled "Run!" before drawing his modest weapon and meeting their charge. Stunned and reeling from the eruption of danger, she had snagged Lillith's wrist, lifted her skirts, and run with everything in her. They led their pursuers a chase through the streets and back alleys . . . hiding behind wrecked carts and ducking around corners. But the soldiers finally caught up with them and seized Lillith, who lagged behind. And when Thera wheeled to help her, more soldiers pounced on her from behind.

Now she was being taken to their camp to suffer God knew what degraded—

The sound of pounding hooves broke in on her thoughts, and her abductors quickly shuffled their column to the side of the road, cursing the two figures bearing down on them . . . assuming they were fellow soldiers, riding hell-bent for camp. But as the two riders drew almost even, they reined up sharply.

Swords suddenly appeared in their hands as they charged the soldiers, their blades flashing. Two soldiers went flying from their horses before the rest could even drag their blades from their scabbards. The burst of angry shouts and clanging blades caused Thera's horse to rear and plunge. It was all she could do to hang on to the saddle and keep her seat; she had no time to be afraid or even to search for Lillith.

In the confusion, a dark form swooped down by her mount's head and jerked it into a frantic run across the grassy fields away from the road and the invaders' camp. Hanging on to the saddle took every bit of her strength, but as they streaked across the grassy slopes she did manage to turn her head long enough to see a second dark form riding hard behind them, and to catch a glimpse of Lillith's blue gown and dark cloak flying on the wind.

How long they rode she could not say, nor did their twists and turns allow her to judge in what direction they were being led. Fear, amorphous and unreasoning, spread through her thoughts as the world careened around her. For the second time—no, the third, or was it the fourth?—she was being dragged away against her will, and, again, she was utterly powerless to do anything about it. Only when the horses' sides began to heave did her new abductor slacken his desperate pace. As they slowed, she struggled upright in her saddle and looked frantically at the one leading her mount.

Her overtaxed heart gave a lurch as her captor straightened in his saddle. At first all she could see was a massive back crossed by an ornate scabbard, a wide leather belt, and a tangled mane of dark hair. Then her gaze slid downward to an ornate dagger, a heavily muscled thigh, and a fur-banded boot that seemed surprisingly familiar. The rocking motion of her mount stopped, and she stared with her throat constricting as that big body gathered, flexed, and swung to the ground ahead of her.

A long, airless moment later, she found herself staring down into glowing green-gold eyes set beneath thick brows. Large sinewy hands reached for hers, and as she felt them working the ropes that bound her to the saddle, her eyes slid to the center of that bush of hair on his face . . . where she glimpsed a full, healthy set of teeth bared in a knowing grin. It was *him*—her rescuer from last night! Relief erupted through terror, sending a welcome tide of warmth through her icy limbs.

But her relief was regrettably short-lived. When he lifted her down, her knees buckled, and he supported her for a moment with his body, looming well above her, crowding her, looking huge and dark. She instantly recalled more from the night before: the feeling of being trapped against his big body and the unthinkable price she had been forced to pay for her freedom. New fears threatened to overwhelm her, and she stiffened and summoned every scrap of authority she possessed to combat it.

"Y-you," she croaked the minute he removed the rag from her mouth. She staggered back as far as the rope would allow.

"Me, indeed," he said, winding the rope around his hand and reeling her closer, bit by bit. "We meet again, demoiselle."

His smile broadened and she found herself staring fixedly at his mouth, which she was shocked to recall in intimate detail: wide, broadly curved lips with the texture of coarse satin . . . surrounded by a soft, dark beard. As he pulled her closer, she caught the scent of him—male heat and sweat, leather and horse—and suffered a rogue wave of remembrance that swamped her thoughts and left her floundering between sensations past and present.

"Let me go—take your filthy hands off me!" Lillith's voice broke in on Thera's shock, and she whirled to find the countess struggling in the hands of a burly brute of a man with long dark hair and a full, red-brown beard.

"Lillith!" Thera called out hoarsely. Lillith spotted Thera and with a frantic lunge broke free and rushed to insert herself between Thera and the hulking barbarian who held her captive.

"Run, my lady!" she cried, attacking his broad chest with her bound fists.

"Gasquar—take this one!" Thera's rescuer grabbed Lillith by the shoulders and thrust her back into the arms of his companion, who seized her by the waist and hauled her back, kicking and flailing. The sight of Lillith captive in a barbarian's arms shocked Thera's regal self-possession back into place and brought her protective instincts crashing to the fore.

"Let her go, you!" She strained toward Lillith, but her own captor grabbed her by the waist also and hauled her back against him, hoisting her so that only her toes touched the ground.

"*Bon Dieu*, Gasquar, we have not one but two angry cats on our hands!" He panted a laugh while wrestling with her. "Here, here, *ma chatte*. Is this any way to show gratitude to your rescuers?"

Thera wriggled for a moment longer, surrendering only when it was humiliatingly clear that she could never prevail against his superior force. With her back as stiff as a fire iron against him, she hissed: "Rescuers?"

"Do you doubt it, demoiselle . . . after last night?" he said in a taunting tone.

Lillith froze with horror, her eyes widening on their captors' dark shaggy heads, bared and bulging torsos, and odd leather braces and belts. "Merciful Mother of Heaven! These are the same barbarians—"

"Who *rescued* your lady last night," Saxxe declared with a vengeful curl to his mouth.

Lillith gasped and looked to Thera. "Is it so? *They* rescued you?"

Thera's face burned with humiliation at being caught in a half-truth she had never expected would be made into a whole one. "It's true. He was the one," she spit out, struggling to conquer the turbulent emotions that admission caused. After a tense moment she forced herself to be calm and demanded once more: "Release me."

"I will indeed release you, demoiselle . . . as soon as I am paid for my trouble."

"Paid?" Wrenching violently, she burst from his restraining arms and scrambled as far from him as she could with the tether of her bound wrists still caught fast his hand. In the crackling silence, his gaze fastened on her mouth, reminding her pointedly of the kiss he had taken from her, then drifted lower on her body. She straightened and drew royal hauteur around her like a cloak.

"Then I fear you will be gravely disappointed. I have no coin, no jewels . . . no possessions at all. Your fellow barbarians were most thorough . . . they took everything." She lifted her chin, pleased to have cheated his greed this time. "I have naught but the clothes on my back."

She was utterly unprepared for his slow, determined smile or his response.

"Fair enough," he declared, stalking closer and planting himself before her with his fist at his waist. "They look to be worth a considerable sum . . . silk and wool woven together, unless I miss my guess." He pinched the cloth at the neck of her gown, rubbing it back and forth between his fingers, and she sputtered and jerked away. "And your cloak is lined with silk." With a lightning-quick movement, he jerked the ties and the heavy garment slid from her shoulders to remain in his hand. "What say you, Gasquar?" He held the cloak up to his companion with a triumphant flourish. "Worth a goodly pouch of silver, eh?"

"Perhaps more than one, *mon ami*." His burly companion grinned.

"I'll take them, demoiselle," he declared, fixing her with a heated look as he unwound her rope tether from his other hand. "Take them off."

Her jaw dropped.

"Take them off, demoiselle . . . unless you prefer I do it myself," he insisted, his voice filled with the threat of determined greed. He tossed her cloak onto a nearby boulder and stared at her expectantly. He was serious, she realized. He'd take the very clothes from her back!

"Y-you . . . unprincipled . . . wretch!"

"Yea, I am that. It is part of our barbarian oath. We vow to behave as despicably as possible on all occasions," he said with a mocking edge, nudging closer, filling her sight with his fierce, dark visage and glowing golden eyes. "Especially to foolish females."

"Your greed knows no bounds," she charged, backing straight into a rock ledge that jutted out of the uneven hillside around them.

"Right again," he said, piercing her confidence with that keen, predatory gaze. "I do nothing without taking a profit, including rescuing demoiselles in distress. And since you have nothing else with which to pay me . . ." His voice dropped to a compelling rumble. "Take them off."

When she made no move to obey, his eyes narrowed and he came toward her with his big hands rising, reaching.

"I owe you nothing! I didn't ask you to rescue—Don't you dare lay a finger on me, you monstrous ox!" she ordered, sliding along the rock face, jerking at the ropes still binding her wrists. She hadn't a prayer of resisting him without the use of her hands.

"Run, my lady!" Lillith cried.

"A waste of time and effort, demoiselle," he warned, watching her like the hawk does the hare. "I can run faster, and farther, and longer. I once ran for two days and nights . . . with a legion of howling Turks right behind me . . . on horseback."

He read her intention in the dart of her eyes, and the instant she bolted, he pounced, slamming his arms against the rock ledge on either side of her, pinning her there with his body. A traitorous ripple of fear ran down her spine, and her heart beat in her throat as he overwhelmed her with his heat and weight. After an agonizing interval, he straightened his arms and pushed back enough to run a speculative eye over her elegant curves.

"But then, I might be persuaded to forgo your

clothes ... if you offer me something better," he said with the glint of fresh calculation in his eye. "Your father is wealthy, eh, demoiselle? Holds a castellany at least ... a rich fief, perhaps, or even an earldom. Perhaps he would pay well for your safe return. Tell me who he is and I will arrange to collect my reward from him instead ... in cold hard silver."

Cold hard silver. His offer to escort her home was a thinly disguised ransom demand! He was unprincipled and greedy and unpredictable ... a barbarian who had obviously turned against his fellow plunderers in hope of securing more gain for himself. Imagine what he would do if he were to learn she was the crown princess of a wealthy, peaceable kingdom!

"Let you take me home?" she declared tautly, intending to divert his curiosity about who she was and where her home was located. "Suffer your stench and your foul barbarian ways for days on end?" She made a face of disgust. "In your care, who is to say I would ever see my home again? For all I know, I could be drowned in a river ... imprisoned and held for ransom. It is a foolish sheep indeed who makes the wolf her protector."

Her open scorn for his person and her denial of the valor of his deed and his right to a reward turned his countenance thunderous. It infuriated him that he'd violated his own mercenary principles and rescued her with no guarantee of profit, only to encounter her temper and arrogance yet again! He stepped back, appraising both her garments and what lay within them with a scathing glare. And with both his manly and his mercenary pride ablaze, he vowed to have what he wanted of her.

"On second thought ... how do I know your old father would be pleased to see a troublesome, ungrateful chit like you? Like as not, he'd show me the sole of his boot for hauling you back to him." Stroking the beard around his mouth, he leaned back on one leg, watching her sputter. "Since I have no assurance of future gain, I must take what profit I can now. And you have nothing, my stubborn little cat, except ..."

He paused, letting his gaze fasten hotly on the elegant lines of her body, and smiling with a carefully calibrated blend of greed and lust. "There is one other thing that would satisfy your debt to me, demoiselle," he said slowly, drawing out the words. And demanding it, he realized, might very well convince her to change her mind about promising him a reward in silver.

"A night with you." With vengeful satisfaction he noted that the color began to drain from her reddened cheeks. "Spend this night with me, in my blankets, and I will consider your debt paid."

"You cannot be serious—"

"Oh, but I am, demoiselle," he said calmly. "And I am determined to have a reward."

"Sleep with you? In your blankets?" she snapped, feeling panicky at the thought. "I'd sooner sleep in a hog wallow." She tried to shove past him, but he contracted around her, trapping her back against the rock once more with the force of his body. She shrank from contact with his massive chest and arms, and found herself pressed hard against the rock.

"Unfortunately for you, the nearest pigsty is miles away, demoiselle. I am the next best thing. I'll have your clothes," he declared irritably, "or your presence in my blankets this very night."

This night. The full sense of his demand suddenly smacked her square between the eyes. *One night!* She felt Lillith's shocked gaze on her but dared not meet it. Thera was achingly aware that "Countess" was more than Lillith's title . . . it was also a description of her foremost duty as royal companion.

Throughout the sprawling reach of the Church of Rome, there were still disputes about what constituted a binding marriage . . . both in law and in the Church's eyes. But in Mercia, the question had been settled long ago. If a man and a woman spent seven nights in each other's arms, it was considered proof of both desire and commitment, and the couple were declared legally wedded. Seven nights made a marriage; no more, no less.

But since the royal heir's night-partner would also become king or queen of the realm, verification was required. The heir's nights in a lover's arms had to be confirmed by an appointed court officer . . . the official "counter" or "countess" of the realm. Thus, of all the things the huge barbarian could demand of her, nights were the most costly . . . for Countess Lillith would be there to *count* them.

Thera raked a desperate look around the barren, rock-strewn hillside, realizing she had no idea where they were or how she and Lillith would get back to their mountain home, even if they could escape. The insufferable barbarian was as big as a barn, as quick as a ferret, and as strong as an ox; she hadn't a prayer of getting away from him. Worse still, he was ruthless and greedy, and something about the way his golden catlike eyes roamed her made her feel naked and vulnerable. And there was nothing she hated more than feeling out of control . . . and at another's mercy.

She seemed to have no choice. A night. She would have to agree to his cold-blooded ransom and try to find some way to get out of it before the sun went down.

"Very well, you shall have your night," she said through clenched teeth. Lillith's gasp echoed in every chamber of her heart. "But on one condition."

"And what is that, demoiselle?" he said, surprised by her capitulation.

"That you find the road to Brittany and set us upon it, come morning," she brazenly demanded.

"Consider it done," he said, his gaze assessing her rising resolve. Brittany, he thought. At least now he knew her destination. But he still had no idea whether she was running to or from her home.

"Now"—she held out her hands to him, once more in control of herself—"cut these cursed ropes and help me back onto my horse."

He was caught speechless for a moment. She'd just been forced to surrender in a fierce clash of wills, and with her next breath she was issuing orders as if she'd been born the Queen of Constantinople! He reached for her hands and one of his daggers. When he had sawed through the ropes, he held her wrist a moment longer to make her look at him.

"Your name, demoiselle. I would know what to call you when I meet you in my blankets tonight." The flush of her cheeks was the only hint of emotion as she jerked her hand from his.

"Thera," she said shortly, annoyed that she was unable to control her blushing. "Thera of Aric." She turned on her heel and stalked on unsteady legs to her horse. She waited by the stirrup for a hand up, then turned to see what was keeping him. He was standing with his fists propped at his waist, studying her.

"And do you not wish to know the name of the man who will hold you in his arms this night?"

"Nay," she declared flatly, tossing her head and praying the duplicity in her heart didn't show in her face.

But he caught a glimmer of distress in her eyes and sensed that she resisted his name to annoy him . . . and perhaps as a charm against thoughts of what would pass between them that night. With that insight he refused to rise to her baiting, and he picked up her cloak and strolled closer, holding it out to her.

"This is Gasquar LeBruit." He swept a hand to his barrel-chested companion, who grinned and jerked a nod. "And I am Saxxe Rouen." His voice lowered as he leaned a hairbreadth closer. "Mark the name well, demoiselle. By morning you will be sighing it with pleasure." When she snatched her cloak from his hands, he laughed and turned to Gasquar.

"You'd better give your demoiselle back the use of her hands, my friend. We have a long way to ride this day. And I wish to make camp *early* tonight."

"Lost her again?" the Duc de Verville roared, flinging a full cup of wine against the silk-draped wall of his tent, outside the city of Nantes. He thrust to his feet and glowered at the captain of his personal guard, who gripped his scabbard and braced.

"My men found her fleeing the city and seized her . . . and another woman with her. Two of the men with her were killed. Two others were wounded . . ." Scallion's emotionless eyes slid from his liege lord's florid face, and the duc pounced on his hesitation like a striking hawk.

"And the others? How many were there?" he demanded.

"I am not sure, *mon duc*. Three, perhaps four others." He swallowed hard. "They . . . escaped."

"Damnation!" de Verville exploded. "Can those pissheads do nothing right?"

"They did capture the demoiselle's trunks," Scallion offered warily.

"Trunks? What in the dregs of Hell would I—" He halted halfway through overturning a small folding table and set it back down as a canny look stole over his face. Straightening, he tugged down his gold-embroidered black tunic and took a deep breath. "Have the trunks brought to me at once."

De Verville spent more than an hour sorting through the elusive demoiselle's belongings. Nothing in those three vessels bore her name or the seal of a known royal house, but he did manage to learn a surprising number of things about his lovely quarry.

All of her gowns were made of the finest silk, delicately embroidered, and her surcoats were made of an ingenious blend of silk and wool and were trimmed in silk cording embroidered with gold wire as thin as angels' hair. Every garment in her trunks was white. A curiously aesthetic taste, he thought, and one which demanded a fat purse. She wore chemises made of tantalizingly thin silk, and her girdles, crispinets, and slippers were all of intricate, sometimes whimsical, design . . . decorated in a style he had never seen before. Her jewelry was simple but elegant, and she groomed herself with a beautiful silver brush and hand mirror . . . adorned with a crest unfamiliar to him, but containing elements used as royal devices.

If she was not royalty, she was certainly close to it, his "princess" in white.

He lifted one of her chemises into the shaft of light streaming through the tent opening, and conjured the sight of soft naked curves wrapped in that diaphanous cloth. A powerful gust of desire shuddered through him, and he crumpled the weblike silk in his fist. Rising from his cot, he shouted for Scallion. When the grim captain ducked into his tent, moments later, the duc shook the garment in his face.

"You said they fled to the north? Then send some of your men to search for her. Tell them there will be a fat reward for locating my princess." He paced away, his black eyes darting with calculation. "I had planned to pay the gouty Count de Aveillard a visit next. Even now a legion of my men announce my intentions throughout his villages. When we decamp here, we will march north, into Brittany as planned, and search for her along the way." He halted, savoring his inevitable successes. "The king is occupied in the east and reluctant to move against me. By the end of summer, I shall make most of Brittany my possession . . . and this *princess* as well."

Chapter Five

A *night in his arms.* The words circled in Thera's head, tying both her thoughts and her stomach in knots. As they rode through the gently rolling forests, fields, and upland valleys, she scoured the countryside for signs of an estate or village which might offer refuge or protection from her rescuer. But they encountered only a lone herder's cottage, at mid-morning, and even that was deserted. The endless plodding of the horses and the sidelong glances Saxxe Rouen cast her way began to wear on her nerves.

Past midday, the sun started down toward the hills ahead of them, confirming that they were traveling north by west . . . toward Brittany and her home in the mountains. It irritated her that the wretched barbarian seemed to be fulfilling her condition while she was feverishly searching for a way to escape honoring his. It irritated her even more that her eyes strayed more than once to his muscular thighs, gripping his mount's sides, and his large, corded hands with their leather wrist guards, holding his reins with authority. She shivered and jerked her eyes from those long, bronzed fingers. *At least seven layers of dirt on them*, she told herself.

When they stopped for water by a rocky stream, Saxxe Rouen and his companion dismounted and led their horses to drink without so much as a helping hand for their unwilling companions. They knelt to drink and dunked their shaggy heads, shaking off the excess water afterward. *Like dogs*, she thought.

But as she watched from the back of her mount, her

eyes fixed on the sunlit droplets sliding down his broad, mounded chest and bare arms. She had sometimes seen her subjects working in the fields without their shirts, but none of them looked anything remotely like him. He was massive and bronzed, yet his limbs were smoothly shaped and neatly tapered. When he moved she was enthralled by the way his muscles and sinews worked beneath his skin. Lillith had to say her name twice before she responded and managed a sliding dismount.

"He is as big as a house," Lillith murmured for her ears only as they knelt together on a rock, scooping handfuls of water to drink. She had seen the way Thera's eyes lingered on the one called Saxxe Rouen.

"But he smells more like a stable," Thera countered with a twitch of the nose.

"What will we do, Princess?" Lillith sat back on her knees and dried her wet hands on her fine woolen surcoat, watching Thera closely.

"We shall have to find a way home, that's what," the princess said determinedly, shaking her wet hands, then wiping them on her embroidered surcoat with a pained look. She glanced over her shoulder at the male forms sprawled on the grassy bank across the way. "We seem to be traveling in the right direction, but Heaven knows how far we are from the village of LeBeau." She thought of her loyal subject and agent who ran a tavern and a stable in the village that marked the trading road to Brittany. "If we can make our way there, Thomas Rennet will provide us protection and an escort back to Mercia."

"And what of this night you agreed to . . . with *him*?" Lillith finally raised the question weighing on both their minds. "A night with a man, Princess . . . you have never had a *night* before."

"And I certainly do not intend to have my first with an off-eyed ox who doesn't even know which end of a tunic goes over his head! I shall deal with him . . . never you fear." She cast another glance across the stream at Saxxe Rouen and found her gaze caught unexpectedly in his. His mouth curled knowingly at one end, as if to say that he knew she spoke of him. Jerking her head to break that disturbing contact, she shoved to her feet, muttering for Lillith's ears alone.

"I am a royal princess . . . heir to a throne . . . ruler of a kingdom. I will not be mounted and ridden in an open field like some brood mare." Her eyes narrowed fiercely. "Certainly not by him. He's not wearing *spurs*."

As Thera stepped across the rocks to the stream bank, Lillith stood frowning after her, thinking of the way the barbarian's huge war-horse answered his every command, and muttering: "Perhaps that is because he doesn't need them."

By the time the sun had become a fiery disk sinking into the horizon, Thera's confidence in her ability to avoid spending her first night in a barbarian's arms had begun to sink with it. Since their brief stop at the stream, she had been allowed to stray no more than an arm's reach from Saxxe Rouen, and whenever she attempted to speak with Lillith privately, he directed his mount between them to prevent it. Each lidded look, each subtle gesture of command, reminded her that she was in his power and stung her already bruised royal pride.

As dusk fell, they paused on the crest of a hill while Saxxe and Gasquar surveyed the land for a suitable place to camp for the night. With habit born of long years of fighting, they chose a defensible spot on top of a rocky hill that had slumped and sheared to form a small bluff overlooking a broad, treeless slope. The moment their feet hit the rocky ground on top of that cliff, Gasquar wrested their reins from the women and took possession of their horses, over Thera's protests. Then Saxxe Rouen ordered: "Collect whatever wood you can find."

"Do what?" Thera demanded, watching her only means of escape being led to a patch of grass and tethered well out of her reach. Her back and legs were pinging from her long ride, her stomach was growling, and she was in no mood to be trifled with. "We shall do no such thing."

"Do you wish to eat tonight, demoiselle?" he responded, cocking his head and eyeing her regal stance.

"Of course I—"

"And how do you intend to pay for your supper?"

"Surely you don't expect . . . Simple decency would demand . . ." She ground to a halt. Appeals to his higher nature were futile, she realized. The wretch obviously didn't *have* a higher nature!

"Providing food for you was not our bargain. And I do nothing without being paid . . . remember? Or perhaps you intend to pay with your fine cloak after all."

"I do not!"

"Then gather wood," he ordered, turning back to his horse.

"And just what will you be doing, *seigneur*?" she demanded caustically. But he ignored her and, after removing something from his saddle, stalked off down the slope, the way they had come. She turned on Gasquar with her eyes snapping. "Where does he think he is going?"

"Do not fear, demoiselle, he will be back," Gasquar said with a chuckle. "I am the fire maker . . . he is the hunter. If there is hare or quail within an hour's stride, we will have fresh meat for supper." His brown eyes shifted from her to Lillith and narrowed speculatively as they slid up and down the countess's frame. "Now, whether we eat our meat cooked or raw depends on you . . . and the wood you gather."

Thera glowered and, though it taxed her sorely, withheld her opinion of the man, the menu, and the task she had been given. Once again she seemed to have no choice. The wretch was fully capable of denying them food. She turned to Lillith and motioned toward the shrubby growth on the back side of the hill.

"Princess!" Lillith hissed when they were out of Gasquar's hearing. "You cannot mean to collect wood like a . . . a shepherd's boy!"

"It appears that we do it or we starve," Thera declared, stiffening her spine as she struggled to assert some control in this humiliating situation . . . even if it was only control of the hot words burning the back of her tongue.

"And I don't find the thought of lying starved and weakened along the road especially appealing."

"Then I shall do it for you, Princess," Lillith insisted, turning toward the bushes. Thera hauled her back by the arm.

"No more 'my lady's,' and for God's sake no 'Princess's' . . . or we will certainly find ourselves held for ransom. Only imagine what these vultures would do if they learned about Mercia." She heaved a disgusted sigh. "I shall just have to help." As she turned, the hem of her tunic snagged on some branches and she freed it, hissing at the sight of a small tear. "Come, Lillith."

Gasquar was squatting on his heels by a mound of dry grass, holding bars of striking steel, when he looked up and saw Thera tripping toward him with the hem of her tunic and surcoat caught up protectively in one hand and a small branch held gingerly between two fingers of the other. He hooted a laugh and fell over backward. At the sound, Lillith came rushing up the slope holding up her skirts and bearing a branch that was only slightly larger than Thera's.

"Someone has taken very good care of you, eh, demoiselles?" he said as he wiped his eyes and vented a final chuckle. "We will need ten times that to make a good fire. And many times more to keep coals going through the night and have something to warm our cold bones in the morning." He shoved to his feet and grabbed their elbows to usher them back into the underbrush. "Come, *mes petites*. I will show you what you must do."

By the end of their sixth trip, both Thera and Lillith had scraped hands, smudged sleeves, and sundry small snags in their fine garments. Lillith tried to help Thera brush the bark and dirt from her white surcoat, but her dirty hands only seemed to make it worse. Thera ground her teeth and told her "Never mind," stalking off into the brush again. As Lillith tidied her own tunic, a motion nearby brought her head up and she found herself caught between Gasquar and a large boulder.

"Your pretty gown, demoiselle. Such a shame," he crooned softly, leaning closer and brushing at the debris on her surcoat. After three quick whisks, his hand hovered, then slid down the contour of her breast, sweeping it with an entirely different stroke.

"Ohhh!" Lillith knocked his hand away and lurched back, her dark eyes glinting and her shoulders rising like an outraged cat's. "Keep your hands to yourself, you filthy barbarian."

"Ah, demoiselle." Gasquar laughed, then his blocky features settled into a canny smile. "You have much to learn about the world. Fortunately, I am the most willing of teachers."

"It appears you have a thing or two to learn as well," Lillith said with a contemptuous tone. "I am no demoiselle. I am a widow and a—" She halted short of blurting out her rank and drew herself up as tall as she could. "I have no need of anything you could teach."

His brows rose with fresh speculation and he cocked his head, viewing her from a slightly different angle. "I see the first thing I must teach you, *ma petite widow*, is the difference between a barbarian and a soldier for hire." He stalked closer and closer . . . then sprang at her, knocking her back atop the boulder and landing over her on braced arms. She squealed and shoved furiously at him, but he seized her wrists and held them.

"A true barbarian, *ma dame*, would make you his possession . . . strip your garments and ease his loins in you without a moment's thought. But a soldier for hire asks only a fair price for his services. We have not yet agreed on the price you will pay for *your* rescue. . . ." He licked his lower lip, eyeing hers. "Perhaps a kiss, eh?"

"Nay!" she cried, struggling to bring her knee up. But his mouth swooped down on hers, claiming it with a long, hard-soft possession that robbed her of breath. When he released her and stepped back, her heart was pounding, her legs were weak, and she could scarcely focus her eyes.

Thera returned from the bushes to find Lillith glaring, scarlet-faced, at the one called Gasquar. When she demanded to know what was wrong, Lillith jerked as if startled, lurched back a step, and stammered from behind a hand over her mouth.

"I have just . . . instructed *la dame* in the difference between a barbarian and a soldier for hire," Gasquar explained with a brazen look of satisfaction.

"Oh?" Thera said icily. "There is one?"

"But of course, demoiselle," he said, his smile dimming.

"And which are you?"

The burly Frenchman shrugged, refusing to be goaded. "Saxxe and me . . . we are soldiers, of course. We have fought at each other's backs in every corner of the world. In causes holy and causes worldly . . . in the service of churches and kings, jealous husbands and rightful heirs, noble houses and merchant guilds . . . for whoever would pay to keep our blades well oiled and our bellies full." He thrust his wide shoulders back and tucked his thumbs into his belt. "Now we have come home. My old father died and I came to see to my inheritance. I am of Gascony . . . Bayonne. And Saxxe . . . he is of that mongrel race of Viking and bad French, called Norman. His family is of Rouen and—"

"So this is why there is no fire yet." Saxxe's deep tones sliced through the closing darkness. They turned and found him standing at the far edge of the dim light cast by the struggling fire, holding a bow and a brace of hares in his hands. "You have put it out with your hard blowing, Gasquar."

Gasquar grinned ruefully at what was apparently an old jest between them, then gestured to Saxxe's kill. "By the time those rabbits have lost their skins, my fire will be ready to taste them," he said, kneeling to tend the weak flame.

Thera held her breath as Saxxe turned his gaze on her. The whites of his eyes and the metal boss on his chest glowed as he materialized fully from the shadows. And as he knelt and drew one of his daggers to clean their supper, there was yet another flash of something bright. Teeth, she realized. He was grinning . . . watching the way she watched him.

Furious, she dragged Lillith to a seat on one of the large boulders nearby and wrapped her arms about her waist. But even without filling her sight, he found a way to occupy her mind.

Rouen. *Saxxe Rouen.* She heard again the way Gasquar LeBruit had said his name. It began to drum in her head, becoming counterpoint to her very heartbeat. Having a name somehow worked the miracle of making him seem more human. He was no longer just a huge, insolent, malodorous barbarian; he was a huge, insolent, malodorous soldier who bore the name of a town in Normandy. He now had a place of origin, a place where his family . . . Her eyes crept back to him and widened. He actually had a *family* . . . perhaps a mother . . . brothers and sisters.

Her gaze slid over his dark hair and onto his bare shoulder, which glowed like living bronze in the firelight. Last night he had felt hard and warm to the touch. For some reason, she had difficulty swallowing just now. Her lashes fluttered down to hide the way her eyes slid to the bulging mounds at the tops of his arms . . . which swelled and flexed with each movement. She followed them down corded forearms to a pair of large, powerful hands with fingers that—

That were covered with blood. The sight caused her to recoil in horror. She knew what was involved in butchering . . . had observed it, despite that such things were usually kept well out of her royal sight. But there was something disturbingly animallike about him bent over his prey, cutting and skinning it so efficiently, so matter-of-factly . . . something that reminded her of his dangerous nature. Soldier for hire or whatever else he called himself, he fought and killed to make his way in the world. She shuddered and turned away.

It wasn't long before the meat was spitted and turning above a bed of glowing coals. Gasquar produced a pouch of oats and poured each of them a handful, which they washed down with watered wine from a skin . . . in taut, deepening silence. It was a vast relief when Gasquar finally prodded a piece of the meat and declared it done to perfection. He used a dagger to cut portions, and handed Thera a haunch . . . which she promptly dropped because it burned her fingers.

It landed on one of the firestones and she stooped to pick it up with the edge of her surcoat. She halted, motionless, at the sight of a dagger lying on the ground between her feet. She glanced up to find Saxxe Rouen checking the horses' tethers and Gasquar LeBruit hacking off another bit of the meat, then picked up the blade, drawing it within her surcoat. When she realized she hadn't been seen, her heart raced and her knees wobbled as she returned to her seat on a nearby rock. She made a show of nibbling the meat, but her thoughts were consumed by the cold blue steel lying between her gown and surcoat, against her thigh.

Moments later she looked up to find Saxxe Rouen lifting the wineskin and pouring wine into his mouth. Could she use that blade against him? He licked his lips and she found herself staring at his mouth, those broad dusky lips, that pink tongue. Suddenly she remembered the taste of honey . . . the rough, velvety feel of his tongue against her lips . . . the sweetness of his mouth. It shocked her even more now than it had then. How could such a brute taste like honey? Had she just imagined it? What would his mouth taste like just now? Wine and honey blended?

Shivering again, she refocused her eyes . . . on the sight of him stuffing most of a rabbit haunch into his mouth at once. She winced as he chewed doggedly for a moment, then put two fingers in his mouth to fish about and draw out a large bone, tossing it over his shoulder. A piece of gristle appeared next, thrust out onto his lips and spit forcefully to the side. Then he stuffed his mouth with oats and meat so that his cheeks bulged, and he tilted his head back to pour more wine on the mass of food, to help wash it down.

As he lowered the wineskin, still chewing hard, his gaze settled into hers. He stopped mid-grind, reading the disgust in her expression. His eyes narrowed.

"Something wrong with your food?" he demanded, without bothering to swallow first.

"I seem to have lost my appetite," she said pointedly, letting the meat droop contemptuously in her hand and averting her eyes from the one responsible for ruining her meager meal.

"A shame," he said, shoving to his feet and moving around the fire to her. She shrank back against Lillith with her heart in her throat—feeling the dagger branding itself into her thigh. "But it would be more of a shame to waste good food," he said, snatching the piece of rabbit from her hand and carrying it back to his seat. He sank his teeth into it, tearing the meat from the bone with vengeful enthusiasm.

She gave a genteel shiver of distaste. He let loose a resounding belch. She started and cast him a scalding look, which he met with a foody grin, produced amidst a beard glistening with grease. Undeterred by her disgust, he gnawed the rest of the meat from the bone, swallowed it without chewing, then gave another monstrous belch. When he flung the bone aside, he smacked his lips, burping a bit more quietly, and settled back to wipe his beard and lick his fingers with exaggerated leisure. When she jerked her face away, refusing to witness any more of his swinish behavior, she heard soft, taunting laughter and her face reddened in spite of her.

The air seemed to thicken, making it harder to breathe, and her heart began to labor under the double weight of anxiety and anticipation. She glanced at Lillith, who was huddling closer, and saw the way she glared at Gasquar LeBruit.

"Perhaps you are cold, eh? Come share the heat." Gasquar's voice boomed out. "*Les chattes* . . . they always love a good fire."

"And someone to rub against," Saxxe added suggestively.

Thera turned a withering look on him and found him sprawled back on one elbow, watching her with a knowing expression.

"Cats are low, treacherous creatures . . . fit only for witches, villains, and thieves," she declared.

"Then how fitting that we should fall in together, eh, *ma chatte*?" he retorted, drawing a chuckle from Gasquar. "Do you know, demoiselle, in some places they worship cats." He watched her with a hungry eye. "And in some places they eat them."

Unnerved by both the undisguised appetite in his face and the suggestion in his tone, she stood up—taking care to hold the dagger in place beneath her surcoat—and started for her horse. He was on his feet in a flash and spread across her path.

"Where are you going?"

"For my cloak. I am cold," she said with a shiver, taking a half step back. She was indeed chilled, but her shivers had more to do with anxiety than lack of warmth. "That's what most people do when they're cold . . . put on *clothes*." She raked the exposed skin of his broad shoulders with a scathing glare. "You might try it sometime." She held her breath as his eyes narrowed, searching her, and his huge hands curled into fists. But after a moment, he leaned back on one leg and produced a knowing smile.

"I do not usually need a cloak . . . nor will you this night. There is always plenty of heat in my blankets, and I believe it is time we sought them. You have a debt to pay."

Saxxe caught the flicker of strong emotion in her eyes and braced for a deluge of tears, an attack of flailing fists, or at the very least a searing tongue-lashing. More than once, in his mind, he had seen himself having to carry her kicking and screaming from the campfire.

"I have a *bargain* to keep," she corrected stubbornly, "as do you. And how do I know you have been leading us toward the road to Brittany? I have seen no sign of it . . . neither a farm nor a village."

"It lies just over those hills," he said, jerking a thumb over his shoulder. "An easy hour's ride. You will have no trouble finding it. A village marks the trading road."

"LeBeau?" she uttered on a breath. Pray God—it had to be the village of LeBeau!

"I do not recall its name." He shrugged. "It is a small village that welcomes traders and travelers." His mention of the village's hospitality lent credence to his words and bolstered her hope that it was the place she sought.

"And now your part of the bargain, demoiselle," he reminded her, watching the tumult in her light eyes and bracing himself for a pitched battle. She stood for a moment, gathering her defenses.

"Then bring out your flea-ridden blankets," she said tightly, fleeing once more from the loss of control that threatened her more than anything he might do to her. "Just do me the courtesy of remaining *downwind*."

His firm-set jaw loosened a bit, but he turned sharply on his heel and retrieved a roll of stitched pelts and woven blankets from his mount. As he carried them beyond the small circle of firelight, she trailed a few steps after him, then stopped.

"Where are you going?" she demanded.

"This is one night I do not intend to share with anyone, demoiselle"—his voice curled around her in the dimness—"except you."

"Nay, I will give you this night, if I must . . . but here, by the fire," she said testily, pointing to the spot by her feet and praying he couldn't see her hand tremble. "Bring your blankets here."

He stared at her, too surprised to be angry at first. Never in his life had he heard of or even imagined a demoiselle who insisted upon managing and directing her own ravishment! *Stay downwind . . . bring the blankets here.* . . . Then the full, outrageous impact of her audacity struck him. By God, he was the barbarian here, and the ravishing was going to be done on his terms or else!

He scoured the dimness furiously, choosing a spot well away from the firelight behind some small boulders. There he dropped the bundle, jerked the strap that bound it, and kicked it with his foot to unroll it.

"Here. We'll sleep here!" he insisted, jabbing a finger at the ground, then bracing his fists on his hips.

"Nay." Her eyes flicked wide and she stalked back a step, then made herself halt and dug in her heels. "I say we sleep here."

He loomed toward her out of the darkness, looking huge and dangerous and utterly determined. But it was his molten gold eyes that were her undoing. She backed up another step, batting aside Lillith's hands and frantic whispers.

"Do you walk, demoiselle, or do I carry you?" he thundered. It took every scrap of her self-control to meet his threatening gaze for that brief moment.

"It all comes down to brute force with you barbarians, doesn't it?" she said, disdain providing a thin disguise for the quiver in her voice. "If you don't get your way, you bellow and bash and bully . . ." Holding her head high, she squeezed the handle of the dagger through her surcoat and turned to grasp Lillith's hand with a last, tumultuous look. The sum of her own fears was reflected in Lillith's huge brown eyes.

"This night does not count, do you hear?" she whispered desperately. Then, with a toss of her head, she strode out of the main circle of light.

"I fear that is not for you to say, Princess," Lillith muttered under her breath. "In the matter of my counting, I answer to an authority higher than yours."

Rounding the low boulders, Thera walked across the unrolled blankets and sat down smack in the middle of them. But once there, in the shadowy darkness, feeling his intensely male presence closing in, her self-possession began to desert her. She glanced up to find him outlined in firelight as he removed his two daggers, then unstrapped and removed the wide armored braces that crossed his chest. By the time he lowered himself to the blankets, the sight of his naked chest was branded in her mind . . . huge, hard mounds of muscle, a sleek channel down his breastbone, ridges along his ribs on each side, and those shocking patches of crinkled flesh which were so like the tips of her own breasts.

Suddenly she was praying . . . Pater Nosters . . . psalms . . . the intercessories of the saints . . . begging anybody and everybody in Heaven for help!

He paused, kneeling above her, staring down into her eyes. Then he bent and swept her knees to the side, to pull the blankets down and bid her enter them. And suddenly he was beside her, all around her, bearing her back onto the pallet . . . invading her senses as he pulled her into his arms.

"Now, demoiselle," he said in tones that seeped through her every pore. "I'll have what I want of you."

She held her breath and her blood stilled in her veins. As his eyes fastened on hers and he lowered his mouth, she managed to thrust back a few inches and slid the dagger, blade first, between them.

He felt the press of cold steel against his stomach and froze with his mouth only a breath away from hers. In the dimness he sought her eyes and found them filled with determination. He didn't have to look; he knew too well the feel of a dagger against his gut.

"I agreed to a night . . . not a pawing," she said thickly.

"Don't be daft. You agreed to a night in my blankets . . . in my arms!"

"And so I am . . . in your blankets and in your arms," she said, measuring her life one breath at a time as he went taut against her. "And here I shall stay . . . all night . . . as agreed."

"With a dagger between us?" he ground out with a furious laugh. "I think not, my treacherous little cat. I'll not be cheated out of my due." Testing her resolve, he leaned closer and aimed for her mouth. The unyielding blade point pricked more than just his skin . . . it skewered his male pride as well. She meant it.

For one fleeting moment he was tempted to wrench that damnable blade from her and—And what? Pin her to the ground and hold her captive all night long? She already lay within his arms ... reluctantly, but at least of her own will. Anything more, he would have to take. And what he truly wanted from her ... a taste of the luxury and pleasure he craved ... he knew he could never have by force.

"Damn it!" he ground out.

He felt her flinch, and his mind seized that small involuntary movement that betrayed her outward confidence and self-possession. He searched her huge, luminous eyes and moon-paled features. Hidden within that prickly arrogance and bravado he suddenly sensed something softer, more vulnerable. As the darkness heightened his senses, he became aware of the tension in her body and the shallowness of her breathing. He searched those sensations, interpreting them. Anger? Expectation? Anxiety?

"You are a cat with very sharp claws indeed," he said irritably, watching her. "So you think I will not like being scratched and will let you go. Well, you are wrong, demoiselle. You owe me this night and I intend to have it ... even if I must spend it with a knife at my breast."

She looked up into his shadowed eyes, then glanced away, unsure whether she had won or not. He seemed to be forfeiting carnal possession of her ... but how could she be sure? Only time would—The horrible truth dawned on her: though it had succeeded, her brash gambit had just sentenced them both to a very long and sleepless night in each other's arms. A whole night of being surrounded by his big body, feeling the weight of his massive arms, listening to his heartbeat, absorbing his heat. She groaned silently. A whole night of waiting for him to pounce on her.

The silence between them filled with small sounds: the rasp of breathing, the rustling of night hunting birds overhead, the muffled thud of racing pulses. Her body came alive with awareness. Where he touched her skin it seemed to melt, allowing him access to her very nerves . . . becoming a touch more intimate and unnerving than any she had ever experienced. Against the frantic urgings of her better sense, she slid her gaze back to his face and found him watching her with those penetrating eyes.

He felt her shiver of response and realized that while he could not take what he wanted by force, he might yet take it by persuasion. And just how did he persuade his prickly demoiselle without risking a blade in his belly?

When he moved his arm, she stiffened. But he ran his fingers over the braid coiled at the side of her head, searching for and finding the ties that held it.

"What are you—"

"I will take what pleasure I can, demoiselle. You deny me your body . . . then I will have your hair instead."

"My hair? Nay—it is not decent. You cannot—" He hadn't surrendered after all! She shoved against him, bracing back as far as his arms would allow. She was desperate to prevent him from transferring his alarmingly personal touch to her hair. A woman's hair was her glory . . . her maiden's crown . . . the outward link to her most intimate and womanly self. It belonged to a woman's future husband; a gift, like her maidenhead, to be safeguarded until the one who would own her passions claimed it. And as with all those things, Thera had planned never to yield it to anyone!

"Such beautiful hair," he murmured, freeing the braid . . . then inserting his long fingers between the woven strands and dragging them through to the end of the hair. "Silk is coarse beside it—like poor, knotted flax."

All it would take was a slight twist of her hand and the blade would bite into his skin. But for the life of her, she couldn't bring herself to turn that handle and sink that cold, merciless steel into his ribs. Higher and higher he worked his fingers through her hair, until the thick strands were tumbling over her shoulder and breast.

"Ahhh, demoiselle. The ladies of Venice would give a fortune to own such tresses," he murmured, luxuriating in the feel of it.

"Give me back this night and you may take it to them," she whispered furiously, desperate to knit up her frayed defenses. "Think of the profit you could make."

He laughed with a resonant rumble that vibrated through the dagger and up her aching arms. "Nay, Venice is too far away, demoiselle, and you are too close and too—"

Definitely too close, he realized, clamping his jaw shut. And too damned desirable. His body was humming with expectation once again, and his loins were heating at an alarming rate. Her body, on the other hand, was still as rigid as a pike staff. Rising to the challenge of softening her resistance, he shifted slightly, bending his other arm beneath her so his fingers could reach her other braid.

"Nay—" She jerked her head aside. But there was nowhere to go, and his hands were strong and alarmingly nimble. The other bindings soon yielded to him as well, and he shifted slightly, bringing her hair close to his face and breathing it in.

"It smells like roses. And roses suit you, demoiselle." One corner of his mouth lifted. "Beauty, but with thorns."

She stared at him, panicked by the strange push-pull going on in her. Where force would have failed, his unexpected gentleness and the vulnerability of her own overtaxed senses combined to weaken her resistance against him. She had no inner defenses to deal with such feelings or with the turmoil they created in her. Her only hope was to put anger and distance between them!

"You, on the other hand, smell like a stable without a shovel," she said, curling her nose. "And there is enough grease in that disgusting pelt on your face to oil a pair of cart wheels."

His hand clenched around her hair and his eyes narrowed furiously. She could feel his chest swelling so that it pressed harder against the blade and braced for the worst, but, deep inside, she was less afraid of his anger than she had been of his unbearably personal touch.

He made a grating noise through his teeth and released her hair as if it were indeed full of thorns. Then after a moment of sizzling silence, he jerked his arms from her and rolled onto his back to stare angrily up into the night sky.

"Go to sleep," he snarled.

It had worked! He had let her go! She sagged with disbelief and, after several moments, rolled onto her back too, still clutching the dagger with both hands. As moment followed moment in the quiet darkness, her tension slowly began to subside. She stared up at the pale half-moon overhead, feeling every stone beneath her hard bed and aching from the day's exertions. Exhaustion stole over her.

She strained to keep her attention fastened on him, to stay awake and wary. In desperation, she reverted to her habit of counting things: the number of hours left until dawn . . . the number of belches Saxxe Rouen had emitted while eating . . . the number of miles they had yet to travel to reach Mercia . . . the probable number of months it had been since Saxxe Rouen had taken a bath. But always, by the time she reached twenty-seven, she had settled into a lulling, rhythmic cadence and felt her eyes growing heavy.

She chose a new subject and tried again and again as moment was linked to moment and soon an hour had passed. Halfway through a second hour, she had acquired a whole new appreciation of the concept of "eternity." She had to stay alert, had to be prepared. He was unpredictable. He was treacherous. He was— she heard his shallow, regular breathing—he was finally *asleep*.

Her sense of release was overwhelming. Her eyes drifted shut, and though she tried valiantly to reopen them, the effort was too much. She slid into blessed, comforting darkness and did not hear the stones grate and sinews groan, later, as Saxxe rolled onto his side, against her.

In the intervening hours, both his irritation and his desire had drained, leaving him cooler and better able to think. With his eyes fully adjusted now, he could make out her features in the moon glow. He propped up on one elbow, watching the rise and fall of her breast and searching the torrent of hair around her shoulders. She seemed younger, somehow. Softer. More womanly. For the tenth time that day, he wondered who she was. Thera of Aric. He sorted through the names of the French noble houses he had once been required to learn. Aric was not among them.

What he did know of her both tantalized and puzzled him. She was obviously of noble birth, used to the finest of everything. And in the last two days she had been thrust into the worst the world had to offer . . . abduction, near rape, loss of her possessions. Any other demoiselle would have long since dissolved into helpless sobs. But she screamed and fought and bargained and demanded. . . .

His gaze slid down her moon-brightened gown to the steel dagger she held. He scowled and sat up, touching the blade, testing her reaction. When she did not waken, he gently pried her cold, cramped fingers from the blade hilt. It was Gasquar's dagger. He plunged it into the sand at the edge of the blanket with a rueful smile. She was resourceful, his fierce little cat.

But then, inexplicably, his eyes were drawn back to her hands, which even in sleep had continued to clutch that blade hilt with desperation. And for some reason he recalled the odd look in her eyes earlier, the hint of vulnerability and inner struggle. Those impressions now came together. Deep inside, she was also *frightened*.

The insight both surprised and annoyed him.

"*Dieu*, Rouen," he growled softly, running a hand through his tangled hair. "You have to think, don't you? You cannot leave well enough alone. You always have to peek in the box . . . see what is inside. And before you know it, you are up to your stubborn neck in trouble again." He took a deep breath and steeled himself.

"She is none of your concern, this treacherous little witch. Twice you have saved her precious hide, and what do you have to show for it? Sneers and insults, a blade at your belly, and a night of being roasted on the flame in your own loins."

He drew his knees up and rested his arms on them, trying not to notice how alluring she looked in the moonlight . . . with her hair all tumbled around her shoulders. He could ill afford the stirring she caused in his loins. There was something else he wanted, something far more important than merely easing a flesh ache. And how damned close he had come to forgetting it, with her lying soft and desirable against his pleasure-starved body!

She was a noble lady; beautiful, well-born, and wealthy. She could never be more to him than an opportunity to line his purse with silver . . . perhaps enough for a small piece of land. And to receive that reward, he would have to return her to her long-suffering and overindulgent father, undamaged and intact.

"A meadow, an orchard, and a stream," he murmured, like an incantation meant to keep the demons of passion at bay. "Just think of what a reward might buy . . . sweet grass and wildflowers . . . pears and apples so plentiful they bend branches down . . . cool, clear water trickling by. Just think of a hearth and a bed of your own."

The chilled air swirled around his bare shoulders, and he recalled her cold hands and pulled his fur cover up and over her. In that movement, his knuckles brushed her hair and he picked up a lock of it, rubbing it between his fingers and thinking of cinnamon and Saracen sugar. Then he caught himself, groaned irritably, and let the hair fall to her shoulder.

"If you had the sense God gave an onion, you would let her find her own way back to her rich father and his bags of—"

Of hard silver coin . . . spendable profit. Was he going to let a woman's sharp tongue and a troublesome bit of heat in his loins ruin his best chance for real coin in years? Like hell he would. And what would happen tomorrow morning when her "debt" was paid and he had no further claim on her? She had already rejected his generous offer of "help."

"Cross that river when you come to it, Rouen," he muttered furiously, lying back down, then sitting up briefly to drag a musty blanket over his bare chest. "If she won't listen to reason, you can always tie her up."

Chapter Six

Thera roused with a start in the first gray wisps of dawn light. She pushed up stiffly on one arm, feeling sore and chilled and damp. Her hair hung in clumps around her shoulders, and the feel of it hanging free shocked her. A moment later she was jarred further by the sight of Saxxe Rouen sprawled, half naked and half covered, on the dew-covered pallet beside her. Peeling the furs from her shoulders, she melted with relief at the sight of her undisturbed gown and surcoat.

It was time to go, before he awakened and found some other excuse to hold her against her will . . . like deciding she might be worth a fat ransom. Pushing back the cover, she crept quietly from the pallet and found Lillith curled up in her cloak on a blanket by the cold firestones. She was startled awake by Thera's hand over her mouth, but quickly understood her gestures for silence and nodded.

They almost had their horses saddled when Saxxe Rouen started awake. Thera heard his growl of surprise and knew it would be mere heartbeats before they were discovered. "They're awake!" she called quietly, inserting her foot into the stirrup and hopping to gain enough leverage to mount.

"Gasquar!" She heard Saxxe Rouen's roar and with a frantic glance over her shoulder, she saw him untangling himself from his blanket and scrambling to his feet. She kicked her horse into motion and went racing down the hillside and across the wide, treeless slope below the small cliff, with Lillith not far behind.

They rode hard for a while, racing over hills and around thickets of trees, heading straight for the hills Saxxe Rouen had pointed out the evening before. Time and again, Thera glanced back over her shoulder, expecting to see him bearing furiously down on them. But there was only the chilled, gray landscape behind them.

After a while, they found themselves by a clear, rocky stream at the bottom of a steep valley. They dismounted to water their horses and fill their empty stomachs with water. She caught Lillith staring at her disheveled hair and scowled at her.

"Don't ask," she commanded irritably, tossing the soft mass over her shoulder.

"I didn't say a thing." Lillith sniffed, moving behind Thera to drag her fingers through Thera's hair and restore some order to it. She felt Thera shiver at her touch and her eyes widened. "I don't see any bruises."

"Bruises?" Thera stiffened and turned partway.

"Of course, not all men—" Lillith bit her lip and frowned. "But I thought, being a barbarian, he would be—" She halted, flushed, and began to weave Thera's hair into a loose single plait that began at her shoulders. "As soon as we reach Thomas Rennet's, I'll see you have a good warm bath. I'm sure you're sore as—"

"Sore?" Thera frowned, then her eyes widened as she realized what Lillith meant. The consequences of a first mating were not unknown to her; she had received a thorough education in all things pertaining to the life of her people. Lillith believed she had actually . . .

"Lillith Montaigne, I shall say this only once," she said emphatically. "He is a vile, loathsome barbarian. I did not go to his blankets willingly . . . and once there, I surrendered absolutely nothing to him. There was nothing for you to count."

Lillith tucked her chin, looking chastened, but as Thera turned back to her horse, she mumbled: "Your hair says otherwise, Princess. And, whether you enjoyed it or not, you made the bargain. And I have to count it."

Moments later they were splashing through the rocky shallows of the stream. As they started up the other bank, Thera looked up to the hilltop ahead and jerked her horse to a halt, putting out a hand to stop Lillith.

On the crest sat a group of men on horseback, watching them. There were at least half a dozen, all wearing black. With a blink and a squint, Thera could make out mail hauberks ... swords and pikes. Her stomach contracted. *Black*. They were garbed and armed just like the soldiers yesterday.

The one in front pointed to her and said something that set the others laughing. She looked down at her white gown ... so visible. So visibly *rich*. Her heart gave a convulsive lurch in her chest and she wheeled her horse, crying out: "Ride, Lillith! Ride!"

"W-where?" Lillith managed to shout as she too jerked her horse around and dug in with her heels.

Where indeed? There was no time to think, only to act on raw instinct. They were up the first hill and down, with the sound of hooves thundering behind them, before Thera realized where her instinct was taking her. They had only one hope ... only one place to go. . . .

Saxxe had stood with his fists clenched and his chest heaving, watching Thera of Aric racing off across the mist-shrouded hills. She was gone. And with her went all of his hopes for a fat profit. The realization made him as surly as a bear roused in winter. He muttered and snarled as he strapped on his cross braces, belt, and daggers, then kicked his blankets into a messy, dusty roll. Gasquar watched with a scowl as he packed up his own furs and went to saddle his horse.

"Are you angered because the night was so bad, *mon ami* . . . or so good?" he said with a wry chuckle, breaking the fierce silence.

"She's a witch ... with the face of an angel and the tongue of an adder," Saxxe declared, throwing his sleeping roll down beside his horse. "A temptation conjured by the Devil himself to beset and confound mankind. Naught but trouble. We're well rid of her." He spread a felt saddle pad on his mount's back and paused, glaring off in the direction she had ridden. "There is never a profit in rescuing demoiselles in distress. If I forget that hard-won bit of wisdom again, Gasquar—for God's sake, take a club and beat some sense into me."

Gasquar laughed softly, listening to Saxxe's fury and reading in his curt, hot movements the unquenched fires still smoldering in his loins. So he had not taken his pleasure of the fiery demoiselle after all. Gasquar shook his head in both sympathy and disbelief. To have had such a creature in his blankets all night without enjoying her . . . it would ruin any man's temper. "Come, *mon ami*, have a bite of food. A full belly helps you forget the hunger in your loins."

As they sat down on the stones to devour a handful of oats, the rumble of distant hooves broke in on them. They exchanged looks of surprise and straightened to scan the nearby terrain. Suddenly two riders, bent hard to their mounts, appeared over the crest of the hill on the far side of the valley. Saxxe shot to his feet, shading his eyes.

White . . . a blur of *white* was visible on one horse.

"*Dieu*—It's her," he declared, his scowl deepening as he strode toward the edge of the cliff. As Gasquar joined him, the cause for her mad flight appeared on the crest of the hill behind her. Horsemen—a hasty count yielded half a dozen—armed and riding hell-bent after her. "Damnation!" Saxxe roared. "Didn't I tell you? Here she comes—with trouble on her tail yet again!" But Gasquar saw Saxxe's face lighting with a devilish grin.

Thera clung to her horse's mane, praying with everything in her that Saxxe Rouen and Gasquar LeBruit would still be there. And as they spotted the craggy wall of rock and raced straight for it, her prayers were answered. A huge, dark figure loomed up from the top of the rock face . . . shaggy, broad-shouldered, standing with his long legs spread and his huge fists propped on his hips. The archangel Michael couldn't have been a more welcome sight at that moment. Saxxe Rouen . . . all she could think was that they were saved.

"Soldiers!" she called, reining up beneath the cliff.

"So I see," Saxxe shouted down, leaning back on one leg.

"Like the ones yesterday!" she panted out, glancing back over her shoulder. She could see that some of them now brandished weapons.

"So they are," he declared, scrutinizing the men bearing down on them. "You do have a way of attracting trouble, demoiselle." His infuriatingly casual reaction to her peril made it clear that he would not volunteer help this time; she would have to ask for it.

"Well?" Thera's pride flamed. Seeing him in his full, arrogant glory once more, her relief wilted. Perhaps they could still outride . . . She tossed a glance over her shoulder and made out the shapes of the soldiers' helmets and the beards on their faces. She whipped back with a groan. "Will you help us?"

"Yea, demoiselle—for a price."

"Curse you, Rouen—I don't have time to haggle!" Nor did they have time to ride around the hill; the riders were already rumbling onto the broad slope leading to the cliff.

"Then you will have to pay my price, eh, demoiselle?"

"Ohhh—wretch!"

Their only chance was to go straight up the craggy rock itself, she realized, and she slid to the ground, pulling Lillith down with her. "Climb!" The snarls on the soldiers' faces were now clearly visible, and she searched frantically for footholds and handholds in the rock.

"What is it—what do you want?"

"Another night," he demanded, kneeling on one knee near the edge of the cliff, watching her desperate climb. "But this time, a night of *pleasure*."

"Horses! Take our horses inste—Aghhh!" Her foot slipped and she grabbed at the rock, dislodging a trickle of loose stone down the craggy cliff. She glanced down at both the rocks below and the grizzled black-clad forms dismounting. Sweet Mother of—she could see the whites of their eyes! "Clothes. You can have my clothes—every stitch!"

"*Pleasure*, demoiselle—a whole night of it!" His voice rolled down over her, unhurried and seemingly unswayed by her peril. "You may spend this night in pleasure with me . . . or in terror with the lot of them. Which will it be?"

The soldiers' grunts and growls roiled up from below, and she could feel the men reaching, brushing her ankles . . . could almost feel their vile hands binding her limbs and pawing beneath her skirts.

"*You!*" she cried, stretching toward him.

In a flash, Saxxe dropped down onto the edge of the cliff and reached to clasp her wrists. He put his back into it, pulled, and gradually hauled her up and over the rocky ledge. She scrambled back from the edge, her heart pounding wildly, and found herself caught in his arms, staring up into his fierce, glowing eyes.

"A wise choice, demoiselle," he declared with a lusty grin, shoving to his feet and bearing her back to the safety of the nearby boulders. When she looked for Lillith, she found Gasquar LeBruit carrying her to the rocks as well, and she stretched out her hands to clasp Lillith tightly.

Saxxe wheeled and ripped his blade from the scabbard across his back, setting the blue steel ringing. He glanced at the soldiers dragging themselves over the edge of the cliff, then looked back at his friend with a fierce smile.

"Gasquar—we fight!"

They met the soldiers full out, with a roar that made the blood stand still in Thera's veins. The attackers rushed Saxxe by twos, then threes, and he stopped their charge with an expression that could almost have been called pleasure. He wielded his massive blade with both hands, swinging freely, slashing with mighty strokes that originated in the depths of his broad back. Each angle of his blade, each shift of his massive shoulders, was calculated for deadly impact. With her heart in her throat, she saw him fall back under a blow, then, when his opponent lunged inside the deadly arc of his blade, he reversed and darted in like a striking hawk.

The clang of metal striking metal tolled across the hilltop and reverberated in Thera's head and heart. She squeezed Lillith's hands and flinched and gasped with each hit he took ... until suddenly his body wrenched violently and there was a gurgling cry. Her heart stopped until one of his opponents crumpled and fell to the ground with a thud.

Slowly, relentlessly, he took his other opponents down, one by one. But Thera hardly saw the strokes that felled them; she was transfixed by the savage grace of his movements, the raw, elemental power coiled within his body, and the chilling aura of control about him. She had never imagined a human form moving like his, had never suffered such wild, nerve-searing excitement in her life. It was both terrifying and fascinating, and together those seductive feelings eclipsed her horror at witnessing a blade battle at close range. For a few moments her personal peril was forgotten in the hypnotic fury of his fighting.

When his own opponents lay in heaps at his feet, Saxxe stood for a moment with his mighty chest heaving, then charged in to help Gasquar. There was another cry, and she came to her senses in time to see one soldier flailing backward off the cliff's edge ... and another going down onto his knees, then falling over, clutching his belly.

Suddenly all was eerily still, and Saxxe and Gasquar were the only two combatants left standing. They staggered toward each other, panting, scarcely able to keep their feet. The sound of horse hooves drifting up from the slope below sent them stumbling to the cliff's edge. A lone soldier on horseback was racing down the slope away from them. They clapped hands on each other's shoulders, bracing each other up.

"Let us hope he does not have more friends nearby," Gasquar said, drawing a nod of agreement from Saxxe.

Then, remembering, Saxxe released Gasquar and staggered back to Thera, still clutching his red-stained blade.

His bronzed body was slick with sweat and his face glowed like fired bronze. He planted himself before her, staring down at her with eyes that burned darkly with unspent passions.

"Now you are safe, demoiselle." His hot-eyed grin sent a shiver down her spine. "From everyone except me."

"Not a bad fight, eh?" Gasquar declared with a broad gesture as they rode purposefully toward the village through rolling hills and vales of trees edged with the delicate spring-green of new leaves. Lillith made a point of lifting her chin and ignoring him ... which deterred him none at all. "Not the worst odds we have faced, Saxxe and me. In Damascus, once, we stood for two days and nights, defending the tower of the garrison against scores of Turks."

"A likely story," Lillith muttered, rolling her eyes and glancing at Thera, who looked straight ahead, trying not to listen.

"*Alors*, there was the time in Alexandria when we fought with Louis the Pious against the Saracens ... scores of them to each one of us. And another time, in Algiers, when fighting for the Caliph of Shalizar, we each took on a hundred of the sea-raiding infidels."

"I could swear I feel the *khamsin* once again," Saxxe muttered, wetting a finger and lifting it into the breeze. Gasquar laughed.

"You fought with King Louis? In his Crusade?" Thera turned, pinning the boastful Frenchman with a skeptical gaze.

"But of course. Some years ago. It was the start of our travels. To Syria first, with good Louis, then to Damietta and on to Alexandria we went." He sighed at the remembrance. "Our hearts were set on freeing Jerusalem."

"And our heads on making a fortune ... like the brave and stalwart knights of the cross before us," Saxxe added wryly. Thera glared at him, then looked back to Gasquar, shocked by something he had said.

"You fought for an Arab lord? A *Moslem*?"

"A caliph, *oui*," Gasquar corrected with a grin. "And it was also there that we encountered the most memorable odds of our lives." He leaned toward her in his saddle and lowered his voice to a lusty rasp. "In the fat caliph's harem ... there were two hundred women to each of us. We were trapped for days, Saxxe and I, valiantly wielding our *blades*." His dark Gascon eyes twinkled and he chuckled wickedly. "But try as we might, we were unable to vanquish them all."

Thera sat straighter in the saddle, reddening and suppressing the urge to look at Saxxe. But it was no use; in her mind's eye she could still see him as he had been in the early morning sunlight ... his body strung taut one instant and moving with fluid ease the next. Then for one breathtaking moment she suffered a vision of him in a sea of women ... grappling, writhing, his body hot and quivering, his eyes burning as they had in the darkness last night. Merciful Catherine! Did he conquer women with the same force with which he fought men?

Shocked by the thought, she refocused her eyes outward and caught him looking at her from beneath lowered brows ... his eyes dark and oddly penetrating, as if he had read her thoughts. The twitch of amusement at the corner of his mouth annoyed her. "So ... you have fought for infidel Moslems as well as Christian lords," she said, covering her embarrassment with disdain. "Well, that certainly accounts for the nobility of your bearing and the delicacy of your manners."

"Yea, I have adopted a number of vile Moslem ways," he said irritably. "I speak the truth, I take only what is mine, and I always fight to win." After a moment, his ire somewhat spent, he continued: "And of course ... like all good infidel Moslems, I also eat babies and am growing a sixth finger on each hand." When her eyes widened and flew to his hands, he gave a harsh laugh which drew a chuckle from Gasquar.

Her face flamed and she kicked her mount to urge it forward, to ride ahead several paces. Six fingers—like Old Scratch himself was reported to have! It wouldn't have surprised her if it were true, the devil! Yet her pride would not burn hot enough to purge the lingering image of his hungry, knowing eyes. And that taunting vision weighed on her mind, reminding her that she was in his debt once again. Another *night*. Her eyes narrowed. She'd sooner spend the night being pickled at the bottom of a tanner's vat than in his moldy old furs and blankets.

But she wouldn't be just in his blankets this time, she realized. She had pledged him a night of pleasure. Frantically, she thought ahead to the village of LeBeau and Thomas Rennet's tavern and stable. Once they arrived at good Thomas's house, she would have to find something to substitute. Silver, perhaps . . . he had mentioned silver.

With her mind so occupied, she hadn't noticed the sun sliding behind a veil of haze. When Lillith called her name, she glanced up and noticed wisps of gray in the sky ahead. On the breeze she caught a faint smell of smoke. The ring of blade metal sounded behind her, and she started as Saxxe and Gasquar thundered past her with their swords drawn. They rode hard for the top of the next hill, then reined up sharply at the sight of whatever lay beyond it. She and Lillith urged their mounts faster to join them, then stared in disbelief at the village below.

It was indeed LeBeau. But most of the modest houses, cottages, and byres now lay in ruins, their stone hearths and timbers jutting like picked bones from among heaps of smoking cinders. Here and there lay crumpled human forms, and around the two or three structures left unburned, a number of armed men garbed in chillingly familiar black brandished their weapons and bullied a group of villagers.

As they watched, the soldiers entered one of the remaining dwellings, rousting the householders and sending them sprawling into the dust outside. Sounds of women wailing and wood crashing wafted up on the low, disturbing drone of flames as the mercenaries reappeared, carrying out sacks of plunder . . . then set a torch to the house.

"We have to stop them!" Thera choked out, kneeing her mount. But before she had gone two paces, Saxxe wheeled his horse across her path and seized her reins. "Out of the way! Thomas Rennet is down there and I have to help him!"

"Who is this Thomas Rennet?" he demanded, glowering.

"He is one of my—"

"Please, my lady!" Lillith cried, straining to catch Thera's sleeve and keep her from revealing that Thomas was one of her royal subjects. When Thera turned a furious look on her, she answered with a wordless plea that reminded Thera of her own precarious position.

"One of your what?" Saxxe demanded, watching unspoken words passing between them. After a moment, Thera looked back at him, her eyes clear and earnest in a way he had never seen them before. Whether it was because of this "Thomas" or not, she was genuinely distraught over the fate of the village.

"One of my father's agents. He is one of our people," she answered with an urgency that struck a chord of truth in him. "I have to help them."

Saxxe glanced over his shoulder, and his jaw flexed as he studied the grim sights of the ransacked village and motionless forms. His gaze fixed on the soldiers who had wreaked that havoc. "Black again. No colors and no banner. They look to be part of the same force that invaded Nantes. Perhaps an outriding party." He turned a questioning look on Gasquar.

"Or forerunners. They could be on the move," Gasquar offered with a wary frown. "That bull Spaniard said they had battles ahead."

"Who do they ride for?" Saxxe wondered aloud. "Who has loosed this dark scourge on the countryside? Black mail . . ." He glanced at Gasquar. "Do you recall any noble who bestows such armor?" Gasquar shrugged and Saxxe scowled. "And no escutcheons on their shields . . ."

"Stand out of the way." Thera tried to jerk her reins from him, but he refused to release them. Instead, he searched the terrain and pulled her horse into motion, heading for the cover of a stand of trees which was just down the back of the hill, out of sight of the village. "Let me go—"

"And just what will you do, demoiselle?" Saxxe demanded, leaning across the pommel of his saddle. "Ride in and give the score of them a stout lashing with your tongue? You'd find yourself flat on your back in a trice . . . suffering the same fate you narrowly escaped two nights ago."

"You don't understand," she said with a frantic edge. "Thomas has a wife and children. It is my duty to see that his household is—"

"You can do nothing, demoiselle," Gasquar added, shaking his head grimly.

"They speak truly, my lady," Lillith said, pleading with Thera through tear-filled eyes. "There is naught we can do now. Once you are safely home . . . you can get your family to send back help for Thomas and the village."

Once you are safely home. Lillith's pleas finally took hold of Thera's reeling thoughts. By herself, without escort and resources, she could no more defend good Thomas Rennet and his family against violence than she could defend herself. And there was the much larger problem to consider—safeguarding her isolated kingdom.

Thoughts of home produced another devastating realization, the enormity of which swamped her. How would she get home now, without Thomas's help?

Saxxe beheld unguarded feelings in her face for the first time. He watched her transforming with each blink of an eye; from haughty, self-contained noble to passionate young woman to vulnerable maid. Her unexpected softening produced a strange sinking in his chest, and to counter that alarming slide, he straightened in his saddle and scowled.

"Who are you, demoiselle?" he demanded. "The truth. Who is your father, and where are his lands?"

Thera's eyes were as dark as an evening sky, and he could see with startling clarity that she was struggling to raise her defenses. "My father is a . . . baron . . . who holds a castellany in the west for the Duc de Brittany."

"The barony of Aric, then." He rocked back on his saddle and narrowed his gaze on her. There was no such castle or holding in what he knew of Brittany, but he gave a contemplative nod and tilted his head to study her from a slightly different angle. It was probably futile to ask more, knowing she would only lie, but he couldn't help voicing his questions aloud. "And what were you doing alone in Nantes with only your lady companion?"

"I was not alone. . . . I had an escort." Her pride flared briefly. "But yesterday, as we tried to leave the city for home, we were set upon by those devils in black, and my escort—" She looked down at her whitened fingers as they gripped the pommel. "I did not see them again . . . my father's men."

Saxxe shifted on his seat, considering the enigmatic young beauty. What a strange creature she was, this arrogant and infuriating demoiselle who issued orders like a military commander, kissed like the greenest of virgins, and kept her word to sleep in a man's arms, even though it meant holding him at knife point all night long.

There was a great deal he didn't know about her. But he knew enough not to let her slip through his fingers again.

"Then it appears you are without protection, without food and supplies, and without guide or escort," he said, watching her reassembling her self-possession. "And by your own word, you are still several days from home. I repeat my offer, demoiselle." He flicked a questioning look at Gasquar, who merely raised an eyebrow in agreement. "Gasquar and I, we could escort you home . . . for a price."

"A price?" Thera looked up into his dark, bearded countenance and found an acquisitive gleam in his eye. He not only looked and smelled like a mangy wolf, he had the predatory instinct of one as well!

"Another night of pleasure, demoiselle," he announced, cutting into her irritable thoughts. When she reddened and glanced at Lillith, he leaned an elbow on the pommel of his saddle with a half smile that proclaimed his advantage. "You owe me one night already. Give me another and I will see you safely home."

"Another *night*?" she choked, straightening in her saddle and harnessing the heat of her burning pride to fire her wits. "Not a particularly shrewd mercenary, are you? If this is the sort of price you generally require, it is little wonder you haven't a decent tunic to your name." She lifted her chin, pleased by his start of surprise. "Still . . . I suppose barbarians don't have a lot to work with." She elevated her nose so that she could look down it at him.

"Perhaps you need a bit of help in coming to an advantageous arrangement. You were correct in thinking my family wealthy, Rouen. They are indeed. And they will pay well to have me returned. I can see you receive a hundred silver groats when we reach my home. Pure silver . . . fine, new coins, straight from Venice itself."

"A most reasonable offer, *oui*?" Gasquar broke in, urging him to accept.

"A hundred silver groats?" Saxxe echoed, surprised and thinking fast. A hundred Venetian groats . . . more silver than he could count . . . more silver than he could expect to earn in ten years of fighting . . . if he lived that long in his perilous trade. Then why did he feel this unsettling reluctance to accept?

His eyes traced the warm, flushed curve of her cheek, slid down the seductive hollow of her throat, and fastened on the gentle swell of her breast. The air he inhaled felt strangely hot and thick. He wanted . . . he wanted . . . *A meadow, an orchard, and a stream*, he repeated desperately. And promise of another night with her, he told himself, would give him a claim upon her person that might be worth a good bit more than one bag of silver.

"A mere hundred to take you home? To suffer the lash of your tongue and the scratch of your claws for God knows how long?" He winced and crossed his arms over his chest, relishing her expression as he turned her earlier words back upon her. "Who is to say I'd even get you there? For all I know, you could be drowned in a river, or thrown by your horse and trampled, or eaten by wolves along the way. And there I would be . . . cheated out of my just reward." He stroked his beard and leaned back in his saddle, watching her sputter. "Nay, my price is firm. Another night of pleasure, demoiselle . . . or you may find your own way home."

She glanced at Lillith and knew too well the cause of the horror in her face. Saxxe Rouen had the upper hand here, and they both knew it. She had no guide, no sustenance, no protection . . . and no choice.

"Curse you, Rouen." She drew an irritable breath, determined to have at least some say in the terms of her surrender. "I'll give you your miserable night, but on one condition. That you collect it only after you have earned it . . . after I am safely home."

He hesitated a moment, turning it over in his mind. She expected him to object or to demand his reward in advance. But, to her genuine surprise, he nodded and handed back her reins.

"Let us be on our way, demoiselle. We have a long day's journey ahead. And I have a debt to collect at the end of it."

Chapter Seven

An unseasonably strong sun bore down upon them as they rode, stinging Thera's and Lillith's unprotected skin and steaming them inside their woolen surcoats. When Gasquar pointed to the billowy white clouds building ahead, in the west, Thera's only reaction was a fervent prayer that she might soon be spared the discomfort of the sun on her hot, reddened skin. And from the way Lillith winced and moved her lips each time her mount set a hoof down hard, she guessed that Lillith was detailing her misery to the Almighty, as well.

By the time they stopped by a stream for food and rest, Thera's eyes burned, her head ached from squinting, and her thighs and buttocks were burning from the constant friction of the saddle. She remained on her mount for a moment, staring at the cool water pouring over the rocks with a longing so fierce that it approached what she imagined must be lust. What she wouldn't give for a bath ... in a lovely warm pool of water ... scented with rose petals ...

Dismounting without assistance, she wobbled to the stream with her horse, then sank to her knees at the edge and made a veritable sponge of herself. When she sat back, moments later, wiping her wet face with her voluminous outer sleeve, she found Lillith beside her, examining her with a worried expression.

"Are you all right, Princess?" Lillith felt Thera's hot cheek and tucked a stray lock of hair back into her braid. "Your poor skin. Oh, I knew we should have worn wimples for traveling."

"You know how I loathe wimples. I always feel I'm in

a cage," Thera said, fanning herself with the edge of her surcoat, then jiggling the high neck of her tunic to admit some air to her suffering skin. "And I already feel like I've been spitted and roasted to a turn." The movement of her gown released a mingling of earthy scents and she made a face. "And well seasoned."

She looked toward the western hills and her kingdom, and thought longingly of the aging body servant she had refused to bring on the arduous journey to Nantes. Her eyes drifted closed as she imagined herself in her own cool, spacious chambers . . . being bathed and scented with fragrant oils. "What I wouldn't give for one of Esme's special baths."

Lillith looked away and mumbled, "You're in debt quite enough already."

"What?" Thera's eyes snapped open.

"I s-said . . . you can bet Esme will have one ready . . . when we return." Lillith pulled her chin in and her face reddened more beneath her sunburn. "*If* we return," she added dismally.

"We'll return, all right," Thera said, setting her hands in the small of her back and arching over them. Slashing a dagger of a look at Gasquar and Saxxe, on the opposite bank, she let out a harsh breath. "Saxxe Rouen will see we get home, if only to collect his wretched *reward*."

"About his reward," Lillith ventured, relieved that Thera had raised the subject weighing heavily on her mind. "How will you explain to Cedric and the Elders that you must take him to your bed? Surely they will learn of—" She halted as Thera's expression became a glower.

"You never cease to amaze me, Lillith. Can you honestly believe I would take that crude, violent churl into Mercia's royal palace—into my very bed?"

"Well . . . you did agree." Lillith's eyes widened. "And there is tonight . . ."

"I do not intend to spend another single moment trapped against his loathsome, overheated body, ever," Thera whispered vehemently. "Not tonight, not any night. I found a way to escape it last night . . . I'll find a way to get out of it tonight, too." But instead of being comforted by those words, Lillith seemed genuinely disturbed.

"But, Princess, you gave your word. And the royal word is sacred. Once given—"

"I did not *give* it, it was dragged out of me . . . coldly and callously coerced from me. I'll not be bound by such an ill-begotten bargain," Thera declared, annoyed by Lillith's shock. "Don't you look at me like that, Lillith Montaigne. I shall see him well paid in silver, and he will have to be content with that."

Lillith dropped her gaze to avoid Thera's, and the disappointment that rounded her shoulders weighed on Thera's already burdened conscience. She didn't like the idea of bending her word any more than Lillith did, but she liked the notion of surrendering to Saxxe Rouen even less. Imagine giving herself up to a crude, half-naked soldier for hire—little more than a barbarian! It would be a disgrace to the throne and an insult to the men of Mercia.

"Trouble upon trouble," Lillith said, breaking into Thera's thoughts with a hushed whisper of portent. When she looked up, she seemed oddly pale beneath her sunburned skin. "It's the prophecy. 'With trouble and contention ripe . . . ' It has begun, Princess. And if you break your word, the troubles will only grow worse and—"

"Stop that!" Thera demanded. "Not another word, do you hear? I'll not have you flailing me with that wretched prophecy! I've quite enough to cope with as it is!" She pushed to her feet and made her way to the bushes, some distance away.

Saxxe heard her raised voice and wheeled with his hand on the hilt of his blade . . . in time to see her stalking off toward the underbrush with her face aflame and her lady companion staring after her with a chastened look. He hadn't caught her words, but something about the way Lillith quickly turned to look at him raised prickles of alarm along his neck. He stretched taut, to his full height, and followed Thera into the bushes with his gaze. Alone and afoot she couldn't go far, he knew, but he struck off after her anyway.

Thera's skin, her pride, and her conscience were all ablaze, and the resulting heat combined with the merciless sun to bake her inside her clothes. She made a quick stop in the bushes, then went to the stream to wash, trying not to dwell on Lillith's claim that these troubles were a result of her solitary throne.

It was ridiculous, of course, to think that her coupling with a man would have the power to temper winter gales, ensure plentiful rain, set blossoms into fruit, and produce a bountiful crop of spring lambs. It was just tales and superstition . . . the thinking of the Old Ones. Male and female in conjunction. Pagan, really. A relic of the old life-ways.

But all the learning and logic of the intervening Christian centuries had not dimmed those stubborn beliefs in the ancient prophecies . . . any more than they had eliminated the desire for the old custom of the rites of May or the tradition of the seven nights for a marriage. And, infuriatingly, it was her wisest and most educated nobles, her Council of Elders, who seemed to hold the deepest convictions about the old prophecies. Now even her countess was haranguing her about them. Their present difficulties were the start of the fulfillment of the prophecies, she said. Why couldn't they see it was all mare's nests and pigeon's milk . . . pure *nonsense!*

But even as Thera shook her head and purged those thoughts, she was left with a vaguely unsettled feeling that she couldn't entirely banish.

She emerged from the shrubby growth onto a grassy bank and stood looking at the clear water bubbling through the rocky channel. Every ache in her overheated body intensified at the sight. On impulse, she kicked off her shoes and gathered the folds of her voluminous surcoat and tunic about her knees, then waded barefoot into the flowing water.

"Ahhh." Ripples of pleasure raced up her legs as she searched for footholds on the rocky bottom and edged deeper into the stream. "It's wonderful," she groaned, wading back and forth to let the swirling water soothe her. The cool comfort of it lured her in deeper and deeper, until she was up to her knees, holding her skirts up in a droopy bundle around her thighs. Soon she was kicking and splashing about with abandon, fairly dancing in the water.

For a few brief moments it was almost like the old days in Mercia . . . when she had time for gamboling in streams, and picking wildflowers with her mother and the court ladies, and lying on her back in the gardens studying the clouds. A bead of sweat slid down her neck and between her shoulder blades, causing her to wriggle her shoulders. If only she could strip off her stifling clothes and plunge her whole sticky body into—

"Go ahead," came a voice from the bank behind her. She whirled and found Saxxe Rouen standing with his arms folded over his chest, watching her. Even from a distance she could see that his eyes glowed oddly and that his stance radiated a sultry, alarming heat. "Take them off, demoiselle, and dive in."

She froze, stunned that he had read her mind, then she fumbled with her skirts, lowering them to cover her knees. "I-I was hot . . . and saw the water . . . and . . ."

"Hot?" A slow grin spread over his mouth. He bent down and hooked her soft-soled leather shoes on two fingers. "There's a simple remedy." He pulled his eyes from her slippers and raked them down her form. "Take off some of those clothes."

The intensity of his stare made her feel that he was doing that very thing . . . in his mind. She felt a worrisome contraction in her stomach as she realized she was well out of Lillith's sight, possibly even out of hearing distance. The privacy she had relished only moments before now represented a potential threat.

"Remove my garments and go half naked . . . like you?" she said with a sniff of distaste. "Nay . . . I prefer civilized raiment." Picking her way along the rocky bottom, toward the bank, she glanced irritably at her shoes dangling from his fingers and wondered how much of a struggle would be required to get them back. "You call yourself a soldier, but you dress like a brute barbarian—like one of those vile Mongol warriors from the east," she charged. "You shouldn't be at all surprised when you are treated like one." To her surprise his big shoulders quaked with a gentle laugh.

"Indeed . . . that is the point, demoiselle." He leaned back on one booted leg, watching closely as she climbed onto the grassy bank. His eyes lingered on her lower legs even after she had dropped her tunic and surcoat to cover them, then he jerked his head up, to spear her gaze with his.

"The Mongols and half-bred Mongol-Slavs are known to be savage fighters. If I look like them, my opponents will believe me a force to be reckoned with, and that gives me an edge against them. A soldier for hire needs every advantage he can claim."

She watched him straighten, and it seemed to her that he grew, filling her senses. His eyes were an odd, earthen color, almost golden. In the strong sunlight his dark, shoulder-length hair had faint threads of crimson running through it, and his shoulders glowed like warm, polished oak.

Her breath shortened as she realized he was scarcely more than a foot away. Then she heard her slippers drop to the ground beside him.

"Everything I wear has a purpose, demoiselle." His voice came soft and deep, stroking her very nerves. "These leather guards around my wrists"—he lifted one massive hand before her eyes, turning it so she could see the wide leather band studded with metal— "they strengthen my hands so that I may wield a blade longer in battle." He made a fist and demonstrated the way the sinews of his arm and hand worked inside the leather.

She tried to swallow and couldn't.

"And these cross braces . . ." He dragged that same hand down one of the wide leather straps that crossed his chest diagonally, then seized her wrist and brushed her fingers along the reverse of that path. "They are lighter and more comfortable than mail . . . and just as good a protection. On crusade, in the desert heat, some knights died of festering burns from the sun searing their mail armor. This metal boss"—he shifted his grip on her hand to press her fingertips over the intricate pattern on the metal disk that held the leather braces together—"protects my heart."

The powerful thudding from inside his chest sent warm vibrations up her arm.

"This belt"—he slid her hand down to his waist and along the heavy leather band around his middle—"supports my back so that I can swing a blade harder and lift great weights . . . and carry young demoiselles to safety."

His wry grin became a full, irresistible smile that made her knees go weak.

"And my breeches are made of deerskin, which glides over the flesh and is easier to bear on long rides than woven cloth would be. Feel." He directed her unresisting fingers downward, along his hipbone. Her fingers burned at the feel of his hard, sinewy flank and she tugged on them, only to have him hold her hand tight against his body.

Her heart was beating wildly, erratically.

"My boots are laced tight to keep them from trapping my foot in mud or filling with icy water. And I wear long hair and a beard, and skins and furs in cold weather, because they make me look bigger and more savage to my enemies." He paused and searched her upturned face, then ran a possessive finger along her jawline. "So, you see . . . I wear nothing I do not need, demoiselle. I suggest you do the same."

"The same?" she whispered, her throat tight. He laughed softly.

"This outer gown . . . you will be cooler without it."

Before she could react, he was unfastening the hooks at the bosom of her heavy surcoat, sliding his hands under the shoulders of the sleeveless garment and peeling it down her arms. She gasped, feeling the first ripples of alarm. It was as if he stripped her inner defenses from her along with her overgown.

"And these sleeves . . ." He ran his hands down her arms in a blatant caress, then lifted her hands between them. "If you open them, your arms will be cooler." He began to unlace the long, tapered sleeves of her tunic, from wrist to elbow. Each time his fingers pulled the laces, she suffered the remembrance of his doing the same thing to her hair.

The feel of him holding her, performing the personal service of a body servant, stunned her. His touch was not at all like old Esme's efficient ministrations, or Lillith's careful handling, or even her mother's occasional pats and strokes. There was no reverence in his hands . . . only a surprising gentleness and a dexterity that spoke of experience with such delicate tasks. Rearranging and removing garments; he had obviously rendered such intimate service before, to other women. The realization slowly surfaced among the sensations inundating her: he was treating her like a woman, not a princess.

A woman. This warm, liquid feeling developing in her middle and spreading downward through her abdomen and legs . . . was this what women felt when men stood close and touched them? Was this fertile, absorbing awareness of every line and contour of her body the result of being touched and treated like a woman? Every incidental brush of his fingers as he rolled her sleeves up her arms sent tingles of pleasure skittering along the underside of her skin.

"There," he murmured. "Is that not cooler?" He smiled into her eyes and began to draw circles over her lips with a languorous, knowing finger. Her blood seemed to rush to meet his touch. She parted and wetted her lips with her eyes fastened on his.

Taking her by the shoulders, he pulled her closer and

lowered his mouth. She found herself plunged into a warm, foaming sea of perception. Wherever their bodies touched, her skin burned with a strange, liquid heat that seeped slowly through her limbs and into her loins . . . like honey set aflame . . .

"My lady?" came a voice, far off but approaching. "Where are you? You cannot wander off like this, you kn—Ohhh!"

A fall down a well would have jarred Thera less than the sound of Lillith's voice at that moment. She jerked her head back. A moment passed before she collected her wits enough to understand that she was caught hard against Saxxe Rouen's big body and was being kissed within an inch of her virtue . . . and that she wasn't struggling. Indeed, she had never felt less like struggling in her life.

A blink, a gasp, and a sputter later, she realized that it wasn't Saxxe Rouen she was annoyed with . . . it was Lillith! And the realization sent her twisting out of his arms and staggering back toward the edge of the water with her pride burning and her face aflame.

"My lady?" Lillith choked out, drawing her startled gaze.

"I was . . . helping your lady with her garments," Saxxe said in a voice as thick and engulfing as night fog. "She was . . . overwarm."

Thera could only gape at him, then groan with impotent fury. No reasonable explanations were possible; what had happened was painfully obvious. The only course left open to her was escape.

She snatched up her skirts and shouldered him aside to pick up her surcoat and thrust her feet clumsily into her shoes. But as she stalked back along the stream toward the horses, the full horror of what had just happened came crashing down on her. She had been entranced, ensnared, and then kissed . . . which was bad enough. But what was worse—she couldn't seem to summon a single shred of outrage about it!

She licked her reddened, thickened lips and felt her

knees going weak at the realization that her tongue was retracing the path of his. He had swirled and laved her lips . . . slid his tongue . . .

Agghhh! She headed straight for her horse and fumbled to empty the sand in her shoes, then to insert her foot into the stirrup. Lillith hurried after her, calling her name, but she clamped her jaw and waved her hand in a curt gesture of forbiddance. She didn't want to speak of it, didn't want even to think of it. But when Saxxe approached from behind, seized her waist, and boosted her into her saddle, she couldn't resist one quick glance . . . and was confronted by both his tawny eyes and the terrible truth about what was happening inside her.

She was enthralled by him. The way he was shaped and moved made him absorbing to watch and strangely exciting to be near. And his appallingly suggestive talk had a way of stirring things inside her . . . making her feel hot and flushed and a little light-headed. He had treated her like a woman instead of a princess . . . and she had responded like one.

Saxxe Rouen made her feel like a woman. With a woman's desire.

The thought nearly knocked her out of her saddle. He was filthy, half savage, and greedy beyond all bounds. He was violent and boastful and ignoble and profane. But he was also *male* in an extravagant and unfettered way that she had never experienced before, and there was something dangerously appealing in the supremely confident sexuality he exuded with every movement of his big body.

She wanted him.

In that moment, her own traitorous desires joined Fate and Saxxe Rouen on the list of things she had discovered were outside the realm of her royal will.

Kicking her mount into motion, she charged across the stream. As she rode hard toward the hills with the others in her wake, the sultry air pulled some of the heat from her glowing face and burning pride, and her princess self reassembled around the newfound gaps in her sense of authority. She might have no control over the humiliating lust he generated in her, but she certainly didn't have to act on it. She was a princess, after all. And he was little more than a barbarian.

As a precaution against possible confrontations with the soldiers in black, Saxxe and Gasquar led them away from the trading road ... despite Thera's heated protests. The terrain grew difficult, becoming rocky hills and steep, densely wooded valleys inhabited by small, swift-flowing streams. They were forced to proceed slowly through thick stands of trees, struggling from hilltop to hilltop where they could catch glimpses of the sun to guide them. The puffy clouds had billowed steadily higher, past midday, and by dusk they loomed like great city walls in the west. Then the towering masses began to move eastward ... borne on gusty, changeable winds that whipped them higher and higher, until they spilled over into the rest of the sky, blotting out the sun.

Saxxe finally halted them on a slope overlooking a thick stand of woods, and together he and Gasquar studied the sky and upturned leaves, then began to search for shelter. Thera watched their faces as they exchanged terse words and felt a sinking in her chest.

"We're lost, aren't we?" she demanded loudly, over the rush of the rising wind.

"We are not lost," Saxxe called back irritably. "We are near the Brittany road." He swept the thick trees in the valley below with a dark look and added under his breath: "Somewhere."

"We should have kept to the road itself," she declared. "We're in no further danger from those marauders— there is naught between us and the western sea that is worth taking." Except her hidden jewel of a kingdom, she thought. "The great Charlemagne himself found nothing in Brittany worth conquer—"

A huge drop of rain smacked her on the forehead and slid down her nose. She gasped, shocked by the force and coldness of it, and suddenly there was another on her cheek, then another; huge, hard drops that stung her skin. She fumbled for the cloak draped over the back of her saddle and glanced up to find Lillith doing the same.

"It's starting," Saxxe called, looking skyward, and the wind-driven drops began to pelt them from all sides. "This way—into the trees!" He charged off down the hillside. There was no time to argue, only to sling their cloaks around their shoulders and give their mounts a heel.

Before they had gone a hundred yards, the rain was coming down in knifelike sheets, tearing at their clothes and battering their faces. They made it to the edge of the trees just as the first fork of lightning ripped through the sky. Dismounting hurriedly, Thera grabbed Lillith and headed for the shelter of a huge old oak, where they huddled miserably as the elements heaved and clashed around them. The rain drove relentlessly through their garments, until they were trembling from both cold and fright.

A huge furry beast reared unexpectedly out of the gloom and charged them . . . trapping cries in their frozen throats. Then it retreated as abruptly as it had come, and it took a moment for Thera to realize that it had been Saxxe, and that he had thrown a skin cover of some sort over them. The cover repelled the rain, and as they braced it with their arms, they were soon able to wipe their faces and catch their breaths.

"I h-hate storms," Lillith said from between chattering teeth.

"As if we didn't have en-nough t-trouble . . . now this," Thera gritted out, trying not to shiver inside her cold, wet garments.

"Trouble." Something in the way Lillith said it made Thera look at her.

"Don't even think it . . . much less speak it!" Thera commanded, knowing that when the word *trouble* tumbled from Lillith's lips, the word *prophecy* could not be far behind. And she was too miserable to suffer being harangued about the calamities caused by her royal virginity.

As the lightning and thunder passed, the relentless rain lingered, saturating every wormhole and animal burrow, and filling every depression in the ground ... sending them scrambling up onto the exposed roots of the huge old tree. Then came the final stroke as darkness fell over the rain and mud, compounding their desolation.

Saxxe appeared once more out of the gloom, startling them. This time he brought Gasquar, a few sharpened branches to prop the skins upon, and the dismal news that there could be no fire to cook the grouse he had taken earlier. Cold and wet and hungry, Thera couldn't even summon a protest when Saxxe and Gasquar invaded the makeshift shelter and removed their wet, shaggy cloaks.

A moment later she was glad to have held her tongue, for they hung their garments up along the sides to further block the rain, creating a surprisingly effective shelter in the steady downpour. Then before her aching eyes, they produced a half-filled wineskin and a bag of rolled oats, and passed them around. When she took the wineskin from Saxxe, her whisper of thanks was embarrassingly genuine.

"Well, I cannot have you either freezing or starving before we reach your home, demoiselle," he said with a wry half grin. "Else I will have no reward for my efforts." His mention of her debt caused her to stiffen and wrap her icy fingers tighter around the wineskin. He must have read her thoughts for he settled a searching look on her. "Speaking of rewards ... I believe I was to claim one this night." He made a *tsk* of disgust. "I fear we shall have to settle that particular debt another time, demoiselle."

Thera nodded and sank back against the tree trunk, feeling as if a huge weight had slid from her shoulders. Suddenly the rain didn't seem quite so relentless or the darkness so gloomy . . . for these clouds did indeed have a silver lining.

"*Entendez*. This rain . . . it is nothing," Gasquar declared with an expansive wave of his hand. He settled himself on the protruding tree root beside Lillith, causing her to huddle toward Thera, and wiped his wet beard and chest, slinging the water casually aside. "Why, once when we were in Venice, it rained for twelve days and nights. The water . . . it came higher and higher . . . and there came such a flood that the goldfish in the doge's palace pond escaped and made a fortune teaching the rats in the bishop's palace to swim." He flashed a wicked grin and Thera couldn't contain a giggle of surprise.

"Lies and falsehoods . . . every word," Lillith grumbled, turning an indignant look on Thera. "The wretch hasn't a truthful bone in his body."

"*Non*—I swear, it is true, *ma belle dame*." He edged closer to her, his eyes dancing in the gloom. "It was a sight to see. I watched from the roof of a great house, and I laughed so hard that I slipped and fell into the floodwaters and was drowned myself. *Alors* . . . I was washed all the way to the sea . . . where I was caught in a fishing net, sold for a flounder, and fricasseed back to life by the cook of a convent in Naples." His face nearly split with a grin. "To this very day I have a great reverence for fat nuns, saucepans, and gravy."

Saxxe and Thera burst into laughter, but Lillith raised a cold fist and shook it at him. "You!" Her dark eyes snapped. "Each lie is more outrageous than the last! Is there not a single drop of shame in you?"

"Draw in your claws, demoiselle," Saxxe said with a final chuckle, settling on a root near Thera's feet. "When Gasquar gets started, he blows like the *khamsin* . . . and just now we can use all the heat we can get."

Thera bit her lip to stifle yet another unexpected laugh. It didn't seem possible that she was sitting in the midst of a howling storm, drenched to the bone, faint with hunger . . . and laughing. She glanced at the glowing white of Saxxe's teeth and eyes, and felt her face warming.

"The *khamsin*? What is that?" she asked.

"It is the desert wind that sometimes blows through Egypt and the Holy Lands in the spring and summer," Saxxe answered, toying with the oats in his hand. "It is hot and salty and as dry as a drunkard's cup. When it begins, everything in its path stills in trembling expectation . . . even flies in the marketplace stop their buzzing." His voice quieted. "All nature holds its breath. For in its wake, the *khamsin* leaves dust-choked springs, crops withered and stripped, and tents buried under shifting mounds of sand. It can be a terrible and fearsome force."

Thera suffered a chill at the dark current of memory she sensed flowing beneath his words. "And you have felt this desert wind?"

"I have." He turned to meet her gaze, and his shaggy hair and woolly beard seemed to fade into the dimness, so that his glowing eyes filled her vision. "When you are caught in its stinging fury, there comes over you a curious sense of peace at being held by a power so much larger than your own. You cannot fight it, and so you must let it carry you where it will. The desert tribesmen . . . they shrug and say you must drive your tent peg wherever the *khamsin* sets you down."

Thera was silent for a moment, pondering those unsettling words . . . an oddly poetic bit of insight from a crude and opportunistic soldier for hire. Then her eyes slid into his, and she glimpsed unexpected depths of experience and reflection in them, and she felt an odd stirring in her chest. The desert . . . she had read about it. Egypt and the fabled Holy Lands . . . she had listened to her trading envoys describe them at length, and had often felt a pang of envy that they had traveled so far and seen so many wonders with their own eyes.

Saxxe Rouen had seen them, too . . . had felt the hot desert wind and learned to call it by its name. What other things had those canny green-gold eyes seen and that powerful frame experienced? She wasn't sure it was wise, but she had to ask.

"And where has this *khamsin* carried you, Saxxe Rouen?"

There was a change in his expression. She had no idea what it meant and held her breath.

"To the four corners of the world, demoiselle. Beyond the Pyrenees, the Alps, and the Carpathian mountains . . . across the Agean and the Adriatic and the Black seas . . . along the mighty Rhine, the Jordan, and the Nile rivers. It has carried me into bedouin tents and caliphs' palaces . . . into both prisons and cathedrals . . . into mighty castles, rich burghers' houses, and simple cottages. There is little I have not seen"—his voice lowered to a rough whisper—"and done."

"And your tent peg? Where have you driven it?" Thera focused intently on his reply. She had to know. Did he have a home? A wife? A woman? His teeth flashed in the darkness . . . a grin that said he knew full well what she asked.

"Gasquar and I have never stayed in one place long enough to set up . . . a tent."

That earnest claim produced a small slide of relief in her . . . which must have shown outwardly, for Saxxe's smile broadened. Their gazes met, and she shivered and glanced away, humiliated by her curiosity about him. She raked a critical look around their rough shelter.

"Nay . . . your tastes clearly run to cruder lodgings."

He shifted and scowled, considering his response.

"I love the taste of luxury as much as the next man, demoiselle," he said with vengeful calm. "Why else would I bother with you?"

The truth in his voice stung Thera sharply. Until that moment, she hadn't thought about *why* he might want her. She had just assumed . . . A taste of luxury? Was that what she was to him? Heat bloomed in her face and she huddled back against the tree trunk, drawing her knees up under her sodden cloak and wrapping them with her arms. The prospect that he found her wealth more alluring than her person dealt an unexpected blow to her fledgling womanliness, and she retreated instantly into her princess self. He would play hob getting a taste of *anything* from her, the off-eyed ox!

Gasquar rubbed his beard, watching the pair glowering and bristling at each other in the strained silence, and chuckled. "Ahhh, demoiselle . . . if you think this is poor shelter, you should have been with us once in the Agean Sea."

"Not again." Lillith rolled her eyes.

"The galley on which we sailed was rammed and sunk, and we were forced to take refuge in the belly of a whale," he continued, bracing his arms on his knees and leaning into his tale. "Regrettably, nine other soldiers— six Turks, two Spaniards, and a one-eyed Dane—had taken shelter there ahead of us. Now, it is a well-known fact that a whale cannot hold more than eight men at a time. A fight broke out over which of us would have to leave, and the thrashing and bashing were so fierce that the poor whale . . . he grew annoyed, sailed straight onto the beach, and spit us all out!"

Lillith hissed and he raised his hand in self-defense. "I swear by my old father's beard—it is true!" His eyes twinkled. "And as the whale swam out of sight, we heard him grumble that the Spaniards had left a foul taste in his mouth."

Thera tried to stifle her laughter with her hand, but some of it escaped. And with that small encouragement, Gasquar launched into yet another fishy tale.

The time passed as the patter of falling rain and Gasquar's banter continued apace. Each monstrous tale deepened Lillith's annoyance, but strangely dispelled Thera's. As her tension subsided, a deep chill invaded her limbs and she was grateful that Gasquar's bawdy, irreverent talk kept her from thinking about their miserable situation.

But inevitably her eyes fell on Saxxe, who now sat with his arms propped across his knees and his chin on one fist, seeming untroubled by the wet and the chill. The dim light lent a dark luster to his bare shoulders, and she could almost see the heat radiating from his half-naked body. She blew a drop of water from her nose and closed her eyes, hearing his voice: *There is always plenty of heat in my blankets.*

As she slipped from the realm of conscious will, she thought of the desert wind Saxxe had spoken of . . . dry and hot . . . imagined it blowing against her skin, then into her mind, bringing with it vivid images from afar. The sound of bells and cymbals . . . distant chants and the rustle of tents in the wind . . . the mingled scents of cinnamon and saffron . . . She slipped into unguarded dreams, where those exotic sensations blended with memories of his warm eyes . . . the feel of his hands sifting through her hair . . . and his moist breath trickling across her lips.

He became one with the four winds . . . one with the warmth of the sun . . . one with the whispers of her desire. And somewhere in the darkness of that night, in the depths of her heart, he became much more than just a barbarian.

That same night, two days' ride away, the Duc de Verville sat in a large, silk-draped tent that was warmed by ornate braziers and lighted by fine beeswax tapers that had once graced the altar of a nobleman's chapel. He sipped port from a silver goblet and, with an imperious finger, sorted through a mass of tarnished metal and ill-cut stones spread on a blanket before him.

"A pathetic lot," he said, wincing. "Times are bad indeed when all you can get from raiding a nobleman's treasury are his lady's rings, a pearl or two, and a few odd links of silver. It's a wonder the good earl didn't die of humiliation well before I parted him from his head." He flipped the edge of the blanket over the jumble of metal and waved an imperious hand that set three servants scrambling. "Put this dross in one of my chests with the rest of the plunder."

"*Mon duc—*" The tall, palorous Scallion shouldered partway through the tent opening and paused, waiting for permission to approach his master. "A bit of news that may sit well upon your ears." The duc beckoned him forward with a narrowing stare, and he turned back for a moment, then dragged a disheveled soldier through the opening and shoved the fellow onto his knees before the duc.

"Tell the *seigneur* what you told me," he ordered.

"My comrades and I were scouting the countryside . . . whilst our captain and the rest of our party took a trading village on the Brittany road. We found nothing of interest and were about to return to the village when we spied two women . . . riding unescorted." He swallowed dryly and received a prod from the stern captain.

"Tell him what they wore," Scallion demanded.

"Wh-white, Duc . . . one wore white. And they rode fine horses."

The duc was on his feet in a trice, his dark eyes suddenly hungry with expectation. "The one in white . . . was she fair, with burnished hair?" When the soldier nodded, de Verville's mouth curled into an unpleasant smile. "It's her . . . my princess. It must be. What happened to her? You didn't let her slip through your fingers?"

"We gave chase and cornered them by a cliff—" He halted and licked his parched lips, glancing at Scallion. "Then out of nowhere bladesmen appeared . . . there must have been a dozen of them. They attacked us, and of the seven in my party, I alone escaped." The anger in the duc's aristocratic features jolted him. "We fought hard, but . . . the others are all dead."

"The village, man—what was the name of the village?" the duc demanded.

"Le-LeBeau, *seigneur.*" The soldier trembled visibly, watching the fires of pride, passion, and greed forging a cold smile on his liege's countenance. Sweat broke out on his dirt-streaked face.

"LeBeau . . . on the Brittany road." De Verville's dark eyes darted as he thought, then they turned on Scallion. "It is more than your scouts have been able to report. Send out another party. Who is your best tracker?"

"The Spaniard, El Boccho. He and his men . . . they follow a scent like dogs, but they bite like jackals."

"Then send them off to this LeBeau place . . . and tell them there will be a fat reward for the man who brings me the name and location of my princess in white." Scallion dragged the terrified soldier to his feet and shoved him back out the tent opening, but de Verville's voice stopped the captain as he made to exit. "And Scallion . . ."

The captain stiffened at the menacing purr in the duc's voice and turned back.

"See that man punished for his cowardice. A good flogging, I think. We haven't had one all day."

"Cowardice, *mon duc*?" Scallion questioned before he caught himself.

"Obviously." De Verville raised one eyebrow, reminding Scallion how easily his ire could be transferred. "If he wasn't a coward, he would have stayed there and died along with the others."

Chapter Eight

Water dripped from the leaves overhead in a soft patter, and the woods fairly steamed around them as Saxxe and Gasquar led Thera and Lillith through a forest the next morning. The sun had come out behind the retreating clouds, but so far had only managed to heat things to a swelter, not to dry them. Despite her cloak and the makeshift shelter, every stitch on Thera's body had gotten wet. Now as the sun swelled the fibers to a prickly mat, both her body and her temper began to itch.

When they came to a swift-flowing stream at the bottom of a steep, narrow valley, Saxxe chose a shallow place to cross and started up the other side. Thera stared at his unfatigued shoulders resentfully. She was wet, hungry, and tired to the bone . . . and if she didn't find a clear spot in some bushes soon, she was going to give a whole new meaning to the words *great flood*.

"We are not stopping?" She pulled her horse to a halt on the rocky stream bank.

"Nay," Saxxe said over his shoulder, riding on.

She glared. The man was a pettifogging tyrant!

Gasquar looked back and reined up at the sight of Thera taking her foot from the stirrup and swinging her leg over to make a sliding dismount. "*Non*, demoiselle, we do not stop here." He made a noise of disgust and turned back, and Saxxe reined up and turned in his saddle. Thera had tossed her cloak onto her saddle and was peeling her surcoat from her damp, disheveled tunic. He ground his teeth and turned his horse, too.

"I am parched and saddle sore and in dire need of . . . relief," she declared, propping her fists on her waist.

"And I won't go on until I've had a stop in the bushes and some water to drink." She lifted her hem and went sailing off down the bank, into the tall weeds and scrubby bushes that lined the stream. Before Saxxe could decide whether to retrieve her bodily and tie her onto her horse, Lillith was joining the mutiny, shedding her surcoat and following Thera into the bushes.

There was nothing for Saxxe and Gasquar to do but wait, mutter, and eye the muddy currents in the swollen stream. By the time Thera dragged herself back to the water's edge, the stream was filling with mud and looked significantly less appealing. She ignored Saxxe's order to remount and instead scoured the waters for a clearer pool from which to drink.

"What are you doing?" Saxxe demanded as she removed her slippers, hiked up her gown, and waded across the knee-deep stream to a small side pool the silt hadn't reached. "Get back on your horse . . . it isn't safe. Don't you see the mud?"

"There's no mud here—this water is perfectly fine!" She cast him a willful glare and knelt to drink from her hands.

Lillith emerged from the bushes just as Saxxe and Gasquar swung to the ground muttering furiously, and a moment later all four of them froze in place. Saxxe and Gasquar went taut, Lillith gasped, and Thera's head came up as the rumble reached them.

It was low and deep, and seemed to come from the rock and soil on all sides, as if the earth itself were growling. The small stones and wet sand beneath their feet suddenly came alive, jiggling furiously, and the escalating vibrations raised the hair on the back of their necks. Thera shoved to her feet, glancing across the water at the others with a look of alarm.

The rumble suddenly focused upstream, transforming into a low roar that grew louder and more complex: dull, droning thuds combined with sounds of wood crashing and snapping, and a broad churning that was unidentifiable, yet chillingly familiar.

Suddenly there it was. *Water*—a whole boiling, churning wall of it, at least ten feet high—sweeping down the valley toward them. Saxxe shouted Thera's name and waved his arm—ordering her to run for the hilltop, up the bank behind her. But as he charged down the bank for Lillith, and Gasquar raced to the panicking horses, Thera just stood at the far edge of the stream, frozen by the sight of that torrent of water bearing down on her.

Boulders rolled ahead of that rampaging flood, unseated and driven along by its force, and in the water's path trees were snapped and toppled like mere twigs. Thera's eyes fixed on the terrifying sight of water, as brown as earth, rearing into a rumbling, foaming wall. Saxxe bore Lillith up the hillside and dropped her on her feet with the order "Climb!" Then he turned to find Thera struck motionless by the sight of the oncoming destruction, and he went running back down the slope, bellowing her name.

The sound of Saxxe's voice, roaring above the sound of the floodwater, finally penetrated her shock. It was too late for her to dash back across the stream, and she looked around frantically, searching for an escape. Then she saw Saxxe waving her up the hillside behind her, and for once she obeyed, scrambling madly up the bank.

The spray hit first, lashing with the force of daggers . . . then came the main force of water, slamming and crushing everything in its path. Thera's feet just missed being sucked into that foaming white wall of terror, and Lillith screamed as she watched the waters tugging at Thera's gown. But a critical instant later, Thera was still on her feet, climbing up the shrubby growth, and Lillith clasped her hands over her heart and groaned in relief.

Thinking the worst was past, or perhaps too stunned to think at all, Thera paused where she was . . . and then it happened. The torrent of water behind the initial tide surged unexpectedly, slamming into her with tremendous force. She was knocked to her knees, then toppled straight into the swiftly flowing current.

"Thera!" Saxxe's body lashed taut at the sight of her

disappearing into that muddy torrent, and his heart contracted powerfully, then stopped dead, until her head bobbed up. When she screamed, he heard more anger than pain in her cry and his heart convulsed with relief and began to beat wildly in his chest. "Stubborn little witch," he bellowed, racing toward her. "Don't you dare drown on me!"

Her thrashing kept her head above the torrential flow, but the water was moving so swiftly that she was already past him before he reached the water's edge. In a split second he changed course. His muscles contracted, his legs pumped, and he was suddenly on horseback and racing downstream, dodging trees and stumps and plowing through treacherous underbrush while yelling at the top of his lungs.

"Swim, damn it, swim!" What were the chances that she had learned something as useful as swimming in her pampered life? "You owe me, Thera of Aric—and I don't intend to let you die without paying!" What were the chances she would rather drown than spend a night making love with him? "If you die on purpose, I swear I'll follow you straight into Hell to collect!" What were the chances that they would end up in the same place in the Hereafter, even if she was as aggravating as the Devil?

At least half of eternity seemed to pass before the valley broadened and the rampaging waters slowed. Her head still bobbed above the surface, but her arm movements were slowing and her calls for help were growing weaker and less frequent. In desperation, he plunged his huge war-horse straight into the muddy water.

"Keep your head up—use your feet! I'm coming!"

The current was powerful, and he feared at first that he couldn't make up the distance. But she had managed to kick her feet and use her arms to stay afloat, and had thrashed her way out of the strongest part of the current. He slid from his horse's back and began to swim for her, stretching out his powerful limbs to close the distance, focusing all his energy on reaching her small, vulnerable form . . . and praying it would still be at the surface when he got there.

The feel of his arms was foreign and she fought it at first, thinking she was caught on some floating debris and would be dragged under. But through the water and the roar in her ears she finally heard his voice calling "I've got you—don't fight!" and understood that he held her. Her struggles slowed and he managed to roll her onto her back and swim with her toward shore.

The mud-laden water weighted Saxxe's limbs; it was like trying to swim in pitch. He had to fight for every yard they gained toward the shore. But finally his feet touched bottom near a stand of trees that were half submerged, and he scooped Thera up in his arms and waded toward the water's edge. She was cold and limp, and as pale as the dirty white silk of her gown, but she had honestly never seemed more beautiful to him than she did at that moment. He paused to catch his breath, thigh-deep in the water, and savored the feel of her body against him and her arms around his neck. She was safe. After another moment, she shivered and raised her head, trying to focus her dark sapphire eyes on him.

"It *is* you," she said hoarsely.

"Yea, it is me . . . risking my own skin to pull your troublesome hide out of danger yet again. A particularly generous deed, I think, since it was ignoring my orders that got you into it in the first place." It was nothing short of an invitation to a verbal brawl, and it was a measure of her shock and exhaustion that she didn't accept.

"It was so cold. I kept hitting into things and going under . . ." She coughed and clamped a hand over her mouth, doubling up in his arms. Her whole body quaked with each contraction of her waterlogged lungs. "I nearly . . . drowned."

"Nay, you would never have drowned," he said with a wry grin. "Not while I was there. Besides, it is a known fact that witches float." She scowled, struggling to reassemble her scattered wits and make sense of his comforting tone and his odd reference to . . . When the insult struck her, she gasped and wriggled weakly, trying to get down. He tightened his hold on her and chuckled as he carried her out of the water. "You see—you're almost back to your prickly old self already."

Moments later, Thera was seated on a log, hugging her knees to her chest and shivering, despite the warming sun. Saxxe's horse, Sultan, had made it to dry land ahead of them and came running to his whistle. Saxxe untied his sleeping roll and two large, oiled leather pouches from behind the saddle. Sorting through his sleeping roll, he located a dry blanket that had been tucked inside the others and threw it around her. From one of the pouches, he produced a striking steel and an oiled bag filled with dry grasses and set about making a fire.

"Wh-what are you d-doing?" she demanded, pulling the blanket up under her chin and watching him collecting stones into a ring near her feet. "W-we don't have time for that. Lillith will be frantic with worry. We sh-should just ride—"

"*Dieu*—even half drowned you spit orders like a mad Turk. Lillith can wait . . . warming you cannot," he informed her, mounding the grass and using the striking steel. "You'll be half dead by morning if we don't get you out of those wet clothes."

No amount of reason would prevail against him. By the time the sparks caught and a small orange flame appeared, she was more than glad to see it. Her limbs felt even colder and heavier than they had in the water, and her body had begun shaking uncontrollably. When he glanced up from laying small branches onto the new flame, he pushed to his feet to hover over her.

"Take that wet gown off . . . now. Take all your garments off and wrap up in the blanket again."

"I m-most c-certainly will n-not!" she insisted, squinting up at his blurry face and wishing he would quit weaving back and forth like that. It was making her sick to her stomach.

"You are a stubborn chit," he said with a voice somehow both rough and tender. "I don't know why I bother with you." He dropped to his knees and pulled open the blanket and dragged her against his chest, so he could reach the lacing at the back of her gown.

"Because I'm rich," she muttered thickly. "And you're . . . greedy."

He stared into her half focused eyes. "Yea, that is surely it. Thanks for reminding me."

He pulled her back against him and worked at undoing her laces. She wanted to push him away but couldn't seem to make her arms move properly. And with all the water that was suddenly roaring in her ears and the strange, spongy darkness constricting the edges of her vision, she somehow forgot just what it was she needed to resist. His skin beneath her cheek was wet—but oh, so warm. . . .

A moment later, her face buried itself in his bare chest and her shoulders sagged against him. He ripped the lacing free and peeled the sodden silk from her shoulders. A garment as thin as a spider's web lay beneath it, and a stout linen band, tied around her breasts, lay beneath that. He growled and shifted her back, and she slid unexpectedly down his arms into a heap. With a rueful smile, he laid her gently in the grass and continued his work without further interference.

"We have to go after them!" Lillith demanded, standing on the hill overlooking the flood-ravaged crossing where Thera had been swept away, and glaring at Gasquar. He lay sprawled on the ground with his feet crossed, his brawny arms tucked beneath his head, and his eyes closed. Three horses were tethered nearby . . . one bearing Thera's cloak, surcoat, and shoes. "She is probably drowned by now. He probably just let her go heels-up and sink like a mackerel!"

Gasquar's mouth curved in a lusty grin and he popped one eye open to scrutinize Lillith's ripe, womanly form. "If her heels are up, *ma chatte*, then you can be sure she is enjoying it. *Mon ami* Saxxe . . . the women find him very pleasant." He pushed up on one elbow and plucked a piece of grass, sticking the stem in his mouth. "Of course"—his hand swept his brazenly displayed body—"not as pleasant as they find me."

Lillith felt the blast of dry heat that radiated from his thick, sinewy frame and recoiled as if he had a forked tongue and scales. His dark eyes glowed with lights she recognized too well. "That is despicable!" she hissed, tucking her arms around her waist and taking another unsteady step back. "My pr—mistress is carried off in a flood and may be lying at the bottom of the river, or fighting for her life at this very moment, and you—all you can think of is your base, disgusting appetites!"

When he shook his head with an indulgent chuckle, she groaned and started for her horse. In a trice he was on his feet and blocking her path.

"Out of my way, barbarian!" she demanded, her hands falling into determined fists at her sides. "You may not care whether my lady lives or dies, but I do . . . and I'm going to find her!"

"*Non, ma petite chatte,* you will not." He took a step toward her, then another, crowding her with his intensely male presence. "Think . . . when Saxxe has rescued your lady and returns, you will not be here. Then we would have the sad task of searching for your deliciously argumentative self. And losing you would grieve me sorely. Do you have any notion of how long it has been since I had such stirring disagreements with such a"—his eyes swept her like a caress—"handsome woman?"

At such close range, mere inches from his bronzed and bearded face, Lillith could not completely hide her involuntary reaction to his bold flattery. *Handsome woman.* The pleasurable feel of his sensual interest widened her eyes and reddened her cheeks. She stalked away and turned back to glower at him, hoping it would hide her blushing.

"That wicked tongue of yours again," she said in clipped tones. "First lies and now flattery—which is no more than lies bent to the service of greed."

"Lies? And which is the lie, *ma dame*? That you are

handsome?" He laughed softly at her embarrassment. "You have a great liking for the truth, I see. But truth is a hard master. There are times when a lie is kinder, even nobler. And a lie is almost always more enjoyable."

"Blasphemy," Lillith pronounced with quiet vehemence.

"*Non*. Merely the truth, *ma dame*. Surely you recognize the truth when you hear it." A slow smile appeared on his face. He had her there, and they both knew it.

Lillith caught herself staring fixedly at his wide, generous mouth, feeling an unwelcome trickle of excitement winding through her stomach and below. She lifted her chin and stepped back again, wondering how they had gotten into such sticky personal territory and remembering Thera's plight with a flush of anxiety.

"I cannot just sit here and do nothing while my lady is in peril—"

"By now your lady is well rescued," he assured her. "And *mon ami* Saxxe is claiming a sweet reward."

"Reward?" Lillith turned to search the valley and follow the swollen waters downstream with a horrified expression. "Merciful Lord! Let us hope not!"

The fire was a flickering, yellow-gold island in a sea of darkness when Thera awakened. When she righted her vision and realized she was lying on the ground, beside a fire and under a blanket, her first impulse was to rise. Halfway up, she made a strangling noise and dropped back down. Beneath the blanket she was as naked as a newborn babe.

"You're awake," came Saxxe's voice from nearby, startling her. She clutched her cover tightly beneath her chin and looked up to find him sitting by her head, watching her. Behind him, spread neatly on a bush by the fire, were her garments. How they got there was something she didn't want to think about.

"How do you feel?"

"Like I've been trampled by a herd of very fat, very rude cattle," she said, groaning as she rolled onto her side. "And I have a sore spot for each of their nasty little hooves. Three score and seven . . . at least."

"You've counted?" He laughed with surprise.

"Of course." She tried not to smile; it hurt too much. "I always count."

"You do?" He grinned. "I shall have to remember that. Hungry?" he asked, smiling. When she nodded, he rose and cut a piece of rabbit from a makeshift spit on the far side of the fire while she struggled to both sit up and remain covered at the same time. She managed to hold the blanket securely and sit back against a log, stretching her cold, aching legs out before her. When she accepted the food, she found the meat was wrapped in a thin oatcake, recently made. She looked up at him with surprise and he cocked a look at her. "Is something wrong with the food?"

"Where did the oatcake come from?" she asked. "You?"

He looked outraged. "I am a greedy, sword-yielding, Mongol-bashing barbarian, it's true. But to accuse me of hearth tending—" He growled good-naturedly. "Put your tongue to better use, demoiselle. Eat." Burying the urge to smile in her food, she did as she was told, and he got to his feet to check her garments. When he saw her watching him with a frown, he announced: "They're not quite dry. But soon." He rejoined her by the fire and knelt by her feet. "And what about you? Are you warm enough?"

Her mouth was full, so she nodded. Food had never tasted so good to her. When she had trouble swallowing that bite, he handed her a half-filled wineskin, telling her to drink well. She did just that, between bites of food, and no sooner had the food settled to her stomach than she began to tremble and her teeth began to chatter again. He must have been watching for that very thing, for he slid to her feet, threw back the blanket, and took her feet onto his lap. Shocked, she tried to jerk them away.

"What are you doing? Let go—"

"Hold still." His grip on her ankles allowed no resistance. "I'm going to rub them to get the blood flowing in them again. It's a trick I learned from an old Swede who . . . served in my father's house." He engulfed one of her feet in his big, warm hands and ran his thumbs down the bottom of her foot, from toe to heel. She squirmed as tiny needle pricks danced up her leg. When he did it again, she braced and winced, but the third stroke produced an entirely different sensation. A sensuous wave of heat traveled up her leg and she nearly melted. It was stunning . . . like having him reach into her very sinews to brush away the discomfort.

"Rubbing and kneading the body can warm the blood and ease the aches. It's a valuable thing to know in my trade. After a long, hectic day swinging a blade in battle, your back and shoulders tend to get hellish sore." He flexed them, drawing her eyes to them. "And your hands—*Dieu*, how they cramp from gripping a blade for hours on end. But worst of all are the aches in your legs and feet.

"In the east, they say that the humors from all over the body meet in the feet and that rubbing and stroking them is the most effective way to restore the entire body. I don't know if all that is so . . . but there have been times I would have sold my soul for a good foot rub." He looked up with a roguish twinkle in his eye and grinned. "Alas, I have never met anyone willing to make that trade."

She stared at him, at his big hands and his broad, sun-bronzed shoulders, and suddenly saw him as a man . . . who spent his life in hard, punishing labor in a violent trade . . . who suffered very human aches and pains and felt a very human need for comfort. A barbarian with sore feet. She almost laughed aloud. As he massaged her feet slowly and methodically, reducing her tremors and discomfort to warm, steamy release, she wondered who, in truth, had taught him such a lusciously civilized thing? Then it struck her that he had spoken of his home.

"And what else did you learn in your father's house?"

He looked up from massaging her toes, one by heavenly one, and his smile dazzled her. "Oh, the usual barbarian things. Deceit. Treachery. Mayhem. The arts of war . . . and of course, the Seven Deadly Sins." He waggled his brows in parody of wicked delight. "My favorite—and the one I was always best at—was lust. I had a great talent for inventive and prolonged debauchery, it seemed. Wine, women, and the arts of pleasure . . . in quantity."

"Now you sound like Gasquar," she said, hugging her blanket a bit tighter.

He grinned, watching her lick a stray crumb from her lip, and felt a rustle of response in his sinews.

"But, come to think of it, *gluttony* was a close second." He reached for her other foot, to give it the same treatment. "They said that was why I grew so large . . . I ate everything that didn't eat me first. Still do . . . when there's food worth eating." A faraway look appeared in his eyes. "I have tasted the food of many far-flung lands, and some of it is fine indeed. But there are times when I actually dream about Saracen sugar. Have you ever tasted *sugar*?" When she shook her head, he sighed. "Sweeter than honey, if you can conjure that in your mind. But a pure sweetness . . . no other taste to it. The Turks make a wondrous hot drink of sugar and mint. And their cooks mix sugar with cinnamon and bake it into sweet, buttery cakes . . ."

His gaze wandered over her and fastened on her hair. "Have you ever tasted cinnamon?"

She managed to nod and realized that his hands had stilled on her foot and he was staring intently at her.

"Do you know . . . your hair is exactly the color of cinnamon."

"Is it?" She realized with a start that her hair was loose around her shoulders again. She reached for a lock of it and looked at it in the light, frowning.

"Wet hair is a sure passage to lung sickness," he explained. "I loosened it and dried it as best I could."

How did he manage to read her mind like that? she

wondered, experiencing a chill that he must have felt all the way down in her toes. She nodded again. Every inch of her skin was suddenly humming with awareness of him. She felt warm and well tended and . . . womanly. And he looked so big and bronzed and male. Her pulse drummed faster in her veins and a flush of heat began rising into her cheeks. She wanted this moment to go on and on . . . to hear him talk . . .

"What was your home like, and your family?" she asked, watching his eyes beginning to glow in the firelight.

His smile tightened, but he shrugged and looked down at her slender feet. "Oh, the usual barbarian hovel . . . skins, twigs and straw, and bedding down at night with the pigs." He paused, waiting for the quip that didn't come, then looked up. "And much too crowded at the trough." Still there was no barb, and he felt a strange melting sensation in his core.

"And your father?" she asked, her voice a little breathless.

"A monumental barbarian . . . tough as pickled bull hide and fierce as a badger. Why once, when our hovel was attacked, he jumped up on the bailey wall with only a three-legged stool in one hand and an ill-tempered hen in the other. And by the time . . . he was . . . done . . ."

He ground to a halt, staring into her jewel-bright eyes and feeling something wriggling against the prominent bulge in his breeches. In the course of his talk, whenever he halted his massage, she had wriggled her toes in his grip, entreating more. Now her feet had slid into the crevice of his lap, and his hands were stroking her shins. But her toes—*bon Dieu!*—they were still wriggling! Did she realize what she was doing?

Every nerve in his body vibrated with sensual awareness of her . . . sitting there with her face flushed with pleasure, her eyes glowing with curiosity, her lips wine reddened. The top of the blanket had drooped open, baring the pale skin of her throat and a slice of her upper chest. He recalled too well the swell of her breasts, the curve of her waist, and the elegant taper of her thighs. He had tried not to look at her as he stripped her garments, knowing the sight of her nakedness would haunt him and weaken his determination to forgo her womanly pleasures in favor of hard silver coin.

A meadow, an orchard, and a stream, he repeated desperately. That was all she could ever be to him. But her slender foot was sending tantalizing trickles of sensation through his susceptible male parts, and they were insisting that there was more, so much more to be had. A shudder racked him, and he froze. *Dieu*, he was afraid to move for fear of pouncing on her!

Thera had watched his gentle ministrations with awe, and had felt the tension of longing replace the chill and exhaustion in her limbs. Now she savored every perception of him . . . the way his long, dark hair hung around his shoulders, the intense concentration on his face, the subtle flexing of his shoulders, and the surprising skill of his touch. Watching his hands sliding up and down her shins, then cupping and kneading the backs of her calves, she found herself scarcely breathing . . . imagining the feel of them rising up her thighs, then her waist. Her unbound breasts felt heavy and sensitive, and tingling heat collected in their tightly drawn tips.

When his hands withdrew from her legs, she started to protest, then looked up and sucked in a shocked breath. His eyes were molten, his features fierce with what seemed to be anger.

"Take your foot from my lap, demoiselle," he ordered, his voice deep and raw. "If I am forced to remove it myself, you will find yourself on your back, paying your debts in full . . . and then some."

She jerked her foot back, gathering the drooping blanket tighter around her. After a long, tense moment, he shoved to his feet and made straight for her drying garments. He carried them back to her and dropped them in her lap.

"Put these on . . . and be quick about it. I'll check Sultan and be back soon."

He left the circle of firelight, and for a moment she could make out his outline against the pale gray horse. Then he strode off into the moonless darkness, and she sat looking after him with conflicting feelings of dismay and relief. What had caused such a drastic change in him?

She should be immensely grateful to it for keeping her from finding herself on her back paying her "debts." Instead, she felt a disturbing sense of loss and a longing for the unexpected warmth that had bloomed briefly between them. He had watched over her today, and fed her tonight, and tended her chills and aches in the most disarming manner.

And when she asked questions of him, he managed to answer in ways that revealed little of substance but left her with the feeling that she knew him all the better for it. He possessed a droll wit and a breadth of experience that left her burning with both envy and curiosity. And at the base of it all was a battle-honed confidence in his own strength and skill, and a sense of mastery in every situation. Just look at the way he had taken charge of her wretched situation.

The notion brought her up short. Her eyes widened. He had more than taken charge of her predicaments, he had taken advantage of them, time and time again! And here she was going all warm and soft and womanly inside . . . longing for his roguish smiles and aching for the feel of his hands, forgetting everything but the seductive pleasure of his presence.

She had to stop letting her womanly feelings get out of hand . . . had to somehow regain control of herself and the situation. To do that, she had to put and keep a safe distance between them. She looked down at her exposed skin. And a few clothes between them wouldn't hurt either!

Letting the blanket fall around her hips, she sucked a shocked breath at the cool air and hurriedly drew her thin chemise and long tunic over her head. Then, clothed but chilling again, she pulled the blanket back around her and scooted toward the fire. The flames were so hot that she inched back, farther and farther, then finally stretched out in the dewy grass . . . halfway between roasting and freezing.

Chapter Nine

T hat was where Saxxe found her: safely clothed, curled around the fire, her front half scorched and her back cold enough to set her shivering. He broke several branches over his knee and added a few to the fire, trying to ignore the pathetic way she quaked. But she looked so small and miserable, huddled on the ground, seeking the fire's heat and yet unable to get close enough to assuage her need for its warmth. The sight generated a powerful surge of protective impulses in him . . . to gather her up in his arms and warm her, to surround her with his . . .

With a huff of disgust, he strode back around the fire, slung a blanket over his shoulders, then lay down behind her, fitting his body to the curve of hers, spoon fashion. She gasped and tried to squirm away, but he pulled her back against him.

"Hush and lie still," he ordered gruffly, slipping one heavy arm beneath her head, like a pillow, and tucking the other around her waist. "I'm only here for warmth. Go to sleep."

Less than an hour after her vow to stay as far from him as possible, Thera found herself lying stiff and wary in his arms. But the slow rhythmn of his breathing and the generous warmth of his body gradually melted her chagrin. He made no move to rouse or caress her, and it began to seem that he intended simply to sleep with her.

Sleeping. Together. It was an entirely new idea for her, sleeping with someone. Not once, in her entire life, had she shared a bed with anyone . . . not her mother or her nurse, not her cousins or companions . . . not even Lillith.

Comfort and warmth slowly claimed her. And her last coherent thought was that sleeping with someone was unexpectedly pleasant . . . on a cool night . . . someone who was big and warm and made her feel safe.

Saxxe laid his head beside hers, on her soft hair, and made himself think of apple boughs laden with ripe fruit; clear, rindling streams; and meadows full of tall grasses, wild daisies, and newborn foals. But as he drifted toward sleep, Thera of Aric climbed up into his apple trees and gleefully sank her teeth into his juicy apples . . . then splashed about, mother-naked and shameless, in his stream . . . and picked armsful of his daisies and nestled her delectable bottom in the middle of his grass, making a coronet of flowers. And for the first time in many years, he went to sleep with a smile on his face.

Thera awakened the next morning to the noisy chirping of birds. The sun was scarcely up and the fire had long since died, but she was grandly, luxuriously warm . . . and she owed that warmth to the heavy blanket of flesh wrapped around her. She came suddenly alert, recalling the bizarre conditions under which she had started the night and a little surprised to find that she had slept so soundly. She shifted gingerly onto her back and turned to look at her night-partner . . . and found him staring at her with a heavy, just-wakened look to his eyes.

She blushed furiously at being caught in the midst of appreciating his nearness, when she should have been avoiding it. But somehow she couldn't make herself move away from him.

"Good morning, demoiselle," he murmured with a huskiness to his voice. "You slept well." It was a statement; he had apparently been watching. "Your feet and legs . . . how did they fare? Can you move them?"

She wriggled her toes, then shifted her legs experimentally. "I can."

"And your arms and hands?" He slid his arm from

her waist and sent a knowledgeable hand down her arm, testing, caressing. "There is no damage?"

"Nay, only stiffness," she whispered, watching the shifting lights in his golden eyes, breathing in his musky scent . . . while he toyed with her fingers and threaded his own through them, gently mating their palms. That interweaving of their hands joined the sensitive valleys between their fingers and gave focus to the desire growing between them for a larger and more intimate union. Then he slid his other arm from beneath her head and raised onto his elbow above her.

"Your shoulders"—he ran his fingers along her collarbone—"are trembling. And your lips"—he drew a finger around her jaw and up, over her mouth—"are much too warm." Both his gaze and his voice were filled with smoky sensuality. "A strange malady. I have seen it before . . . once in Paris and again in Venice. Fortunately, I know the cure," he whispered, leaning over her, lowering his head, and claiming the moist, yielding bow of her mouth.

There was no resistance in her, for her night had been filled with potent dreams of hot wind and cinnamon . . . Arab sugar and thick, sweet kisses. Soft to soft, like honey poured into cream, the feel of his mouth on hers was delicious. And each slow, silken brush of his lips spread before her a sensual repast of sensation; the tickle of his breath against her skin, the sweet saltiness of his mouth, the tantalizing swirls of his tongue around hers. She wound her fingers through his hair to cradle his head and urge it closer to hers, deepening both the contact and the pleasure.

He shifted his chest over hers so that the edges of his leather braces raked her hardening nipples. She arched into that delicious friction, seeking more, drinking in the size and weight of him against her. But a moment later his weight was replaced by his hands, moving in sinuous spirals over her unbound breasts, and the steady, progressive flow of pleasure was suddenly interrupted by a jolt of sensation that shook her bodily.

He lifted his head just enough to say against her lips, "Are you cold?"

She managed to focus her eyes on his. She nodded, then shook her head, then looked confused. He laughed softly against her lips, sending sensuous vibrations all through her.

"What a troublesome creature you are, *ma chatte* . . . always in need of rescuing or feeding or warming." His hands slid to her fitted sleeves and began to undo them. "Who warmed you before I came along?"

His words tumbled about in her head on currents of expectation as he fumbled with her laces. They had been damp when she tied them, and overnight had dried and shrunk so that the knots were drawn as tight as clam shells. His moan of frustration broke through her swirling thoughts, and a moment later he was sitting up and pulling her into a sitting position, too. The cold air gliding over her bare back and her abrupt change of position somehow righted his words in her mind.

Who warmed you before I came along?

No one. No one had ever warmed or touched her like this. Until Saxxe Rouen, she had always been "Princess Thera" . . . never "demoiselle."

The next moment that thought shocked her to the ends of her being. She *was* "Princess Thera" . . . *not* "demoiselle." The sense of what was happening between them rattled her to the core. The shock of it warred with the desire for it, but not for long. Distance—she had to put distance between them. She jerked her wrist from him and skittered back on her knees.

"What is—"

"I'm quite warm enough," she said, clasping her arms around her shivering shoulders. "In future, Rouen, be so good as to keep your hands to yourself."

In her jewel-clear eyes he glimpsed a raging conflict of longing and alarm. Inside she was half melted, vulnerable . . . and her desire for him horrified her. He understood all too clearly, for he was experiencing that same painful clash of emotions. Every fiber of his body was swollen with need for her . . . and the strength of his desire appalled him.

The thwarted heat of his arousal set fire to both his conscience and his pride. What in hell had gotten into him, making love to her . . . endangering his hopes of a fat reward? *She* had gotten into him, he realized, staring at her huge blue eyes, tousled hair, and kiss-swollen lips. *Dieu*—how she had gotten into him!

He bounded to his feet, giving the blankets a contemptuous kick, and stalked off toward his horse.

Fearful that she might have angered him enough to make him leave without her, she called after him.

"Rouen! Where are you going?" She was relieved to see him jerking his bow and quiver from his saddle.

"Hunting!" he roared back. "And if I have any luck, when I get back you'll have something to sink your claws into besides me!"

Thera slid her arms around her waist and stared after his retreating form in a mild panic. She was alone with him now, and vulnerable in ways she hadn't dreamed she could be. All he had to do was talk to her in that roguish, teasing manner, or touch her with his disarmingly gentle hands, and all her bones seemed to melt . . . starting with her backbone.

What was the matter with her? Why couldn't her princess self just issue a royal edict and banish her unholy feelings for him to some neat little chamber of her mind where they wouldn't be any trouble?

Because the woman in her wanted him. Because the woman in her found him interesting and strangely warm and companionable. And because the woman in her was every bit as stubborn as the princess.

Furious at her inability to control her own feelings, she stalked off into the bushes, then ventured down to the water's edge. She washed her face and rinsed her mouth and rubbed her teeth with a soft, frayed twig, then set to work trying to draw and tie the lacing at the back of her gown. The laces were stubborn and the holes through which they threaded seemed to have both raveled and shrunk. Wrenching and contorting her shoulders and fighting her hair out of the way again and again, she managed to pull the edges together at least halfway up her back . . . then could reach no more and had to abandon the effort.

Feeling thwarted and angry that she would have to ask for the use of Saxxe Rouen's hands—after she had just told him to keep them to himself!—she ground her teeth and snatched up a lock of her tousled hair. Here, at least, was a task she could manage on her own. But she needed something to work with. Then her eyes fell on Saxxe's leather pouches. What were the chances he would have something as civilized as a comb or brush in his possession?

She dragged the bags over to the blankets, knelt, and opened the first one, gingerly drawing out the contents. Various lengths of rope, a number of metal fishhooks, metal arrow tips, striking steel, two cups and a metal bowl, a flat bit of metal for use as a griddle, and a small pouch of coarse salt inhabited the first one. Nothing but the rude essentials for procuring and preparing food, she thought, wincing. How like him.

In the second bag she encountered more personal items, including a pair of old leather wrist guards, an aged tunic that bore stains and cuts that looked unsettlingly like wound marks . . . and a few bits of crumpled, faded silk that looked suspiciously like pieces of ladies' veils. Then her fingers raked something large and hard and oddly shaped in the bottom of the second pouch. She seized it, drew it forth, then began to remove the chamois wrapping.

From inside the soft skin came the dull clink of metal on metal. She laid back the last fold of cloth and stared at a pair of gleaming spurs, simply but beautifully crafted. Golden spurs. The arched metal bore the soft patina and occasional nicks that came from use. She sat staring at them for a long moment, then ran her fingertips over their cool luster.

In Mercia there had been no need for knights for a long

while, though a few crusty old relics of a bygone era still survived. But Thera knew full well that throughout France and the German provinces and Italy, a true knight was identified by his golden spurs . . . and that the only way a knight was parted from them was by death itself. What were these doing in Saxxe Rouen's bag?

There were several possible explanations, she told herself. Perhaps they had been given to him in payment for his services, or they had belonged to the knight in whose service he had crusaded. There were also less honorable possibilities: he might have taken them from an enemy . . . or scavenged them on a battlefield . . . or *stolen* them.

"What in Seventh Hell do you think you're doing?" came an angry bellow, startling her so that she fell over onto her rear. Saxxe, his eyes blazing, stood holding a brace of hares in one hand and his bow in the other.

"I . . . I . . ." Her face flushed crimson at being caught going through his bags, but only because they were *his*. As a princess, she had never been forbidden access to another's possessions in her life; it never occurred to her that he might consider it a violation of privacy. She raised her chin and pushed to her feet, her fingers curling around the cool metal she held. "I had to have something to set my hair to rights and while I was looking for a comb, I found these." As she held out the spurs, his mien went from thunderous to volcanic.

"Damnation!" he roared, slamming the hares and his bow on the ground and striding forward with his fists clenched. "You wait until my back is turned and plunder my things and take whatever strikes your eye!" He took another step, then another, and halted himself. "And you call *me* a barbarian!"

"I was not plundering," she declared, scrambling to meet his unexpected fury. "I—I told you: I needed a comb or brush and thought perhaps . . . I would never take anything that didn't belong to me." She lifted her chin, casting him a look that said she doubted the same could be said about him. "Where did you get these?"

"Give me those," he growled, snatching them from her hands and dropping onto his knees to shove them back into the pouch. He quickly stuffed the other things back as well, then hauled up the blankets and headed for his horse.

Every movement was like a whip crack, each glance like a dagger flung her way. The raw, honest fury of his reaction shocked her.

"You didn't answer," she charged when he went back for his bow and the game he had taken. She crossed her arms over her chest and tried to tell herself that she had no reason to feel guilty; she wasn't a thief. "Is that because you stole them?"

A wall of floodwater had less impact on her than the look of compressed anger, loathing, and hurt on his face just then. He strode to the cold fire and gave the stones and ashes a hard kick that sent them flying, then stalked back to his horse and finished loading his possessions. Inserting his boot in the stirrup, he swung up into the saddle and sat there for a long moment, staring straight ahead.

He was gut-churning furious. *Dieu!* He'd spent half the day and night tending and warming her . . . only to have her riffle his possessions and accuse him of stealing! The fear he had felt when he saw her swept away and the pleasure he had experienced at having her safe and warm in his arms all night now embarrassed him to his mercenary core. She truly believed he was a low, thieving barbarian. The dull, squeezing pain that realization caused was an appropriate punishment for forgetting that she was a means to an end . . . a pampered, arrogant female who was redeemable for cold silver.

He turned and settled a hard look on her. "I suppose you wish to ride. Well, I guess it could be arranged . . . for a price."

Thera's crossed arms slid to her sides. He was angered and now intended to make her pay for it. And whatever price he demanded, she vowed not to pay it.

"I have decided that your manners could use a bit of improving, demoiselle. Say 'Prithee please, sir' and you may ride," he declared, smacking the spot just behind his saddle.

"My manners?" she said hotly. "How dare you presume to judge me . . . when you look like a wolf with mange, act as greedy as a jackal, and have the manners of a boar hog in a wallow. Just who do you think you are?"

For a long moment they faced each other, eyes hot and pride crackling.

"I know precisely who I am, my savage little cat," he said, his voice thick with roused pain and pride. "The more pressing question is: who are you?" When she remained defiantly silent, he supplied an answer. "You're a pampered, arrogant noblewoman," he continued, "who should learn how it feels to pay respect to someone else for a change. Say 'Prithee please, sir' and you may ride."

She looked down at her bare feet, recalling her defiance when removing her shoes before the flood and hoping she wasn't making the same mistake. She looked up at the glint of vengeful purpose in his gaze and squared her shoulders.

"I'll walk."

And walk she did. Through thick grasses, over rocky knolls, and along cool, wet beds of leaves on the forest floor; she followed him all morning long. By the time they paused by the swollen stream to rest and have a bite of food, she was parched, bone-weary, and her feet were pricked sore from the stubble and stones. She was too miserable to appreciate how effectively she had managed to put distance between them. She might have been in the far reaches of the Egyptian desert, as far as he was concerned, and the reason for her exile settled a weight in her chest every time she thought about it.

She had all but accused him of stealing a pair of knightly spurs, and the turmoil in his face still burned in her mind.

The thought that she might have injured him with her words was somehow devastating to her.

One moment he was a lustful, swaggering brute; the next he was a warm, teasing swain. One moment she wouldn't trust him with a silver groat, and the next she was trusting him with her life.

She honestly didn't know what to think of him anymore. She only knew that she wished he would talk to her again . . . or at least look at her.

As if feeling her eyes on him, he glanced back, paused, then declared that they would stop for a while. When he untied the bag of oats from his saddle, she recalled the delicious warmth of the oatcake she had eaten only the night before and felt a terrible emptiness inside her that had nothing to do with hunger.

She carried a handful of oats down the stream bank, out of his sight, and collapsed onto a boulder, staring at the dry groats. She was tired, hungry, and dispirited . . . sitting on a rock in the middle of God knew where and wearing a dirty, tattered gown that wasn't even laced properly. Her skin was sunburned, her long hair in tangles, and her toes bruised and scratched from trudging barefoot behind a man who seemed to wish she didn't exist. Now she was sunk so low that she was eating the same food as a horse . . . fed to her by the same unwashed hand!

She'd never been so miserable in her life or had so little control over her circumstances.

Her eyes burned as she thought of her beloved Mercia and of her outrage at having to marry and give up part of her precious authority to a husband. It seemed a thousand years ago. Since she last saw her home, she had rejected a suitor . . . been caught up in an invasion . . . been abducted and nearly raped, robbed and chased by marauding soldiers, caught in a downpour, swept away in a flood, almost drowned, forced to bargain away her virtue, and regularly humiliated by her own venial impulses.

She sniffed and wiped her tears with her sleeve. Until

a few days ago she hadn't even known she *had* venial impulses.

Troubles. She'd had nothing but troubles since that night at the Earl de Burgaud's when she roundly rejected the porcine Duc de Beure. The voice in her head suddenly became Lillith's. *Troubles and contention.* And the next word she heard was *prophecy.* For the first time, when those words fell in the churned and receptive ground of her heart, they began to take root.

Compared to all that had happened to her in the last few days, having to marry and share a throne seemed a paltry complaint. If she ever got back to Mercia she was going to—

If? She halted with her chin quivering, feeling that emptiness in her growing to cavernous proportions. She *had* to get back to Mercia. Battling back a smothering wave of anxiety, she straightened her shoulders and stuffed a few of the dry oats into her mouth, chewing doggedly. She struggled to swallow and glowered at the grain in her hand.

"And when I *do* get back to Mercia, I'm never going to eat another oat as long as I live."

When they set off again, Saxxe turned in his saddle, patted Sultan's rump, and made her the same offer: "You may ride, demoiselle . . . for the price of a 'Prithee please, sir.' "

Thera strode to the horse's head, took hold of his bridle, and looked the huge beast straight in the eye. "Prithee please, sir . . . may I ride?" The horse snorted and shook its great head, and she jolted back. Saxxe chuckled, and she realized from his wicked smile that he had probably done something to cause the horse's reaction.

"If you wish to ride, demoiselle, you'll have to say it to *me,*" he advised. "I collect all Sultan's debts for him."

And to think that mere moments before she had been racked with guilt for always assuming the worst about him! She groaned and set off along the ridge overlooking the flooded stream. She didn't care how sore her feet were or how hungry she became, she did not intend to be in Saxxe Rouen's debt any more than she was already.

By midday, both Saxxe and Sultan had grown impatient with Thera's slogging pace and they ranged ahead for a while, then paused by a large stand of trees on the side of a hill overlooking the stream. When she caught up, she found Saxxe lying serenely beneath a tree with his arms crossed and his eyes closed. Feeling sweaty and gnat-bitten and not to be trifled with, she planted her fists at her waist and demanded:

"How much longer until we reach the place where I was taken by the flood?"

"I have no idea," he muttered, not bothering to open his eyes.

"Well, how far was I carried downstream?"

"I was too busy at the time to take note."

"Then how do you know Lillith and Gasquar will still be there when we get there?"

"I don't." With that, he did at least open one eye.

"Then what in Suffering Stephen do you know?" she shouted, dropping her fists to her sides. That opened his other eye.

"I know enough not to hazard walking barefoot through such treacherous country when I could ride and make much faster time," he said with an arch smile.

"Oooh." She vibrated with the urge to kick him. Instead, she whirled and picked her way down the hillside to the stream bank and found a place to wade in the shallows.

As her feet and her temper cooled, she looked upstream, along the debris-strewn banks, and tried to recall what the crossing where she had been swept away looked like. The flood had happened so swiftly and violently that her recollections were now shrouded in a churning muddy torrent of water. Her shoulders rounded and she expelled a tired breath.

She had no choice but to depend on Saxxe to get her back to Lillith, then on to Mercia. But she did have a choice of whether to cling to her pride and waste precious time and energy or to give him his wretched "prithee please" and save both delay and her poor feet. Her duty to get back to her people was more important than her personal pride.

She rinsed her feet and started back, resolved to make the required sacrifice. Halfway up the bank, along the edge of the rock ledge, she felt something heave beneath her bare foot and she recoiled with a gasp. At her feet lay a huge, mottled brown snake . . . its coils shifting and sliding.

Her scream of terror brought Saxxe bolt upright from his nap. He was on his feet in a heartbeat, drawing his dagger and charging down the hill. He found her crouched on a narrow rock ledge, gripping the stone behind her with whitened fingers and staring in blanched horror at something in the grass.

"There!" she cried, pointing to the grass at the bottom of the ledge. "A s-snake! A huge one!" Her entire arm trembled as she punched her finger accusingly at the place. "There it is! It's still there . . . I can see it." A shudder racked her as she announced: "I s-stepped on it!"

Saxxe straightened out of his defensive stance, looking around the sloping hillside. A snake? There was no other source of immediate peril, so he sheathed his dagger and strode a bit closer, craning his neck to see through the knee-high grass. There it was: a prime, well-fed rat snake that had crawled out of its den in the rocks to do a bit of sunning.

"Well, don't just stand there!" she commanded. "Do something!"

"Do what?" Saxxe leaned back on one leg, watching Thera channel her fear into imperious anger. He had seen it happen before several times, he realized, but never quite so plainly. For the first time, he truly understood: when she was frightened, she reacted by taking charge and giving orders.

"Kill it, for Heaven's sake!"

Her command had a truly desperate edge. The more

frightened she was, the fiercer and bolder her orders became, he realized. It made a bizarre bit of sense, somehow. Every time he'd expected terror and tears from her, he'd gotten a sharp-clawed cat who hissed orders instead.

"Well? Are you going to do something or not?" she demanded.

He tucked his thumbs in his belt and edged nearer, giving the snake a closer look. Letting out a low whistle, he backed up a step. "That's a big one, all right. I don't mind telling you, demoiselle, I don't much care for snakes. Treacherous creatures. You never know what you'll get into when you tangle with one. Why, I remember once in the caverns of Crete . . . Gasquar and I came across a snake as big around as a man's—"

"Curse you, Rouen," Thera choked out. "This is no time for one of your idiot tales! Just kill the vile thing before it gets . . . one of us!"

He paused, drew in his chin, and shook his head gravely. "I don't know, demoiselle. Snake fighting can be a dangerous business. Before I tangled with it, I'd need to know I'd be well paid for the effort."

Her eyes narrowed as she realized where he was leading. "You're already being paid to protect and escort me to M—my home!"

"True. But nothing was said about snake fighting. I'd have to have an additional reward for that. Say . . . another night of pleasure."

Another night? There were *two* snakes in the grass in front of her now!

"Spit and roast you, Rouen," she ground out. "I'll do no such—Aghhhh!"

The snake was moving . . . straight toward her perch. She screamed and thrust back as far as she could against the rock behind her.

"Another night of pleasure, Thera of Aric. It will either be a night with me or a quick kiss and cuddle with your legless friend here. But then, I seem to recall you once said you'd prefer a snake's kisses to mine. . . ."

Thera's heart raced and her stomach churned as she watched those fat brown coils unwinding and sliding toward the edge of the ledge, looking for all the world as if they were headed straight up the rock toward her place of refuge. Closer and closer it slithered. She looked up at Saxxe's broad shoulders and glowing eyes . . . and was furious with him.

"All right! Another night of pleasure." Her throat constricted and she was barely able to squeak out, "Now do something! *Hurry!*"

With a fierce grin, he brandished his dagger and curled into a crouch. "Stay where you are . . . keep back," he called, and she flattened further against the ledge. He charged through the grass with a great bellow, and she screamed. Then at the last moment, he halted and made a lightning-quick stomp. There were thrashing sounds, then all went deathly still. Her heart convulsed in her chest. He was holding the snake's head in one hand, letting its thick body writhe in his grasp . . . and he was grinning.

"Well, that wasn't too bad a fight," he said, sheathing his unused dagger.

Wasn't too bad a fight? It wasn't a fight at all! Chagrin burst red-hot against her skin as she watched him look the vile beast in the eye, shrug as if in apology, then whirl it above his head and send it sailing into the grass far down the hillside.

"Y-you picked it up?" she demanded hotly, rising from her huddled perch. She'd been had. "You just reached down and picked the cursed thing up?"

"I didn't get a good look at it, at first," he said with a less than penitent expression. "It turned out to be a fine, fat rat snake. Not dangerous at all, really, unless you happen to be a field mouse. A fine bit of luck, eh?"

"*Luck?*" Her eyes widened and her fists clenched. "You knew all along, didn't you—you greedy, unprincipled cur!" Climbing down from the ledge, she shoved furiously past him and stalked back around the hillside with her face aflame.

Saxxe's laughter lapping at her back was the last straw. He had taken advantage of her ignorance to coerce yet another wretched night from her. This was the last—the very last—time he would do such a thing to her. She swore it on Mercia's sacred scrolls; she wouldn't be held for ransom again, no matter what the cost!

She marched straight to Sultan, hiked her tunic well above her knees, and jammed her foot into the tall stirrup. It took several hops, but she managed to catch on and push up to a seat behind the saddle, where she sat with her back as straight as an arrow shaft.

Saxxe had a feeling she was saving her anger up for him, but he couldn't help the small smile that overtook him. Taking advantage of her fear of snakes was a canny, opportunistic, and mildly despicable thing to do . . . a bit of work any mercenary would have been proud to claim. It was a relief to know he hadn't gone totally soft where she was concerned.

She now owed him three long nights of pleasure: a considerable obligation and not the sort of debt a wealthy father would wish to see satisfied. It was more the sort of thing a wealthy father would wish to pay off in silver . . . large, spendworthy pouches of silver. And it couldn't be much longer, three or four days at most. If he could just keep his distance from her . . .

As he strode back up the hill, he stopped dead at the sight of her sitting astride his horse with her tunic pulled taut over her ripely curved buttocks and tucked around her shapely thighs. His gaze slid down her naked lower legs and his hands curled around the remembered feel of them.

It was another infuriating dilemma: did he walk in order to keep a distance between them, or did he pull her from his horse and make her walk? Growling irritably, he climbed onto the saddle and gave Sultan a knee to set him moving . . . having forgotten all about making her say "Prithee please."

Chapter Ten

When they finally stopped for a rest and a drink, it was nearing sunset. Saxxe studied the sky and the abundant tree cover and announced that they would make camp there, above a wide spot in the still-flooded stream.

"Make camp here? We cannot stop now . . . there is plenty of daylight left," Thera insisted in a ragged voice. "We could locate Lillith and your braggart of a friend at any time now . . . it can't be much farther."

Saxxe halted in the midst of a broad, muscle-rippling stretch and turned a narrow look on her. All afternoon he'd suffered her disdainful propriety. She had taken great pains not to touch him or speak to him in any way, except to demand they go faster, and her stubbornness had begun to wear on him.

"There is water and dry wood here, and trees for shelter. We'll go on after we've had a hot meal and a night's rest. Not before," he said firmly.

"I don't need to rest," she declared, ignoring the aches in her legs and back that said otherwise. "I need to travel on . . . toward Lillith and my home. And I hardly think you've been overtaxed this day. You've done nothing but sit on your horse, take naps under trees . . . and take advantage of another's fears and misfortunes."

She gave him a scathing look. She'd had all afternoon to nurse her irritation and bolster her nerve, and now intended to have what she wanted: a quick end to this wretched journey.

"Lust may be your favorite of the Deadly Sins, but I can say with certainty that you show remarkable aptitude for *sloth* as well. All I've had to eat all day are a few berries—which I picked myself, along the way—and a handful of oats." Her eyes glinted like blue Damascus steel. "It occurs to me, Rouen, that I am not getting much value for the exorbitant price I am paying for your services."

He reddened beneath his dark beard and copied her arrogant pose. She'd conveniently forgotten about the times he had hazarded life and limb to rescue her, and about the way he had fed and revived her and warmed her . . . just as she'd forgotten about the debt of pleasure she already owed him. However, she had managed to remember his gentle, teasing revelations of the night just past, and now used them to gore him. And for some reason he couldn't just shrug off her disdain as he had before.

"So you think you've been ill served and neglected, do you?" he said, ire rising. "Well, perhaps you will do better yourself." He turned to his horse to retrieve his bags and the hares he had taken earlier. "Here's your supper." He dropped one fat, gutted rabbit on the ground before her and leveled a vengeful half smile at her.

"You cannot be serious," she said, backing up a step.

"I assure you, I am. And you will need something to drink." He turned back and fished about in one pouch to produce a crude metal cup, which he tossed onto the ground between them. "Never let it be said that I didn't provide." He swept a hand toward the stream. "There is plenty of water that way, demoiselle."

"See here, Rouen. You promised to escort me and that means providing for me."

"I am escorting you. And providing food for you." He turned away and began searching the ground for downed branches and bits of firewood.

"If I cook it!"

"Yea, if you cook it." He paused, watching her stare at the rabbit with undisguised horror. "I suppose you'll need something to skin that. Here—" He drew one of his daggers and sent it thudding into the ground beside the carcass.

"S-skin it?" She blanched.

"Before you cook it . . . unless you have a taste for singed hair," he said with a glint in his eye. "Trust me, demoiselle, that is a taste that takes getting used to."

"This is absurd. I'll do no such thing." She turned on her heel and strode off into the bushes, then returned in time to see him removing the last of the skin from his hare and sharpening a stick from the pile he had gathered.

She plopped down on a nearby log, her arms tucked adamantly around her waist, trying not to watch as he used the striking steel to set some grasses afire. He added twigs and larger branches, and soon the smell of roasting rabbit wafted across the small clearing. Her mouth watered and her stomach growled.

"Hungry?" he said, making a show of tending and checking his meal.

"Nay." Starving was more like it.

"Having trouble, demoiselle?" He cocked a look toward her untouched meat. "I could arrange to help you," he said solicitously. "For a price."

Sitting on the wrong end of a hornet couldn't have brought her to her feet quicker. *A price?* The insufferable lout! Not again. Never again.

She sank to her knees and picked up the knife in one hand and the hare in the other. The knowledge of what she had to do made her feel a little sick, but she swallowed her stomach back into place, muttering: "It's you or me."

She flinched as she made the first cut, then closed her eyes, seized the fur, and pulled. Nothing happened, and she opened her eyes and tried again, then finally picked the cursed thing up for better leverage. She tugged, then yanked hard, and the carcass popped out of her slippery hands and landed in the dirt a pace away. She gasped and blinked. For a moment her chin quivered with frustration, then she pounced on the hare, straining and pulling with a vengeance . . . persevering until her supper began to relinquish its furry coat.

By the time she finished, the creature still had the odd patch of fur here and there and a puffy tail, but she told herself she could just eat around them, and she cut a stick and sharpened it to make a spit.

She looked up from her work to find Saxxe standing nearby with a stack of branches in one arm and the striking steel in the other. "You'll need a fire."

"Don't be ridiculous." She pointed to the flames crackling nearby. "That's—"

"*My* fire," he said.

She was stunned at first; she couldn't imagine that he would be so barbaric as to deny her access to a fire. It was the most basic of human sufferance . . . sharing the means of warmth.

"Fine!" she declared, snatching the steel from his hand and sinking to her knees by the stack of branches. How difficult could it be to lay a fire? She'd seen her palace servants do it a thousand times.

More difficult than she had guessed, she soon learned. She huddled and struck and blew on the sparks until her fingers cramped and her back ached and she was light-headed from blowing. It took half an hour just to set a bit of dry grass alight . . . a good while longer to feed the flame into coals hot enough to cook.

When she finally did get her pathetic dinner over the flame, her eyes stung from the greenwood smoke and her hands trembled from strain. After a few moments, she sat back with a feeling of relief and looked up to find Saxxe lolling on his side by a glorious fire, tossing the bones from his meal aside and licking his fingers with exaggerated relish. When he saw her looking at him, he smiled cheerily and raised a bone in salute. Glowering, she turned back to her meal.

The bottom of her meat and the stick on which it was spitted were both on fire.

"Nooo!"

Panicking, she picked up a branch and tried to beat out the flames . . . which sent both meat and stick crashing into the fire. Smoke and ash billowed in her face and she jolted back, coughing and fanning herself, until she realized her hard-won supper was going up in smoke. Seizing a stick, she poked and prodded the meat out of the flames. As she assessed the damage, the pungent smell of singed rabbit hair rose from the half-charred wreck.

An odd noise from Saxxe's direction caused her to jerk around, and she found him sitting with his face in his hands, his shoulders shaking violently as he made muffled, hiccuplike sounds. The wretch was laughing at her! She sat for a moment on her knees, her face flaming and her throat tightening . . . feeling small and inept and vulnerable. Then her royal pride caught fire and she refused to give in to such humiliation.

"I skinned and cooked it. By the saints, I'll find something to eat on it," she muttered furiously. She began pulling off the ash-covered outer part and discovered some nicely cooked meat below.

It was a bit dry and a little burned in places . . . but if she held her breath and didn't look too closely . . . it was almost tasty. Better yet, it was filling. And best of all, it was all hers . . . debt free. She had done it herself. She carved and nibbled and gnawed, not stopping until she had eaten every part that wasn't too blackened or too raw.

Saxxe sprawled on his side, watching her devour her scarcely edible meal. He had expected her to rant and rail and berate him, then to demand, and finally to dissolve in tears and give in to his offer of help for a price. But she hadn't. She had gutted it out . . . stuck with each dirty, disagreeable task until she finished it. And now she was enjoying the fruits of her own labor, perhaps for the first time in her life.

His righteous ire was eroding dangerously. She had surprised him just now with her tenacity. She was pampered and arrogant beyond any female he'd ever encountered. But there were hidden depths inside Thera of Aric . . . resilience, a quick wit, and a remarkable strength of will for a woman so young. He watched her sitting back, wiping her mouth on the back of her hand and licking her fingers. Yet, for all her outrageous self-possession, there was a girlishness about her that roused protective impulses in him, and an artless, untutored sensuality about her that he found irresistible. He watched her intently, studying every movement, hungry for another glimpse inside her.

The question of who she was and what she was doing charging off into the high wastelands of Brittany returned to him with new urgency. Was she indeed going home? Or to meet a forbidden lover? Or—a new thought struck him—to participate in some dynastic intrigue?

Dieu! She was a puzzle—one he ached to solve. As she arched her back, he caught a glimpse of her body through her thin garment and smiled wryly. That was not all he ached to do. She pushed to her feet and he called after her.

"Where are you going?"

She halted and looked at him, her guard rising.

"For some water. I believe you did suggest it," she said loftily, lifting the cup in her hand. When she turned back toward the stream, the sound of his voice slowed her.

"You'd better take a knife, demoiselle. You never know when . . . or against what . . . you may have to defend yourself."

He was declaring that he didn't intend to come to her rescue again, she realized. Not without a healthy price. Well, she had managed to feed herself. She could certainly manage to draw a bit of water. But after a moment's hesitation, she did turn back for the dagger.

By the lowering light, she picked her way down the gentle slope. Choosing a sheltered spot among some rocks, she lifted her tunic and waded into the stream. In the soft evening light, it seemed peaceful. Swallows swooped in the sky and frogs sang in the distance. Mud laid down by the retreating floodwaters covered the smooth stones on the stream bottom, and as she ventured farther out, she relished the way the mud squished between her toes. For a few moments she felt oddly content, kicking around in the water, answerable to no one for these unfettered moments.

Then she turned and found Saxxe standing on the bank not far away with his fists on his hips. His scowl caused her shoulders to rise defensively. "What do you want?" she demanded, but even as the words left her lips, she realized that his dark look was aimed past her. She followed his gaze toward something behind her, something emerging from the shadows beneath an overhanging tree. There it was . . . in the water . . . a sinister dark ribbon, floating.

She froze, thinking of her terrifying encounter that afternoon . . . and of Saxxe's warning moments ago. "S-snake!" she cried. Her head snapped around and she spotted the dagger where she had left it . . . on the boulders downstream. With a frantic glance over her shoulder, she lurched toward her weapon in the knee-deep water.

But the mud made treacherous footing, and she slipped and flailed wildly . . . and fell into the stream with a horrendous splash. The cold and the fall knocked her breathless, and for one terrifying instant she sat with a face full of water, watching the slithering beast closing in on her . . . unable to summon even a scream.

"Don't move!" Saxxe bellowed, charging into the water with his dagger drawn, then rising up at the last moment and striking mightily. All went deathly still and after a moment he made it to his feet with a strange look on his face. And as she sat clasping her hands over her heart, he turned and lifted something out of the water with a smile that broadened and deepened into booming laughter.

"Here is your snake. Just a branch . . . a bit of driftwood!" He laughed so hard that he had difficulty heaving the deadwood onto the bank. Then he turned to her with his eyes dancing. "You should see your face." And he went off in another spasm of mirth at her expense.

"It looked like a snake!" she choked out, her face burning. He had no right to laugh at her, the smug, insufferable . . . barbarian! She was sitting shoulder-deep in water, and when her hands doubled into fists, they curled around heaps of mud. There he stood, his big body vibrating with laughter. She looked at that impervious expanse of bronzed chest . . . and hauled back a fist full of mud and flung it at him.

"Wha—" He sobered instantly and looked down at the splat of mud that had landed square in his chest. "Troth—and I suppose you see no cause for laughter in what just happened," he said, unbuckling his cross braces and giving them a rinse before tossing them onto the bank. He rinsed the rest of the mud from his chest, then lifted his head to challenge her silence. And—*splat*—a second handful of mud pelted his bare shoulder.

"What in the name of thunder do you think you're doing?" he demanded.

She honestly didn't know what she intended . . . only that it felt wonderful. Filling her hands with cool, slippery mud and flinging it against his broad chest was the most satisfying thing she'd done in weeks . . . maybe years. And without a thought for the consequences, she loaded both her hands again and delivered two more well-placed blasts.

"It's nothing to get upset about, Rouen," she taunted sweetly. "Why, it's hardly noticeable amongst all the other dirt." He jerked sideways to dodge her next handful, but got caught by the one after that.

"What the—"

As quickly as she fired, she dredged up more ammunition from the mucky bottom. Her eyes glowed with mischief. "My only regret is that I'm not sitting in the midst of a cow pasture!"

"Why, you little witch!" He crouched and scooped up two handfuls of mud and tossed them at her. One broke up before reaching her, but the other hit her square in the shoulder, muddying her beleaguered white tunic.

"You wretch! This is my only garment!" she said with a groan. But there was an entire armory at her feet, and she retaliated in kind.

The battle was joined.

"Take that, Rouen!" she shouted triumphantly, throwing at him and eluding his missile.

"You've asked for it, demoiselle! I warn you"—he heaved another ball of mud—"in battle I show no mercy!"

"Ha! When do you *ever* show mercy? I certainly haven't seen any of it! Ohhh! Ugh!" She had to pause to wipe a splat of mud off her jaw and fling it away.

To both their surprise, she displayed a marked talent for slinging mud. She scored hit after hit while managing to dodge many of his throws. She would have thought he wasn't trying except for his crimson face and mutters of disbelief. Somehow she managed to keep her feet and to scramble into deeper water whenever he got too close.

Her taunts gradually turned to laughter as she loped about in the water, eluding him, teasing him. She loved it—the cool mud, the buoyant water, the sticky ooze down her gown, the way the mud clung to his skin. It was like nothing she'd ever experienced before. There were no rules or decisions, no preparations or protocols. It was pure abandonment.

But for Saxxe it was pure astonishment. He was losing both battles . . . the one with her and the one with himself. He hungrily absorbed the grace of her nimble movements, the mischief and pleasure shining in her eyes, and the arousing sight of wet silk plastered against her nubile young curves. She was a river sprite . . . a wicked, elusive imp . . . an innocent seductress. Each rise of her knees or jiggle of her breasts sent a shock of excitement through him that interfered with both his reflexes and his aim.

Experience had long since taught him that brute force often succeeded where skill had failed. He simply abandoned slinging mud and launched himself through the water at her in a blinding spray. She squealed and fell back, but he grabbed the tail of her tunic as she scrambled toward the bank. She stumbled and fell in the shallows, and in a trice he was on top of her, pinning her on her back in the mud . . . then rising up, astride her wriggling form.

"No—stop—don't you dare!" Her eyes widened on a huge handful of mud he was holding, and she tried valiantly to block his aim. But he overcame her flailing hands and brought it down square in the middle of her chest. "Ohhh—you'll be sorry for that!" She grabbed a handful of mud and smashed it into his ribs, rubbing it around on him as much as possible.

Instead of flinging mud, they now wrestled in it— sliding and grappling for the upper hand in the slippery muck. They tussled wildly and rolled and splashed until she was suddenly on top, her ripely curved form pressed forcefully against his bigger, harder one. Then, to maintain her advantage, she pushed up to sit on his lower belly, holding handfuls of mud over him.

"Beg for mercy, Rouen," she demanded.

"Never!" he growled, with a deep resonance that sent tantalizing vibrations up the inside of her thighs, where they were pressed against him.

"It's time someone taught you better manners, barbarian. Say 'Prithee please, my lady' and you'll be spared!" she declared.

"Do your worst, demoiselle. Barbarians have no need of manners," he ground out, seizing her wrists and holding them. Straining and shoving downward, she managed to squash the mud over his chest. But when she started to pull away she found her hands suddenly trapped, splayed in the cool mud slathered over his hot flesh. She tugged forcefully, then began to writhe against him as she demanded he release her. Her movements brought her hard against a swelling at the base of his belly.

Inexplicably, they both went still.

She sat astride him with her sodden tunic pushed up around her hips and her hands splayed across his chest . . . feeling a hard ridge beneath her sensitive woman's flesh. His hands slid slowly up her arms, then over her shoulders to cup her breasts, his palms only a layer of wet silk away from her sensitive skin. The heat of his hands seeped through that thin garment and into her cool breasts, and her breath stopped.

The water lapping gently around their bodies was the only evidence of the passing of time. She slid her hands down his chest, the mud an excuse for a touch long desired. Down his breastbone and around a dusky, crinkled nipple she drew one finger . . . leaving a streak of bared skin glowing through the mud.

He began to trace the shape of her breasts through the thin silk, lingering over their tightly budded tips, stroking, rubbing them to hard, aching points. Then his hands quested downward . . . to her waist, her hips, and her strong, shapely thighs, which were spread temptingly against him. Her body felt warm and firm beneath his fingers. And he sought her face with his eyes.

The darkness was deepening around them, but her sapphire eyes glistened in the purple twilight. There was no anger or disdain in her expression now . . . only the warmth of rising desire. He shoved up on his arms, face-to-face with her as she sat astride his lap, and he rinsed his hand to wipe some of the mud from her cheeks.

"Come. The light is gone and the air grows cooler." He slid her from his lap and stood up, then took her hand and led her deeper into the stream. There, he scooped water and poured it over her, gently washing away the mud. The contrast of the chilled water and his warm hands sent shivers through her. His eyes were soft, lighted from within by desires she recognized and needs she couldn't begin to know.

Out of the rising mists of feeling inside her came a new and compelling need to give. Never before had she washed or comforted or touched someone in intimate service. She scooped water and began to wash the mud from him with long, wonder-filled strokes. He was so marvelously made; solid muscles stretched over wide shoulders and ridged over lean ribs . . . raw power visible in the cording of his arms . . . determination etched in the underlying angularity of his frame . . . sensuality imbedded in the haunting strength of his beard-cloaked features.

The current curled around them, tugging at their feet, wrapping them in a liquid, elemental awareness of each other. He pulled her close, then bent at the waist and lowered her hair into the rippling water, combing the dirt and mud from it with his fingers. Then, setting her back on her feet, he drew his dagger and cut the stubborn laces of her sleeves and lifted her half-laced tunic and her chemise up and over her head.

She watched, stunned, as he rinsed the mud from her garments, then picked her up in his arms and carried her to the bank. He left her there, holding her clothes, while he waded back out and dunked himself under the water, rinsing his hair thoroughly and giving his breeches a rubbing. Then he retrieved his cross braces and her dagger, and led her back to their camp.

"My fire has gone out," she said hoarsely, nodding toward her cooking fire, now nothing but ash. He laughed.

"Mine hasn't."

He unrolled his sleeping pallet and wrapped her in a blanket, then laid more branches on the fire. Spreading her tunic on a nearby bush, he stripped off his belt and breeches and hung them beside it.

She averted her eyes, but not before she saw the scars on his legs and the startling column of rigid flesh that nestled in a swirl of dark hair at the base of his belly. She stiffened as he approached, but he sank onto his knees beside her as if it were the most natural thing in the world to be there with her, unclothed. Taking the edge of her blanket from her, he began to rub her hair with it. After a long moment she turned to look at him, and he gave her a wry, heart-stopping smile.

"I wish I had a comb for your hair."

His quiet words stunned her with their genuineness, and she felt a strange, sweet fullness in her chest. What a paradox he was, this barbarian whose hands knew how to ease pain as well as inflict it . . . who spent wishes on a comb for a woman's hair when he had no possessions of his own. As he ran his fingers through her hair, over and over, untangling it, she felt her last defenses slide.

This intimacy was too precious to resist. When he took her face between his hands and looked into her eyes, she let the blanket fall away and raised her arms around his neck to pull his head closer.

This was what she wanted, what she had ached for . . . the feel of him taking her mouth with his . . . a hundred, a thousand, sensations pouring into her heart, invading her blood and marrow. She wanted his power and his heat against her, around her, within her. For the first time she felt full force the sweet pain of longing that was desire. Its fever set her trembling with an urgency for joining, and in that tumult, logic and reason failed and flesh exerted a wisdom of its own.

The world receded to the edge of consciousness as they sank together onto the blankets, bathed in the fire glow and in the heat of their rising passions. Their mouths blended in hot, languorous kisses, hungry but unhurried.

Then he slid, bearing his weight to one side, and shifted his caresses lower . . . to her throat, down her chest, to her breasts. He ran the rasping softness of his beard across her nipple, again and again, bringing her taut and quivering with each stroke. Her hands fluttered like birds . . . then sank into his hair to urge him on. His kisses became nibbles and sharp tugs that made her shiver with pleasure.

All her perceptions seemed to melt and fuse . . . leaving her only the deep and primal sensation of touch. Her skin came alive with a tactile hunger bred by a lifetime of regal restraint. Every part of her cried out for his touch . . . tiny strokes, bold caresses, gentle kneading, and just the delicious pressure of his weight upon her . . . she wanted it all. And as she greedily sought those sensations, his hands drifted lower on her, down her stomach and between her legs.

Her breath stilled in her throat as his fingers stroked her inner thighs, then slid to the tender cleft at the top of them. Her heart stopped as she waited, not knowing what she waited for. Then his gentle fingers invaded her woman's folds, exploring and teasing that sleek, tender flesh, and she shuddered and tensed as his fingers brushed the throbbing center of her response.

Slowly, he traced circles around that burning, sensitive point . . . brushing by it but not touching it directly. And with each rounding of his fingers she felt herself drawing curiously tighter inside, growing hotter. A delicious ripeness seeped into her womanflesh; she felt swollen and expectant. Pulsing waves of pleasure mounted like a swelling tide that pushed her steadily higher, toward some unknown peak. Giving herself to it, she gripped his shoulders with frantic hands, arching, tensing, seeking whatever it would bring.

Higher and higher she was carried, borne on hot currents until she went tumbling into breaking, churning waves of release . . . calling his name.

Lillith picked her way down the dark slope, toward the stream, muttering to herself and scrutinizing every bit of ground before she set her foot on it. The sharp snap of a stick startled her and she wheeled, clutching her throat.

"Where do you go, *ma chatte*?" Gasquar's broad smile and glowing eyes appeared out of the darkness, and his wiry beard and thick shoulders materialized next.

"Into the bushes for a bit of privacy," she said, hurling each word. "You do know the word *privacy*. . . ."

"Ahhh, but it is night . . . *dangereux* for a woman alone." He crept closer on silent feet. "The wolves, the bears, the badgers . . . there are many who hunt by night. Yet you do not listen, *ma petite*. What will I do with you, eh?"

"You'll let me go . . . or I won't be responsible," she said, gritting her teeth. He sighed and backed up a step, letting her go.

A while later, as she stood staring at the steeply eroded stream bank, wondering how she could get down to wash, she spotted a flicker of light on the far side through a stand of trees. She blinked, then gasped. Thera!

She ran along the top of the steep slope calling out, "Thera! Thera! My lady—is that you?"

Gasquar, who had been covertly keeping watch, charged out of the nearby trees and intercepted her.

"It's a fire—it's them!" she insisted, pointing across the water.

"Perhaps," he uttered with quiet force, craning his neck to catch a glimpse of the dim light. "But it may also be someone else . . . travelers . . . or a band of cutthroats and thieves. Hold your tongue until we are certain. Come."

Together, they slid down the bank to peer across the rushing stream. Through the trees, they indeed saw a campfire. Not far away stood something large and pale . . . a horse. "Sultan!" Gasquar declared with relief.

Together they began to shout and call above the noise of the water.

The sound of Thera's name fanned through the mists of pleasure swirling through her senses. At first she thought Saxxe had said it, and she smiled and pulled his head up to hers, offering him her mouth. He slid a knee between her thighs, nudging them apart, and slowly transferred his weight onto her soft, resilient frame. She gasped against his mouth and he cradled her head between his hands and drew back, smiling, reassuring her. His eyes were rings of molten gold encompassing black wells of desire, his skin hot, his body hard and heavy . . . focused fiercely on containing the need straining inside him. He arched and rubbed slowly against her, sliding his swollen shaft against her still-throbbing flesh and—

It came again, louder and recognizable.

"Thera! Thera, is that you?" Then: "Saxxe—*mon ami!* Where are you?"

They froze, waiting until it came again . . . slamming into them like a wall. With hearts pounding, they drew back to look at each other, anguished by the intrusive call of reality. But there was no choice; already they were retreating from the edge of Paradise.

"Damn you, Gasquar," he cursed softly, rolling aside and pushing to his feet.

"Lillith?" Thera sat up, clutching her pounding heart, and caught a glimpse of Saxxe heading for the stream. She scrambled to her feet and hurried after him, going back for a blanket only when the night air raised gooseflesh over her heated body. She found Saxxe standing in the moonlight, scouring the far bank, and when she approached he pointed to two indistinct figures across the way. She could make out what seemed like a face and an arm waving, but Lillith's voice was unmistakable.

"It *is* you!" Lillith cried, waving wildly. "Thank the Heavens! I had such a time getting this great horse's arse to come searching! Are you all right?"

Thera hauled the blanket around her haphazardly and waved back, calling out, "I'm fine! I almost drowned, but Saxxe rescued me and—" She suddenly realized he was naked . . . clearly visible from the other bank . . . as was she. With a gasp she pulled the blanket around her shoulders and pushed Saxxe toward the cover of some nearby trees. "All is well, Lillith . . . truly!"

It was too late. Across the way, Lillith's eyes were widening with shock. "Naked?" she choked out, grabbing Gasquar's arm. "Holy Mother—are they both naked?" She dragged him this way and that, craning her neck, frantic to get a better look. "I saw her bare shoulders and bosom. And he is naked—I'm sure of it! Saints! I could see his . . . his . . . from here!"

Gasquar laughed and grabbed her shoulders to restrain her. "This is a bad place to cross, *mon ami!*" he called out. "And treacherous in the dark. I am glad to see you both survived. We will see you by sunlight and find a place to join you. Sleep well!"

"We shall not!" Lillith declared hotly, struggling to break free. "I have to cross right now. . . . I have to be there with her, this very night, all night!" He slid an arm around her waist and hoisted her off her feet. "Put me down! Let me go—I have to see what they're doing!"

"Why concern yourself with their pleasures, *ma chatte*," Gasquar said raggedly, grappling with her defiant form, "when you should be concerned with your own."

"I'm her cou—chaperone, her *dueña*. I have to know where she is sleeping."

With a squat and a heroic heave, he boosted her across his shoulder. She squealed and smacked his back with her fists, demanding her release. He paused, sensing that her panic was genuine. It had been her task, he realized, to guard her lady's virtue. "You must know where she sleeps this night?"

"It is my sworn duty!"

"But that is simple, *ma chatte*. She sleeps with *mon ami*, of course. She has no cloak and no shoes . . . she must stay warm. And Saxxe . . . he has a great fire for her in his loins, *non?*"

"Dearest Lord—let me down!" She wriggled and shoved and raked her nails down his bare, thickly muscled back. He flinched and growled, but kept his hold on her.

"Ahhh—the sharp claws of the cat." He gave her upended bottom a warning smack that drew a choked squeal from her. "*Alors*—you remind me. Once, when we were in Egypt, we came across a lost temple dedicated to the ancient cat goddess, Bast. We were trapped there for three days with a score of very beautiful and very lonely priestesses. *Dieu*—so many hungry claws! Our backs were a month healing."

"Heathen!" she hissed.

He laughed wickedly as he climbed the hill toward their camp. "Perhaps you need something to dull your claws, eh, *ma chatte*? As the lovely priestesses soon learned . . . I make a very fine scratching post."

Chapter Eleven

Across the way, Thera climbed the bank and went straight to the bushes where her wet tunic was spread. As she reached for it, Saxxe's hand closed over hers and she pulled back an arm's length, clasping her blanket together. When she looked up, all she could see was his compelling green-gold eyes and all she could feel was a raw, pulsing ache of need. She tried to reach her tunic again, but he would not let her go.

"Please, let me," she whispered.

"Nay." His voice came thick and laden with unspent emotion. "You'll catch lung sickness. Leave it till morning. You will not need it to warm or protect you." He paused and a flicker of pain went through his countenance. "That is my task."

"Saxxe . . ." The soft stroke of longing she gave his name betrayed her inner turmoil.

Lillith's and Gasquar's untimely interruption had saved her from surrendering her body totally to him. But the true barrier of her innocence had already fallen; the wall which for much of her life had forbidden intimacy between herself and others—the gulf between monarch and subject—had been utterly and irrevocably breached. In one shatteringly sweet moment in Saxxe Rouen's arms, she had been paradoxically both reduced and elevated to human dimensions.

She was a woman . . . who wanted a man. For a few splendid moments they had been in a world of their own . . . the only two people in Creation. . . .

But that moment was past. The real world had caught up with them, shattering that sweet illusion of Eden and reminding her of the barriers of rank and wealth and person that still lay between them. And as she looked up into his eyes, she knew it had come just a few heart-rending moments too late. What she had surrendered to him could never be taken back, could never be given to another man. Saxxe Rouen would always hold the key to her passions and the deepest stirring of her woman's heart.

For a moment he wavered, wanting to wrap her in his arms and cover her trembling lips with his. It wouldn't take much to make her respond again, and he knew that for a while he could make her forget her waiting lady and her waiting home. But the morning would come, and they would still face the fact that she was a wealthy young noblewoman, while he . . . he was . . .

He led her back to the fire with a pained expression. "Take what sleep you can, Thera." He pressed her down onto his pallet. "We have a day of hard traveling tomorrow."

She gave a silent nod, keeping her eyes averted, and lay back on the skins. He took a deep, shuddering breath and drew a cover of stitched pelts over her. Then, pulling a blanket around his shoulders, he went to sit by the fire.

As the dew fell, he stared into the golden flames, seeing in their wanton destructiveness the pattern of his own life. All day her question had echoed in his mind, opening doors long closed and raising thoughts and feelings long buried.

Who do you think you are?

He was a hireling, a man who spent his strength and blood fighting for other men's importance and worth. He ate like a wolf when there was food to be had and slept with one eye open . . . in sour, rotting taverns when he had a bit of coin, and on frozen or muddy ground when he had none. He was a man who lived each day in death's shadow . . . who carried his past in a leather pouch . . . who had no future, only a dream.

There had been a time, years ago, when he had worn fine mail and plate armor and kept a squire to see that his hair was neatly cropped and his face was close-shaven. He had worn fine woolen tunics, trained in the company of knights and nobles, and dined by the head of a great table. He glanced down at his cross braces, lying nearby, and ran his callused fingers over the scarred boss.

This single plate was all that was left of his fine armor, and the tempered strength of his body was all that was left of the years that had passed between then and now. And the desperate craving for a scrap of land—a meadow, an orchard, and a stream—was all that was left of his dream of a land and a title . . . a kingdom of his own. The ache in his chest approached unbearable, but he had never shrunk from pain in his warring life and he made himself face it squarely.

His knightly armor and his knightly manners and graces had been pared away by the years of hard living. He was left with only the hard-fighting, surviving core of himself. He was indeed little more than a barbarian. And he now knew with dread certainty that the only title he would ever hold was Prince of Dreamers.

As the night wore on, Saxxe laid more branches and a good-sized log on the fire, then, rising quietly, he crept onto the pallet and slid beneath the skin cover with Thera, curling his body around hers and pulling her gently back against him. He held his breath for a moment, and when she didn't stir or protest, he slowly tightened his arm around her. It was sweet pain, lying there with her, knowing it was for the last time. He laid his head on her damp hair and sank gradually into a dreamless sleep, not seeing the tears that slid from between her closed eyes.

Gasquar's and Lillith's shouting had roused not only Saxxe and Thera; it had alerted other eyes encamped in darkness on the nearby ridge. At their first call, three dark-clad forms scurried along the crest of the hill behind Lillith and Gasquar. Catching sight of the people below and of the tantalizingly pale forms on the far side of the stream, the burly black-clad soldier with ratlike eyes had pulled the others down into the bushes with him.

"*Silencio*. We listen first."

When the greeting was past and the two pairs below parted, each to their own campfire, the leader's eyes narrowed with cunning. "Two women. No doubt the ones we seek." He paused and thought for a moment. "They may not cross the river tonight . . . but we will."

He motioned sharply with his hand and instantly they were creeping back along the ridge to their horses and backtracking to a crossing not far downstream. Soon they lay on the opposite hilltop, looking down into their quarry's camp with glistening eyes.

"They are naked, eh?" one whispered breathlessly.

"*Sí*," another snarled, watching the dark-haired giant warming himself. After a while, he joined the girl, curling around her and holding her tight against him. "*Sacre Christo*—why do we just lie here? We could surprise them and take the woman for ourselves."

"And have the duc flay us alive?" the leader growled in a thick Spanish accent. "We are sent to find her . . . nothing more. You know the duc. He does not like to share." He turned to one of the others. "Sleep while you can. At sunrise you will ride to the duc's camp and make a report." He turned his gaze back to the flickering fire and settled down in the tall grass to watch and to wait for dawn. "And while you are gone, we will follow to learn where she goes . . . so that we may lead the duc to her when he marches into Brittany."

The next morning Saxxe and Thera rode along the stream, uncommonly silent with each other as they looked for a suitable crossing. They were reunited with Gasquar and Lillith at the same place where Thera had been swept downstream two days before.

Lillith ran to Thera, embracing her, then holding her at arm's length to inspect her. "Your gown—it is filthy!" she wailed. "And your hair!" She looked down at Thera's bare feet and blanched at the sight of her unbound breasts straining her silk tunic. With an accusing look at Saxxe, she bundled Thera off into the bushes to tend her needs and right her clothing.

"That brute—what you must have been through!" Lillith said, her eyes flashing as she seated Thera on a log.

"He saved my life, Lillith. And he warmed and fed me . . . and helped me get back to you," Thera said tersely, feeling Lillith's eyes measuring every part of her body for some evidence of what had transpired in the nights just past. Her cheeks reddened, but she knew she had to face Lillith with the truth before the countess's fertile imaginings made it into something to count.

"Last night, when you came upon us, I had been washing in the stream and fell into the mud. I had to remove my tunic and . . . he . . . washed it." When Lillith's eyes widened with expectation, Thera frowned and turned away. "Nothing happened between us." She dismissed it with the wave of a hand and reached for her shoes. "Put it out of your mind entirely. There is no need to speak of it again."

But even as she ordered Lillith to forget about her time with Saxxe, she knew she would never forget what had happened between them. She would forget only when thoughts of him no longer roused pleasure or desire or sadness in her. And she couldn't imagine ever thinking of him without feeling some of the sweet womanly longings he had stirred in her.

Lillith, too, would have a difficult time forgetting . . . a royal command notwithstanding. She kept recalling the sight of Saxxe Rouen's nakedness, a glaring omission in Thera's explanation. She searched Thera's glowing face and luminous eyes. Something had indeed happened between them; they had been naked, and he had warmed her. Gasquar's bawdy conjectures about what sort of fire Saxxe would use came back to Lillith with a vengeance.

The standards by which she was constrained to count were strict and explicit. From what she had observed, the two nights would have to be counted. And all together, that made *three*.

Three nights spent—Lillith groaned and rolled her eyes—and two yet promised! For once she prayed that Thera had some sort of devious, unscrupulous plan in mind . . . for by the terms of her charge, she was forbidden to reveal her "count," lest she influence her princess's decisions. Thus, as much as she wished to, she could not warn her princess that the count of her nights had already begun and was rapidly mounting.

The tensions between the foursome eased as they spotted the dwindling track that was the trading road through Brittany and they were able to orient themselves once more. They climbed a nearby hill and Thera spotted a gray-tinged ridge among the peaks in the distance. She pointed to it, saying her home lay near those slopes, and they struck off across the uninhabited hills.

It was only when they had eaten and lain down to sleep that night that Thera allowed herself to look at Saxxe again. She found him staring thoughtfully at her, as he had much of the day. As she pulled her cloak and blanket tight about her and closed her eyes, she felt oddly desolate. And she knew in her deepest heart what sort of warmth she was missing.

Across the fire, Saxxe watched her turning and shifting and curling up into a ball as she tried to fall asleep. She was disturbed by what had occurred between them, he knew, but he sensed that her tension also had to do with approaching her home. She probably worried about what would happen when he confronted her father with his demands. He intended to tell her that he would make no mention of the nights and would ask for the hundred in silver that she had once offered him instead. But there didn't seem to be an opportune moment. She seemed to be avoiding all contact with him, and, as much as it annoyed him, he told himself it was probably just as well. This dull ache inside him was difficult enough to live with.

But as they went on the next day, he saw her biting her lip and glancing nervously his way when she thought he couldn't see. And his own tension began to rise as he thought of what she might be keeping from him . . . a jealous father, perhaps, or a vengeful bridegroom. He began to scour the cliffs and rocky, boulder-strewn hills for signs of danger, and his sword hand began to ache with anticipation.

They paused just past midday for water and a rest, and as they sat on the rocks, there came a scraping, rustling noise from a ledge above them. Thera had gone off for a bit of privacy and Saxxe shot to his feet, looking around for her, then up toward the source of that sound.

He thought of dire possibilities—bandits and thieves . . . or those black-clad soldiers. Though they had seen no sign of the marauders for several days, he sometimes felt a prickling at the base of his neck, as if he were being watched. It was a familiar warning sense that had saved him more than once in treacherous situations; he could not ignore it. Drawing his blade as silently as a passing breeze, he motioned Lillith to be silent and beckoned Gasquar along with him.

They climbed onto the rocks, broadly circling the source of that noise. Thera was returning just at that moment, skirting some boulders, when she caught sight of them climbing up the hillside . . . crouched and moving stealthily, their blue blades glinting in the sun. Her throat constricted and she flattened back against the rocks. Scraping and thudding broke out and she saw Saxxe signaling Gasquar to attack—at the same moment she spotted wild goats on the ledge beneath them. Her shout of warning was too late; Saxxe and Gasquar were already hurtling down the rocky slope with fierce cries, preparing to jump onto the ledge and do bloody battle.

The goats panicked and took flight in all directions. Saxxe managed to change course at the last moment and slam against the rocks, narrowly missing the bleating, lunging animals. Gasquar, however, was not so lucky. He fell straight in the path of a frightened buck and was nearly impaled on a nasty set of horns. Only his quick thinking—using the flat of his blade to bash the beast away—saved both him and the wild-eyed animal from disaster.

It was over in an instant. All four of them froze in stunned silence as the sounds of scrambling, clopping hooves faded. Then Gasquar pulled himself upright, grinning. Saxxe joined him, and Lillith came running.

"Goats—it was only goats!" Gasquar roared. And they laughed, even Lillith.

"Hazardous country in which you make your home," Saxxe said with a twinkle in his eye as he helped Thera remount her horse. "I shall have to speak with your father about these dangerous, marauding goats."

Thera managed a smile, but it was more relief than humor. Her knees were weak with the realization that those goats could have been some of her shepherds in search of stray lambs . . . and that Saxxe's great blade might not have been stayed so easily if his quarry had proved human.

As they rode on, she remembered the sight of him fighting the soldiers that first morning on the cliff top. The power and savagery of the fight came back to her with a focus that her original perceptions had lacked. Now she saw not just Saxxe but also the slashing blades, the faces contorted by fury, and the gore that seeped from the still, silent forms.

There was a fierceness bred into his very sinews, a thirst for fighting that had been deepened by years of experience into a habit of violence. Despite his stunning lapses into gentleness, the urge to draw steel was ever-present in him . . . and alarmingly near the surface.

The hills became steeper and more deeply fissured, and they had to travel single file along narrow paths that led ever higher. They stopped in the late afternoon in a small clearing in the midst of craggy stone walls and massive boulders. Thera recognized the place and sent Lillith a speaking look as she announced that they were yet a day's ride from her home. Lillith's dark eyes widened, then lowered, to hide her reaction to the half-truth.

In fact, as Thera and Lillith both knew, they already stood on Mercian soil. And when Thera ventured away from the others, stretching her legs, she glimpsed confirmation of the fact carved in stone. On a huge rounded boulder just outside the clearing, the crest of the royal house of Mercia, a circle of oak leaves encompassing two entwined hands and set beneath a crown, was hewn into the rock. The emblem had been erected on stone markers or carved into rocks to identify the outer borders of her kingdom.

She stood looking at it, running her fingers over the smooth, delicate design, and the full impact of their arrival came crashing down on her. The journey was over; Saxxe had indeed brought her home. Her mind flooded instantly with images of her people, her lands, and her city, and they pointedly reminded her of who and what she was. Crown Princess Thera of Mercia, heir to a throne and ruler of a people.

In that moment, facing the duty embodied in her own royal crest, she felt the mantle of her responsibilities settling upon her shoulders once more. The sense of it stunned her, for in order for her royal obligation to fall upon her again, she must have shed it somehow, somewhere.

Saxxe Rouen had gradually peeled away her "princess" shell, and for a brief but memorable time . . . two days and nights in the wilderness . . . she had been a woman. "Thera," not "Princess." She had gone barefoot and cooked food for herself, had a mud fight in a stream, and discovered the merits of shared body heat on a cool night. She had explored the depths of her own pride and will, and experienced life without the protection— or interference—of her royal status. But, most important, she had learned what it was to want a man . . . to share her bed and her self with one.

That thought brought her up short.

In all her railing against the uselessness of husbands and the hatefulness of marriage, she had never considered that she could possibly *want* a man as mate or companion. And now that she wanted one with all her heart . . . it was the wrong one! Not a sober and godly man of noble birth, not a man of fine education and courtly manner, not someone who could be an example for the men of Mercia—she groaned silently—or even someone who bathed occasionally! Some hideous conspiracy of the Fates had paired her with a crude, lusty, powerful, and utterly irresistible barbarian!

In her mind she saw bold, greedy, and unbridled Saxxe Rouen swaggering into her peaceful, orderly kingdom . . . striding amongst her diligent, immaculate, and sheltered people. It would be like turning the wolf loose in the sheepfold!

She glanced down at her broken nails, unkempt hair, and dirty, tattered tunic, seeing them suddenly as signs of her abandonment of duty. Look at the wretched effect he had on her, she told herself: dirt and disorder and neglect of duty. It was the worst that could befall a monarch: abandoning one's obligation to one's people. And if he had such an effect on her, just imagine what havoc his violent, unpredictable nature could wreak in her isolated kingdom!

He was the very embodiment of the dangerous, unpredictable world she had vowed to keep at bay. And she had led him straight to Mercia's doorstep.

She had to reassemble her princess self, to somehow seize control again. Her obligation to her people came before her own personal needs and desires. No matter how much she wanted him, duty demanded that she never let Saxxe Rouen set foot beyond the mountain passes that isolated Mercia from the rest of the world. She pressed a hand against the stonecutting, drawing strength from the symbol or perhaps the rock itself. She had to think of a way to leave him and to substitute silver for—

"There you are." Saxxe's voice startled her, and she whirled, leaning back against the marker to shield it from his eyes.

"You surprised me," she said thickly, her hand over her pounding heart.

"You were gone for so long that I began to wonder."

"I was just returning," she said, a bit too quickly. She lowered her eyes and said no more, for her throat tightened.

"It won't be long now," he said quietly. "You will be back with your family." He took a step toward her, and she stiffened and pressed against the rock, feeling the royal crest burning into her back . . . into her very heart. "About your debts . . . three nights, by my count . . ."

"*Three* nights?" Lillith's voice sounded from behind him. He turned to find her staring at him with some part indignation, some part alarm. "Blackguard! My lady has promised you only *two*!"

"There was a little matter involving a snake while we were separated from you," he declared. "Was there not, demoiselle?" His piercing look said he expected Thera might try to deny it.

"There was," she declared, then flinched at Lillith's gasp. "Never fear, Rouen, you'll be fully paid."

Saxxe opened his mouth as if he would say more, then expelled a disgusted breath and turned back to the horses, leaving her to face Lillith's horror alone.

"There was a snake, Lillith," Thera insisted, "as big around as a man's leg. And he fought it and"—the half-truth stuck in her throat—"rescued me again."

"For a price," Lillith supplied, scowling.

"For a price," she echoed, her cheeks reddening. "But you needn't worry that he'll ever collect it." Stepping aside, she revealed the crest she had shielded with her body. Lillith melted with relief at the sight. "We're home."

Dawn crept red and golden into the narrow rock-lined passage where they had spent the night. When they made camp the evening before, Thera had wrapped up in her cloak, settled down by Lillith as usual, and promptly gone to sleep . . . or so it seemed.

Through her lashes she watched Saxxe and Gasquar, waiting for them to fall asleep so that she and Lillith could seize their mounts and steal away. But Saxxe and Gasquar had remained awake most of the night, taking turns scaling the rocks and keeping watch over the surrounding area in the moonlight. She tried to stay alert, but her eyes grew heavy as the night went on, and soon her guise of sleep became sleep in earnest.

She dozed fitfully on the hard ground until she was awakened by a muffled growl. Her head popped up and her heart lurched until she realized it was Gasquar's snoring, and she sagged with relief. She spotted Saxxe sprawled against a rock with his head bent, and sat up slowly, looking at him . . . his long, muscular legs, his wide shoulders that gave off half-visible heat, his callused but gentle hands as they lay across his thigh, and his dark, tousled hair. She closed her eyes to trap the sight of him inside her, and felt a dull, stabbing pain near her heart.

Quietly, she got to her knees and awakened Lillith with a hand over her mouth. As they readied their horses, every creak of saddle leather seemed to be magnified in the crisp air, but neither Saxxe nor Gasquar stirred. Then with a last look at Saxxe, she took a deep breath and led her horse as quietly as possible up the narrow path between the rocks.

The thud of hooves striking stone echoed off the rock faces as they led their horses along, and Thera prayed that the sound would not carry far behind them. All went well until they rounded the first major bend in the winding path. Lillith caught the edge of her cloak underfoot, stumbled, and cried out in surprise before she could clamp a hand over her mouth. Thera looked back with a frantic expression. "They may have heard . . . mount up and let's ride."

Behind them, Lillith's cry had indeed reached Saxxe, and he bolted upright, straining to catch a repeat of the sound that had awakened him. When there was continued silence, he eased and took his hand from his

dagger. Then he spotted the empty blankets where Thera
and Lillith had spent the night, and lurched to his feet,
looking around for a sign of them. His eye fell on the
horses; two were missing.

She was gone. He couldn't believe it. How could she
just steal away—after all they had been through, after all
he had done for her, after all that had passed between
them? It had been a long time since he had opened a
part of his inner self to a woman. And now that he had,
she stole away in the dead of night! The betrayal struck
deep into the feeling so recently revived in him.

But as he stood staring at her empty blanket, he realized she hadn't just stolen a bit of his heart; she had also
taken his hopes for a reward . . . a future. And the aching
emptiness began to fill with anger.

"*Dieu*, Rouen," he muttered furiously. "Again you are
left without a denier to show for all your efforts. Will you
never learn?" He ruthlessly stuffed his ragged feelings
back into a corner of his heart. "This time it will be
different," he declared. "I swear to God . . . this time I'll
track her down and make her pay."

"Wake up, Gasquar—they're gone," he growled, giving
Gasquar a shake, then a hand up. "And we're going after
them. The little witch owes me and I intend to collect!" He
grabbed the blankets and rushed to saddle his horse.

In minutes they were riding through the narrow, rock-
lined passages that carried them upward toward the
mountaintop. Then, following what appeared to be a
trail, they descended toward a shallow, forested valley
which was bounded on the far side by another high,
rocky ridge. They paused to take their bearings and
were reconsidering their direction when Gasquar spotted
something in the distance, something moving among the
rocks on the far ridge. He shielded his eyes against the
sun for a better look.

"It's them!" he declared, pointing.

The next instant they gave their surefooted mounts
free rein down a steep graveled slope toward the woods
below. Once in the trees, they rode hard, picking their

way through the dense woods on what seemed to be an overgrown path. It seemed forever until they reached the base of the far ridge and began to climb. Far above, Saxxe caught sight of Thera's dark cloak and horse moving against the pale sandstone, and he gave Sultan the knee and charged ahead.

"It's them!" Lillith said frantically, pointing to the figures on horseback far below.

"The wretch!" Thera groaned, muttering, "He's part wolf, part badger, part ox . . . and now part blooded hound as well. Faster!" she called to Lillith. "We'll have to lose them in the cliffs!"

But as they entered the mazelike trails higher on the ridge, they could see Saxxe and Gasquar gaining on them. They raced through the narrow passages, jostling and changing direction twice in an effort to throw their pursuers off their trail. But when they emerged on the far side of the mountain and hurried along the paths that led down into the valley, Thera found the tenacious pair leaving the stone passages and starting down the steep trails after them.

"Nooo!" she wailed, kicking her horse to breakneck pace down the steep incline with Lillith close behind. As they reached the trees and located a well-used path, they galloped full tilt through the forest.

Saxxe was close enough to see Thera's reaction, and the sight of her distress spurred him on. He was going to catch her and haul her up short . . . and . . . Well, he wasn't sure what he intended to do to her, but it wouldn't be pleasant. And he was going to enjoy it, by God!

Leaning with his mount, he raced down the rocky slope and into the trees after her. He was so intent on the sight of her ahead of him that he scarcely took note when they emerged from the dense trees into lush green meadows filled with wildflowers and dotted here and there with clusters of fat, indolent sheep.

They left the road and streaked across thick grass, their hoofbeats muffled thuds reverberating through the moist earth. Over hillocks and around clumps of trees, they raced until they reached a snowy forest. Saxxe reined back slightly, disoriented by the endless expanse of white above thick, green grass. After a moment he realized it was trees in bloom . . . hundreds of them . . . growing in rows. The air was heavy with spring perfume as he plunged through the orchards after her.

Beyond the blossoming trees lay cultivated fields, a patchwork of varying hues of green and brown . . . crops newly sewn and newly sprouted. They raced through the midst of those fields on a road bordered by huge old oaks, and when Thera went splashing straight through a stream, he went splashing right through it after her.

Her hair was flying like a banner behind her, and the wind had torn at her cloak until it came undone and was blown from her shoulders. He focused doggedly on her image; her white surcoat, her burnished hair flashing in the morning sunlight.

He was so intent on riding her down that he didn't realize she had led him straight to the edge of a small city. He raced pell-mell toward the stone buildings and neat half-timbered houses, oblivious to all but her wind-whipped form. He managed to bring his horse abreast of hers and dove for the reins she held. In moments he had pulled her horse to a halt and was on the ground, pulling her from the saddle.

"Nooo!" she cried out, kicking and flailing with everything in her. Trapped now, she went stiff and bashed his chest with her fists one instant, then went limp and tried to slither out of his grip the next. "Unhand me—"

"So—you thought you'd run off without so much as a fare-thee-well!" He grappled with her thrashing form, then, in desperation, gave her a powerful spin and hauled her back against his chest. With her back to him, caught hard against his body, there was little she could do but shove at his arms around her waist and kick at his shins. "Owww! Damn it!" he howled, spreading his legs to avoid her heels. "You owe me, my wicked little cat. And you're going to pay . . . like it or not!"

Another thing Saxxe had failed to notice was the people in the fields they passed along the way. The people, however, had noticed them, and now came running across the fields and up the road, calling to each other. Soon there was a score of them rushing toward Saxxe and Thera . . . men in work clothes, women in fine woolen tunics and kerchiefs, and bright-eyed children in tidy smocks and wooden shoes. And as word spread, people in the houses at the edge of the city began to pour onto the road as well, streaming toward them.

Whether it was the sound of the people approaching or the fact that Thera gasped and stilled against him . . . something caused him to look up. For the first time, the sense of where he was registered in his mind.

They were in a broad valley set between high, steep hills, and standing on a road not more than fifty yards from what appeared to be a small city. The buildings were all made of the same finely cut stone and were set along cobbled streets. In the distance, he could see a spire, several round towers, and what appeared to be domed roofs supported on columns. Brightly colored pennants flew above some of the taller buildings, and he could see treetops among the houses.

The sight of a city here, in these craggy, forbidding hills, astonished him. And such a city . . . cut stone, spires, towers . . . it was nothing short of beautiful. But as unexpected as the sights were, it was the sounds that burst upon his ears that left him speechless.

"Huzzah!" the people were calling as they came. "Princess! Welcome home!"

The entire city was turning out to meet them, surrounding them with scores of smiling, bobbing faces and waving hands. "What was the journey like, Princess?" a grinning, ruddy-faced fellow called out. "We have a dozen new foals, Princess—wait till you see!" cried another. "Was the city of Nantes as beautiful as they say, Princess?" another voice asked above the din.

Princess. The word rang like a clarion through Saxxe's head. These people recognized Thera, he realized; this place must indeed be her home. But they addressed her as "Princess." *Bon Dieu!* His pampered, arrogant, and deceitful demoiselle was a *princess*? As he grappled with that shock, he felt her trying to wriggle away and instinctively tightened his hold on her.

"Let me go!" Thera demanded through gritted teeth while discreetly trying to pry his arm from her waist. But it was no good—she was caught, trapped. Her attempt to escape and to keep him out of Mercia had utterly failed, and now she would have to deal with not only his presence but also his wrath!

She looked around the circle that had formed about them and saw the sunny smiles on a number of faces turning to quizzical frowns. She froze in his arms, reddening, forcing a smile she hoped would divert their attention. But their eyes only widened and they crept closer, scrutinizing Saxxe's appearance and the forceful way he held her.

This was the ultimate degradation, she thought furiously: being held against her will in front of half her kingdom by a huge, greedy, violent mercenary intent on taking her body as payment for services rendered!

But she had only begun to plumb the depths of humiliation, for the throng suddenly parted to make way for a contingent of older men and women robed in rich garments the color of lapis lazuli. They were all shapes and sizes; some quite elderly and frail, and some robust and in the prime of life. All carried about them an air of great dignity and all bore at least a trace of silver in their hair. She groaned silently.

The elders.

The moment the elders spotted her, their expressions of concern changed to beaming smiles. Chancellor Cedric came rushing forward, ahead of the others, his rounded form bounding enthusiastically and his dark eyes shining with pleasure.

"Princess!" He halted abruptly and made a courtly bow from the waist, which was copied by every man present and was accompanied by curtsies from the women. "Thank the good heavens you have returned safely!" he said breathlessly. "We said the prayers . . . every day . . . for . . ."

Halfway through both the bow and the greeting, he halted. His gaze had fallen on the tattered, mud-stained hem of her tunic. As he straightened, his eyes traveled upward, widening on the sight of her rolled-up sleeves and the dirt, ash, and stains on her once elegant surcoat. Thera felt him taking in the smudges on her face and the wild tangle of her hair, and her face reddened.

Then he dropped his gaze to the huge, sinewy arm clamped around her waist. Following that thick band of flesh, his gaze slid to a massive shoulder and a dark, shaggy head and forbidding scowl. Some of the color drained from his ruddy cheeks. Thera had been dreading that very look on his face.

"And this . . ." Cedric drew himself up straight, obviously scrambling for a diplomatic response to so unexpected a face and form. "This must be the duc." He bowed again, discreetly waving his hand at his side to draw the other elders down with him. "Your Grace, on behalf of all Mercia, we wel—"

"The duc? Nay!" Thera choked out, trying to force Saxxe's arm from her waist without alarming Cedric and the others. How could they possibly mistake Saxxe for a nobleman . . . even a *Norman* nobleman? "He is most assuredly not the duc, nor even a *seigneur*. He is . . . he is . . ."

She looked at Cedric's expectant expression, then at the trusting faces of her people, and felt a stinging chagrin that she had behaved so unworthily . . . indulging in unthinkable intimacy with a violent soldier for hire and then leading him straight into the heart of her kingdom. Retreating into her princess self, she collected that horror and flung it straight at Saxxe.

"He is a *barbarian*."

"Oh." Cedric pulled back his chin and clasped his hands tightly, looking thoroughly bewildered. "But why did you bring home a barbarian instead of a duc?"

"Well, it was hardly by choice!" she declared, thinking how to explain, while still trying to escape Saxxe's hold. "As we left Nantes, we were set upon by . . . rogue soldiers. Countess Lillith and I were separated from Captain Pernaud and the rest of our escort," she said, avoiding the disturbing details of her numerous abductions. Her words unleashed gasps and murmurs through the crowd. "This . . . barbarian . . . agreed to escort us home and I was . . . he was merely . . ." She scrambled for words, trying to decide how to explain their shocking position without revealing that she had been trying to escape her resulting debt to him.

"Nay, I did more than agree to escort her home!" Saxxe's deep voice boomed out as he took up the tale himself. "I *rescued* her . . . from an army of pillaging mercenaries." Cedric and the other elders started at the force of his voice and edged back a step.

Saxxe's shock at learning Thera was a princess had momentarily eclipsed his anger at her desertion. But it came flooding back to him as she issued a ringing dismissal of him as a barbarian. After he had feared and fought for her, made pleasure for her, and brought her home safely, she turned haughty and arrogant and *royal* with a vengeance.

"She owes me a sizable debt for saving her," he declared defiantly. "And I'll not leave here until I have the reward I was promised!"

"Cedric!" She turned to her adviser, frantic to be rid of Saxxe and praying that his greed was greater than his desire for vengeance. "Send straightaway to the treasury and bring two hundred silver groats in traveling pouches . . . so that he may be on his way." She had just doubled her highest offer to him, and now held her breath to see if he would accept it.

Two hundred silver groats. More money than he could count . . . more than he could even imagine, Saxxe realized. His lifeblood had been poured out on foreign battlefields for a few deniers, and she was offering him two hundred silver groats. A small fortune. Enough to buy a dream.

His legs began to tremble. He looked around at that sea of curious, bright-eyed faces, then lifted his gaze to the inviting little city in the distance. His arrogant, pampered demoiselle was not just a noblewoman; she was a *princess*. That fact explained a great deal. And it also widened the personal gulf between them to vast proportions.

Just then, loud voices came from behind them, and Saxxe turned Thera partway to find Lillith and Gasquar tussling toward the center of the crowd. "Let me go, you disgusting brute—"

Gasquar had Lillith by the wrists, and she was hissing like a cat caught in a rain barrel. When she glimpsed Thera, she made a last valiant twist in Gasquar's hand and wrenched free. She rushed toward her mistress, but stopped in her tracks at the sight of Saxxe's arms around Thera and the shock on the elders' faces.

Lillith's arrival had given Saxxe another moment to think. All he had to do was let it happen. *Hard silver coin.* Wasn't that exactly what he had always wanted? Now, somehow, it didn't seem enough. . . . Before he could completely sort it out, he heard Thera repeating her order, and saw the one she called Cedric bow and turn away. And though he still held her bodily, he somehow felt her slipping away.

"Nay." The booming sound of his own voice startled him. "Silver was not our bargain. And your lady knows it."

A storm of confusion swirled through the crowd as Cedric turned back to Thera with surprise. "Is this so, Princess?"

"We discussed silver," she insisted hotly, wresting about in Saxxe's arms to glare at him. "Two hundred is more than generous, considering the service rendered. *Go, Cedric,*" she commanded.

"*Stay, Cedric!*" Saxxe countered in an even louder voice.

The chancellor stood rooted to the spot and cast a glance at his fellow elders, whose expressions mirrored his own shock at the way the fellow handled their princess bodily and presumed to countermand her orders.

"Well, then, if I may be so bold . . ." Cedric addressed Saxxe directly. "Just what did Princess Thera promise you?"

Saxxe pinned Thera with a vengeful smile and declared boldly: "Three nights of pleasure!" And he braced for an explosion.

None came. The common folk, the blue-clad elders, and Cedric all just stared at him, unmoving, unblinking . . . as if unable to believe their ears.

"Three nights of pleasure," Saxxe repeated firmly, adding, "with her."

In any other kingdom in the known world, Saxxe knew, such a claim would elicit an order for his arrest, a blade challenge, or at the very least a punishing blast of fatherly outrage. Thus, he was understandably confused when Cedric roused from shock, glanced anxiously at the rest of the group of elders, then inched forward with an expression of intense concern.

"Only *three* nights?" he asked.

Saxxe stared at the little fellow. "Yea. It was three nights," he answered. Cedric crept even closer, ignoring Thera's high-pitched groan of outrage.

"Three. Not four or six or . . . *seven*?" Cedric ignored her sputters to focus fiercely on Saxxe's response.

"Nay, I have said *three* was our bargain," Saxxe insisted, bewildered by the fact that Cedric and the others seemed more relieved than outraged, and more concerned with the number of nights than with the passion they implied. When Cedric turned to Lillith for confirmation, Saxxe's jaw loosened.

"Countess . . . is this true?" the chancellor demanded. "The princess has promised this fellow three nights with her?"

Lillith lowered her gaze to avoid Thera's and answered so quietly that the contingent of elders had to lean forward with their ears cupped in order to hear.

"Upon my vow . . . it is true. She has indeed promised him three nights."

Cedric looked a bit pained, tugged the neck of his tunic with a pudgy finger, and cleared his throat. "Well, then." The weight of his chancellor's responsibilities settled heavily on his shoulders, rounding them. "There is naught for us to do but welcome you as our guests until our princess's debt is settled."

"Guests? In my palace?" Thera finally succeeded in pushing free of Saxxe's slackening hold and backed away, glaring at him as if he possessed horns and a long red tail. "And what if I re—"

She caught back the rest of that shameful notion before it was fully out. It wasn't possible for her to refuse. It was a matter of royal honor now. Her people would be mortified to learn that the thought of breaking her royal pledge had even crossed her mind. She was caught . . . trapped by her own word.

Ever the soul of courtesy, Cedric introduced himself with a bow—"Cedric of Cyan, Chancellor of Mercia, chief adviser to Her Highness Thera of Aric, Crown Princess of Mercia"—then began to introduce the dignitaries behind him. "These are the elders of Mercia: Elder Fenwick, Elder Audra, Elder Mattias . . ." By the time he reached "Countess Lillith, whom, I believe, you already know," Thera's temper was at a slow boil and Saxxe was hearing only one word in three.

The little chancellor and the others behaved as if they expected Thera to actually honor her outrageous debt to him, Saxxe realized. He slid his hand to his dagger and searched the crowd for soldiers or guardsmen who might be summoned to cart him off to imprisonment. But he saw nothing more ominous than an occasional scowl in the crowd, and released his blade hilt in furious confusion.

What the hell kind of place *was* this?

Chapter Twelve

A very odd sort of place, Saxxe learned shortly, as Cedric and the elders dismissed the crowd, then escorted their princess's party into the city. The streets were wide enough for several horsemen to ride abreast and were paved with flat slabs and cobblestones. There wasn't an open gutter, a heap of rotting garbage, or a pile of animal dung to be seen anywhere. The houses and shops, owing to their thick stone walls, stood straight along the tidy streets, their upper stories freshly whitewashed and painted. Bright-colored boxes of cooking herbs and flowers hung beneath nearly every window. In the two open squares they crossed, stone-lined wells provided fresh water and large trees provided natural awnings for a number of merchants' brightly painted stalls and carts. He had never seen such an immaculate place in his life.

As they passed through the streets, the people came out to see their dirty, rumpled princess and the wild-looking strangers accompanying her. Their curious stares made Saxxe acutely aware of the dried mud in the creases of his boots, of his wild bush of a beard, and of his dusty and sweat-streaked body.

He returned their scrutiny and found their faces well scrubbed, their hair neatly cropped or capped, and their tunics handsome and well made. The men were clean, close-shaven, and weaponless, and he began to feel oddly out of place . . . walking along half naked, with daggers bristling at his sides and a great blade hilt looming over his shoulder. He was bigger, darker, and dirtier than anyone he laid eyes upon, including the hounds that frisked in and out of the royal party as they passed.

But if the city had surprised him, the palace truly shocked him. They crossed a small greensward and came to a broad set of steps leading onto a terrace. Looking up, Saxxe stopped in his tracks, dumbstruck. Before him lay a magnificent stone structure topped by several graceful domes supported by stone arches and pillars. It looked much like the great church of Saint Etienne, and all around lay plots of well-tended earth and wild roses, interspersed with oaks of varying ages.

The party crossed an arched portico and entered the palace through two massive carved doors. At the end of a short passage, they entered a soaring hall covered by a grand dome, and Saxxe halted again, staring in wonder at the marble columns, ceiling paintings, and finely crafted silk weavings which hung on the walls.

Thera knew the instant he stopped; she was achingly aware of every motion he made, of every direction he glanced. He stood in the center of her main hall, his fists on his hips, surveying the size and richness of her palace. He stood a head taller than the people around him and his huge, bronzed shoulders seemed to fill the space. As he turned slowly, his heated gaze fell on her, battering her strained defenses, and she felt crowded by his massive presence.

Turning to Cedric, she declared in regal tones: "I shall retire to my chambers now. But this evening I shall dine with you and the elders." She tossed a scathing look at Saxxe. "See that he and his hairy friend bathe and get decent clothing," she said with a fierce wave of hand. "I will not have him stalking about the city . . . fouling the air and frightening the women and children." She was gratified by the stiffening of Saxxe's big frame.

"Where shall I put him, Princess?" Cedric asked, clasping his hands.

"Anywhere," she declared. "As long as it is far away from me."

She turned on her heel and glided off in a sea of chattering females, leaving Cedric to deal with the hulking, unwashed barbarian she had just roundly insulted. The beleaguered chancellor swung his gaze to Saxxe's forbidding countenance with a grimace of a smile. "The east hall, I think," he muttered, gesturing to a broad passage opposite the one Thera had chosen. "This way, please."

Still stinging from Thera's barb, Saxxe glared after her for a moment before motioning to Gasquar and striking off after the chancellor. As they followed Cedric down the passage, Saxxe gradually became aware of movement behind him. He suddenly stopped and wheeled into a defensive crouch, drawing a dagger with practiced speed.

A wide-eyed serving man was scurrying after him with a metal pan and a short-handled broom . . . brushing up the dried mud that had fallen from his boots onto the pristine floor. When the little fellow saw Saxxe's blade, he dropped the pan with a clang and froze in terror. Saxxe reddened, sheathed his blade, and strode on, steaming from the realization that the servant had been cleaning up behind him as if he were a hound that had messed the hall!

By the time they reached two sets of doors on opposite sides of the passage, Saxxe was sunk into a foul mood and berating himself for not taking Thera's bribe. If he had, he told himself savagely, he would be well on his way to Paris now, with a dream jingling in his pouches. What in hell had gotten into him—demanding those cursed three nights with her?

She had gotten into him, he realized. Again. He wanted more from her than just cold, impersonal coin. The stinging male pride in him wanted to make her admit that he had been more to her than just a means to an end. He wanted to make her deal with him as a man . . . *as a man she wanted*.

"These will be your chambers, goodly sirs," Cedric said, breaking into Saxxe's thoughts as he gestured to the two sets of doors. He pushed back the great oaken planks and entered one chamber. Saxxe sent his hand to his dagger and glanced at Gasquar, whose shoulders were tensed with the expectation of treachery. Each took a harsh breath, braced, and entered.

There was no hidden force, no attack . . . only a handsome chamber with polished stone floors, colored glass windows, and a dry stone-lined pool sunk into the floor at the far end of the chamber. Saxxe watched the chancellor hurry across the chamber to a second set of doors, which led to a columned and terraced courtyard beyond. Warm light flooded the chamber, revealing the richness of the furnishings: a carved chest and table, several pillowed benches, and richly colored hangings on the walls. To one side stood a large bed draped with thick, patterned satins and swathed in sheer silk that flowed from the high ceiling like a waterfall.

"Your quarters are across the hall, sir," Cedric said to Gasquar, waving a hand toward the door. Without waiting for escort, Gasquar rushed into the hall and Saxxe heard him throwing back the doors with a crow of delight. "The bathing pool has not been filled for a while," Cedric said in apology. "We have no visitors in Mercia, and it has been a long while since these chambers were filled with royal children and family." He looked up to find several serving women huddled in the doorway and he beckoned them inside to do their work, frowning at the way they giggled and eyed Saxxe as they scurried past.

"They will soon have it cleaned and filled for your bathing. There is linen in the trunk . . ." He frowned uncertainly and tapped a finger against his chin. "But as to clothing . . . I am not certain we have anything in the palace that would fit—"

"I need no other clothes," Saxxe declared. Cedric's dubious smile said that he believed otherwise but was content to let it go.

"By what name are you called, sir?" Cedric asked, dragging his gaze up Saxxe's formidable frame, then meeting his challenging expression with a thoughtful air. Years of serving and advising royalty had given the chancellor a special fluency at reading other men's characters in their faces. Interesting eyes, Cedric thought. Intelligent.

"Saxxe Rouen," Saxxe said, bristling at the chancellor's scrutiny. "And my friend is Gasquar LeBruit."

"Rouen? As in the Norman town of Rouen?" Cedric's gray eyes lighted with recognition.

"Yea, I was born in Rouen and my father's name was . . . Rouen."

"I was in Rouen once, as a lad. My father was Mercia's agent of trade in his early days, before becoming chancellor. I thought the trading fair was wonderful. And the horses . . . such horses!" He seemed transported by memory, then, after a moment, came abruptly back to the present. "And are you a warrior, sir . . . or . . ."

"Gasquar and I . . . we are soldiers for hire," Saxxe answered, feeling a sudden need to explain himself and his unusual demands to this remarkably even-tempered fellow. "The city of Nantes was overrun by an army of mercenaries and hired barbarians, who captured your princess. She has a way of attracting trouble, that one. And if she cannot find any, she makes some herself." Cedric choked on an unexpected laugh, then bit his lip.

"Indeed," he said, smoothing both his dignity and the embroidered front of his tunic. "And what sort of trouble did she make for you, Saxxe Rouen?"

"Every sort of trouble and annoyance a woman can cause a man. She is spoiled, ungrateful, and stubborn to a fault," Saxxe declared, daring Cedric to contradict him. But he got no argument from Cedric on that. "She has less sense than my horse . . . spouts orders she can never enforce . . . and refuses to listen to sound advice or even warning.

"I not only rescued her from barbarians and soldiers *three times*"—he jerked a thumb toward his chest—"I also saved her from being drowned in a flood and rescued her from a man-eating snake! Then I fed and warmed and tended her pampered hide for days on end!" He realized he was nearly shouting and halted to get a grip on himself. "She owes me," he said with quiet vehemence. "And I intend to collect."

"I see." Cedric gave a restrained nod. In fact, he saw more than Saxxe could have guessed. Here was a man who had gone to a great deal of trouble to rescue and care for a woman who had scorned and annoyed and exasperated him . . . a man who had refused a small fortune in order to claim three nights of pleasure with that same woman. What sort of *barbarian* would do such things? Thera had caused him every annoyance a woman could cause a man, he said. That bore thinking about, for Cedric knew from experience that there were some annoyances wrought by women that were very sweet indeed.

Saxxe's mind was racing. The chancellor's mention of children and families had raised the dread prospect of Thera's father. If she was a princess, then her father had to be a *king*. And he had seen enough of the workings of temporal kings to know how jealously they guarded their power and possessions . . . including their daughters. It was scarcely believable that he hadn't been hauled before the throne or tossed into a dungeon straight away.

"When will I see the king?" he asked, glancing toward the door.

"Oh, I'm afraid that won't be possible," Cedric said, clamping his hands on his embroidered surcoat. "The old king, Princess Thera's father, has been dead for over seventeen years now. And we will not have a new king until Princess Thera marries."

The news hit Saxxe like a fist in his gut. She was to be *married*. "And just when and to whom will that be—her marriage?"

Cedric sighed and shrugged. "The Council of Elders has been asking those same questions for some time now. The answers, I fear, are entirely up to Princess Thera." He turned to survey the chamber. "I believe you will be comfortable here. Food and drink will arrive shortly." He paused. "Perhaps it would be best if you joined us for supper. I shall send someone for you." When Saxxe didn't respond, Cedric nodded and withdrew.

Saxxe stumbled to the bed and sat down. The soft feather mattress billowed around him, and he ran a callused hand over the fine linens, then down the silken bed hangings. In all his travels, he had never seen anything more appealing than this unexpected little jewel of a kingdom. Mercia, they called it. He had never heard of it, he suspected few people had. Not even in his dreams of a kingdom of his own, had he—

A kingdom of his own.

He shoved abruptly to his feet and made a circuit of the chamber, touching the colorful weavings and stroking the polished stone and wood. His hands began to tremble and his heart beat faster.

Marriage. King. The chancellor's words echoed in his head and heart. A kingdom of his own was his heart's desire, and this ripe little plum of a realm had a *royal vacancy*! All that was required was marrying its prickly but eminently desirable princess.

That thought stopped him cold.

"*Dieu*, Rouen, you are a dreamer. What could possibly make wealthy, refined Thera of Aric marry a crude, penniless barbarian like you?" He gave a pained laugh at the horror that prospect would conjure in Thera, and answered himself: "Only a bloody miracle."

Cedric hurried straight from Saxxe's quarters to the council chamber in the north wing and found the place in turmoil. His fellow councilors were pacing and arguing, shaking fingers and heads at one another. They descended on him with a vengeance the instant he stepped through the doors.

"Did you speak with her?" Elder Mattias demanded.

"Three *nights*! What in God's name possessed her to promise him such a thing?" fastidious Elder Gawain proclaimed. "Why, it's indecent!"

"What sort of man would go about without a tunic?" Elder Margarete declared. "And that beard—he looks like he's carrying around a litter of hedgehogs!"

"Is he locked in—are we safe?" ancient Elder Agnes asked in her reedy tones.

"Sons of Thunder—did you see that sword?" barrel-chested Elder Hubert crowed, shaking an exuberant fist. "Longer than a man's stride. Now there's a worthy blade!"

Aghast at the turmoil of the usually dignified council, Cedric raised his hands in self-defense and headed straight for the chancellor's chair. "Let us have order here—*order*!" He held up his hands for silence. "Look at you, acting like quarrelsome children." After a stunned moment, the chaos subsided and the elders retreated to the circle of chairs with mutters and reddened faces.

"I have spoken with our . . . guest. He was left to bathe and don proper garments"—he nodded to Agnes—"well away from here, in the east wing. From my brief encounter with him and the fact that he has brought the princess back to us, safe and sound, I do not believe we need fear him. He is a soldier for hire, born at Rouen in Normandy, and is called Saxxe Rouen. And it seems he rescued Princess Thera not just once but at least five times . . . from at least three different perils."

"I said she never should have gone on that journey," aged Elder Fenwick declared, raising a gnarled finger. "Said it would bring naught but trouble."

At the word *trouble*, every person present had the same thought leap to mind. It was the chief woman among them, Elder Audra, who gave voice to their common thought.

"It's the prophecy, that's what," she said, rising from her chair. "The ancient scrolls do not lie. The princess's difficulties on the journey were but a partial fulfillment of the prophecy. Mark my word, there will be more trouble in the days ahead . . . caused by her empty marriage bed and empty throne. This barbarian she has brought back to Mercia is only the start of our difficulties."

"She should have stayed in Mercia and married amongst her people," Margarete insisted, "and not meddled with the outside world."

Stout, ruddy-faced Hubert rose to his feet and punched a thick finger at Audra. "You and those wretched prophecies," he said with disgust. "Did you not hear Cedric? The man is a soldier . . . a fighting man, not some wild savage."

"And perhaps it is a stroke of good luck, not bad, him being here. After all, he did *rescue* the princess five times," Elder Mattias added. "I personally accompanied his horse to the stables and—saints!—it is a most magnificent animal. A great Norman stallion . . . gray as fog, with hooves as big as cart wheels and ballocks the size of melons! If we could get the fellow to stay a fortnight, we would have a crop of foals next spring that would—"

"You and your wretched horses!" Margarete snapped. "We are speaking of our princess's virtue, Mattias! That great brute has laid claim to it."

"Well, I say let him have it," Mattias said irritably, drawing gasps of outrage from a number of the women councilors. He pulled in his chin defensively. "Well, a fat lot of good it has done us to have her hoard it!"

"Mattias may be right," Hubert declared. "After all, it was her that promised him the nights. And she cannot refuse to honor her word."

"She loathes the barbarian . . . anyone can see that," Margarete insisted. "How could she possibly bed him even once, much less three nights!"

"And three nights . . . that is almost halfway to seven!" Elder Jeanine declared.

Seven. The number gave them all pause. If Thera did honor her word, the barbarian would be almost halfway to being their king.

Margarete turned to Cedric. "You spoke with him. Is there any chance he might be persuaded to take something else as his payment instead?"

Cedric sighed, thinking back to Saxxe's righteous anger and emphatic words. "Princess Thera has already tried that, I believe, and succeeded only in rousing both his anger and determination. I believe he intends to make a point of holding her to her exact word." Around the chamber, there was sighing, fidgeting, and shifting on seats.

"Well, I for one do not intend to sit by and watch our future queen devoured by some lustful beast," Audra declared, crossing her arms. "I say we should search the sacred scrolls and prophecies for guidance. They have always provided it. There must be some way for her to escape so vile a bargain . . . some exception to the rule of Truth. And we must find it. Who goes with me?"

Shortly, a small contingent of women led by Elders Audra and Jeanine were traipsing out of the council chambers, headed for the kingdom's archives, located in the maze of caverns below the church. Cedric watched them go with a sigh. He held out little hope for any help from the sacred scrolls. In his experience the voices of the ancients were more likely to make trouble than to alleviate it.

"What do you think, Cedric?" Elder Gawain asked as the remaining elders drifted to other parts of the palace and out into the city, still arguing.

"I think," Cedric said with a thoughtful expression, "that there is a good bit we do not know about this 'barbarian' and our princess." He thought of the possessive way Saxxe had held Thera against him and of the nights of pleasure she had promised him. And he wondered about her nights on the journey. His face lighted slowly with a small, cherubic smile. "And I think it will be most interesting finding out."

Just at sunset that evening, as the Vesper bells rang drowsily over the valley and servants hurried about the private dining hall, setting torches and oil lamps high on columns around the walls, Thera emerged from her chambers. She had spent long, restless hours that afternoon trying to adjust to her reimmersion in royal life. It should have been wonderful, being back in her spacious, comfortable quarters, bathing, resting on her huge feather-soft bed, eating something besides dry oats and charred rabbit. But it wasn't wonderful, and it didn't take a sage to understand why.

He was here, in Mercia . . . in her palace and in her mind and heart. And his presence changed things in ways she didn't want to think about. She had fully intended to leave the woman in her outside Mercia's borders, and he had come barging in after her, dragging her womanly desires with him. What in Heaven's name was she going to do now? How was she to deal with him and his unthinkable demands?

By the time she called for Lillith and left her quarters for her private dining hall, she was gowned in her finest embroidered tunic and her most royal-looking surcoat, made of white silk and spun gold woven together. Her burnished hair was braided with strands of pearls and wrapped into elaborate coils at each side of her head, and she wore her ceremonial coronet . . . a thick circlet of gold embellished with small, stylized oak leaves. She intended to appear as regal and dignified as possible tonight, for she knew the elders would have questions about her abduction and the outrageous reward she had been forced to promise her rescuer.

Waving aside the page at the door, she entered the large dining chamber where generations of Mercia's kings and queens had dined with their Councils of Elders. In the center of that hall stood a great circular table designed to allow the royal couple to see and to converse with all of their advisers and guests without straining. Tonight the table was draped with fine linen, set with silver goblets, and festooned with garlands of evergreens.

A number of her elders stood near the door, waiting, and they met her with words of welcome and relief. She greeted them warmly, one by one, until she lifted her gaze and halted mid-word.

On the far side of the chamber, standing like a dark colossus, wearing cross braces and skin breeches and not a bit more, was Saxxe Rouen. His legs were spread, his massive arms were crossed, and he was staring at her as if she were tinder and he intended to start a flame with his gaze. Her face reddened in spite of her and she turned on Cedric, who had just hurried to her side.

"What is *he* doing here?" she demanded.

"The council requested his presence, Princess . . . to hear a full accounting of your journey and valiant rescue," Cedric answered diplomatically, searching her reaction to her rescuer. She could scarcely refuse the council's request without it seeming she had something to hide. She turned a narrow look on her earnest chancellor.

"Did I or did I not give instructions that he was to be bathed thoroughly and clothed decently?"

"Indeed you did, Princess," Cedric said with a pained glance at Saxxe's near nakedness. "I sent Ranulf, the chief steward, and Edwin, my own body servant, to see to it." He paused, swallowed hard, and leaned toward her with an apologetic whisper. "He threatened to bite off their ears and have them for supper if they so much as laid a hand on him."

She studied Saxxe's savage appearance and defiant pose, and honestly couldn't blame Cedric's men for running in fear of their lives. Saxxe looked as if he was ready to rip out one of his daggers and carve someone into ribands. And from the glare trained on her, she could guess who he would prefer to make his first victim.

Saxxe was equally annoyed by Thera's appearance. He had just arrived and was surveying the handsome carved chairs and the fine silver and linen on the unusual table, when he looked up to find her floating into the dining chamber like a vision . . . stately and regal and utterly untouchable. The warm glow of the oil lamps cast a golden radiance over her skin and turned her hair to a burnished halo that rivaled her crown. The gold wire embroidery of her elaborate surcoat shimmered with every movement she made, like the sun dancing on waves. She was breathtaking . . . out of the reach of ordinary mortals. And the look she had just given him proclaimed him far below "ordinary" in her estimate.

As soon as Thera was seated, the elders took their places along the great table for the serving to begin. Saxxe and Gasquar were shown to seats directly opposite Thera. They sank onto the chairs as if straddling a bench, with their legs braced for fight or flight.

Thera was fiercely aware of Saxxe's glowering gaze trained upon her, but was determined not to let it make a difference to her. She turned to Cedric, and when she spoke, other conversation in the chamber damped considerably.

"On the journey home, we found the village of LeBeau overrun by a band of cutthroats and thieves. They had burned and looted the houses, and I am sure some of the villagers were killed." Cedric and her elders reacted with shock and dismay, and she had to raise her hands for silence. "I cannot say what might have happened to Thomas Rennet and his family, but we must send help . . . food and covering for those who survived. And we must bring Thomas and his family back to Mercia straightaway."

Cedric nodded soberly. "Some of our traders will surely want to go. They have all stayed with Thomas on their journeys and are used to traveling that road."

"A good thought. They will need food and blankets," she said, looking to Elder Margarete, who lowered her head briefly, accepting the task. "And whatever tools may be spared for rebuilding," she charged burly Elder Hubert, who nodded gravely. Then she turned to Elder Mattias with: "And pack animals and riding mounts for Thomas's family."

In a moment it was settled, a quick and regal bit of command and delegation . . . a glimpse of the imperial Thera at the duty for which she had been born and raised. The scowl deepened on Saxxe's face as what he had just witnessed shed new light on Thera's conduct on their journey. Picked up by fate and set down in circumstances that would have undone most other mortals, she had maintained her self-possession and tried to assert whatever control she could in the situation. Her arrogance, her determination, her stubborn secretiveness . . . they all made sense to him now. She was a princess. A ruler.

He felt a strange, spreading hollowness in his chest.

The servants had entered with pitchers of wine and terrines of soup and trays of bread, and when he was served, he hauled the servant back by the arm and took the wine pitcher from him, filling and draining the delicate silver goblet twice, as if trying to fill that disconcerting emptiness inside him. And when the soup, a tasty brewet, was poured into the écuelles, which were normally shared by two diners, he seized the nearest vessel, hoisted it, and began to devour its contents without benefit of a spoon. As the aromas of barley, sage, and chicken filled his head and the soup filled his belly, his tension subsided and his thoughts shifted to more immediate and comforting concerns.

"Food," he said with a low groan, and Gasquar grinned back at him. "Whatever else happens tonight, we'll eat like kings!"

But in fact, as everyone else present would later attest, they ate like barbarians . . . and starving ones, at that. They tore hunks from loaves of bread, rubbed them around in a nearby crock of butter, and stuffed their cheeks, chewing doggedly. When the braised trout was served, they each snagged several and were so entranced by the buttery, peppery flavor that they consumed the fish without much regard for bones or for the niceties of using an eating knife or finger towel.

As the courses rolled on, whatever was on a platter or in a terrine when it reached them became their portion, and they consumed it down to the last morsel. Eating utensils lay unused on the linen as they stuffed and slurped their way through the greens, the stuffed quail with cream gravy, and the pottage of leeks, apples, and cabbage. They preferred their own huge daggers when hacking off pieces of steamed capon, and their fingers when fishing around in the gravy for bits of roasted pork. Platters, bowls, soggy trenchers, and bones accumulated on the table and the floor around them . . . even as horror collected on Thera's face.

It was bad enough that she was forced to suffer him at her table, she thought with a groan, but she had to watch him making a glutton of himself as well. In recent days, she had forgotten his brutish behavior of that first night they were together. Now, seeing her elders' reactions, her first impressions of him came back to her with a vengeance. She flushed and downed the rest of her wine as she recalled the reasons for her forgetting . . . the fact that she had taken pleasure from those hands and lips— now covered with grease and gravy.

"Dieu!" Saxxe crowed minutes later, sinking his teeth into a pasty filled with apples and raisins. "This reminds me of that fruited roll they make in Bern," he addressed Gasquar with a mouth full of sweetmeats. "What did they call it?" He swallowed and took another massive bite.

"I cannot recall. *Stuben* . . . *struzen* . . . something," Gasquar answered, engulfing another mouthful of the stuff.

Saxxe paused to cut off another hunk of mild white cheese and suddenly became aware of the intense silence around him. He froze.

Raising his head, he found more than a score of faces turned his way, bearing expressions ranging from astonishment to disgust. He looked to Thera and found her eyes glowing with angry heat . . . and realized that he was bent over his food, with his mouth stuffed so full that his cheeks bulged. As he straightened, his awareness widened to include the vessels and platters, the bones, crusts, and debris piled on the table and floor around him.

Red crept up his neck and into his face. It had been so long since he had eaten at a civilized table, in civilized company . . . and the food had been like a long-awaited dream come true. . . . He glanced at Gasquar and found him stuffing his face, saw the pastry juice joining the grease glistening on his beard. Suddenly he had difficulty swallowing.

"More wine for our guests." Thera's voice, though not loud, seemed to ring out over the silent chamber. She pinned him with a piercing glare. "And by all means, they must have another platter of pork . . . there must be a pig left somewhere in the kingdom undevoured."

Her words stung. Embarrassed by his great hunger and crude manner, and feeling shamed in a way he hadn't experienced in years, he raised his stoutest defense . . . which was, of course, his most barbaric behavior.

"Nay, that will not be necessary," he declared. Glancing at wide-eyed Elder Hubert, who was seated closest to him, he smiled wickedly. "This good fellow seems to have lost his appetite. And you know how I feel about wasting food."

He leaned brazenly over a stack of soggy trenchers to spear the roast capon on Hubert's trencher with his dagger, and he proceeded to devour it with zest as a shocked murmur raced around the chamber.

But when he looked up at Thera moments later, his vengeful pleasure dimmed. Deep in her eyes, amid the anger and disdain, was a small but undeniable glimmer of distress. He halted, mid-bite, realizing it was evidence that her feelings toward him were not so calculated and indifferent as she would have it appear. But even as a bit of hope bloomed at that insight, it was quelled by the realization that his display of crudity had just undercut his determination to make her deal with him as a man.

Barbarians might not need table manners, but *men* did.

Dieu—couldn't he ever get it right? Why did his behavior and his circumstance never agree? He seemed doomed to act nobly when he should have been more tough-minded and mercenary, and to be his most crude and hard-nosed self when a bit of nobility would serve him better! Glowering, he tossed the bones onto the table and shoved back in his chair to lick his fingers.

The strain between them caused the air in the chamber to thicken.

"Most excellent food. A far cry from the rabbits and the oats, eh, Princess?" Gasquar said, watching both Saxxe and Thera. He wiped his mouth with the back of his hand and took another draught of wine. "Do you know," he said to Cedric and the elders, "that your lovely princess learned to skin and cook a rabbit on the journey?"

"Indeed?" Cedric said with genuine surprise, turning to Thera. "Perhaps you will tell us more of what happened, Princess . . . the story of your rescue and of this remarkable journey. I am certain we would find it fascinating."

Thera scowled at him. "I told you of the village. There is nothing else to tell," she insisted. But the whitened knuckles of her hands as they gripped the table said otherwise. And Cedric had astutely caught the brief but intense exchange of glances between Thera and Saxxe, and sensed that an even more important question was in order.

"Indeed?" Cedric nodded politely, seeming to accept her statement. He turned to Lillith, who was seated on the far side of Thera. "And what say you, Countess? Is there anything for *you* to tell?"

Not a breath was expelled for a full minute after those fateful words died away. Lillith's face drained of color as every eye in the chamber turned toward her. Most keenly of all, she could feel Thera's gaze, expecting her to confirm before the elders that nothing of official interest had occurred.

She squirmed in her chair and drew a deep breath, avoiding Thera's cautioning frown. "There was . . . indeed . . . not much to tell," she said with deliberation that spoke of words chosen carefully. "There was riding and wind and rain and sun . . . and more riding. The food was terrible and the company"—she tossed an irritable glance at Gasquar—"was worse. I have no desire to make another journey, ever."

Cedric nodded, then flicked a glance at Elder Audra, Elder Margarete, and ancient Elder Fenwick, who were now on the edges of their chairs, watching Lillith's ill-disguised discomfort.

"Tell us, Countess," Cedric said carefully. "Was there anything to *count*?"

Lillith sat with her eyes downcast, her turbulent silence confirming the elders' growing suspicion that there was indeed more to report. "What I can say, Chancellor? We slept . . . under the stars . . . together . . . the princess and I . . ."

Thera watched Lillith with growing alarm. "Lillith," she demanded, "tell them."

"Well, you must understand that there were s-special c-conditions . . . beyond my lady's control," Lillith stammered, halting as murmurs swept the great chamber.

"Lillith?" Thera said, gripping the arms of the great chair.

Saxxe watched in confusion, knowing that Lillith's answer was important but unable to fathom why. It was Gasquar who saw clearly what was being asked . . . for it was Gasquar who knew that Lillith was the trustee of Thera's virtue and the guardian of her nights. It took only a logical step to conclude that the elders were asking if Thera had spent nights with her rescuer.

"My lady was washed downstream in a great flood . . . she nearly drowned," Lillith reported obliquely, struggling with the conflicting demands of her roles as countess and confidante. "Saxxe Rouen rode after her and pulled her out . . . and she was in no fit condition to travel . . . and . . ."

"And?" Cedric demanded in a voice hoarse with tension. "Did she or did she not spend nights with this Saxxe Rouen?"

Gasquar watched Lillith squirming, avoiding the truth she had so piously championed at every turn. His eyes narrowed. The little hypocrite! She had scorned his best stories and most inventive lies. Yet now, when she was put to the test, she obviously found the truth a good bit less desirable than she had proclaimed it to be.

"But of course she did!" Gasquar declared in a booming voice, shoving to his feet. Gasps and mutters rose around the table. He snatched up a towel and wiped his beard and hands. "Several nights your princess slept with *mon ami* Saxxe . . . warmed by the fire in his eyes and in his loins."

Lillith shoved to her feet, her shock turning to anger as she faced Gasquar. "How dare you interfere?" she cried, trembling.

"I dare because they seek the truth, *ma chatte*. Truth . . . is that not what you have bludgeoned me for lo, these many days and nights? Now that you hear it, you do not like the way it sits upon your pretty ears, eh?" He cast a canny gaze around the circle of elders, reading the importance of his revelation in their blanched faces. "The princess . . . she slept in *mon ami*'s arms three nights . . . once to fulfill a bargain and twice more when he rescued her from the flood."

"I-is this true, Countess?" Cedric choked out, his rounded face crimson. Lillith lowered her eyes, unable to face him or Thera.

"Yea," she admitted angrily, "it is true." And she held up three fingers. "I have counted three nights."

A lightning bolt streaking through the room could not have caused a greater reaction than those fateful words.

"Nooo!" Thera jolted to her feet, and across the ring of tables Saxxe did the same. The elders began to talk all at once, demanding an explanation, and Cedric clapped his hands on the sides of his face in shock.

"Three nights?" Elder Audra declared hoarsely. "But she has promised him three nights. And that would make . . ."

"Six," Cedric supplied with visible shock.

The word exploded in their midst like a sorcerer's spell, cutting off every exclamation mid-stream. Abrupt and ominous silence reigned as the elders stared at each other, then turned to Thera, who was suddenly as pale as the silk of her gown.

"But—I did not truly sleep with him!" she declared desperately.

"Oh, but you did, demoiselle," Saxxe said in his deep, commanding tones. "Three nights. In my arms."

"Don't be ridiculous!" she said with rising panic, turning to the elders near her. "I admit I did share his blankets, but I only did so for safety and warmth."

Saxxe had glanced at the faces of the elders as Thera spoke. Strangely, it did not seem to be the presumed loss of her virtue which concerned them . . . there was no talk of sin or defilement. They seemed to believe it was her right to spend her nights as she pleased. It was something about the number of the nights that upset them. He wasn't sure what it meant, but he knew it was important to have the nights they had spent together *count*.

"She speaks the truth," he said, seizing their undivided attention. "She did share my blankets for warmth and safety . . . at first. But ask her if she also found pleasure in my arms." He pinned Thera with a penetrating look, and their gazes locked. "Tell them, demoiselle, about the night after the flood when I warmed you . . . and the following night, when we bathed in the stream." When she remained silent, trembling visibly, he reached for her with his eyes, the way he had that night, baring the desire inside him and calling to hers, daring her to deny what had happened between them.

"On your honor, can you swear that you took no pleasure in my arms?"

She felt his gaze burning into her, reducing her defenses to cinders, summoning remembered sensation. Once again she felt his strong hands on her feet, the cool mud and the warm laughter, the shattering release of a climax that was a little like dying and being reborn. The bittersweet pleasure of those nights was written forever on her heart, and now was clearly readable in her softening countenance. There was no denying it. For the honor of both the woman and the princess, she had to speak the truth.

"No, I cannot swear," she said in a whisper that sounded like a whip crack in the silence.

The chamber erupted in tumult.

The elders were galvanized by the news. Cedric and the men of the council were astounded by the thought of their choosy, headstrong princess joined in passion to this great strapping horse of a man . . . and the women of the council were appalled to think of their learned, refined future queen being defiled by a crude barbarian.

If Thera refused to satisfy honor and pay her debt to Saxxe Rouen, she would be breaking their revered law and custom. On the other hand, if she fulfilled her pledge, the barbarian would be only one night away from being their *king!*

Thera realized it too. Three nights counted and three promised—dearest Lord!—she was *three-sevenths married!* With as much dignity as she could summon while in a royal panic, she lifted her chin, picked up her skirts, and sailed out the doors.

Lillith gasped and stammered and tried to explain the unusual and extenuating circumstances, but the chaos caused by her admission was too overwhelming. When she caught sight of Gasquar's insufferably smug expression, she snatched up the trailing hem of her tunic and headed straight for Thera's quarters.

Saxxe watched Lillith go and caught Gasquar's arm, motioning toward the door. Together they strode out after her. Adopting an instinctive stalking gait, they surprised her in an arched colonnade that led to the west wing.

"Ohhh!" she gasped and pressed back against a stone column, her eyes luminous in the moonlight as they closed in on her.

"A word, if you please, Countess," Saxxe said, edging closer, easing his stance.

"I have no words for you, sir," she hissed, then gave Gasquar a fierce glare. "Nor for you . . . except that, if you so much as touch me, I'll scratch your eyes out!"

"I have only one question." Saxxe propped one arm against the stone pillar beside her, blocking her last route of escape. "These nights . . . what do they mean?" She remained stubbornly silent. "Why did you count the nights we spent together? Why does the number of them matter more than the pleasure in them?" Lillith stiffened noticeably and Saxxe knew he had struck the heart of the matter. "What will happen if I claim these nights she has promised me?"

"That is not *one* question, Rouen . . . you count no better than your friend does," she said furiously. She tried to duck under his arm, but he dropped it to prevent her escape.

"What will happen if she spends *six* nights with me?" he asked, lowering his voice to a husky, persuasive stroke. Then it occurred to him that there was one traditional consequence of nights of passion that Thera and her elders might find equally appalling: "After the six nights, will she be forced to wed me?"

The catch in Lillith's breath was slight, but it resounded thunderously in Saxxe's mind, answering his question as surely as if she'd spoken aloud. He slid his hand from the wall and straightened. With a groan, she snatched up her skirts and darted around him, running for the doors at the end of the colonnade.

Saxxe stood with his arms dangling at his sides, staring into the moonlit garden. The ramifications hit him like a war hammer in the gut. It wouldn't take a miracle to make her marry him at all. It would only take three nights. And if he married her, he would be *king*.

"Did you see the way he ate? Snatched the food right off Hubert's trencher!" Audra cried to a chorus of feminine support. "And Heaven knows what more he'll snatch before he's through with Mercia. I say we have Hubert escort him out of the kingdom at once!"

"It is not for us to break Princess Thera's word, woman!" Mattias answered, echoed by a predominantly male contingent of the council. "I take it you found nothing in the sacred scrolls that might release her from her pledge."

"We have not yet finished our search," Audra said irritably.

"Just as I thought," Mattias said. "You found nothing because there is nothing. She is bound by her word, and breaking her pledge would certainly bring a greater disaster upon us than keeping it. I say, let the princess deal with the fellow herself."

"He'll make a morsel of her!" Jeanine protested.

"Princess Thera? A morsel?" Old Fenwick gave a crusty laugh. "She is a queen in all but name. Have you forgotten how stubborn she can be? I say, let her decide whether to give him the nights or not. After all, they are hers to give. And if he manages to claim them . . . then perhaps he is a better man than we know."

"Wise counsel!" Mattias declared with a smile.

"Foolish counsel!" Audra objected, a sentiment shared by a number of the leading women. "Can you honestly imagine that uncouth barbarian as our king? Sitting on the throne occupied by generations of orderly and dignified kings . . . belching, scratching, and licking his fingers? Good King Aric would turn in his grave." She turned on Cedric. "If you will not do something, I will!"

Audra and her party excused themselves and headed straight for the kingdom's archives, determined to find some way to relieve Thera of the burden of keeping her royal word. If there was nothing in the sacred law, they decided, there would surely be something in prophecies.

As Cedric and the rest of the councilors departed the chamber, the wide-eyed servants began to remove the remains of the half-eaten supper. Later, they departed to their houses, hearths, and taverns in the city, and the word radiated from the palace like ripples on a pond:

Mercia had three-sevenths of a king!

Chapter Thirteen

In her quarters, Thera paced and wrung her hands, struggling to contain her reeling emotions. It was bad enough that her councilors knew she had spent three nights with an unwashed soldier for hire who ate like a starving army and licked his fingers afterward like a hound. But to have to admit before her dignified elders that she had taken pleasure from it was too embarrassing for words.

Now she faced three more nights with him in order to redeem her royal pledge. And he had served bold notice that these three nights would be filled with passion. She shivered and clasped her shoulders. Saxxe didn't belong in Mercia; his behavior tonight proved that. And he had already broken through her princess shell and stolen her desires and part of her self-control. What more would she lose to him in three tumultuous nights of pleasure? Part of her kingdom? The rest of her heart?

The trust of her councilors and her people's welfare were at stake; she had to find another way to settle this wretched debt. The longer he stayed and the more he saw of Mercia, the harder it would be to get him to leave . . . and the harder it would be to watch him go. What would it take to make him go and forget he had ever set eyes on her and her kingdom?

There was only one way to find out.

Lillith came rushing into her quarters, out of breath and visibly distraught. "I am so sorry, Princess . . . I didn't want to tell. I mean, he asked me . . . I didn't really say, but he guessed . . ."

"What's done is done, Lillith," she said, assuming Lillith spoke of her revelations to the council and waiting to hear no more. Shedding her surcoat, she placed her coronet in Lillith's hands and headed for the doors.

"Wait—where are you going?"

"To beard a badger in its den," she declared. "If I am not back in an hour . . . call out the palace guard." And she sailed off, leaving Lillith clutching the crown with a look of horror.

"Palace guard?" Lillith said in a choked whisper. "You mean Elder Hubert and his two nephews? What could they possibly do against Saxxe Rouen?"

Saxxe lay on the bed in his quarters, his hands propped behind his head, staring up into the sumptuous silk that formed a soaring canopy overhead. The golden light of two oil lamps flickered over the bed drapes and the silk hangings on the walls, and a light breeze wafted through the open door to the courtyard garden.

"*Dieu*, Rouen," he swore softly, bewildered by his luck. He glanced around him and wondered if he was indeed in some sort of trance, from which he would awaken abruptly if he began to enjoy it too much. "Excellent foods and wines . . . fine, soft beds . . . the promise of three long, steamy nights of pleasure. For once in your wayward life you've a chance for something of value. What more could a man ask for?"

But there was a thorn as well as a rose in his blossoming fortunes, and both bore the name Thera. His grin faded as he thought of the way she had looked at him tonight . . . as if his crude manner and rough ways had just crushed whatever tender feelings she might have had for him. She was not only a princess, she was the ruler of this kingdom, and he was beginning to appreciate just what that meant. What if she truly had changed? What if she honestly didn't want him now?

The doors were flung open just then and he vaulted over the side of the bed, his hands going for his daggers before he even glimpsed the invader. A heartbeat later he found himself crouched defensively and facing Thera with his blades drawn. The sight of her sent a surge of pleasurable confusion through him. In the golden light, her skin seemed warm and touchable, her jewel-clear eyes radiated a soft, womanly allure, and her hair shone like a halo. She was a vision. And, standing there without her coronet and glittering royal robes, she was an approachable vision . . . a demoiselle once more.

But was she still *his* demoiselle?

"Welcome, *ma chatte*," he said with a flicker of a smile, straightening and replacing his daggers in their loops.

"I am not your *cat*, Rouen. I am the Crown Princess of Mercia."

"So you are. A detail you managed to overlook when telling me who you were," he charged.

"What is your price, Rouen? How many pieces of silver will it take to make you leave and forget you ever set eyes upon Mercia?"

"Oh, I could never forget this place, demoiselle." He glanced around him with genuine wonder. "Your palace is like a precious jewel . . . all cut stone, adorned with carvings and set with colored glass." He swept a hand around him. "And these bathing pools . . . I haven't seen anything like them since the old Roman baths in Constantinople. Did your own masons do all this?" He grinned at her. "*Dieu* . . . the bishop of the cathedral at Saint Denis would be green with envy at the sight of your windows."

"I could make you a very wealthy man," she said, sliding her crossed arms down to her waist.

His smile took on a lusty curl as he strolled a bit closer and let his eyes fasten on the lush velvet of her lips.

"And I could make you a very satisfied woman, demoiselle."

"I am not a demoiselle!" she said, dropping her hands to her sides and bristling. "You will address me as 'Princess' or 'Your Highness.' "

"You will always be 'demoiselle' to me, Thera of Aric."

He couldn't have chosen any words that would strike more terror into Thera's heart. Against her better judgment, she looked up into his heated golden eyes. The beat of her heart quickened. He began to fill her senses . . . his broad shoulders, his hungry gaze, his pleasurable mouth. A crush of longing went through her. For one brief and terrifying instant she wanted to *be* just a demoiselle. *His* demoiselle.

"Three hundred . . . and not a bit more, Rouen!" she said, recoiling from that dangerous feeling and backing around the bathing pool. "Don't be a fool. Think what you could buy with three hundred in silver."

"Three nights . . . and not a bit less, Thera of Aric," he answered in husky tones that engulfed her in a deep, swirling tide of temptation. "I have traveled far and wide . . . have learned the pleasure secrets of many lands. Think what delights you would discover in three long nights of passion."

Coming here had been a terrible mistake, she realized. At the mere suggestion of delights, her knees were weakening. "I do not intend to spend another moment in your presence, much less three nights!" She started for the door, but he lunged and snagged her wrist as she passed.

"You count . . . your countess counts . . . even your councilors count. And *six* is a number you all seem to find most interesting," he said, searching her tensed frame. "Why is that?" Her eyes jolted wide.

"All right—four hundred!" She twisted in his grip, trying to divert him. "That is almost half of my treasury. Take it and leave. Forget both me and Mercia!"

"After our three nights of pleasure, I will leave . . . if you still want me to." He reeled her closer and, after a brief struggle, caught her around the waist with his free arm and pulled her hard against his body. "But nothing could ever make me forget the feel and the taste of you." He ran a knuckle down her cheek. "Your skin is like sun-warmed marble, so smooth and sleek."

His words snared her senses, holding them for a ransom of pleasure, while his hand slid to her buttock and cupped it possessively, pressing her against his rousing flesh. Wherever their bodies touched, she began to ache for even closer contact.

"And you taste like Saracen sugar to me." He lifted her hand to his mouth and dragged his teeth over the sensitive pads of her fingertips. Gooseflesh rose all over her.

"I want you, Thera of Aric. More than I have ever wanted anything in my life."

Each word carried the seductive resonance of truth. The feel of his body against hers combined with the relentless persuasion of his voice to overwhelm her beleaguered defenses. When he lifted her chin on his finger, she looked up into his shadowed face and held her breath.

No, please . . . not this, she thought desperately. *Anything but this. . . .*

Then he lowered his head and dropped a kiss on the corner of her mouth, her chin, the tip of her nose and each of her eyes. It was a tender assault . . . meant to enlist her own desires in breaching the walls of her will, and the fears she had harbored about him were no match for that subtle invasion. With a moan of surrender, she turned her face for him, entreating his kisses.

"And you want me," he murmured with equal measures of awe and certainty.

It was true. She melted against him and her arms slid around his neck. She drank in the salty-sweet taste of his mouth, the sensations of his tongue tracing her lips, and the pleasure of being held in his powerful arms.

"Give me this night, Thera," he growled, so softly it was almost a purr. "And I will give you Paradise."

Conflict lodged in her throat: the *yea* her heart clamored for and the *nay* her reason demanded. She couldn't speak, and in the interval her body answered, leaning into him, seeking his heat and power. He shifted and clasped her tighter against him, mating his contours with her soft curves. Instinctively she parted her legs to nestle her thighs against one of his, an intimate touch that would soothe the sweet burn beginning in her womanflesh. He was so hard and hot, and his hands were tracing sinuous patterns over her sides and back and buttocks. It was what she had dreamed of, what she had longed for . . . this pleasure with him.

Neither heard the voice from the half-opened door. But the sense that someone had called her name gradually penetrated Thera's consciousness.

"Princess?" It struck a nerve. It wasn't Saxxe; he never called her that. But it was very familiar.

She managed to drag her lips from his and turn her head. Cedric stood in the middle of the chamber holding a pair of worn leather pouches and wearing a startled expression.

"Princess, I . . . well, the door was open and I . . . didn't expect to f-find . . ." He stammered to a halt, crimson-faced, and simply held out the pouches as evidence of his mission. "These were on Saxxe Rouen's horse. Mattias brought them to me, thinking he might have need of something . . . clothing, perhaps . . ."

The shock in his face was like an icy blast against Thera's heated frame. She was suddenly aware of Saxxe's arms around her, and of her body . . . so hot and molded so tightly to his that they were nearly fused. Another few moments and Cedric would have interrupted them in the midst of—

Oh, Lord! The impact of her position—in Saxxe's chamber—shattered her enthrallment and she pushed back in his embrace. He had done it to her again; beguiled her senses, robbed her of her wits. She gave him a harder shove and freed herself unexpectedly, so that she staggered back.

"I believe your princess is about to pay part of her debts," he said, his voice husky with arousal. "If you will be so good as to close the doors on your way out . . ."

The presumption that they would take up where they left off, after such a humiliation, fanned the flames of her royal pride.

"He is wrong, as usual, Cedric," she declared, coming to life. "I only came to—to—" She glimpsed the bathing pool behind him and, on impulse, gave him a hard shove. He flailed with surprise and fell back into the water with a tremendous and satisfying splash. "To make sure he had a bath!"

Saxxe sputtered and scrambled to his feet in the waist-deep water. It took a moment to wipe the water from his eyes, and by the time he cleared his vision she was storming out the door. The sound of her angry footsteps mingled with the lapping of the water. He looked up to see Cedric's head shaking as he deposited the bags on the foot of the bed and started for the door.

"Chancellor!" he called out, halting Cedric. He pushed back his wet hair and vaulted out of the pool. Standing in a growing puddle with his hands on his hips, he fixed Thera's chief adviser with a piercing gaze. "I want to know about these *nights*. Will she be forced to wed me afterward?"

Cedric studied him for a moment, thinking of the sight he had stumbled upon and considering the unlikely match they made, his princess and her fierce barbarian. He took a deep, unsettled breath, deciding to tell him.

"Nay, Princess Thera would never be forced to wed. Our sacred law declares that a marriage is made by seven nights . . . spent willingly in a lover's arms. If Princess Thera chooses to spend the rest of seven nights with you, then you will be her husband. And you will be crowned our king, even as she is crowned queen."

Saxxe felt Cedric weighing him as a man and a potential ruler. "Seven nights," he said thickly. "We have already spent three together . . . and she has promised me three . . ." Cedric nodded, watching the play of emotion in Saxxe's face carefully.

"We have need of a king, Saxxe Rouen. Whether or not you are the one we need, I cannot say. I can only pray that our princess will make the right choice . . . for herself and for our people."

The chancellor turned and strode out, closing the doors quietly behind him.

Saxxe stood for a moment, staring after him.

King. Despite all his talk of a kingdom, he'd never truly considered it a possibility . . . until this very moment. And he'd never given any thought to what was involved in being a king. Kings presided over populations, customs, and banquets; made decisions and issued judgments; collected taxes and spent money; went to war; and fathered heirs. Done rightly, ruling required courage, cleverness, authority . . . and a certain kingly bearing.

He hadn't been born to the crown, as Thera had; it wasn't in his blood. And he certainly hadn't been reared in a palace or fostered in a royal house or trained in the things he supposed a ruler might be. He thought of Thera tonight . . . the effortless authority of her tone, the grace of her bearing. What made him think he could ever be a king?

He grabbed the cover from the bed to wrap around his wet body and the leather pouches Cedric had brought fell to the floor with a thud. They had jarred open in the fall, and when he picked them up, a golden spur fell onto the stone floor with a clink.

He stood looking at it, then picked it up and sat down on the bed, turning the spur over and over in his hands. It brought painful memories boiling to the surface. But instead of shoving them back into his core as he usually did, he allowed them to take shape and substance in his mind.

Long ago, in another lifetime, he had lived in a different world . . . among titled men and refined women. He had been born the younger son of a noble house, lived as a nobleman, and won his spurs as a knight. And though he had long ago ripped the spurs from his boots, not even long years of desperate, violent living had been able to rip the knightly code from his heart. Forever hindered by those wretched noble impulses, he had made a mediocre mercenary. But was there enough of the knight left in him to resurrect? Enough to make him into a proper king?

In the long night that followed, he lay in bed, looking up at the billowing silk overhead and searching for answers. Just as those silken folds were gathered to a point far above him, he saw his entire past narrowing and focusing toward one fateful encounter in an alley behind a tavern . . . toward one proud and headstrong young princess. And in that same instant, he saw that the rest of his life would be shaped by that same determined and utterly irresistible woman . . . by her acceptance or rejection.

It all came down to Thera.

He wanted her with everything in him. And barbarian or hire-soldier; crude, greedy, or opportunistic—whatever she thought him to be, she still wanted him. He couldn't let her dismiss him from his life. He had to claim the three nights she had promised and use every bit of pleasure in them to reach her heart.

It wouldn't be easy. She could be unholy stubborn and she had more than a queen's share of pride. He would have to be utterly mercenary about getting her into his bed . . . then noble enough to get her to stay there for the rest of their lives.

A noble mercenary. His scowl slowly faded into a wry smile.

Perhaps he was just the man for the task.

On the hilltops overlooking the city, two pairs of eyes watched the dawn rising over the valley. For much of the previous afternoon, the Spaniard, El Boccho, and his countryman had prowled the hills above Mercia, looking for some trace of the travelers they had been trailing. After several frustrating days of staying concealed and being forced to keep their distance, they awoke to find that the women and their watchful escort seemed to have vanished with the morning mists.

The pair had finally discovered a design cut into stone next to a path, and followed that trail up onto the mountaintop, trying every possible pass until they found a route through the stone passages to a thickly forested valley. It took them still longer to discover a route through the trees which bore the marks of recent passage, and to follow it to a second high ridge topped by a maze of deeply fissured rock.

By sunset, they had left their mounts to climb over the craggy summit on foot. And in the distance, shrouded in evening haze, they finally spotted the winking lights of a small city.

"*Christo y Diablo!*" El Boccho muttered. "Who would have thought to find such a place here? Look at it . . . a spire . . . bell towers . . . many houses and shops." He pointed to the church and the palace. "Even great domes. It is a full city."

His accomplice nodded, adding: "A city . . . but without walls."

"By the Devil's beard . . . the duc will be pleased indeed." El Boccho rubbed his grizzled chin and his ferret-quick eyes darted in calculation. "We have not only found his woman, we have found him a rich prize. We must search out a better way into the valley. When he marches into Brittany, we must be ready to lead him straight into the heart of this city."

The palace was astir early that morning. By the ringing of Prime, at sunrise, the palace kitchens had long been bustling with activity. Into that organized chaos stepped Saxxe Rouen, his hair still damp and his face and hands freshly washed. He strolled through the kitchen with his thumbs tucked into his belt, staring at the great stone hearth with its hooks and spits and griddles, then at the baskets of wintered vegetables, crocks, barrels, and grain sacks that lined the walls.

Every hand froze and every eye widened as he passed the huge worktables, headed toward the glowing hearth. This was the one they had heard of, the barbarian who had rescued their princess, the one who was three-sevenths king. When he paused to survey the great stone chamber, they regarded him and the huge daggers at his sides with a mixture of awe and anxiety.

"I've come to see the one responsible for that sage-dusted brewet last night," he declared. The servants nearest him scurried back, their faces blanching. Every eye still capable of moving turned to a large, thickset woman with cheeks like polished apples.

"Yea, sir?" she said in a voice Saxxe guessed would never be so timid in addressing another. "I am head cook, Genvieve . . . it was my seasoning in the brewet."

"Then I must tell you, good woman, that I had a vision of Heaven itself, the first drop I took of it." A broad smile unrolled across his face. "I have eaten the foods of many distant lands, but I have never tasted a finer dish." He gave her a bow that dropped her jaw and set the kitchen sculls behind her tittering.

"And I was wondering if you've any of it left . . . to line my belly this morning?" he asked with a flattering light in his eyes.

"None left, Yer Grace," she declared hastily, "but I got plenty of other tasty fare with which to break yer fast."

Shortly he was seated at a worktable with a tankard of fragrant ale and a heaping platter of sausages, bread and butter, and several whole boiled eggs, which the cook thoughtfully sprinkled with a pinch of ground black pepper. He groaned and rolled his eyes with pleasure, and began to speak of dishes he had eaten in his many travels.

The cook and her helpers collected around him . . . albeit at a safe distance . . . marveling at him and his talk of spices, almonds, dried figs, and olives heaped up like mountains in the halls of the Arab spice merchants in the east.

By the time he departed to examine the rest of his potential realm, the kitchen was aglow with flushed faces and excited whispers. This barbarian, the kitchen folk decided, was a wondrous man indeed; they could see why Princess Thera had chosen him to be their new king.

More than three hours later, Thera sat at a parchment-strewn table in her chambers, listening to Cedric's report of what had occurred in Mercia during her absence.

Birthings, tilling and planting, deaths and tree harvesting . . . she heard it all with half an ear. In truth, it was another report that occupied her mind . . . Lillith's report on Saxxe Rouen's whereabouts.

"What? Sneak and snoop and pry?" Lillith had protested when Thera dragged her out of bed at dawn that morning with orders to spy on their unwanted guests.

"Exactly. I should think it would be second nature to you by now," Thera said with a narrow look. "I want to know what he does and where he goes, and the instant he tries to leave the palace."

She did not have long to wait. Mid-morning, just after the bells had rung Tierce, Lillith came rushing into her chambers, red-faced and out of breath. "Saxxe Rouen . . . he's poked and peered into every corner of the palace . . . the kitchens, the wine cellars, the cisterns and drains, the workrooms and gardens . . . even the audience chamber. Now he's left—headed for the streets!"

Alarmed at the prospect of Saxxe abroad in her fair city, knowing his admitted greed and his alarming propensity for violence, she grabbed Cedric and Lillith by the sleeves and dragged them out of the palace, across the terraces, and into the streets, searching for Saxxe.

She found him in the central market square. His dark, shaggy head was visible well above the crowd that ranged before him and trailed after him. From cart to stall to shop door he went, inspecting the wares and speaking with the merchants and craftsmen. Even from a distance she could see the sparkle in his eyes and the brilliant flash of his smile . . . and she knew too well what a devastating effect those devilish agents could have on a person. Her knees felt a little weak at the thought of confronting them again.

When she could tear her eyes from him, she examined the people around him. Men, women, and children alike . . . their faces glowed with excitement. They almost never saw strangers and, Heaven knew, they had never seen anything even remotely like Saxxe Rouen. They gawked unabashedly at his long hair and beard, his huge sun-browned chest and powerful arms, and his wicked-looking daggers. Whichever way he stepped, they scurried out of his path, and whenever he spoke they strained to hear.

She pulled Lillith and Cedric along with her to find out what held them so enrapt. A few people at the edge of the crowd noticed her and gave place, bowing as they removed themselves from her way. But she was stopped a few feet from him by a number of backs fitted shoulder to shoulder, oblivious to her presence.

"A fine bit of workmanship and a prudent style!" he was saying, holding up a leather slipper from the cobbler Albert's stall. "I tell you . . . in Venice they now wear shoes so long and pointed you could pick your teeth with them." There was a murmur and a number of incredulous giggles. "Troth—I swear it is true! Some of their shoes are so long, the wearers must put bells on the tips so they can find their toes in a fog." When he grinned at his own jest, their titters became laughter. And he moved along to the chandler's stall and the tin-smith's shop, pausing to examine the goods or to point to a house or building and ask about it.

Thera followed, listening with burning ears to his out-rageous talk. But when she started to tap people on the shoulders and make her way through the crowd, she heard him asking about what crafts and trades they pursued, and stopped. Why would he wish to know about their occupations? Someone spoke up, revealing that some were farmers and tradesmen, but in some respect they all were involved with the city's main indus-try . . . weaving cloth. When he asked what kind of cloth they made, they proudly responded: both silks and wool-ens . . . serges to whisper-thin silk veiling.

"I would like to see your looms. With my own eyes I have seen the great looms of the Saracens and the Venetians, and have watched the way they dye yarn and cloth and mark their patterns. . . ."

As he spoke, a number of little boys who had made their way through the legs of the crowd pushed toward him, until one of them dared reach out and touch his dagger from behind. He felt the movement and whirled into a defensive crouch, catching the offender by the tunic. The other boys went squealing back into the crowd, and the adults muttered nervously.

"What's this?" he said in his sternest voice, and the boy trembled in his grip. "Not a thief, I hope." A voice from the crowd answered.

"It were a child's prank, sarr. Them other boys dared 'im to touch yer blades."

"Is that so?" When the lad nodded, Saxxe eased his grip and studied the boy's ruddy face and neat, bowl-cropped hair. "I have a way of dealing with such brazen deeds!" He pulled out one of his long daggers, and there was a collective gasp. Then he offered it, hilt first, to the boy with a wry grin. "Bravery should always be rewarded. Go on . . . hold it for a moment."

The boy took it with shaking hands and reverently turned it over and over, then glanced warily up at Saxxe. Audible sighs of relief came from the mothers and fathers. And soon a number of children were creeping from behind their mothers' skirts, venturing closer. Saxxe knelt down on one knee, studying them even as they studied him. One intrepid little fellow with his tongue protruding from the corner of his mouth reached out a finger to touch Saxxe's beard. Just before he made contact, he glanced up to find Saxxe staring at him.

"Take care, lad," he warned, jerking a thumb toward his face. "I've had as many as six little boys lost in this beard at one time. They fall in and can't find their way out. I usually have to send in a brace of blooded hounds to find them!" Surprised laughter came from the adults, and Saxxe couldn't help chuckling as he offered his beard for examination. "Go on . . . feel." It might have been the glint of amusement in his eyes or the warmth in his deep voice . . . something charmed the boy past his fears.

"It's soft!" he cried out with an excited grin, ruffling his fingers through it.

Thera stood to one side, having finally pushed through the crowd. She watched Saxxe teasing the children and felt a melting sensation in her middle. Seeing his manner with them reminded her of how breathtakingly gentle he could be. Then she caught the admiring glances he cast toward the mothers, and watched the mothers' cheeks glow as they lowered their eyes. Little boys were not all that got caught in that wicked beard, she realized with a rush of irritation.

Her people were like children in many ways . . . skittish, easily charmed, and alarmingly eager to please. Her protective impulses rose as she recalled his oft-repeated declaration that he did nothing without expecting a profit. What could he expect to gain from her sheltered people?

"What do you think you are doing, Rouen?" she said, stepping forward. He turned and she caught—full force—the devastating impact of his tautly reined power. She felt the sweep of his gaze like a physical sensation, and quelled a shiver. Then she drew her shoulders up straighter and demanded, "You have no business here."

"I am curious about your kingdom and your people. And I have nothing better to do . . . unless, of course, you are ready to start paying your debt to me." When her mouth tightened into an angry line, he smiled. "I thought not." And he swaggered off to continue exploring. The Mercians studied their princess's sudden ire, then struck off after him. She had to hurry to keep up with them.

He paused before a large, round stone structure built without windows. "What's this?"

"One of the granaries, Yer Grace," came a man's voice from the crowd.

Thera blanched at the way they addressed him. "Your Grace" was what they sometimes called *her*! She pushed through the throng and planted herself between him and the granary door.

"There's nothing of interest to you in there. Now kindly remove yourself back to the palace. . . ." But his eye was already lighting on a large shop across the way.

"What's this?" He stared at the bush on the signboard above the door and was surprised to recognize it. "A vintner!" He headed straight for it and ducked inside, greeting the shopkeeper and plying him with questions about his grapes and the wine they imported from the Champagne region.

"He doesn't need to see your stores, Howard Vinton," she told the proprietor, planting herself in the doorway to the cavernous cellar below. Saxxe peered around her, told the fellow "Another time," and ducked back out the door with an infuriating smile.

The apothecary was next, then the harnessmaker and one of the bakers. Whatever he picked up, she snatched from his hands; whatever he wanted to see, she tried to shield from his view. By the time they started down the third side of the market square, she was steaming visibly, and his enthusiasm for his explorations had become a thinly disguised rebellion.

He entered the church and walked boldly toward the beautiful rose-windowed chancel—without a proper genuflection!—then stood admiring the ceiling and altar and breathing in the heavenly scent of beeswax tapers.

"No less than a bishop must be responsible for so beautiful a nave," he declared. "I'd like to meet him."

"That will be impossible," Thera snapped, striding to the front. "He's been dead more than a hundred years. Now, do you mind leaving?"

"Yea, I do mind," he answered, standing in the sanctuary with scores of her people looking on. "You know, you are sorely lacking in hospitality, Thera of Aric. What sort of example is that for your people?"

It was as if someone had poured scalding water over her head.

"How dare you stand there and criticize my conduct toward my people or my example before them . . . you, who won't bathe . . . or even cover your nakedness with decent clothes?" she blazed, stalking recklessly close to him, her chin thrust out. "It has nothing to do with hospitality!"

"Then perhaps there is something here you don't wish me to see. What are you trying to hide?"

Everything! she wanted to scream. She would hide her entire kingdom from him if she could.

"No one knows better than I how profit-minded you are, Rouen. I do not intend to let you take advantage of my people. I won't let you take their trust . . . then use it to take their money or their possessions."

His eyes lost their roguish glint and narrowed. She didn't want him to have any contact with her people; she was trying to protect them from him! It stung—her belief that he might purposefully misuse these good folk for his own profit—and he reacted angrily.

"The only thing I intend to take in your precious kingdom, Thera of Aric," he declared in a voice at the bottom of its range, "is *you!*"

There it was, baldly stated. He wanted her and he intended to take her. And the part he left unspoken was clearly readable in his eyes: it was only a matter of time.

How dare he stand in front of her sexton and her priests and her people—in a church, no less!—and say such a thing to her? The man hadn't a drop of shame in his entire body!

"I would rather bed with the swine than with the likes of you, Rouen." She dragged a furious glare down his sparsely clad frame. "The smell would certainly be better!"

Again, his reaction was unexpected. He edged forward and loomed over her with a cool, vengeful smile.

"You didn't seem to mind my smell last night, demoiselle."

She jerked her chin back and tried to summon a retort. Her lips moved, but not a single word issued forth.

A murmur of excitement went through the people crowded into the back of the church as his words and her lack of them were relayed to those still outside. They couldn't recall another single time when Thera of Aric had been rendered speechless!

Wheeling, she found herself facing a score of faces filled with undisguised fascination. She was halfway out before she recovered enough to realize that she might have no control over him, but she was still *their* princess. Immediately, she spread her hands and began to sweep her people along with her.

"You have better things to do than stand around gawking! Sext hasn't rung yet," she declared. "Go back to your work, all of you!" As they lowered their eyes and turned back to their labors, she tossed a glare over her shoulder at Saxxe, adding: "And you'll do well to stay clear of him and his hairy friend. Trust me . . . they will bring you nothing but trouble."

Saxxe paused on the step just outside the church doors . . . appreciating the womanly sway produced by her determined stride, but also roundly frustrated by her superior, mistrustful attitude toward him. He might manage to claim her passions, but she had just served notice that a fleeting pleasure was all he would have. She still treated him like a dirty, greedy, uncouth barbarian who strode about half naked and didn't belong in her precious kingdom. He clearly had his work cut out for him.

As he stepped onto the street with a thoughtful frown, he glimpsed several men wearing leather aprons, standing nearby and staring at him.

"Can you tell me where I could find your forge?" he addressed them. "I wish to see how your smith does his work."

"Yea, sir . . . this way, sir," one said, jolting forward.

The others looked at each other and hurried along behind them. And as they watched Saxxe's powerful, manly gait, they gradually drew their shoulders up straighter and a hint of his swagger crept into their strides.

Chapter Fourteen

The forge was located at the far edge of the city, tucked amid a number of wooden sheds and pens of horses and other hoof stock. As Saxxe's party passed houses and shops along the way, people paused in their labors and stuck their heads out their doors and windows to see him. Word of his destination spread, and a number of men excused themselves from their benches, stalls, and shops to trail behind him . . . insisting they too had business with the smith.

"This is it? Your forge?" he asked, standing before a modest stone structure with a single hearth. "One hearth for so many people? And how many smiths do you have?"

"Two," came another voice.

"Unless you count Edward, who is really a tinsmith," said his guide.

Saxxe scowled and ducked inside the building. By the hazy light coming from the open windows he saw stacks of buckets and barrels and tinware needing repair. As he looked around, he found hammers and tongs and rods of brass and bronze lying idle on benches. At the rear of the structure he finally spotted numerous wooden bins filled with the things he would have expected in a smithy: pieces of iron in recognizable shapes . . . hinges, pokers, spade heads, harness pins, and cooking spits. There was an air of neglect about the place, lent by the incongruous tidiness of the floor and worktables.

His guide called to the head smith, and just as the strapping fellow entered from the back room another visitor arrived. He drew his robust, gray-templed form up as tall as possible and introduced himself to Saxxe as a member of the Council of Elders and the captain of the palace guard . . . Elder Hubert.

Saxxe frowned. "I don't recall seeing a palace guard."

"Well, you may certainly see them now," Hubert said with great dignity. "I have brought them to meet you." Saxxe's hand went instinctively to his dagger. But Hubert beckoned to someone outside, and two tall, broad-shouldered young men ducked through the door and stood clasping their wrists before Saxxe. Hubert gestured to them. "The best marksmen in all Mercia. And"— he added with considerable pride—"my two nephews. Castor and Pollux."

Saxxe acknowledged them, and when they returned the nod, he could have sworn they blushed.

"And if I may be so bold . . . I have something of a request, sir." Hubert drew himself up with a reassuring pat of the short sword which hung at his side. "When you drew yon blade in the square, we thought we glimpsed . . . *blue.* If you would permit it, we would deem it an honor to examine your steel, sir." The head smith and the other men crowding into the smithy echoed that request.

Saxxe drew his daggers and laid one in Hubert's hand, the other in the smith's. There was an immediate murmur as the steel was held up to the dusty light and examined with great reverence. The burly smith looked transported.

"Damascus steel. It truly is blue! And see the wave pattern in the blade? I have heard stories of it, but never thought to see it myself. And you have a sword . . . is it the same?" When Saxxe nodded, a mist rose in the burly smith's eyes.

"I'll show it to you tomorrow, if you like." He turned to Castor and Pollux. "Now, perhaps you will return the favor and show me your garrison."

"Garrison, sir?" one of the pair said. "We have no garrison."

"Then who mans your walls?"

"Walls, sir?" the other said with a quizzical look. "We have no walls."

Saxxe was struck speechless. Indeed, they had no walls. He had been so preoccupied as he rode into the valley and so shocked as he entered the city that he hadn't given notice to the lack of walls and fortifications. Now, as he gazed at the palace guard—a force of three—he made the additional discovery that only Elder Hubert carried a weapon, and that but a small, ceremonial sword of ancient bronze.

"We would be honored, sir, if you would join the young men tomorrow after the ringing of None, midafternoon," Elder Hubert said. "A number of them participate in trials and games and archery practice on odd days . . . and tomorrow is odd."

Saxxe nodded, thinking that every day in this place was a bit odd. He probably already knew the answer, but he asked anyway: "And where is your armory . . . and your armorer?"

"Armory, sir?" Elder Hubert said with a wince.

"We . . . have . . . no . . . armory," Saxxe pronounced, along with the rueful elder.

He continued his explorations with the city stables. The stone-walled structure was large enough for scores of horses, but there was an air of disuse here as well. Gasquar was there, seeing to their mounts, and as they looked around the main stalls together, they were approached by another breathless, blue-clad elder, who had just arrived. Hubert introduced him as Elder Mattias.

"I have been admiring your steeds, good sirs," Mattias said. "Magnificent animals. Truly inspired breeding. Did you train the big gray yourself, sir?" When Saxxe answered in the affirmative, he sighed. "Once, these stables were filled with fine racing stock. Now, we are reduced to plow horses and palfreys. *Useful* animals are the order of the day. I don't suppose you would care to see?"

But he did care. Saxxe made a thorough inspection of the premises, and despite Mattias's gloomy assessment, found a number of fine mares in the lot of saddle horses. The elder's long face lit with hope as Saxxe and Gasquar ran their hands over several animals and pronounced them promising.

"It is not only the bloodlines . . . important as they are. It is also the training," Saxxe said. "My family raised and trained horses for many years . . . some of them fine, fast animals. Every horse has bursts of speed in its sinews. It takes but the right sort of training to bring it out. With a bit of work, some of these animals might surprise you."

"You think so?" Mattias said, brightening visibly.

Saxxe's eyes twinkled as he glanced at Gasquar. "I'd be willing to *wager* on it."

When they left the stables with Mattias and Hubert, Saxxe rubbed his chin and declared, "I've a powerful thirst. What say we find a tavern and have a draught of ale?"

"Oh, I fear that won't be possible," Mattias said apologetically. "Sext, the midday bell, has not rung . . . and it is hours until the Vesper bell and the close of the day's work. The alehouses will not open for some time."

"The taverns are closed?" Gasquar echoed, glancing at Saxxe in astonishment. "*Sacre Bleu!* The people . . . what do they drink?"

"Home ale," Mattias said. "Or water. We have very fine, clean water."

"The taverns do not open until Vespers?" Saxxe said in a strangled voice. "*Bon Dieu*—why?"

"Well . . ." Mattias glanced at Hubert in confusion. "That is the time for drinking ale in company . . . after work is done. Just as None is the time for a bit of food."

"And Prime is the time for rising and Tierce is the time for the opening of trade," Hubert added. "There is an order of things, you know. A place for everything and everything in its place." He exchanged nods of conviction with Mattias.

When Saxxe looked to Gasquar, that hard-drinking son of Gascony looked as if he'd been impaled.

"Water?" he gasped. "They drink *water*?"

It *was* a most peculiar place. With his thirst and incredulity growing, Saxxe visited the tannery, the pottery, the mill, and the carpenter shop, and the place grew more peculiar still.

Wherever he went, people paused to greet him shyly and answer his questions. But he began to notice that whenever he or Gasquar picked something up and set it down, the tradesmen or clerks quickly straightened and readjusted it the moment they turned away. In fact, the whole population were constantly sweeping, dusting, and arranging and rearranging things. In his entire, eventful life, he had never seen anything like it. It was a veritable frenzy of tidiness; they couldn't allow a bit of dirt, confusion, or disorder anywhere.

Second only to their compulsive orderliness was their penchant for counting. They numbered the beans in a bag, the pegs in the sole of a shoe, the hours of the day—rung out by bells—and the strokes required to mix dough in a baker's trough. And they argued about their counting . . . how many more customers one merchant had than another on a given day; how many paces it took from one point in the town to another; how many sneezes constituted a true illness; how many individual raisins constituted a selling measure.

He stood in complete bewilderment as Mattias and Hubert argued whether he had seen five-eighths or four-sixths of the ninety-seven buildings in the city . . . and whether Saxxe had paid them seventeen compliments or twenty-two. He exchanged looks with Gasquar, then headed for the seat of their industry: the weavers' street.

He spent a long while watching their busy looms and the exhaustive patience they took with marking their patterns and setting their looms. Then he moved on to their warehouse and examined the bolts of cloth stacked there from the winter's weaving, awaiting the trading mission that would carry them to the Hot Fair at Troyes in midsummer. The fabric was extraordinary work; colors as deep and vivid as any he had seen in the east, and patterns and finishes to rival anything in Venice. Their finest goods were a blend of silk and wool, which they wove with great ingenuity into a single cloth that felt as soft as the exotic velvets of the Persians.

They paused in the doorway of the spinning house and he was astounded by a drone of counting—scores of voices—as the raw wool yarns were being wound onto skeins on pairs of hands. Each loop of yarn was tallied the instant it was created; numbers were flying hot and thick!

"What are they doing?" Saxxe demanded, stumbling back into the street.

"They are counting the windings, to make the skeins even," Hubert said proudly. "After they are dyed, they will all be of the same length . . . the perfect size for our looms."

"Why don't they just wind it on one large spool and cut the yarn to length later?"

Hubert blinked, seeming unnerved by the suggestion. "But that would not be . . . as orderly. And if weaving is anything, sir, it is an orderly undertaking."

Saxxe stared at him. Orderly. What sort of people maintained orderliness above practicality? And what sort of people welcomed strangers so warmly and eagerly? As he and Gasquar strode through the city, there was not a door or a face closed to them.

He began to see why Thera had behaved with such fierce protectiveness toward her people. They were a gentle, courteous, impressionable folk who had an endearing but worrisome innocence about them. They had developed their weaving to a high art, but it seemed to be the only trade that truly flourished among them. Their metal craft and masonry had fallen into disuse, their stables needed work, and they had no forge capable of the ironwork necessary for weapons or large tools like iron plowshares. Most important, they had no defenses; no walls, fortified towers, or ramparts . . . no garrison, no guard, and, from what he had seen, not even a warrior class. Mercia, like its sensual little princess, was a juicy plum . . . just ripe for the picking.

He began to see why Cedric said they needed a king. There were a number of things that required a man's doing in Thera's unusual little kingdom.

"Bells or no bells," he declared with a gleam in his eye, "I need some ale!"

He and Gasquar strode through the streets to the main marketplace and pounded on the doors of the first tavern they came to until they were opened. With a combination of wicked flattery and good-natured guile, Saxxe talked the wide-eyed proprietor into serving him and Gasquar . . . and everyone else in the throng who felt a bit dry.

Only one or two Mercians dared wet their throats with tavern ale at such an hour, but the tables and benches were soon packed with people eager to experience Mercia's visitors. As the drink began to flow, so did Saxxe's talk of his travels and Gasquar's outrageous tales. Before long, half of the busy square had collected at the tavern and the crowd came alive with excitement.

In the midst of a story, Saxxe gestured broadly with his tankard, sloshing ale on a nearby table, and a tavern maid rushed to wipe it up with a cloth. The movement brought a scowl to his face and his apparent displeasure settled a hush over the crowd. The little maid froze.

The Mercians' unholy penchant for cleanliness, Saxxe realized, afforded him a shameless opportunity. His expression softened and the twinkle came back to his eyes, melting the tavern girl's fear.

"You are without a doubt the cleanest, most orderly folk I have ever seen," he said, looking around him. "Are they not the most fastidious of peoples, Gasquar?"

"*Alors*—the streets of Heaven itself could not be any cleaner than these!" Gasquar agreed, wiping the ale from his beard with a brawny fist.

There were grins of relief and proud nods all around. Then Saxxe spotted Lillith at the edge of the crowd again, watching him suspiciously, and he smiled. All morning and into the afternoon, wherever he had gone, Lillith had appeared . . . scrutinizing his interactions with Thera's people. It wasn't hard to guess why she was there or who had sent her. Counting that his words would reach Thera's ears, he winked at the women standing nearby, setting them blushing and smiling.

"Your city is so fair and pleasant, and your people so diligent and exemplary . . . I swear you have converted me!" He jerked an emphatic nod. "Indeed. *To cleanliness*."

Widened eyes, stifled gasps, and delighted laughter greeted his pronouncement. He raised his hand with a wickedly solemn face. "I have decided to mend my slovenly and unkempt ways, for good. But I fear there is one difficulty . . . one that it shames me to relate."

All glanced at one another and held their breath, edging closer to hear.

"It has been so long since I bathed . . . I believe I have forgotten how." He aimed a look that blended roguish seduction and boyish petulance at the women in the crowd. "I believe what I need is someone to show me what to do and to help me do it properly." He turned to a plump, bright-eyed matron on his right.

"Now, who do you suppose I could get to help me?" And she giggled.

That evening, after a long afternoon of listening to the reports of her clerks and councilors, Thera sent a page to invite several of her ladies to dine with her in her private chambers. He came back alone and seriously out of breath. But before Thera could hear his news, Lillith appeared in the doorway, holding her sides as if she had just run a distance.

"Princess! Saxxe Rouen . . . the women . . ." She staggered against a pillar to try to recover her voice. But the few words she had managed to get out were enough to rouse Thera's anxiety.

"Saxxe?" she demanded, grabbing Lillith's sleeves. "What has he done now?"

"In his quarters," Lillith said, swallowing hard and straightening. "They're in his quarters . . . or on their way . . ."

"Who?" Thera demanded.

"The women . . ."

"What women?"

"All of them." Lillith braced. "Nearly every woman in the kingdom!"

Thera rushed for the door with Lillith right behind her. She raced through the arched colonnade leading from her quarters into the public chambers and then jerked to a halt. The great domed hall was filled with women streaming toward the east wing of the palace. Young and old, highborn and lowly, elegantly dressed and modestly garbed . . . there were dozens upon dozens of women . . . all bright-eyed and red-cheeked, talking excitedly.

"They're going to Saxxe Rouen's chambers," Lillith explained, looking a little sick. "He invited them."

"He *what*?" Thera stared at the parade of women with flame in her eyes. Charging out into their midst, she confronted a pair of shopkeepers' wives. "And just what do you think you are doing . . . going to Saxxe Rouen's chambers?"

"He's bathing, Princess . . . and he's asked us to come teach him how," one of the women said with a blush. With a perfunctory curtsy, the pair hurried past Thera.

"Bathing?" For a moment she stood flat-footed in shock, scarcely able to believe her ears. Then she turned back to Lillith with her eyes widening and mouth tightening. "He's taking a wretched bath?" She waved an arm toward the crowd of women. "And they're going to *teach him how*? Like bloody hell they will!"

She snatched up her skirts and strode furiously down the long corridor toward Saxxe's chamber. Pushing her way through the throng outside, she finally made it to the door and thrust inside . . . to find the room equally crowded . . . and awash in "oohs," "ahhs," and sultry feminine laughter.

At the center of that heated throng lay the sunken bathing pool . . . and in the pool stood Saxxe Rouen, waist-deep in water, being scrubbed and attended by half a dozen young women wearing only clinging wet chemises and sloe-eyed smiles.

Thera reached the edge of the crowd and stood rooted to the spot, speechless, as she watched their avid hands gliding over his wide chest and up his thick, corded arms and down his tapered sides . . . toward the parts of him that lay below the water line. The women watching laughed and called advice as the nubile young things acting as his body servants demonstrated the use of a cake of Castilian soap, wielded a pair of shears to trim his shaggy locks to a neat shoulder length, and plied a well-honed blade across his face.

She watched in horrified fascination as they scraped the last of the thick, dark beard from his throat, then splashed water on him to rinse the soap away. Their busy fingers lingered over his square jaw and corded neck, then floated curiously down the trail of dark hair in the center of his chest and stomach, before veering coyly aside.

The back of Thera's throat burned. Her fists clenched. Her stomach felt strangely hot and hollow.

When he ducked under the water to rinse, then rose in a showering spray, she was swamped by a deluge of memories and longings that made it difficult to breathe. She recalled another sort of bathing . . . in a stream at twilight, when they had rinsed mud from each other. She had caressed him with that same wonder, that same sensual hunger. . . .

"By the Sacred Scrolls—there's a fine face under that bush of hair!" came an age-thinned voice from across the chamber. When Thera craned her neck to see, there was old Elder Agnes, grinning enthusiastically at Saxxe. Thera's jaw dropped. Elder Agnes too? "A mirror—we must have a mirror," the old lady decreed.

They passed a polished metal hand mirror through the spectators and handed it to him. "Dieu! It's been so

long since I saw my own chin, I scarcely know myself."
His deep, sensual laughter rolled out over the crowd,
and the sound of his pleasure stripped every nerve in
Thera's body raw, exposing her desires and uncovering
an unexpected greed in her.

"What in heaven do you think you are doing?" She
erupted from the crowd to take a stand near the edge of
the pool, her chin at a combative angle. Saxxe jerked his
head up, then handed the mirror to one of his comely
body servants, and greeted Thera with an infuriating
smile.

"Princess Thera! How good of you to come! You must
be pleased to know that I have decided at long last to
follow your advice ... to *bathe.* And your ladies have
been so good as to—"

"I know what they are doing, Rouen—I have eyes!"
Ogling him! she almost blurted out. And how dare they
gawk and gape at him when he was—he was—She finally said it to herself: *he was hers!* She wheeled on the
women behind her with her eyes blazing. "This is an
outrage ... indecent in the extreme!"

"What? Giving a weary visitor comfort and assistance,
out of the goodness of their hearts, is indecent?" he
declared, pulling her attention back to him. "In every
noble house in France, the women attend their guests'
bathing ... in all goodness and charity." His smile grew
as he glanced around at the women's glowing faces, then
wrapped brawny arms around two of his attendants and
gave them each a blatant caress. "And believe me, your
women are the very essence of"—his eyes twinkled—
"goodness and charity."

The titters that wafted through the chamber raked
Thera's newly exposed nerves like cats' claws. How dare
he smile at them like that—stroke and fondle them right
before her eyes!

"Out!" She turned on the lot of them. "*Out,* I say! This
moment! You too, Agnes!" She blazed at the withered
little woman in imperial blue, then turned to the others.
"Go home—all of you—to your husbands and fathers

and uncles. Go bathe your own men. Out!"

She drove them from the room in a royal fury . . . pushing some by the elbows, dragging others by the arms, staring down one or two stubborn ones . . . sending them all scurrying for the door. With longing and apologetic looks at Saxxe, and startled "ohhhs" and "oh my's," they retreated . . . creating confusion in the corridor as they pushed their way out of the chamber. She then stalked back to the bathing pool and glared at the young girls clinging to Saxxe's obviously naked form.

"You too, Alaine . . . Birget . . . Claudine. Out! *Now!*"

The fire in her eyes set them scrambling for the edge of the pool, and in short order they were wrapped in linen and hurrying for the door. She herded the rest of the women out after them, then slammed the door behind the lot and threw the bar in place. For a long moment she stood glaring at the heavy wooden panels, listening to the turmoil outside and trying to master the turmoil inside herself. Then she turned back to the bathing pool, intending to give him the tongue-lashing of his life.

Halfway there, she stopped. He was still standing waist-deep in the water, watching her with an irresistible, tawny-eyed smile that made her feel as if he could see straight into her heart . . . and knew that her outrage was not caused by concern for her women's sensibilities or by propriety. But that roguish grin was almost all she recognized. The rest of his face, shorn of its dark beard, and his neatly trimmed hair seemed completely strange to her. And devastatingly handsome. She couldn't take her eyes from him.

His cheekbones were high and wide, his jaw was strong, and his chin was square with a slight dent in the middle. In the midst of that astonishing new countenance was a familiar mouth . . . with wide, grandly curved lips that had sometimes felt like warm satin and other times like burning brands against her skin. A shiver went down her spine and she moved closer, drawn to that fascinating new aspect of a face that she had known so intimately.

"After all your complaints, I would have thought you would be pleased to have me bathe . . . perhaps even put on a tunic," he said, watching the play of emotions across her face. "Since you've sent all my helpers away"—he picked up a sponge floating nearby and held it out to her—"I think it's only fair that you take their place." His voice lowered to a finger-tingling pulse. "My back still needs scrubbing, and they hadn't quite gotten to my legs and my . . . feet."

Creeping closer, she stared at him, torn between her rightful ire and her rising need. Her heart was drumming against her ribs, and her whole body was going warm and weak with excitement. Her lips felt thick as she stared at his, and suddenly all she could see was his handsome face, his eyes . . . glowing with desire . . . reaching for her.

She put her hand out to take the sponge, and he snagged her by the wrist and pulled her straight into the water with him.

"Ohhh! Ughh—*y-you!*" she sputtered, wiping her wet face as he dragged her against him. Gasping, she tried to shove away, but he slid his arms around her and reeled her close, laughing.

"Now we're even," he said, staring down into her eyes with wicked satisfaction.

Then she knew: he had planned this all along. She stilled against him. The women, the bathing, the shaving . . . he had been just waiting to pull her into the water.

When his mouth lowered to hers, she realized she had been waiting for it, too.

At that first contact, her arms slipped around his waist and her hands slid up his back as she opened hungrily to his kiss. Her body molded to his, seeking his heat in the cooling water, seeking the sensual power that trembled the very foundations of her being. She drank him in with every breath and absorbed him through her skin . . . hungry for the feel and the taste of him.

His mouth was wine sweet as he toyed with her lips, taking the kiss steadily deeper. He was caressing her, teasing her until she moaned softly and writhed against him, entreating his touch. Just when she felt she couldn't bear the need another moment, he began to run his hands over her back and waist, tracing her shape, working a potent magic through the wet silk of her gown.

Desire rose like a sultry mist inside her, conjured by his heat, then condensed by his touch into a river of need that flowed through her limbs and pooled hotly in her loins. She rippled under his hands, unable to get close enough to him to soothe the ache in her breasts and the burning between her legs.

"Stay with me, Thera," he murmured, cradling her head between his hands. His whispers filled her mouth, then flowed down her throat . . . straight into her heart. "Give me this night. And let me give you all the pleasure you can hold."

Pleasure. She managed to right her gaze enough to look into his darkened, luminous eyes. His heat and presence engulfed her; his desire permeated the air, the water, the entire world around her. She somehow understood. He was a force of nature . . . ordained for her . . . inevitable . . . inescapable.

He was like the *khamsin* he had spoken of . . . hot and powerful and utterly irresistible. Whenever they came together, he swept her up like a searing desert wind, overwhelming her with his passion and his certainty. And as the desert tribes understood of their mighty wind, all she could do was yield to that force and pray that wherever he set her down would be the right place.

"This night is yours, Saxxe Rouen," she said softly, touching his face.

Yours. The word resonated in his very blood and he burst into a huge grin and picked her up by the waist and whirled her around in the water. "Yea, the night is mine, Thera of Aric. And soon the Seven Pleasures of the World will be yours." And he lifted her into his arms and carried her up the steps and out of the water.

Standing her by the pool, he peeled the clinging silk from her shoulders, down her arms, and pushed it over her hips so that it fell into a puddle around her feet. Her thin, knee-length chemise came next, and soon she stood before him wearing nothing but a blush.

With unhurried grace, he reached for one of the folded linens the women had brought for his bath and wrapped her in it, dragging his hands down her shoulders and sides to dry her. Then he reached for a bit of toweling himself and was surprised when she tugged it from his hands and began to ply it over his chest and shoulders and back.

Her fingers strayed from the cloth to stroke his body, skimming his mounded muscles, tracing his tightly banded ribs and narrow waist. He watched patiently as she satisfied her curiosity ... until both her attentions and his desires focused intently on his loins.

"Now, my little cat," he said, pulling the toweling from her hands and shoulders. "It is time for your first lesson." Lifting her, he strode to the veiled bed and settled her in the middle of it, on her knees. Then he climbed up opposite her, smiling in a way that caused her heart to skip beats.

"There are seven pleasures. And the first of them is *the kiss*." He brushed his lips over the ends of her fingers.

"I believe you've already shown me that one," she said, leaning forward to press a lush, open-mouthed kiss on his lips. She didn't want lessons, her darting tongue said; she wanted pleasures. He couldn't help rousing to her provocation, but when she sat back, gasping, he took a deep breath and reined in his response.

"A very nice start, sweetest. But you still have a few things to learn." He pressed her back onto the soft bed, spanning her body on braced arms. "Close your eyes." She obeyed and he made a sound of approval and shifted to the bed beside her.

"You love to count, eh? Then count for me the different kisses I give you ... all the different ways a kiss can make you feel." He kissed her forehead, then brushed his lips down the bridge of her nose to plant a kiss on its tip ... one soft and parental, one teasing and squishy.

"One . . . two," she said with a hint of impatience. Then he covered her closed eyes and cheeks with a steady rain of soft kisses that made her skin glow and made her turn her head to offer him the rest of her face. "Ummm, three . . . perhaps four." And when his kisses trailed back along her ear, they began to invade her sensitive skin in a subtle way. "Definitely four," she murmured. After a number of gentle massaging kisses, he added a short, liquid stroke of his tongue. She shivered. "Five."

"Nay, keep your eyes closed." He chuckled softly. "And concentrate. I'll want you to remember someday."

And he trailed kisses down the side of her throat, leaving a damp trail that made her flesh quiver and brought an emphatic: "Six."

He kissed and licked his way down her shoulders, stopping her breath when he added small nibbles. By the time he reached her tightly contracted nipples and swirled them with his tongue, she grabbed handfuls of the silken bed cover and groaned, "Eleven. Nay— *twelve*." Then he suckled her, flicked her with his tongue, and raked her with his teeth, setting her afire with need. "Fifteen . . . sixteen . . . ohhh, sweet saints in Heaven! Please . . . Saxxe . . . s-seventeen . . . ohhh—eighteen!"

He drew back to watch her writhing in the throes of pleasures she had never known. She shuddered, stiffened, and bit her lip as he plied her with more kisses. Her legs shifted restlessly, her back arched, and her hips rolled in a sweet agony of desire. He knew that need; it was the very thing he was suppressing in his own loins even now. And as his own desires threatened to surge out of control, he took a deep breath and moved down her body.

"Saxxe?" she said softly, then felt a passionate kiss dropped on her navel . . . a series of wet, extravagant kisses trailed down her abdomen. She gasped—"Twenty"—as he veered off to one side to nibble her hipbone and nuzzle the border of her thigh. She could tell that his face was hot, and when she felt his hands grasp her legs, she started. His kisses lowered to her knee, where nibbles made it "Twenty-one," then begin to rise up the sensitive skin of her inner thigh as he nudged her legs apart. She tensed and her hands fluttered anxiously about his head.

Then she felt a touch and a gentle pressure that she knew must be a kiss. Twenty-two. Then something brushed the curls over her woman's mound, over and over, round and round, producing a gentle tickle that vibrated through her entire body. She moaned softly as the turgid heat collected around those sensations and grew into a burning need for release. Then suddenly she felt it . . . like a series of strokes across her very soul . . . that most intimate of kisses, soft and shimmering, building to a shattering intensity.

She lost her breath, lost her count . . . and lost control.

Pleasure crashed through her in huge waves, filling her loins, rising up her spine, curling through her chest, gripping her lungs.

With a convulsive gasp, she threw her head back and arched . . . splintering into a thousand burning embers . . . flung into vast, color-drenched realms of pleasure. Her consciousness filled with brilliant, searing gold and fiery crimson swirling and blending in exotic patterns as tremors shuddered through her again and again. Then as that flash-fire of passion cooled, gentler hues appeared, purples and azure, topaz gold and lush sendal green.

She returned slowly to her senses and found Saxxe holding her close. A calm sense of release permeated her, and she gave him a drowsy, potent smile that made him rustle against her.

"That, sweetest, is the first of the Seven Pleasures . . . the kiss," he said in a soft rumble, stroking her love-thickened lips. "Do you remember how many ways you counted?" When she shook her head, his eyes filled with mysterious promises of delights. "Twenty-three. And I believe, in time, you will discover quite a few more."

"How many more?" she said, shifting to look at him in complete wonder.

"I have no idea." His chuckle vibrated along her ribs and set her tingling anew. "I've never been especially good with numbers . . . and never had a reason to count. You count for me"—he waggled his brows—"and I'll try not to repeat myself."

"And in what part of the world did you learn the wonderful secrets of the kiss? In a Saracen beauty's arms?" The hint of jealousy in her question deepened the glint in his eye.

"Nay, it was no Saracen. The Moslem women seldom kiss . . . they consider it a decadent western practice. I learned kissing from the buxom Norman serving girls of my home, then acquired a few refinements in the arms of accommodating Italian and Spanish ladies." He kissed the edges of her frown and slid a hand up her hip, watching her shivery ripple of response with mild surprise. "So you see, I have traveled the world . . . collecting pleasures to spend on a stubborn princess."

"Then how lucky I am to be a stubborn princess," she whispered, pressing her hip against his swollen male flesh and watching the flare of response in his eyes.

"I see you are ready to begin again." His smile was soft and knowing as he dragged his fingertips down her face, drawing her lashes over her eyes. "Close your eyes, Thera, and learn the ways of the Second Pleasure . . . *the caress.*"

Willingly this time, she drifted into the darkness inside her own head and was slowly overwhelmed by the sensations he produced for her. Her spending had given her release, but had left her on a plateau of lingering excitement. Within a mere few caresses, she was again flushed with rising passion. His fingers were surprisingly supple, and soon she had experienced five wholly different caresses; gentle pressure, stroking, kneading, nuzzling, and feathery brushes. She sighed raggedly as he paused to kiss her deeply, then to run his knuckles down her throat.

"I never imagined touches could feel so different." He cupped and massaged her breasts, gradually working his way toward her tightly contracted nipples. "Six . . . seven . . . ohhh, please . . ." She expelled a long breath that was part sigh, part groan. "Eight."

For all the delicious intimacy of his kisses, his caresses seemed somehow more personal and moving. They reached inside her, to places inaccessible to words and even to the flood of sensual passion. From the first moment they met, Saxxe had touched her often, and with masterful assurance. It was his nature to deal with the world physically, to touch in order to convey and command, and to express his feelings with his hands. And in his tactile nature she had discovered the key to the woman locked deep inside her.

Now, as he focused the intensity of his need for her in his hands, she opened her senses to receive it. Each stroke took on a meaning of its own, and in her deepest heart she began to understand what they said to her. She recognized the awe in his delicate tracings, the possession in his firm caresses, and the playfulness in his tweaks and feathery brushes. There was a deep respect in the way he handled her, and a tenderness that spoke as much of caring as of skill. And as he settled tautly between her parting thighs, she felt his need and understood the restraint he exercised.

They began to move together, body against body . . . his chest brushing the tips of her breasts, his swollen shaft tracing the cleft of her woman's flesh, his heavy thighs rasping softly against hers. A familiar hunger grew within her, roused by the light, erotic contact. The core of her both swelled and tightened in preparation, and her heart pounded wildly as she felt herself propelled once more along that tight, explosive spiral toward climax.

He drew back for a moment, then began the slow joining of their bodies . . . thrusting gently but insistently, again and again . . . invading her like a warm, relentless tide . . . taking her breath and the last of her self-possession. She met his thrusts with hunger . . . wrapping him with her legs, demanding more of him, straining toward the feel of him parting her untried flesh. Battling for control of his own soaring needs, he halted and stroked her face.

"Slowly, Thera. I would not have this end too soon"—he said with a low groan—"for this is the third of the Seven Pleasures, *the joining*."

But their passions had been held at bay too long to be constrained by something as malleable as human will. She undulated provocatively against him, luxuriating in the fullness inside her and demanding the completion her body craved. "Nay, Saxxe . . . now . . . love me now," she whispered, wrapping her arms tighter about his shoulders and taking him deeper inside.

The heat and fullness and friction exploded in her senses and she cried out as she was caught up in searing winds of release and blown toward rare, bright peaks of sensation. He called her name and plunged into that pleasure storm after her, pouring a part of his very soul into her as he filled her with his seed.

The boundaries between them melted, and as they drifted from summit to summit of response, it was impossible to say where one's being ended and the other's began. For the moment they were one flesh, one spirit, complete in a way that neither would ever be again, alone. And as their bodies and hearts were blended, so were their fortunes and their futures.

It was some time before Thera's senses returned to normal. They lay still joined, though he had slanted across her body and onto the bed to spare her some of his weight. His eyes were closed and she reached out to trace his features with her fingertips, just above his skin so that she wouldn't disturb him.

But he sensed the warmth near his face. His long black lashes fluttered open, and she found herself sinking into the luminous depths of his eyes. "What are you doing?" he asked in husky tones.

She paused, then continued her explorations more directly, drawing her fingers up his temple, ruffling his eyebrow, then down the slope of his nose to his lips. "I just wanted to touch your face. I love looking at you.

Without your beard, you look so very different, so . . ."

"Civilized?" he supplied, watching her reaction keenly.

"Well . . ." She lowered her lashes.

"Fighting and warring are not particularly civilized pursuits," he said softly, "despite all the grand pageantry of knighthood and the code of chivalry. It has been a long time since I've had a reason to shave my face and wear burghers' clothes."

"And you have a reason now?" She held her breath.

"I have," he said softly. "You."

"Me?"

He nodded. "I would go a long way, Thera, to have you look at me just as you are now." He lifted her other hand, kissed it, and placed it on his chest. "To have you touch me like this." He smiled and slid her hand toward his belly, then slowly, experimentally, to his hardening shaft. His eyes closed as her fingers curled around him. "And like that."

He wrapped his arms around her and rolled onto his back, carrying her with him, so that she lay half on top of him, her breasts pressed against his chest. She was caught deep in another of his toe-curling kisses when the sense of his words registered in her mind. She lifted her head and whispered, "When?"

"When what?" he countered hoarsely between nibbles of her throat and shoulder.

"When did you dress like a burgher and shave your face?" A visible barrier rose in the backs of his eyes and the sight caught her off guard.

"I once fought for nobles and merchant guilds, remember? I have dined in great houses as well as on battlefields and in forests. And to dine at a great man's table . . . you generally have to wear clothes." He produced a beguiling smile and drew her head down to continue their kiss. She raised it again and frowned.

"Saxxe, where did you learn to fight? Who was your lord when you rode on the Crusade?"

"I learned to fight from a crusty, annoying old fellow who lived with my mother when I was a child. And I rode under King Louis. Who else? It was there I met Gasquar. We sailed the same galley on the way to Alexandria and spent most of the voyage hanging over the rails together." He flashed a distractingly dazzling grin. "It was a wonder either of us could lift a sword by the time we arrived. I tell you, we were so sick that the fish following the ship stuck their heads out of the water and begged us—"

"Saxxe!" She gave him a shove. "Be serious." She pushed up onto her elbow beside him, searching his face. As always, he spoke easily of himself without revealing much. The need to know about him became as compelling as her physical need for him. "Tell me about your home. Tell me all about you. I want to know." After a moment's silence she added softly: "Prithee please, sir."

He raised onto an elbow and studied the intensity in her face, searching for something. "Why do you want to know?"

It was the very question she had avoided asking herself. There were at least a hundred ways to answer . . . but only one truth. And it took every bit of her courage to say it.

"Because every time we're together you make my knees go weak and my skin ache for your touch. Because I just gave to you what I should have saved for my lord husband. And because I am coming to care a great deal for you, Saxxe Rouen." Emotion tightened her throat, reducing her voice to a whisper. "And I can't seem to stop it."

His face nearly split with a grin, and in an instant he kissed her breathless. Before she could recover, she found herself on her back, being showered with jubilant kisses and rousing caresses . . . which made it impossible to remember what she had just been so intent on knowing.

Much later, they lay together with their legs entwined, wrapped in the swirl of her hair and the cocoon of his warmth.

"I love your pleasures, Saxxe," she said drowsily, nuzzling the hand he brought up to stroke her cheek.

"As much as you love me?" he said, watching her eyes close and feeling her sliding toward sleep.

"Not quite that much," she whispered, with a ghost of a smile. "More like . . . four score and six worth."

He felt her relax against him and realized she'd fallen asleep. His chest felt marvelously full as he gazed at her dewy skin and pleasure-softened features. She had just admitted for the first time that she cared for him, even if it had been in a roundabout way. His broad, joyful smile slid into a laugh.

"*Dieu*. She counted."

Chapter Fifteen

Gasquar opened his door the next morning, at sunrise, and found Lillith seated on a stool outside Saxxe's door, her head against the wall and her eyes closed. He shook his head and gently scooped her into his arms and carried her back into his chamber. She wakened as he lifted her, but instinctively threw her arms around his neck to steady herself.

"Where am—?" She glanced around in newly wakened confusion and, as Gasquar deposited her on his bed, she suddenly made sense of where she was. "J-just what do you think you're doing?" she demanded, making straight for the far side of the bed. Gasquar was around the corner post in a flash, intercepting her.

"You are tired, eh, from your long night's vigil?" He planted himself before her so that his knees trapped hers against the bed. "I thought perhaps you would rest better here."

"Your bed, of course," she said. "Stand aside. I have to be there when she comes out of his chamber."

"Still you poke your nose into others' pleasures," he said, wagging his head. Her mussed hair, sleep-heavy eyes, and cherry-red lips lent her a just-wakened allure that he found irresistible. "Very well, then . . . but hurry, *ma chatte*. When you have finished counting your princess's pleasures, I would have you begin to count your own. Yours . . . and mine."

Before she could protest, he pressed a quick kiss on the tip of her nose. Her eyes flew wide, and as she drew back, he followed and captured her lips with his. Holding her with only the force of his kiss, he pulled her slowly upright and deepened that possession . . . tantalizing her mouth with slow, lavish strokes of his tongue.

She groaned softly, unable to pull away, mesmerized by the feel of his mouth on hers. It was as if she had been plunged into swirling hot water . . . she could scarcely get her breath. When he finally pulled away, she swayed and blinked.

Her hands were curled tightly over the front of his belt, her fingers trapped against his taut belly, and her body weak with a strange and delicious hunger she had glimpsed more than once in Thera's face. As the impact of her position washed over her, she snapped straight, her face crimson and her pride on fire.

"Let me up."

"Are you certain you wish to go? If I know *mon ami*, they will not rise from the bed before midday. He is a man for . . . morning pleasures." His eyes danced over her. "In that way, we are much alike."

"This is an outrage!" she said, shoving him back and struggling to her feet.

"Nay, the outrage is that you were paired and mated with a man old enough to be your grandsire."

"How did you—"

"I wanted to know." He shrugged. "I asked. He was well past his manly prime when you were wedded, eh? And I would wager you have not taken a man to your bed since he died. It cannot be from lack of wanting, *ma chatte*. You have the burning in your loins, I can tell. I feel the flames licking my lips when I kiss you."

"How dare you?" She tried to move toward the door, but he blocked her path.

"I dare because I, too, have wasted many years . . . wandering and fighting. I would waste no more time, Lillith of Montaigne." His words bore the weight of truth as his dark eyes softened, allowing her a glimpse of a side of him seldom seen. He leaned closer and drew a knuckle gently down her chest, across the tingling tip of her breast, and down her belly to her woman's mound, where he fitted his palm over her femininity. It was undoubtedly a crime against her dignity—but she couldn't make herself pull away from that tender, claiming touch.

"I could fill your blood with fire, your sweet belly with children, and your heart with laughter, *ma chatte*," he said earnestly, "if you would let me."

Pleasure, children, and laughter . . . for a brief moment she glimpsed an unexpected yearning for those things in his gaze. But she honestly could not say whether it was his longing or the reflection of her own. Never in her life had she wanted anything so much as she wanted what he offered her at that moment. And the power of that desire sent her into a full panic. She drew back with a jerk, bit her lip to keep from speaking, and darted around him for the door.

Gasquar watched her retreat and sighed heavily. He'd never met a woman so determined to deny herself pleasure. What would it take to make her come around?

Lillith raced out the door and ran smack into Cedric and a collection of bleary-eyed elders who had come to investigate the rumor that Saxxe Rouen had claimed the first of his three nights with Thera. She huddled back against the door to Saxxe's quarters and avoided meeting their eyes. They had seen her hurtling from Gasquar's chambers just now, and as they studied her rumpled form, they drew unfortunate but understandable conclusions about how she had passed the night as well.

"Really, Countess!" Elder Audra declared with an indignant glance at Gasquar, who had heard the voices and was stepping into the passage from his open door. "You have a duty. You must see to the princess's nights before engaging in your own!"

"Audra!" Cedric's glare silenced her before he turned to Lillith with a somber mien. "We have come to learn if what we heard is true. What is your count, Lillith Montaigne?"

Lillith bit her lip and searched their faces. Then, with

Gasquar's gaze prodding her to render up her precious "truth," she held up four fingers.

The elders hurried from the palace carrying with them the news of Thera's night with Saxxe. And the word spread like wildfire through the city: *Mercia had four-sevenths of a king.*

When the sun was fully up, Saxxe uncoiled from Thera's sleeping form and stood by the edge of the bed, taking pleasure in the hair curled around her body like errant sea waves. He had never met a woman like her in his life, never imagined one could exist. She was a fascinating blend of monarch and maiden; a determined noble, a devoted ruler, a commanding presence . . . but also a bright and clever young woman, a richly responsive lover. She called to things deep within him, feelings and responses that had long lain dormant . . . the need to defend and uphold, to give freely of himself. For the first time in a long while he had something of his own to strive for . . . something fine and good . . . something that involved the depths of his heart as well as the might of his arms.

The fullness in his chest grew so that he felt he would burst if he didn't move. And in Mercia there was a great deal that needed doing. To do something for Mercia, he sensed, was to do it Thera . . . for her heart and soul were bound up with her people. And in that moment, he knew that was the key to her.

He pulled on his skin breeches, laced up his boots, then strapped on his cross braces with his trembling hands. Moments later, he stepped into the passageway and peered through Gasquar's open door. There sat his garrulous friend in a circle of serving women and maids, teasing them with his scandalous talk. Saxxe beckoned him, and a chorus of protests rose as he joined Saxxe in the corridor.

"*Alors*—you have had your night," he said, studying the satisfaction in his friend's face. Then he started as he realized Saxxe's face was now naked. "*Sacre Bleu*! I will not ask how it was." He rolled his eyes. "I can see for myself . . . she has singed and plucked you for roasting!"

"It's called *shaving*, Gasquar," Saxxe said with a laugh. "Part of barbering, remember?" When Gasquar shook his head in mock ignorance, Saxxe gave the end of his beard a flip. "I tell you, old friend"—he leaned close with a wicked grin—"I had forgotten what an effect a clean-shaven face can have on a woman."

"Your face perhaps, *mon ami*." Gasquar chuckled, stroking his wiry beard dolefully. "My naked chin has never been known to send women into fits of passion."

Saxxe clapped him boisterously on the shoulder and drew him along. "Come with me. I have a thousand things to do today, and I have to start by finding a tailor."

"A tailor?" Gasquar stopped in his tracks, searching Saxxe's expansive mood with genuine horror. "First the shaving . . . now the putting on of clothes. *Sacre Mere!* Next you will be eating soup with a spoon!"

"Perhaps I will," Saxxe said. "But then . . . I believe most *kings* do."

He turned and strode on, leaving Gasquar gaping after him. A moment later the burly Frenchman caught up and flashed him a grin of understanding. "*Alors*, it has been a long while since I have seen my chin, also," Gasquar mused, falling into step beside Saxxe with a glint in his eye. "Perhaps it has improved. After your tailor, *mon ami*, perhaps we will find me a barber. . . ."

Out of the sweet heaviness of sleep Thera roused to a lush feeling of warmth . . . the heat held by the soft bed around her and the low, patient burn of the embers of desire banked within her. She came slowly to life, stretching, arching, shifting her arms and legs languidly, aware of every delicious inch of her body in an entirely new way. Lying naked in a bed that bore the subtle scents of a night of loving, she felt like the culmination of femininity . . . whole, encompassing, supreme . . .

connected to all that was fertile and productive and sensually alive. And the one responsible for these marvelous new feelings was Saxxe Rouen.

From the strong light filtering through the half-open garden doors, she guessed it must be midday at least. She sat up and looked around, finding the rumpled bed, then the bedchamber, empty. Where had he gone? Why would he leave her alone in his bed?

But the sting of disappointment quickly gave way to relief as she thought of what she would say, how she would face him after her wild, uninhibited behavior of the night.

Her garments, which lay damp and crumpled on the floor, were beyond wearing. She pulled a sheet from the tangled bed linen to wrap around her instead. Then she paused and leaned her head against one heavily draped post, seeing in her mind's eye Saxxe's newly shaven face. Such handsome features. They could lure a kingdom of women from their hearths and husbands . . . or entice a stubborn princess to his bed.

She'd spent another night with him; that made *four.* She wasn't sure how she felt about that, but what she had experienced with him had dispelled many of her doubts about him. He was a knowledgeable and considerate lover, a tender and passionate man . . . and the one person in the world to whom she was a woman first. Between them, there were no rules or boundaries, no protocol. He placed no expectations on her, demanded nothing except her honest response. She wanted him and had begun to understand that in some ways she needed him as well. In their passionate bond, she felt a personal freedom that was a rare and precious thing in her royal life.

A hesitant rapping at the door startled her and she whirled with her hand at her throat. The hinges creaked and Lillith's head appeared.

"Princess? Thank the saints you are awake! I had to come and tell you . . ."

Thera pulled her inside. "What is it? What's happened?" she demanded. But instinct told her that the first words of Lillith's explanation would be . . .

"Saxxe Rouen. He's in the city . . . going this way
and that . . . poking into everything . . . bursting into the
closed shops!" She paused to take a breath and Thera felt
herself going a little light-headed. She grabbed Lillith's
hands and squeezed.

"What shops?"

"The tailor . . . he pounded on the tailor Lucian's door
just after Prime. Then he and his miscreant friend barged
into the barber's stall and then called the bootmaker to
open his shop—the whole of the marketplace was in
an uproar! And then he went into the weaver's row
and caused a commotion in the spinning and weaving
rooms. . . ."

Uproar. Commotion. Thera struggled for a grip on her
reeling emotions. He had left her sated and safely tucked
out of the way, in his bed . . . while he took advantage of
her absence . . . and her people? How could he? Humiliated heat poured through her, reddening her from head
to toe. How could she have been so gullible?

She was halfway out the door when Lillith caught the
tail of the sheet she wore and pulled her to a halt.

"Princess, please . . . aren't you going to put on some
garments first?"

Saxxe had arrived in the city like the rising sun that
morning, rousing the inhabitants and spreading his vital
energy throughout the streets. He had indeed invaded
Lucian's tailor shop just after Prime . . . with a request to
be measured for a tunic and hose. The little tailor was as
delighted as he was shocked, and set about marshaling
his apprentices to see to Saxxe's request immediately.
And Lucian's good wife, Faye, set her hearth aglow to
provide them something to break their fast.

By the time Saxxe and Gasquar stepped out into the
street again, a crowd had gathered. With a growing
escort, they went to the barber Stephan's stall . . . where
Gasquar was shorn of a winter's growth of wool. From
there, they visited the bootmaker Robert's shop to order

a pair of soft boots for each of them. And when parsimonious Robert dared inquire about payment, Saxxe told him the king of Mercia would stand good for the debt and gave him a wink.

His comment was passed by those who heard, and soon every person in the crowd that trailed them through the streets knew that bold and handsome Saxxe Rouen planned to someday be their king. They began to call questions to him, begged him to tell of his travels, and offered him samples of their foods and wares at every turn. They blushed at his direct looks and glowed with pride as he examined and complimented their workmanship . . . and their hearts swelled as he lifted their little ones to ride upon his broad shoulders as he strode along.

As he paused to clasp the men's hands and tousle the children's hair, he was suddenly swamped by an unexpected wave of protectiveness toward them. They were a gentle folk, generous and trusting, and much too vulnerable. They needed a champion, a defender.

Within the burning fullness in his chest, within that poignant rise of the desire to gird and uphold, he somehow understood . . . the knight in him was being reborn.

He strode on, meeting their curiosity and their enthusiasm with a heartfelt desire to do good among them. Finding himself in the weaver's street, he made his way to the spinning house and, with a delicacy worthy of an ambassador, suggested ways to speed the winding of the skeins. His broad, winning charm finally made them bend their tradition of counting every loop of yarn as it was created, to try something new.

Then, in the weaving house itself, he described the kinds of shuttles and reeds and the variation of wrapping yarns that allowed the weavers of Paris and Florence to conceal the warp of a cloth entirely and produce a rich, tightly woven fabric with an identical pattern on both sides. By the time he departed, Benelton, the head weaver, was ecstatic about the possibility of trying this new sort of weaving, which Saxxe called "tapestry." And

Mercia's looms would never be quite the same again.

Thera raced into the city with Lillith at her heels. She had hastily donned whatever garments she came to first in her cabinets and had to be constrained bodily so that old Esme could coil her hair into a proper crispinet. Then, girding herself for a battle royal, she headed for the streets to find Saxxe and see for herself the damage he had wrought.

But instead of the tumult they expected, she and Lillith found the marketplace virtually empty. The ware shelves, stalls, and workbenches were abandoned. With anxiety rising, Thera hurried toward the weaver's street, where she found the spinning house strangely silent. And in the weavers' hall, the looms were motionless and the workers were gathered around to watch the head weaver and several of his master weavers trying out Saxxe Rouen's idea of a new way of wrapping yarns. She intervened and sent them all back to work, then burst from the weaver's hall to stop passersby and demand the whereabouts of Mercia's missing citizenry.

She found her people, as reported, gathered in the lane and on the corral rails around the smithy. Far above, on the roof that covered the main building, stood Saxxe and Gasquar and two other fellows . . . armed with iron pry bars and picks, popping wooden planks from the roof. She elbowed her way through the crowd and stood aghast. On the ground lay pieces of the shed roof that had covered the forge's hearth, and all around lay stones from the hearth itself, which was being dismantled with iron picks and chisels and hammers.

"What in God's name are you doing?" she roared. "Stop that—this instant!" They looked at her and lowered their tools, then turned to look up at Saxxe . . . as if seeking his direction. Their hesitation and the way they looked to Saxxe set her blood on fire. "Saxxe Rouen!" she yelled at him. "Come down immediately!"

He located her on the ground near the front of the onlookers, and waved. A moment later he was sliding down the sloped roof, and dropping from the eve to the ground. "Well, what do you think?" he asked, gesturing with a broad hand.

"I think you're mad," she declared, shaking a fist and almost bashing him with it. "You've wreaked havoc in the city all morning and now you're dismantling our forge! Are you determined to destroy my kingdom as well as my peace?"

"Well, there's gratitude for you," he said with a scowl, dusting his hands together and propping them on his hips. "We are not destroying anything. We're merely rearranging things . . . to make room for two more hearths." He nodded toward the half-demolished stonework. "One hearth is not sufficient for an entire kingdom."

Thera mastered her anger enough to note a number of her carpenters clustered nearby with split planks and beams, adzes and chisels, and several of her aged stonemasons examining the stones taken from the hearth and making measurements with the knotted cords they had not used in years.

Indeed, it appeared that they *were* preparing to rebuild as well as wreck the forge!

"Our forge is more than adequate," she insisted hotly, though with a bit less fire than before. "One hearth is all we have ever needed."

"Your old hearth wasn't large enough for proper ironwork . . . hardly enough to repair what tools and cooking irons you have." He turned to Randall, who stood nearby with a frown, for verification, and the smith nodded reluctantly. "And it's certainly not big enough to make armor or weapons or tools as large as iron plow blades or vessels as large as iron cauldrons for making dyes."

Her eyes flew wide with alarm. He spoke of weapons and armor—of arming her people!

"We don't need armor or weapons." She matched his determined pose, putting her fists on her hips. "Our mountains are our defense . . . we need no other. You build that hearth and roof back exactly as they were!"

He stared at her flushed face and angry stance, his

irritation rising. Then something roused in the back of his mind, delaying his angry blast for an instant as he searched her eyes. Orders. And there it was . . . the shadow of the fears she was channeling into a stream of royal commands. What was she afraid of? The need for weapons? The changes he was working? His effect on her people?

"But you do need plowshares and tools and iron vessels," he responded, sidestepping the volatile question of arms. "You send your traders off with your fine cloth, and they must spend much of the profits of your labors to buy things that could be made here, by your own smiths. They are fine craftsmen, but their skills are often wasted because they have so little space and so little iron to work. Two more hearths, a smelter, and a few more strong backs would give them what they need to do such work here."

Thera felt oppressed by his logic. How neatly he had turned it all around and made it seem there was a compelling need for things they had gotten along without for years.

"Please, Yer Grace." The smith approached with a courteous bow. "He speaks truly. Harold and me could do much more . . . if we had more hearths and a bit more raw iron. Collier, the head plowman—he only got two iron plowshares, and durin' the plowing just past, he had to bring me them old wooden blades again an' again for patchin'. They near lost the plantin' moon because of it." Nearby stood Collier and several of his men, nodding agreement and looking urgently to her for approval.

She felt the eyes of her people on her, searching, waiting for her decision. And when she looked at Saxxe, there was a challenge in his expression that said to choose anything other than enlarging the forge would be to slight her people's welfare. But why would he care? And what could he expect to gain from such a development? She was furious at the way he had taken her sensual surrender of last night as a license to meddle in the affairs of her kingdom, but just now she couldn't think of a way to counter both his conclusions and her people's support of them.

After a long, tense moment, she announced her decision. "Very well—build your new hearths." Joy flooded the smith's ruddy countenance, and at the edge of her vision her plowmen whooped and began jostling and dancing about. "But you will spend your efforts on tools and plows and implements for living and working, not on weapons or armor," she admonished, turning a determined look on Saxxe. "I will not allow Mercia's forge to be used to produce implements of death and destruction."

"No weapons? That's absurd," Saxxe declared, angered by her stubbornness in the face of what her recent experience should have taught her. "You need weapons every bit as much as you need tools!" But she was already leaving.

"You've heard my instructions," she said to Randall, then turned to the crowd. "And you . . . have you nothing better to do than to stand around gaping and gossiping? You've left your shops and benches idle, and the day is wasting."

When she lifted her skirts, the crowd parted to let her pass, then followed her dutifully back to their houses, workbenches, and looms. But as they went, they glanced back at the half-demolished forge and at victorious Saxxe Rouen, and smiled at his masterful handling of their strong-willed princess. He might have only four-sevenths of their princess's nights, but in their hearts they were more than ready to crown him king.

Six elders were required to sit with Thera to hear cases brought before the royal court each month. But by the ringing of None, mid-afternoon, there were still only five elders in their places on the dais of the marble-lined audience chamber . . . and those were all women. Thera had sent pages to fetch some of the other elders, but they hadn't returned, and in exasperation she sent Lillith to look for them. When Lillith didn't return, she finally decreed the court convened and had Cedric call the first claimant.

The case involved a dispute between two merchants, each of whom claimed the same space in the market and had erected a large signboard to protect his claim. Each now called his neighbor's sign a public nuisance. But when their names were called to appear, they were not to be found.

"You're sure they knew their case would be heard today?" Thera said, frowning.

"Most certain," Cedric answered, shaking his head. "I'll send for them. Meanwhile, I can call another case. Stephan the barber brings Michael the baker to the court . . . a matter of nonpayment for a bit of wart removal, cupping, and bleeding." But when they were called, both proved absent from the mostly empty supplicant benches outside the audience chamber doors.

Five more cases were called and only one could actually be heard. Either principals or witnesses in the others failed to appear to give testimony.

"My elders . . . the supplicants to the court . . . the witnesses . . ." The weight of so much truancy collected at the edge of Thera's awareness until it toppled her thoughts into the dread conclusion: "It's him again. I'm certain of it." She pinned Cedric with a glare. "Saxxe Rouen, where is he?"

Cedric shrugged; he had no more idea than she did. Thera shed her coronet and robes of state and headed for the city with her shoulders set and her eyes ablaze. Lillith met her before she reached the market square, bearing news that many of the city's people were on the lower valley road on the far side of the city . . . where Saxxe Rouen and Elder Mattias had organized a number of horse races.

"Horse races?" Thera nearly choked on the words. She grasped her skirts and went flying through the streets, with Cedric and a number of her elders trailing along.

Surely enough, the road leading to the lower valley was lined with jostling, noisy people, craning their necks to see when the next pair of horses would begin thundering down the road. It wasn't long before another pair of fleet-footed mares came racing down the course, headed straight at Thera. She grabbed Lillith and darted to the side just in time, bringing other spectators scurrying to inquire if she was all right.

"I'm fine," she declared indignantly, tugging her tunic and girdle back into place. "Which is more than Saxxe Rouen will be when I find him!"

As it happened, she didn't have to find him; he found her. He had been riding one of the horses that had careened past her and now turned his mount and raced back to her. He dropped to the ground at her feet and grasped her shoulders, looking her over with a harried expression.

"Are you all right?" He seemed surprised when she smacked his hands away and huddled back as if he were a viper about to strike.

"You're responsible for all this, I presume," she charged, waving her hand at the crowd and the lathered horses. "Arranging horse races! I might have guessed. It wasn't enough for you to tear down part of my city. You have to lead my people into idleness and vice as well!"

"Vice?" He jerked his chin back. "There's nothing sinful about enjoying a horse race . . . or making a bit of a wager on one."

"Princess!" Elder Mattias came running up, red-faced and glowing with excitement. "Was it not marvelous? A true horse race. And did you see—they flew like the wind!" When she glared at him, he drew back, buffeted by her towering displeasure at something he had awaited so eagerly.

"No more, do you hear? Pulling folk from their labors to stand around in the hot sun . . . frittering away their time and worldly goods. How much did you collect from them today, Rouen?"

He straightened, his shoulders swelling as his defenses rose. "If you must know, I made not a single wager. I did it to show Mattias here and some of his young men how to handle a horse in a race. And I did it for amusement, entertainment . . . fun. You do recall what *fun* is?" He stalked closer and, since she could not retreat, loomed over her. "How long has it been since you did something just for the joy of it, Princess?"

"What I do and don't do are not at issue here!" she insisted, humiliated at the way she had to drop her head back to continue to meet his gaze. The heat from his chest migrating into the tips of her breasts reminded her of more intimate and pleasurable encounters with him, and she had the feeling he knew it . . . that it was part of his strategy.

"Oh, but they are. In fact, I believe that is exactly what is at issue here. When did you last laugh and gambol and play, Thera? Can you recall the time?"

The intense focus of his eyes prodded her to recall something specific . . . and in a heartbeat she realized he meant their time together on the riverbank . . . having a mud fight . . . romping and laughing . . . and experiencing her first full taste of pleasure. The memory ignited her anger even as it weakened her knees. How dare he drag something as precious as that moment into an argument over a horse race?

"Your people are the most diligent folk I have ever seen. They work hard . . . just as you do . . . and they deserve a bit of amusement, a chance to escape the tyranny of those wretched bells now and again."

"What right do you have to tell me what my people need?" she demanded, stalking back. "Why are you suddenly so concerned for their welfare?"

Why? It was a question with an edge far sharper than she could have imagined. His face took on the semblance of stone.

"Because in three more nights this will be my home as well as theirs," he declared fiercely. "Three more nights and they'll be my people and I'll be—" He caught himself before he said it, but not a person within hearing couldn't have finished his sentence.

Their king. It rang like a cymbal in Thera's head. He

knew about the nights, she realized. He knew that if he managed to claim them, he would have both her and the right to half of her throne. And this sojourning among her people . . . he was laying claim to her kingdom, bit by bit.

She looked at the faces trained on them in expectation. He was insinuating himself into Mercia's heart and soul the same way he had invaded hers . . . with the tantalizing sense of freedom he created all around him, with his irresistible passion for living for the moment. Her people liked him. They wanted him. He laid claim to them with only a smile and a swagger . . . and she resented the ease of his conquest, when she had spent years earning their respect and preparing to rule wisely. How could her people be so accepting of someone they knew nothing about?

Then it struck her: why shouldn't they accept him on faith? She had brought him among them and given him her passion and her nights. She was their ruler, their future queen, whose duty was to put their welfare before her own. They accepted him, she realized, in part because they trusted her. They had no way of knowing the dangers he posed for them . . . or the conflict he stirred in her heart.

For the first time in her life, she wondered if she was worthy of their trust.

When she looked up at him, the determination in his angular face made her heart quiver. When she spoke, her voice sounded strangely full.

"There will be no more horse races . . . until I say it may be so."

Saxxe watched her turn on her heel and stride back toward the city. He was unsure of all that had happened in those brief moments, but she hadn't retreated in outrage or attacked his arrogance and presumption. There was indeed hope.

In the cool twilight of her walled garden, Thera sat listening to the sound of the frogs in the nearby fish pond and smelling the delicate fragrance of lush new growth all around her. She had sent all of her attendants away the moment she returned to the palace, and had cloistered herself in her chambers to think in peace. It had taken a while, but she had managed to regard her situation in a somewhat more rational manner . . . and decided that it wasn't a particularly rational situation.

"Pardon, Princess," her page said quietly, startling her so that she turned on the bench. "Elder Audra and a number of the women elders are at your door. They say it is urgent that they see you."

Thera took a deep breath and nodded, granting them audience.

More than half a dozen women soon collected into a defensive knot before Thera's bench. Their faces were grave and a number of them held hands, as if to bolster their courage.

"Princess." Elder Audra stepped forward to speak for them. "We bring most distressing news. Hearing your impossible debt to Saxxe Rouen . . . we took it upon ourselves to search the sacred scrolls for a provision or codicil which might release you from your vow."

Thera shoved to her feet. "You did what?"

"Please, Princess, don't be angry," Margarete said, coming to peer at her over Audra's shoulder. "We could not abide the thought of you being forced to . . . endure such a fate at a crude barbarian's hands. Prithee forgive us, Your Highness . . . we meant no offense."

Thera turned away and stood tautly for a moment, staring into the encroaching purple shadows of night. She didn't know whether to be indignant at their presumption or to be grateful for their concern.

"And did you find a way?" she said, turning to study their faces. Audra glanced at Margarete and fidgeted uncomfortably.

"Nay, Princess, we found nothing to release you from your word. We found . . . something far worse."

"Worse?" Thera clasped her hands hard; they were beginning to tremble.

"Not in the laws, but in the prophecies...we found..." Anxiety progressively constricted Audra's voice until she halted and nudged Margarete to make her take it up.

"We found another prophecy, a dire one," Margarete said in somber tones.

"A prophecy?" Thera blanched and took a step backward. It had to be trouble if those wretched prophecies were involved; the cursed things were filled with gloom and portents of destruction.

"You know of the prophecy that catastrophe will befall if the heir to the throne does not marry and the thrones remain empty," Margarete continued.

"Every wretched word," Thera said irritably. "By heart."

"Well...there is yet another prophecy that pertains." Margarete turned to Elder Jeanine and held out her hand for the scroll. "We copied the words and phrases for you." She began to speak them from memory as Thera opened the scroll and stared in dread at the dim figures.

" 'The very stones weep for Mercia...for this hour of travail that comes upon her. All that was will be no more. In the days of an unmarried ruler, in the time of empty and troubled thrones...a dark and powerful prince... a man of steel, a man of blood...will come upon fair Mercia,' " Audra said in a drone filled with portent. " 'With his dark hands he will wreak destruction...with his dark heart he will work schemes and treachery among us...with his dark might he will spread conflict and chaos throughout the land. Weep for the proud mountains who have faithfully guarded the kingdom...for they will be breached...and the three-headed beast of war, famine, and disease will stalk the land...devouring the people...' "

Thera could not see the writing, could scarcely feel the stiff, dry parchment in her hands. She didn't want to hear such a thing, didn't want to acknowledge it. But it was there in her hands and in her mind.

"If you fulfill your word and grant him the remaining nights, then you will likely wed him," Audra said in a hoarse whisper. "And if you wed him, the kingdom will be in grave danger, Princess."

"How can you be sure he is the man?" Thera protested.

"He is dark . . . a man who bears steel at his side and above his heart," Jeanine said.

"He is a man of blood . . . a warrior accustomed to battle and to killing," Margarete added, biting her lip at the sight of Thera's growing distress. "And yours is a solitary bed, which leaves the thrones unfilled. The conditions are the very ones laid forth in the prophecy."

"He wants you, Princess, and will trade upon your desire for him to win a place at your side," Audra added. "If you give yourself to him, half of the throne will be his, and he will begin to spread chaos and destruction." She exchanged worried glances with the others. "There is one way to be sure: test the prophecy against whatever happens . . . watch for the signs."

"The signs?" Thera's heart stopped.

"A man is known by his works," Jeanine said softly.

The parchment began to tremble in Thera's hands.

"Princess?" Audra took a step toward her.

"Leave me, please," she ordered, shrinking back. "Just go."

As they curtsied and withdrew, she sank onto the bench, holding the parchment so tightly that it began to crumple in her hands. She had never given credence to the old prophecies, until the mounting troubles she encountered on her ill-fated journey began to seem like a punishment for her avoidance of marriage. And at times, she had to admit, Saxxe seemed like a plague the fates had set upon her. Now those feelings combined with this rediscovered prophecy to give focus and weight to her vague fears about him and his effect on her people.

A dark prince. Saxxe wasn't precisely a prince, but he was dark. And he was indeed a man of steel; he never went anywhere without his wretched daggers. And with her own two eyes she had seen him shed blood. A man was known by his works, Audra said. Well, just this morning she had caught him tearing down their forge and this afternoon he had led her people to abandon their honest work. And he had all but proclaimed that he intended to take her in marriage and, through her, the throne.

But even as the weight of circumstance joined against him, her heart rallied to his defense. He might be dark and powerful, but there was nothing sinister or treacherous about his dealings. He was appallingly open about his desire for her and for making her kingdom his. She thought of his loving, then of his smiles and how gently he had touched the children yesterday. There was a gentler side to him; he could be so very generous and tender.

The conflict between her desires and the good of her kingdom suddenly seemed overwhelming. For more than an hour she wrestled with it, pacing and thinking and laying out the facts and the prophecy side by side. But it all led her into a desperate circle of hope and doubt. What she needed was an objective ear . . . someone wise and experienced and not easily swayed by emotion or overawed by the power of the Sacred Scrolls. She turned to the one who had always advised her in times of difficult decisions; she sent for Cedric.

But her page returned from Cedric's house at the edge of the palace grounds with word that he hadn't returned home for supper. His good wife believed him to still be in the palace somewhere. Thera sent the page to search the council chamber and audience hall and private dining chamber. After a time, he returned wearing a dubious frown. The chancellor, it seemed, was in the kitchens with Saxxe Rouen and a host of other men. And when pressed about what they were doing there, the lad rolled his eyes and said that she had best come and see for herself.

Chapter Sixteen

Noise from the great, stone-walled chamber reverberated along the corridors to meet Thera as she hurried to the kitchens. She could make out voices, shouts of merriment and laughter, and there was music—the drone of vibrating strings and pipes. A billow of heat rolled from the doors, laden with odors of ale and warm bodies. She squared her shoulders and forged into the glow of burning tallow and hearth flames.

The kitchens were full of men lolling around the food-laden worktables with large metal tankards in their hands . . . drinking prodigiously, roaring crude songs, and calling encouragement to those of their company who were engaged in bouts of arm wrestling. There were her chief artisans and craftsmen, her clerks and clerics, and her leading merchants . . . laughing, shoving, and poking each other like boys truant from a priest's school bench!

She halted as her narrowing eyes caught on a clump of vivid blue to one side . . . Mattias, Hubert, Marcus, Raymonde, old Fenwick, Gawain, Arnaud, and her sensible Cedric. Virtually all of the men who sat on her council were present, and like the others, they were beet-faced with drink.

In the midst of it all sat Saxxe Rouen, crowing the words to a reedy tune . . . something about Spanish ladies with accommodating knees and squeezes, squeals, and upturned heels. A number of the others apparently knew the ditty, for they bellowed what seemed to be a refrain about rolling over and over in a patch of clover. Then Cedric took up the lyrics and sang with gusto about a demoiselle with very large ears, very big eyes . . . very broad lips and very *wide* thighs. . . ."

They were swine-drunk, the lot of them! Even Cedric. And just when she needed him most.

Saxxe spotted her first and thrust to his feet, weaving, then raising his tankard aloft. "Thera—welcome! Come an' tilt a cup with us—somebody fill 'er a tankard!"

"High-ness?" Cedric staggered about in surprise, spotted her, and lapsed into a silly grin. "There ye are! D-did ye come to wet yer whis-tler?"

Wet her whistler?

She closed her eyes.

When she recovered enough to open them, she turned on her heel and strode straight out the door.

As she lay in her bed that night, feeling burdened and abandoned and utterly alone in her fears and responsibility, she heard a sound coming from the garden outside. She held her breath and sat up, staring at the bright shaft of moonlight coming through the half-open garden doors. The sound grew louder and became a voice, and the voice became familiar.

Saxxe's ale-roughened tones floated toward her . . . surrounding her with their warmth and vitality. It was a low, melodious tune . . . a ballad. Heaven help her—it was a love song. Her chin began to quiver and her eyes stung. The lout. She didn't know if he was just drunk and lost, or if he was actually trying to serenade her.

"Curse you, Rouen!" With tears trickling down her face, she dragged a feather pillow from the head of her bed and threw it at the open door, causing it to swing shut. "Why can't I ever be sure of anything about you?"

No bell sounded the hour of Prime the next morning for the first time in anyone's memory. The church sexton had been among the drinkers carousing in the kitchens the night before, and his head was pounding so that he couldn't bear to pull the bell rope. And without the bells, the people didn't rise, the hearths stood cold and empty, the cows bawled for milking, and the shops and stalls didn't open.

Thera was livid when she heard of it, and she went charging into the great council chamber to give her wayward councilors a thorough scolding for their own less than exemplary conduct. But the few men who had managed to drag themselves from their beds to the circle of council chairs were moving as if they feared their heads might topple from their shoulders. One look at Cedric's bleary eyes and suffering expression, and she was too furious to trust herself with words.

It was Saxxe again, Lillith confirmed a short while later in Thera's chambers. It seemed that after the horse races the previous day, Saxxe and Gasquar had led the men to the alehouse in the market square and pounded on the doors until the tavernkeeper opened to them. They spent the rest of the afternoon in "celebration," and when the sun went down, Saxxe led them to the palace kitchens, where he cajoled head cook Genvieve into providing them an impromptu feast and persuaded Ranulf, the palace steward, to unlock the wine cellars.

Thera endured as much of Lillith's report as she could, then rose abruptly and escaped into the gardens.

She sank onto a bench with her hands knotted into fists. What was she going to do? Through the long and sleepless night, she had been haunted by the words of the old prophecy the women had uncovered. *Chaos and destruction.* There was no denying that his every action seemed to result in some sort of confusion and disorder in her realm. But was he the dark prince of a looming apocalypse . . . or simply a lusty mercenary soldier whose unrestrained impulses were at odds with the orderliness of her society?

She lifted her eyes to find a page standing nearby with an anxious expression and a message that the chancellor and a contingent of her elders waited just beyond her doors, seeking an audience with her. Whatever her personal trials and tribulations, the business of the kingdom was always there, demanding her energy and attention.

Preparing herself, she nodded permission.

Elder Hubert led an all-male contingent into her spacious chambers. They bowed stiffly and old Fenwick staggered dizzily when he straightened. Mattias and Gawain reached out to steady him with taut looks of sympathy.

"Princess, may I say that you look lovely indeed this morning," Hubert said with determined cheeriness.

"You may say that if you wish, Elder Hubert," she answered, leveling a daunting look on him. "But I assure you, 'lovely' does not begin to describe my humor."

Hubert's smile faded and he looked to Mattias for help. "We come with a question, Princess," Mattias said, fidgeting under her stern gaze. "We respectfully request . . ." He swallowed hard, glanced at the others, then started again. "It would be helpful to know. That is, if you could tell us . . . perhaps . . ." When he ground to a halt, old Fenwick huffed in disgust and blurted it straight out for them.

"How long till ye've paid yer full debt to the fellow, Prissy?"

The others froze. Only old Fenwick, whose advanced age entitled him to a few liberties, dared call her by the pet name from her girlhood. When she didn't erupt straightaway, they took it as a positive sign.

"That is none of your concern," she informed them in clipped tones.

"Oh, but it is, Princess," Mattias said, edging ahead of the others. "You see, there's the ceremony of confirmation and wedding feasts to arrange . . . and then the double coronation to plan. It has been many years since we crowned a king and queen. We'll need to study the records to see how it's done and . . ."

They spoke as if it was a foregone conclusion that Saxxe would claim a full seven nights with her! As she searched their faces, she was stunned to realize that they seemed none too distressed by the possibility of having a bare-chested barbarian as their king.

"I will discharge my wretched debt to Saxxe Rouen when and if I see fit to do so. Not before," she insisted.

"If?" Hubert lurched a step forward, his eyebrows rising and hovering like startled birds. "But you are honor bound to fulfill your word, Princess."

"May I remind you that my debt will be fulfilled after *six* nights, not *seven*."

"But after six nights with the fellow," courtly Gawain said in a discreet hush, "where else would you find a husband? And you must marry, Princess . . . and produce an heir."

"You would have me wed a common hire-soldier?" She drew herself up with regal indignation. "One who eats with his fingers and stalks about half naked?"

"Oh, haven't you seen? He's wearing a tunic today," Marcus interjected.

"And hose . . . very fine hose," Gawain added, exchanging nods with Marcus. "He looks quite civilized. And Robert, the bootmaker, is laboring day and night to finish a most marvelous pair of boots for him." They all nodded earnest agreement.

"And that is supposed to recommend him to me as a husband and co-ruler?" she said irritably.

They seemed taken aback by her reluctance toward the man she had already spent four nights with. Lowering their gazes, they shifted feet and smoothed their tunic fronts. Hubert finally elbowed Mattias, urging him to speak for them.

"W-well, we expected that Saxxe Rouen had already recommended himself to you, Princess. After all, he is a bold and manly fellow . . . more than passing handsome . . . and in *four nights* . . ." Mattias winced when she drew a sharp breath.

Marcus took it up. "And he is strong and capable and has an endless stream of notions in his head. He knows horses from withers to hooves . . . and masonry and an astonishing amount about weaving. And he is most generous with his help. He'll show us how to rebuild our stables and put new life into our heavy trades."

"Yea, and he's traveled the world, Princess," Hubert went on, his voice—like their hopes—rising. "He's seen

Egypt and Constantinople, the Holy Lands and the Holy See of Rome. He understands several tongues and has a whole world of learning stored in his head. He's been to the great merchant fairs and can advise our traders so they may strike more advantageous bargains."

"He may be a hire-soldier, Princess, but there is nothing *common* about him," Mattias concluded, drawing agreement from the others.

Their valiant defense of him stunned her. She looked from man to man, seeing in each one's eyes the personal hopes and longings Saxxe had somehow managed to touch. Instead of deficits and difficulties, they saw assets and possibilities in him . . . things they believed Mercia needed. They recognized his strength, his knowledge, his experience, and the natural authority of his bearing. Barbarian, hire-soldier, commoner . . . it made no difference to them. They wanted him . . . just as the rest of her people did.

"He's a strappin' great bull of a man. Never seen finer," old Fenwick blurted out, jostling the others aside as he pressed to the front and looked her over with a less than reverent stare. "But best of all, Prissy, he seems willin' to put up with you. So why not just get on with the beddin' and weddin' and livin' . . . and that be that!"

If it had been anyone but Fenwick, she would have rung down verbal flames of perdition upon his head that would have left him picking cinders out of his scalp for a week! But somehow, from withered, crusty old Fenwick, that crass exhortation sounded more like a blessing than an insult. And it struck the deepest longings of her own stubborn heart, dead center.

The part of her spirit that had been sinking in despair under the weight of the women's fears and distrust had just been revived by the men's faith and pragmatic acceptance of Saxxe. They had provided powerful confirmation of all the good things he was.

"I will give your suggestion some thought, Elder Fenwick," she said with an odd thickness to her voice.

"Now if you will excuse yourselves . . . Cedric and I have several things to discuss."

They hadn't gotten the firm answer they wanted, but at least they were leaving with hope. The elders sighed and bowed and made as dignified an exit as possible. When the door closed behind them, Thera turned to her trusted chancellor.

"I need your advice, Cedric." She beckoned him to her writing table and handed him a parchment, bidding him read. His eyes widened as he recognized the writing and surmised the probable source of the document. He lifted his head with a frown, registering a new understanding of her troubled mood.

"This is from the prophecies, I assume," he said. "Audra and Jeanine and their cohorts brought this to you, didn't they?"

"Yea, they brought it."

"They believe Saxxe Rouen is the one . . . this dark prince."

She nodded and threaded her hands tightly together as he lowered his eyes to the words and read it again. "He *is* a man of steel and blood," she said.

"He is a man of *flesh* and blood, Princess," he rejoined, raising his gaze to hers. "A man who has braved great perils to rescue you a number of times, with precious little reward. And I have always believed that actions speak louder than mere words." He let the parchment fall onto the tabletop.

"But the prophecies never err. Time and again in our past, they have sounded warnings that helped keep our people from calamity."

"Yea, but our ancestors could not have known, as we cannot know, if a given prophecy was meant for their time or another. Hindsight makes each instance seem clear and inevitable to us . . . but I doubt it was so for them. That is what I hate about the prophecies . . . the uncertainty makes them stumbling blocks to reason, logic, and decision, and sometimes allows them to be used as tools for mischief. I would burn the lot, if I could."

"Blasphemy, Cedric," she said with a gentle smile.

"So it is." He sighed. "I fear I have a most lamentable streak of the heretic in me." Then he took her by the hands and engaged her eyes with his. "Do not be afraid to decide for yourself and your people, Princess. Despite the turmoil your barbarian stirs here and there, I believe he has possibilities." He smiled ruefully. "And as Fenwick says, Saxxe of Rouen is willing to undertake you as a wife . . . and that is no small consideration."

When she glowered at him, he chuckled and, unknowingly, gave her the very same advice Elder Jeanine had.

"Give it time, Princess. His actions will prove him, one way or another."

That afternoon, Thera took Lillith and a small party of her elders and rode the length of the valley to check on the newly sprouted crops and the orchards and flocks. The weather was perfect: the sun bright and gloriously warm, the breeze light and flirtatious. For Thera, it felt good to be in her valley and among her people again.

Over and over, she dismounted to walk the land and to talk with her plowmen, orchard keepers, and shepherds . . . listening to their problems and plans. They seemed encouraged by the recent run of good weather after a freezing, wet spring that had made the early work difficult. They were unfailingly polite in asking after her health and journey, but to a person they peered around her as if searching for someone else in her party. And it didn't take much to guess who they hoped to see.

When the royal party paused by a stream that came down through the mountains, some of the women removed their shoes and went wading. Thera stood looking at the water for a while, remembering the last time she had waded. Soon her mind and heart were filled with images of Saxxe as he had been that night by the riverbank.

They started back mid-afternoon, and as they approached the city they spotted a small crowd in a pasture just outside the city proper. Drawing closer,

Thera could make out a number of young men with longbows taking aim against targets across the field.

Archery was the only martial art practiced by her people, and was encouraged more for its exacting nature and aesthetic appeal than for any military benefit. The men all possessed bows for hunting and competition, and they practiced regularly, so the sight of them in the field did not strike her as unusual until she spotted a large group at the far end of the field, near the granary walls.

Her concern piqued, she quickened her pace and rode down the closest cart path to investigate. The rest of her party followed. From horseback, she could see above the heads of the crowd to an open circle of ground in their midst, and in the circle caught sight of violent, jerking motion. The air filled with ringing metal and male shouts of encouragement.

As she nudged her mount through the spectators, she caught sight of Saxxe's dark head darting and lunging, of his shoulders twisting and heaving, then of his blade flashing in the sun. Her heart gave a convulsive jerk as he sprang to the far side of the clearing and she saw Gasquar give a mighty roar and charge after him. In less than a heartbeat, they were engaged in heated blade battle. Their faces were contorted with fierce concentration as they lunged, swung, and slashed at each other in what seemed to be deadly earnest.

Her throat constricted with anxiety. All around her stood men with bows in their hands and eyes gleaming at the sight of the battle underway. Something in the looks on their faces bespoke a hunger, a disturbing desire for the spectacle of fighting, and it rattled her to her very core.

A number of men turned to help her dismount, and she strode straight into the clearing with her fists clenched and her countenance ablaze with anger. "Stop this! Cease fighting this instant!"

Her voice and the flash of her white gown caught the edge of Saxxe's senses, drawing away some of his concentration. For half an instant his motion slowed, but the briefest moment was all Gasquar needed to penetrate his defenses. A tip of blue steel smacked hard against the bronze clasp of his belt and rasped downward, narrowly missing laying him open from groin to knee.

Saxxe twisted back and aside just in time, and the near miss startled Gasquar, who checked his counterswing to prevent further chance of injury. Staggering and panting for air, they lowered their blades and turned to Thera with widened eyes.

"Bon Dieu!" Saxxe roared. "Don't ever do that again—charge into the midst of a blade battle like that! When you broke my line of sight, you broke my concentration." But a moment later, his face lit with a fierce grin at the sight of her angry blue eyes and heaving bosom. "And I came devilish close to losing that part of me which will prove indispensable to my future sons and daughters. . . ."

The laughter his comment and accompanying gesture evoked caused her to redden, and in spite of her, her gaze dropped to the bulging front of his hose. She jerked back as if she'd been scalded, and glared at him.

"It might have served you right."

"Ah, but then I would have served you ill, sweetest." He waggled his brows, grinning, and drew nervous laughter for his audacity. His blood was running high, and the sight of her flushed, wind-tousled form turned his thoughts from military to sensual conquest.

"You have no business blade fighting in the first place, Saxxe Rouen."

"Gasquar and I were merely giving our blade arms a bit of work to keep them fit. Your men had invited us to see their archery training, and we offered to show them some blade work in return."

"Well, no more," she proclaimed. "From now on, you're not to blade fight within the borders of Mercia. I forbid it."

"You *forbid* it?" he said, leaning back on one leg and sending Gasquar an incredulous look. "What on earth makes you think—"

Pushing and jostling occurred beside them, and a number of red-faced fellows pushed through the crowd carrying what appeared to be a set of clothes stuffed with straw to resemble a man, topped with a makeshift stuffed head. Behind them Castor and Pollux, Elder Hubert's strapping nephews, loped up with their bows in their hands.

"Yer Grace—look here! Castor done it—he sunk all five shafts, dead on center!"

Unaware of the volatile scene they had interrupted, they turned merry faces and nods of respect on Thera, then hauled the straw man around so both Saxxe and Thera could see the front. The feathered shafts of five arrows were jutting from the torso of the dummy . . . exactly in the area that on a real man would have contained a beating heart. Thera gasped softly and put her hand to her throat.

"Excellent work!" Saxxe declared, clapping the blushing Castor on the shoulder. "A fine display of marksmanship."

Thera wheeled and pushed her way through the crowd, striding for the archery range. Several men, seeing where she was headed, ran before her to halt the firing. But she didn't have to cover the entire length of the field to see the straw men set up in front of the usual circular targets, or to confirm that they bristled with arrows shot into what on live men would have been arms and legs, torsos and heads. She stood staring at those substitute humans and felt a wave of weakness flooding up from her knees. She had to spread her feet to keep from swaying.

"This is your work," she charged when Saxxe caught up with her. "You had them make straw men and practice shooting at them."

He scowled, unable to fathom what she found so upsetting about a few bits of rag and straw with arrows in them.

"Yea, I suggested it. In my experience, enemies seldom come at you with red circles as big as barrel heads painted on them. I believe it's time they practiced firing at something more like a real archer's target ... something that would do Mercia more good when a defense is needed."

The shock of having her suspicion so openly confirmed left her speechless. Without a word or a nod to any rightful authority, he had taken it upon himself to begin training her men to fight with their longbows. He was spreading his combative experience with the world into their thinking, tainting their manly pleasures with thoughts of battle.

"Mercia doesn't need deadly archers ... or an armed force, or a defense of any kind. For centuries we have dwelt in safety, sheltered within these mountains, and we'll go on that way. Few outside our borders know of Mercia. And even if they did, our valley is inaccessible."

"I found my way in," he countered.

"Nay," she said angrily, "I led you in. That was a grave error. And letting you roam freely about my kingdom was clearly another. But I will not make the mistake of letting you fill my people's heads with talk of fighting and of threats that do not exist."

He gave her a tense, searching look. "Can you truly believe that Mercia is inviolable, that you are completely safe against all harm here? After what you experienced in Nantes and on the road afterward, how can you possibly think there is no threat to your kingdom? *Dieu*—have you already forgotten where I first found you ... in an alley behind a tavern ... in the hands of half a dozen Mongol-Slavs?"

The high color began to drain from her face and she took a step back. He countered with a step forward, determined to make her remember and understand.

"Can you not recall the smell of burning timber as the city was slowly plundered ... the cries of women and children in the streets?" he demanded. "Have you so quickly forgotten what happened before your very eyes to the village of LeBeau?"

Her face grew stiff and pale, her body rigid. When she did not answer, he looked straight into her eyes and saw there the tumult she refused to show before her people. The contrast of her supremely controlled posture and expression and the roiling fear he glimpsed in the depths of her eyes stunned him. His anger and frustration began to melt.

She did remember the horrors of her journey. Indeed, she recalled them all too well. Was he the only one who could see how frightened she was?

For a long moment they stood, gazes locked.

She could feel his tawny eyes probing, reaching inside her to places she didn't want to open to anyone. He had no right to see into her very soul.

But there was no other person in the whole world who could penetrate the barriers that years of training and self-control had built around her emotions . . . no other who could know the deepest doubts and yearnings of her heart. It was only for Saxxe Rouen to know her in that way . . . only for Saxxe Rouen to be the part and counterpart of her soul.

In the softening depths of his eyes she glimpsed a deepening well of understanding. He saw that she was afraid, and yet there was no condemnation in his face, no contempt, and no triumph. He simply accepted it.

Trembling, she tore her gaze from his and backed away.

"I have not forgotten, Rouen," she said, raising her chin. "And I have sworn on my honor that I will never allow any of that to happen here. The terrors and strife of the outside world will never reach past the mountains of Mercia."

She did not wait for a rebuttal; she retraced her steps to her horse. When she had mounted and was riding back to the city, the men turned to Saxxe with questions.

"What will we do, *seigneur*?" "Do we have to stop our training?" and "Can we still use the straw men or not?"

they asked. Then came the most pertinent question of all: "Is the princess right, *seigneur*? Are we safe?"

How could he answer them? He watched Thera's form growing smaller and disappearing into the city. After a moment, he sheathed his blade and flashed them a determined grin.

"The Saracens have a saying: To live in peace, keep your sword sharp. I don't know about you, but I will be here tomorrow afternoon, and each afternoon, training, practicing. I pray your princess is right, that Mercia never needs archers or weapons or warriors. But it is better to have them and never need them than the other way around."

At early eventide, just before the ringing of Vespers, Thera emerged from hearing the songs and recitations of the priests' school pupils in the audience chamber. She paused in the Great Hall for a few moments to speak with the proud parents who had been permitted to attend with her. As she complimented their children's accomplishments, a frightful noise rose outside . . . sounds of rushing and shouting. She hurried toward the front doors, then fell back at the sight of a frantic crowd bearing down on the entrance of the palace. Well before they reached the doors, she could make out Castor and Pollux, Elder Hubert, Gasquar, and Randall, the smith, at the forefront of the throng. They seemed to be straining, as if hauling something.

Cedric materialized at the edge of the crowd and came barreling through the door, huffing and puffing: "Out of the way! He's hurt—make way!"

"Who is hurt?" Thera started forward, alarmed. Then she saw Saxxe lying limp and unconscious in the arms of the group at the front of the crowd, and gasped. "*Saxxe?*" Shock froze her to the spot, so that Gasquar and the others had to shoulder her aside to carry him into the hall. Jostled back to life, she channeled her rising panic into more productive paths and took charge immediately.

"This way! Carry him to my quarters—they're closer. Cedric—show them where!" She seized one of the parents and ordered him to go for her physicians, then hurried to catch up with the men carrying Saxxe. "Is he hurt badly? What happened?"

"He was on the roof of the new smithy . . . when a plank broke . . . and he fell all the way to the ground!" Cedric panted out, bustling beside them. "Don't know how bad it is. No blood . . . but it knocked him senseless."

They carried him into Thera's sumptuous quarters, through the glass-windowed solar, and straight to the bed in her inner chamber. They deposited him as gently as possible on Thera's massive bed, then stepped back as old Esme and Thera anxiously wedged their way between to have a look at him. He wasn't bleeding, and a cursory feel of his limbs seemed to indicate nothing was broken. But the sight of him—so still and oddly pale beneath his sun-browned skin—sent a crushing wave of anxiety through Thera. He couldn't be badly hurt; he just couldn't!

By the time the physicians and the leeches arrived, she was gray with worry. The physicians insisted they slather him with pilasters and pour him full of herbal philters, but the leeches argued that he needed to be bled and purged, not sweated and stuffed. Thera lost patience with the lot of them and sent them all packing, keeping only Gasquar, Lillith, and old Esme to help tend him.

His skin grew hot and old Esme suggested they bathe him with cloths dipped in cool water. It was only then that Thera realized one of the reasons he looked so strange to her: he was wearing hose and a tunic beneath his cross braces . . . real clothes, just as her elders had said. When the cloths and basins were brought, Thera climbed onto the far side of the bed to help Gasquar remove his garments so they could bathe him. They wrestled his cross braces from him, then faced the task of removing his tunic, which had to be drawn up and over his head.

"He would have to choose today to start wearing clothes," Thera muttered as they lifted and tugged and rolled him from side to side to work the garment up and over his head. It took a while longer to remove his boots, then she and Lillith turned aside while Gasquar removed his close-fitting hose and covered him strategically with the linen sheet.

Saxxe's eyelashes parted to reveal slits of canny gold, and when he saw only Gasquar working over him, he opened his eyes completely, startling his old friend. In a blink, he grabbed Gasquar's wrist and signaled him to remain silent with a finger against his lips. When he nodded toward Thera and grinned, the Frenchman's scowl of confusion melted into a lusty grin of comprehension.

"Finished," Gasquar declared a moment later, and Thera and Lillith turned back to the bed. Saxxe's eyes clamped shut once more and Gasquar wagged his head and stared in admiration at his wily friend. Trust Saxxe to find a way to turn a potential disaster into an opportunity for pleasure. "Sacre Mere—I have seen such things before. It may be hours, even days, before he wakes. But he must have water, and when he begins to burn he must have the cool cloths. Perhaps we should take watches . . . to sit with him through the night."

"I'll take the first watch," Thera said. "He's in my bed and . . . I couldn't sleep a wink, anyway." She glanced at Gasquar, then Lillith. "Both of you . . . go and get some rest. I'll call you if he stirs."

With Gasquar and Lillith gone, Thera sent Esme on to her own bed, promising to call the old servant if she was needed. Then she sat alone, watching his slow, shallow breathing, praying with all her heart that he would be all right. All of her distrust of him and all her fears for Mercia faded beside the thought of losing him. Whether to death or to the world outside Mercia's borders if he someday left her . . . it would be like losing a part of her very body and soul.

After a while, she dribbled some wine between his parched lips, then retrieved a vial of rose-scented oil to soothe them. Her moist fingertips floated from his mouth along his bronzed cheeks, stroking and comforting, then trailed lovingly down the corded column of his neck and across the heated mound of his chest. He was so strong, so vital . . . she touched him to comfort herself as much as him.

In the darkness inside Saxxe's head, every sensation was magnified. Her touch was like living fire, spreading across his shoulder and chest . . . then curling around his nipple . . . lapping that sensitive peak again and again. It was exquisite sensual torture.

She felt the catch in his breathing and looked up. His eyes opened and struggled to focus on his surroundings, coming to rest on her.

"You're awake!" she exclaimed softly, her anxiety melting in a hot surge of relief. It was all she could do to keep from throwing her arms around him. "Are you in pain? Where do you hurt?"

"My head," he said in a hoarse whisper.

"Here?" she said, running her fingers over his temples and back through his softly tangled hair, searching. "Or here? You do seem to have a lump." Her fingers found a swollen place at the base of his head and massaged gently, wringing a moan from him.

"My shoulder, too," he said. When she ran her hands experimentally over the sun-bronzed shoulder nearest her, he closed his eyes and swallowed hard. "No, the other one." She began to gently massage the powerful muscles with delicate fingers.

"I don't feel anything . . . perhaps it's just bruised."

Her body was arched over his, moving rhythmically as she kneaded his shoulder. From his vantage point below, he had a delicious view of the curve of her unbound breasts and the tantalizing strain of the silk across her roused nipples. He watched those erotic peaks jiggle and press against her tunic, and some of the heat rising in his blood began to settle in his loins.

"And my ribs," he whispered, touching them with an artful wince.

She slid her hands down his chest, pressing tender-
ly . . . sending quivers of pleasure through his belly and
loins. He grabbed handsful of the coverlet and groaned
softly. "And my . . . hip."

Ahhh, such biddable fingers, he thought, adrift on a
warm sea of anticipation as her touch skimmed his side
and dipped beneath the linen sheet covering his hips. If
only the rest of her were as accommodating. If he had
guessed she would be so concerned for him, he might
have arranged a fall from a roof earlier. The feel of her
cool hands just inches away from the burning center of
his desires registered in his loins with a jolt, and she
paused mid-stroke.

At some point her concern for his health had dissolved
in a rising tide of sensual nuance. She was suddenly
holding her breath, aware of every aspect of her body
in relation to his: the exact distance between her breasts
and his chest, the heat of his body radiating into hers,
and the tangy male scent of him . . . the softening of her
body and the subtle hardening of his. His skin seemed
to grow hotter beneath her hands, and her eyes were
drawn to the lengthening ridge rising up the center of his
belly . . . just inches from her fingers.

Hidden behind a veil of lashes, her eyes traced that
elongating shape, remembering the satiny texture of it,
the pulsing muscularity of it, the exquisite searing heat
of it imbedded in her depths. She blushed and ripped her
gaze away, only to have it catch in his. And the dark glint
of his eyes said he had seen the direction of her eyes and
knew the drift of her longings.

His hands shot from his sides, seized her shoulders . . . and she was toppling onto the bed, across
him, before she could blink. "Ohhh! Sa-axxe—" In
that same smooth motion, he rolled onto his side and
slid her onto the bed next to him. She found herself
on her back with her legs draped over the side of
his hip. He shoved up onto one elbow and pulled
her against his bare chest, grinning like a devil.

"Y-you—but you—" It took her a moment to understand the gleam in his eye. "You're not injured!"

"Ah, but I was. You felt the lump on my head," he said with a low, seductive laugh that rumbled through her body. He seized her hand and raised it to his mouth, pressing a kiss on her palm. "Your hands seem to have banished the pain. Such marvelous hands." He kissed her wrist, then her elbow. "Ummm . . . such lovely arms." He pressed a kiss onto one of her breasts, nuzzling its hardening tip with his nose. "And such wonderful breasts. *Dieu*, woman, you're a feast!"

She opened her mouth to protest, but he quickly pulled her closer, covering her lips with his. His kiss went on and on . . . so soft and liquid, and relentlessly tender . . . impossible to resist precisely because it could be so easily overcome. His gentleness called forth powerful longings in her . . . enticing her to give, to complement that possession which allowed room for a free response. Her whole body began to tremble with need for the completion and certainty she found in his arms.

He began to stroke her with long, leisurely caresses that made her want to hold her breath at the end of each one, praying there would be another. She quivered under his touch and arched into his hands, demanding more . . . a firmer possession, a claiming touch. And he knew the time had come.

"Give me this night, Thera," he said softly against her kiss-swollen lips.

"And what will you give me if I do?" she whispered, her eyes shining. "If I recall properly, you still owe me four pleasures."

He laughed softly. "And you dare call me profit-minded." He rolled onto his back and pulled her atop him, so he could have both hands free. "You'll have your pleasures, Princess . . . and then some."

Chapter Seventeen

Thera's gown and thin chemise were soon a heap on the marble floor and her silken slippers lay in far-flung corners of the chamber. The silk cords and strings of pearls that had bound her braids were lost in the rumpled bed covers. Saxxe ran his fingers through her hair, loosening it, draping it about her body like a veil . . . trapping a handful of it over her breast and caressing both at once.

Sinking onto the bed beside him and into another voluptuous kiss, she both recalled and experienced sensation . . . his moist lips sliding across her closed eyes, nibbling her ears, and parting to string soft, tonguing kisses around her throat like erotic jewels. Excitement unfurled in her like a dew-drenched blossom opening her senses, rousing each nerve to hungry expectation under his hands.

"The kiss is yours . . . and the caress. And the joining will come. Now you'll learn the fourth pleasure," he whispered with a wine-potent stare that made her breasts ache and her womanflesh feel hot and empty. Then he shifted slightly onto his back and took both of her hands in his. "The fourth pleasure is *taking*."

She pushed up onto one elbow, frowning, and his stare muted into a sensual smile. "You have learned what pleasure is. Now learn the ways it can be done. Take what pleasure you want of me. Take my heat, my hardness, my strength . . . take what is mine and make it yours."

He could see the surprise in her face and feel her uncertainty in the stiffening of her frame. With a knowing look, he kissed each of her hands and placed her palms against his chest, covering her hands with his.

"How do you want to touch me? What parts of me would you explore and claim? What kisses do you want?" His voice dropped to a sultry, compelling rasp. "Take them, Thera. To discover this pleasure you must *take*."

Still she hesitated, and after a moment he nudged her head toward his . . . offering his mouth. And she took it. With a depth of hunger that she hadn't known she possessed, she claimed his lips . . . licking, nibbling, teasing his tongue, raking his lips gently with her teeth.

Somewhere in the midst of those feverish kisses her hands began to move over his chest and up his neck, molding to his shape and caressing him, raking him lightly with her nails . . . exploring the textures of his skin. Soon her kisses drifted down his throat and across his chest.

Pleasure cascaded through her as she gave her desires free rein over his marvelous body. Dimly she began to understand what this was about . . . it was *her* desires that drove their loving now. In *taking*, she was learning what she wanted . . . exploring her passions as she satisfied her need for him. And that insight set her free.

Sliding sinuously atop him, she fitted her body to his—reveling in the contrast of their shapes—and began to undulate against him, drawing helplessly responsive movements from his roused frame. She rubbed her breasts down his stomach, gasping at the erotic friction of hair against her nipples, then caressed his hip, his swollen shaft, and his thighs with her breasts. Then she nuzzled the soft-skinned expanse of his inner thigh, and kissed her way up his leg, his belly, and his chest.

"Saxxe," she whispered hoarsely, the flame in her body visible in her eyes as she rubbed her womanly heat against his rigid staff. He knew what she wanted, and it took every particle of his self-control to keep from pulling her beneath him and giving her exactly what she was asking for.

"Take what you want, Thera," he managed, on an inrushing breath.

"But . . . I . . ."

"Claim me. You're very close . . . just claim me." When she gave a soft moan of frustration, he put his hands on her waist and guided her hips downward on him.

Suddenly she understood. Parting her thighs to accept him, she lowered herself slowly, moaning as her body yielded and accepted the heat and hardness penetrating her. Then she stilled, steeping in the liquid sensations, luxuriating in the spirals of pleasure radiating from her body's core. She held him within her, had claimed him . . . had taken him in that most exquisitely primal way.

A new sense of power flooded through her, more rousing than even the lush delights her body was experiencing. She met his eyes, then slowly pushed herself up on her arms, above him. The sight of him lying naked between her thighs, with his flesh imbedded deeply in hers, was wildly intoxicating.

She moved her hips and watched his eyes close and his body tense. Slowly, more purposefully, she rounded her hips again and again. Wave after wave of pleasure crashed over her, pushing her to breathtaking new levels of excitation. She straightened farther, so that she sat upright on him. With every seductive movement of her hips, she pushed his control toward its ultimate limit . . . aware that she was reaching her own limit as well.

With a soft moan, she stretched out on top of him and sank her arms beneath his shoulders, inviting his arms around her. Together, they began to move . . . long, languid strokes that propelled them both higher and faster along a tightening spiral of sensation. All motion seemed to slow, and she plunged, body and soul, into a breathtaking storm of sensation. And as she burst free of sensory bonds, she felt his body gather and arch, then convulse beneath hers.

"Saxxe—oh, Saxxe—now I know." She sighed as she floated on a sea of release, not knowing whether she spoke aloud or not. "Now I know."

It was some time later, when they were lying relaxed and sleepy in each other's arms, that her words finally righted in his mind. "What is it you know now?"

"Why *taking* is one of the seven pleasures," she said languidly. "And I know I've never been happier than I am right now. And I know you're the cause."

He grinned recklessly and drew her close against him, dropping a kiss on her forehead. "I am? I make you happy? Are you sure I don't make you furious or suspicious or embarrassed?"

It was said lightly, but there was a serious undercurrent in his tone. She looked up at him with a soft-eyed smile. "Of course you make me furious . . . and suspicious . . . and even embarrassed, sometimes. But you also make me feel warm and wanted and complete in ways I never imagined possible." She ran a finger down his breastbone and felt him shiver. "Who are you, Saxxe Rouen, to come charging into my kingdom and into my heart like this?"

"Your heart?" he said in a hush.

"My heart. I died a thousand deaths tending you this evening. I was so afraid you would die and I'd never have a chance to—"

His face nearly split with a triumphant grin. "To what? Tell me." He caressed her hip warmly, coaxing her to say it, needing to own her love.

"To do this again," she said, rocking onto her elbow to place a gentle kiss on the corner of his mouth. "Or this." She ran her tongue around the sworl of his ear, wringing an eloquent shiver from him. "Or this." She laid her head on his chest and nuzzled until she found just the right place, then she wrapped her arms securely around his waist. Then, after a few moments, her grip loosened.

When he raised his head to look at her, her eyes were closed and her breathing was settling into a slow, predictable pattern. He laid his head back and closed his eyes with a smile. Before long, he had joined her in sleep.

Hours later, Thera awakened to the sensuous feel of a big warm body curled around hers. The lamp was flickering low, slowly abandoning everything to shades of gray and deep midnight blue.

When she stirred, her hip brushed the fully erect column of his manhood, and she froze. His hands slid inquisitively over her breasts and down her belly. She responded with a languorous arch of her back . . . which thrust her breast more fully into his hand. His unasked question was answered without words.

"Ready for the Fifth Pleasure, I see," he murmured hotly in her ear. His fingers toyed with the sensitive tips of her breasts as he coaxed her passions to ignite again. The flame was not long in catching. She slowly turned in his arms and reached for his kiss.

"The Fifth Pleasure. And what is that?" she whispered.

"*Giving*," he said, rolling onto his back and carrying her atop him again. "As you took pleasures . . . now you must learn to give them." His voice flowed out of the darkness around her, alluring, compelling . . . pure temptation. And the quivering resonance it created in her body must have been akin to what Eve had felt in the Garden of Eden. It was utterly irresistible. "How closely have you been watching?" His voice set her ear humming. "Do you know what will give me pleasure?"

Without a word, she pushed onto her hands and knees astride him. Her tousled mane transformed her into a voluptuous animal, set to devour him. Shaking her hair, she set it tumbling over him like a silken shower. She flexed and swayed so that her body brushed his, ever so lightly, and he inhaled raggedly as her nipples raked his chest and jolted as the liquid heat of her femininity slid across his swollen shaft. The sight and feel of her undulating above him was wildly arousing.

Then she lowered her mouth to his, kissing and nibbling his lips, and began to suck his tongue with soft, rhythmic motions that imitated the way her body would soon demand his. Every square inch of him caught fire.

"My wicked little cat," he groaned as she writhed erotically against him. "You did pay attention, after all."

She had indeed absorbed his every sigh and shiver of response, but it was not memory that now directed her body against his. With a feminine instinct older than memory itself, she simply did for him what had given her such intense pleasure. And it was more than enough.

In the play of hands, the weaving of limbs, and the heated press of bodies, his arousal mounted quickly. She curled over him like a sleek, silken pet . . . rubbing, teasing, bringing him to aching hardness . . . then slowly engulfing his heat with her responsive flesh. With each rise and fall of her hips, he felt the pressure build until he couldn't see or speak, could scarcely breathe. And when the tension grew overwhelming, a jagged bolt of pleasure shot through him, exploding up his spine and searing along his nerves . . . to the very ends of his body.

In a sensual haze, he rolled Thera onto her back and continued his deep, penetrating strokes, raking against her throbbing center until her fingers dug into his back and she arched and stiffened, flung past all sensual limits. For a time she was insensate . . . lost to sight and sound and even touch.

For a time they drifted together, not speaking, content just to be in each other's arms. But even as exhausted as she was, she had no desire to sleep.

"Did I do it right?" she finally said, rubbing her nose against his lightly stubbled chin. "Did I *give* the way you wanted?"

"Umhmm."

"Everything?" she said, teasing, propping her chin on her fist to look at him.

He looked into her love-weighted eyes and had to speak the truth. "Let's just say it was all I'd hoped for and a good bit more. *Everything* will take more than just one night, I'm afraid. We greedy barbarians are notoriously insatiable."

"Oh?" she flirted with him through her lashes. "And what more could I give you, greedy barbarian? More kisses? More caresses? I could hardly give you more enthusiasm. . . ."

"You could give me your trust."

The instant he said it, he knew it was a mistake. But his defenses were down and his longings were too near the surface to suppress. It was what he wanted . . . perhaps more than anything in his life.

Those simple words struck Thera's thoughts like small stones, catching her unawares with their sting. She started and sat up, feeling an edge rising in her. "Trust? A strange request, I believe, considering I've just given you my body and my passions . . . and my heart."

"Part of your heart," he said. "The private part, the woman's part. And greedy barbarian that I am, I want it all . . . the princess part as well."

She looked into his glowing golden eyes and shivered at the raw determination in him. The stormy pleasures of the night had blown through her emotions, sweeping away her old defenses and leaving her with no refuge and no weapons against his honesty.

Abruptly she rolled aside, but he caught her by the arm and held her. "Nay, this time you cannot flee. I would settle this between us, Thera. You make me your mate and lover in the cloistered darkness of your bed, but you dread the possibility that someday I may walk with you in the light . . . as your husband. Why else, except that you do not trust me?"

"My reasons are my own."

"You trust me with your body and your passions, but will not trust me with your people. And until you do, until you share your kingdom with me willingly, I will not have your whole heart, Thera of Aric. There will always be a part of you that doesn't belong to me." He rose onto his knees and overcame her resistance to take her by the shoulders and turn her to face him. "I know how you watch my every step . . . how you try to prevent my contact with your people . . . how you mistrust my efforts to help them."

"You call tearing down the forge and disrupting the marketplace and getting my councilors drunk being help-ful?" she declared, trying to squirm away. "You think teaching my men to shoot arrows at human targets will benefit them?"

"Yea—I do!" he roared, hauling her back and imprison-ing her against his chest. "Your people must learn to defend themselves and their land, and since you will not—nay, you *cannot*—teach them, then I'll do it for you. Mercia needs a new forge, a garrison, fortifications, a number of improvements in the stables . . ."

He halted, staring into her angry face and understand-ing the distrust there in a new way. She could do noth-ing about the defense of her kingdom; she knew nothing about arms and strategy. She was used to doing every-thing for her people herself, and the thought that they might need something she couldn't give them terrified her.

"I swear to you, Thera, you don't need to protect them from me. Can you honestly believe I would ever willingly hurt you or your people?"

She didn't want to believe such a thing, but the longings of her heart were at war with her obligations to her people. Was he her heart's desire or her kingdom's destroyer? Or both? Long-suppressed doubts came roiling up, and she began to tremble.

"I don't know what I believe about you," she said in a desperate whisper. "One moment you're a fierce, hard-bargaining mercenary; the next you're a tender, larcenous rogue who steals my senses and my people's affections. You boast openly of your greed, you ignore every standard of civilized behavior, and you tell whop-ping lies when the truth would suit better. You won't say where you're from—I don't even know with certainty that Saxxe Rouen is your real name." Tears welled in her eyes and clogged her throat. "How can I give you any more of me when I may have already given you too much?"

His fists clenched and his face burned with frustration.

"What would you believe? I rescued you and brought you home . . . I kept my word . . . I cared for you. Everything that is important to know, you already know about me. What proof can I give you, if you will not accept the honesty of my actions?"

Searching the depths of her tear-rimmed eyes, he could see her pained longing for him . . . and he could see that it wasn't enough.

"Damn it!" He released her and rolled from the bed, pacing furiously. Then he stopped, looked at her for a long moment, and began jerking on his hose and jamming his feet into his soft new boots. The fierceness of his motions and the determined set of his features alarmed her. She swiped at her eyes and snatched up a sheet to shield herself as she slid to the side of the bed. But as she reached for her clothes, he lunged for her and scooped her up into his arms.

"Wa-ait! What do you think you're doing?" She dragged the sheet over her, trying to cover herself as he carried her toward the doors. "Put me down— no! No! Have you lost your mind?"

Panicking, she began to squirm and push against him, but it was no use. He kicked open the door, then strode briskly along the colonnade toward the Great Hall. He carried her through the main chambers of the palace and down the east corridor to his quarters. Once inside, he slammed the door with his foot and dumped her in the middle of his bed, snarling an order for her to stay put if she valued her hide. Struggling to wrap the sheet around her bare body, she saw him throw open the trunk at the foot of the bed and pull out one of his leather saddle pouches.

In the dim morning light he came to stand by the bed, looming dark and powerful above her, his eyes turbulent and his jaw muscle twitching. "You want to know who I am? I'll tell you. I am Saxxe Rouen, born Saxxe de Challier, sixth son of the Earl de Rouen . . . the youngest of three who survived to adulthood. My father controlled an estate much dwindled and impoverished by the bold thievery of water from our streams. He had no inheritance for me, no money or influence to send me to foster elsewhere . . . and so made me his own squire. He was a wily old man—strong as an ox and twice as stubborn. He taught me well the skills of fighting . . . then sent me off at sixteen, spurless, into the company of knights pledged to King Louis the Pious . . . bound for the Holy Lands. He gave me a mount and a sword and an order not to come back without spurs.

"I went with King Louis to Alexandria and Damietta and I fought hard and well." He reached into the pouch and drew out the golden spurs, one in each hand. The glimmer of pain in his eyes took her breath. She knew without hearing; they were his. Shame burst hot against her skin as she thought of her arrogance that day by the stream, and of her continuing blindness to the truth about him. Her eyes stung and a hard lump formed in her throat.

"I received them at the hands of the king himself, after the battle at Damietta. And when the Crusade ended and Louis disbanded his knights, I proudly carried these home. . . ." He paused and drew a harsh breath, struggling for control as old memories boiled up inside him.

"Only there was no *home*. In the king's absence, a long-standing rival had provoked a fight over the water rights and killed my father and my elder brother . . . and in the regent's court had taken the land and castle of Challier for damages. My only remaining brother had sought refuge in an abbey with the monks. As a royal knight, I petitioned the king for relief, asking that he set aside the judgment and allow me to reclaim the land, so that the title might be preserved in our line." His hands tightened around the spurs. "But the king had his own problems with greedy nobles and moneylenders and an angry pope; he could not, or would not, be bothered with what he deemed a petty land squabble.

"Such was my reward for honorable and valiant service." He raised his head. "I ripped the spurs he had given me from my boots . . . and I never looked back."

The sight of his pain seared through her tears. She wrapped her arms around her waist, desperate to comfort him but afraid he would not accept it from her now. He was a knight, the son of a nobleman. But somehow that mattered less than the fact that he had opened the rest of his life to her and entrusted her with his past.

"The rest you know. I roamed . . . and fought . . . and sometimes bled. And more often than not, I received the same reward Louis had given me for my troubles. Noblemen have short memories for their promises, I soon learned." Her face burned with shame as she thought of their early encounters and of how she would have escaped her own debt to him if she had found the chance . . . how after all he had done, she was still reluctant to give him his due.

"When my belly grew lean and my face gaunt, I learned to demand payment in advance and to guard my investment until I was fully paid. If that makes me greedy, so be it. I left behind the trappings of knighthood when I renounced my loyalty to Louis. But it is not so easy to leave behind the lessons of knighthood." His voice became a pained hush. "And I never could seem to resist . . . a demoiselle in distress."

As he stood there, his spurs glinting dully in the gray morning light, he realized he had come to a crossroads, but the path he would follow was not his alone to choose. He reached out a hand to her, and after a pause, she laid her hand in his and he helped her to her feet at the side of the bed.

She stood looking up at him, wrapped in a sheet and a mist of sadness. She was a woman, his woman. But she was also a princess, ruler of a people, whose heart was not fully her own to give. He understood that, for the first time. And since she could not freely give her whole heart, he would have to earn it.

"I am a knight without a lord," he said quietly, stroking her cheek, allowing the love that blossomed in him to unfold in his face for her to see. He stood before her as a man and touched her as a lover. And the next moment he went down on his knees before her as a knight. Laying his spurs at her feet, he looked up into her shimmering eyes.

"I offer you my loyalty, my strength, and my heart, Princess Thera of Mercia. I will be your knight. I will fight for your people and make their lives like my own. I swear before God—as I love both Christ and you—that I will dedicate myself to your well-being and theirs . . . that I will uphold and defend you with the last drop of my life's blood. You have only to accept this offering to make me your servant for life."

The next moment seemed the longest in human history. It was the bravest and most foolhardy thing he'd ever done, laying his heart and his future at her feet . . . for he had no assurance that the love growing in her was strong enough to urge her to accept him, even in the role of a knight.

As I love both Christ and you echoed in her heart. She heard the rest, but it paled by comparison. Saxxe loved her. He was offering himself to her, pledging himself freely to her and to Mercia.

She stooped and picked up the spurs, and watched the joy that flared in his expression as she kissed them and clasped them to her breast.

"I accept you, Saxxe Rouen," she said in a voice thick with feeling. "With all my heart, I accept your loyalty. I have no other knights. I want no others. Only you." She placed his spurs back in his hands and curled his fingers over them. "Wear them now . . . for me and for Mercia." She could have sworn his eyes glistened with moisture.

"And with all my heart, I treasure your love. For I love you, too, Saxxe Challier de Rouen." Taking one step, she slid her arms around his shoulders and pulled his head against her breast, holding him tightly. His arms flew around her waist and he held her as well.

For a long while neither moved or spoke. That embrace celebrated something newly born between them . . . a beginning, a new way of being together, a new understanding. And though there were things as yet unsettled between them, from now on there would be no question that they were committed to each other and to Mercia.

He finally raised his face to her. "You love me—you said you love me!" He shoved to his feet, carrying her up with him, and whirled her around, laughing, until his feet tangled in the sheet. He halted, then toppled joyfully back onto the bed with her, kissing her, making her say it again and again . . . and repeating it back to her in a litany that could only be a prelude to loving.

"You realize what this means, my princess?" he said, nibbling her neck. "You have to pay to feed both me and my horse. A liege lord is always obligated to give a knight his keep."

She laughed, a low throaty sound that was like music in his ears. "Then, Heaven help me . . . I'll be beggared before the year is out!"

Lillith looked worriedly at the brightening dawn sky as she hurried along the colonnade toward Thera's chambers. She had been so tired and had slept so soundly that she had slept right through the start of her "watch" over the injured Saxxe Rouen. But when she arrived, she found the door to the outer chamber ajar, the bed empty and well-tossed, and Thera's clothes next to Saxxe's tunic on the floor. It could mean only one thing.

She rushed through the Great Hall and down the east corridor to Saxxe's chambers. She delicately tried the handle, but the door latch had been thrown. She listened and heard nothing, so she put her ear to the door and tried again.

"Still at it, eh?" Gasquar's voice startled her. She jumped and turned with a fierce scowl on her face.

"I went to take my watch at his bedside and found—"

"What I also found this morning," Gasquar finished for her, rubbing his chin out of habit, though his beard was long-since gone. "Evidence of a long night of loving. Your princess . . . she must be a most excellent physician, to have cured him so quickly."

It was an inescapable conclusion; Thera and Saxxe had spent another night together and were now ensconced in his chamber. But for the moment, Thera's amorous indulgence seemed less important than the fact that Lillith was staring into Gasquar LeBruit's bare face and really seeing it for the first time. He had smooth, broadly sculptured features, a generous mouth, and a square but noble jaw.

It took a moment for her to realize that he was coming closer, and then she staggered back a step and smacked into the doorpost. Within a heartbeat, his arms were braced on either side of her shoulders and his thick, muscular body was leaning lightly into hers. A rosy flush of excitement rolled up from where their bodies met into her face.

"*Mon ami* Saxxe, he prefers the slow pleasures. Perhaps I can help you find a way to pass the time, eh?" And he leaned still closer and covered her lips with his.

She jerked her head to the side, breaking that contact, and stared defiantly at him. But there was more amusement than irritation in it, and a moment later she was lost in the dark promise in his eyes.

He did not move. He just stood with his battle-hardened body pressed against her softer frame . . . letting the heat rising between them soften her resistance. And when he felt the tiny downward shift of her body that signaled the melting of her will, he lightly caressed the sides of her breasts and waist, and his hands come to rest on her hips.

She drew a hot, quivering breath as he touched her, then she reached for his mouth with hers. He pressed her back against the wall, and she shifted to mold her body closer to his. It went on and on, until her blood pounded in her head and her body grew hot and her bones seemed to weaken. She was scarcely aware when he lifted his head and turned it slightly.

"*Sacre Mere*—have you people nothing else to do with your mornings?"

Her eyes popped open, and she found herself facing a contingent of elders. They were staring at her in bald shock. She closed her eyes with a strangled moan and wished she could melt down the wall and slither away.

"Countess." Cedric's voice sounded a little choked. "We went to the princess's chambers and found . . ." He halted, but she already knew what he'd found. "What is your count, Lillith of Montaigne?"

Without opening her eyes, she held up five fingers.

And when the word went out from the palace . . . *Saxxe Rouen was now five-sevenths king* . . . weavers and tradesmen left their shops, looms, and workbenches, and women left their stew pots and laundry. The taverns threw open their doors mid-morning, in his honor, and there was dancing in the streets.

Chapter Eighteen

That evening, after Vesper bells, Thera invited her Council of Elders to dine with her in her private dining chamber. They arrived to find Saxxe, Gasquar, and Lillith present as well. Saxxe was wearing a sendal green tunic trimmed in gold silk cording, matching hose, and elegant knee-length boots. He cut a fine figure as he greeted the male elders with sober nods and the female elders with somewhat stiff, but obviously heartfelt, bows. And when Thera called Saxxe from his seat far across the circular table to come and sit at her left hand, not a person he passed on the way failed to notice that he was wearing a very fine set of golden spurs.

Somewhere in the night just past, a major transformation had occurred both in Saxxe and in their princess, the councilors realized. Thera was more relaxed and her countenance was notably sunnier, especially when her gaze fell on Saxxe. And Saxxe seemed infinitely more civilized and assured in his new guise . . . though there was still a rogue glint in his eyes which made some wonder how far those changes extended beneath his surface.

The first test of his new persona came when the serving began. With the image of his former gluttony burned into their minds, all watched as Saxxe began to eat and drink in exemplary—if somewhat self-conscious—moderation. He shared an écuelle with Chancellor Cedric and exercised marked restraint when serving himself from the food platters. Even Thera seemed relieved when Cedric proposed a toast and Saxxe raised his cup with everyone else and drank in a perfectly noble fashion. But the greatest shock came at the end of supper, when Thera rose with a queenly smile and an announcement for the council.

"I would have you know . . . from this day forward, Saxxe Rouen, son of the late Earl de Rouen, shall be known as a citizen and a knight of Mercia . . . sworn to uphold and defend Mercia and her people."

The elders sat stunned for a moment, then reaction broke over the chamber. The men banged the tables and shouted cheers of welcome, while the women turned to one another with widened eyes, then quickly set up a murmur about what it all meant.

But elders Audra, Margarete, and Jeanine didn't have to guess; the significance was all too clear to them. It meant Saxxe Rouen was a great deal closer to being their king, and according to the prophecy, it meant the doom he would ring down upon Mercia was that much closer as well. Through the rest of the serving, they sat with accusing expressions that reminded Thera of those dire words of portent: " . . . a dark and powerful prince . . . a man of steel and blood . . . will spread conflict and chaos throughout the land . . . the people will be scattered . . ."

As soon as the serving ended and entertainment began, Audra and her party excused themselves from the company in silent protest. Thera watched them go with relief and dread . . . until Saxxe's tawny-eyed smile relieved her uneasiness.

Between the minstrels and the dancers, a handful of men appeared at the chamber door asking for Elder Hubert. He excused himself, only to return moments later with a scowl and a group of sheep herders at his back, fingering their felt hats as they gawked at the splendid chamber. "Your Grace, the shepherd Rouset and his men have come with unsettling news. I have asked them to lay their tale before Saxxe Rouen and Gasquar LeBruit." When Thera nodded and waved the dancers to wait, Hubert led the party forward. Saxxe and Gasquar rose to meet them, and the fellows jerked nervous nods as Hubert bade them speak.

"My sons and me, we tend th' high meadows. This day, we come across two of our young sheep . . . dead. In two different spots, near a mile apart. An' they wasn't taken by no animal. Cut clean up the belly . . . wi' th' guts flung aside an' just one haunch missin' on each. Ain't no animal I know what does that. Not any wi' a taste for sheep, anyway."

"Nay, a wolf or cat would eat the guts first," Saxxe said, crossing his arms and stroking his smooth chin. "Cut, you said? Someone was probably hungry and decided to take one or two of your flock."

Rouset scowled and looked at Thera, then at Elder Hubert. "That's what I tho't. But nobody in Mercia need do such a thing . . . not wi' house an' hearth nearby. We all got plenty o' food."

"An' the fire—tell 'em about the fire," the youngest shepherd, Rouset's son, urged.

"We found an old fire . . . wi' grass tramped down an' nary a stone set to guard the flames. It weren't one o' ours," the shepherd declared. "We alwus lay our night fires in the same places . . . and alwus use a ring o' stones."

Hubert frowned and rubbed his forehead. "Killing sheep and building fires . . ." He looked to Saxxe with a knotted brow. "What do you make of it, sir?"

"It sounds as if you may have a visitor in your hills," Saxxe said, and his words blanketed the chamber with silence.

A number of eyes flickered toward the walls of the chamber and the hills beyond. An unseen visitor. One who wastefully slaughtered their sheep at will. A chill went through the room like a night breeze.

Within the hour, Saxxe, Gasquar, and Hubert and his two nephews were riding with the shepherds into the hills to investigate. Thera suggested they wait until morning, but Saxxe and Gasquar insisted that the darkness might help them see a campfire, if indeed there was someone in the hills. They went for their cross braces, daggers, and swords, then joined the others and rode through the valley by moonlight, retracing the route by which they had entered Mercia.

After a while, they climbed into the wooded hills and left their horses at the shepherds' cottage in one of the high meadows. Rouset showed them the carcasses. The sheep had indeed been slaughtered, and Saxxe and Gasquar outlined a plan to separate and scan the meadows from the cliffs far above, looking for signs of night fires. They agreed on signals, then spread out and began to climb the cliffs. After more than two hours of searching, it was Pollux who spotted an odd glint of light high in the woods, above the city, and retraced his tracks to signal for the others.

Their hearts were pounding as they crept down the forested hillside toward the ridge overlooking the city. From this vantage point Saxxe could see almost all of Mercia: the unwalled city, the lush valley dotted with clusters of cottages and byres, the orchards and fields extending in each direction. It was so beautiful, so peaceful, and so disturbingly vulnerable. A shiver raced through his shoulders at that thought, and his face set with determination.

Their goal indeed proved to be a campfire . . . with a lone figure sprawled nearby. Motioning the others to keep to the safety of some boulders and brush, Saxxe and Gasquar began to stalk the intruder in a broad circle, watching his movements, keeping their eyes peeled for others. Closer and closer they stole, with daggers drawn.

From across the way came Gasquar's signal that he was in place. Saxxe curled his shoulders forward, took a deep breath, and went charging out into the small clearing. His quarry reacted with lightning speed, rolling toward a blanket spread nearby, then onto his feet . . . with a snarl on his lips and a blade glinting in his hand. Saxxe had fleeting impressions of a dark countenance and feral eyes, before the intruder charged with practiced fury. Saxxe dodged, then struck back, raking only air with his dagger.

The intruder struck repeatedly, then whirled aside and in a heartbeat was repositioned and ready to strike again. It was the very strike-and-roll strategy that Saxxe himself favored in close fighting, precisely because it was so difficult to defend against. His sizable opponent was obviously no stranger to hand-to-hand combat. Feinting, Saxxe lunged in the opposite direction, catching his opponent off guard. At the last instant he twisted aside and Saxxe's blade narrowly missed his shoulder. In the dim light, Saxxe pressed ruthlessly forward, forcing the intruder to retreat until his heel caught on a large branch and he pitched backward onto the stony ground.

Saxxe was on him in an instant, wrestling, grappling with his upraised dagger, then finally driving his arm to the ground—where Gasquar's booted foot pounced on it, trapping it. As quickly as it had begun, the flurry was over.

"Who are you?" Saxxe panted, scarcely able to restrain the large form beneath him. But the intruder jerked his bearded face aside and spit. "What are you doing here? Are there others?" Saxxe grappled to hold him, realizing that he was large and muscular, and that the dull *chink* that had tugged at his senses during the fight was the subtle rattle of mail. That didn't surprise him; everything about the fellow's quick responses bespoke a soldier's experience.

Gasquar cut strips from the blanket to bind the intruder's hands, and when he was secured, Saxxe dragged him closer to the meager fire to get a look at him. The skin prickled on the back of his neck.

That swarthy face with its closely cropped beard and those dark, sullen eyes seemed familiar. But was that because he had seen this man before somewhere, or because he had seen hundreds, or perhaps thousands, of him in military camps and taverns all over the known world?

"Who are you?" he demanded again. "How did you find your way into the valley?" But even as he said it, he knew he would get no response. An experienced soldier never divulged his circumstances or betrayed his comrades to an enemy, and Saxxe could see many seasons of experience in the craggy face glaring up at him. He turned to Hubert and the others, who were emerging from the bushes.

"No sign of horses or others," Saxxe said, drawing a harsh breath. "Still, soldiers seldom travel alone. He would have no reason to be here unless he were looking for something." Something to steal? Something to raid? Or Mercia itself? Had someone learned of the little kingdom's existence? "We'll search the area before heading back. Then we'll take him to the palace and find a way to loosen his tongue."

From a higher vantage point on the ridge, Juan watched his captain, El Boccho, being hauled away and congratulated himself on having detected the strangers as he was returning to camp. They hadn't spotted him earlier and he had had time to hide in a shallow stone crevice covered by bushes. When they gave the area another search, he pressed deep into the crevice and they passed by him, unaware, yet again.

He waited in the rock hollow until the city dwellers had snuffed the fire and departed, then crept out and gathered up what belongings he could. By moonlight, he struck off for the tree line where he and his captain had left their horses.

As he hurried along, he realized that his burly captain's wretched luck would likely prove to be his own good fortune. They had spent the last three days exploring the hills and had discovered an easier—albeit more lengthy— route into the valley. A fat reward awaited him if he could carry that information to the Duc de Verville and lead him into the kingdom. Yea, it was a stroke of luck indeed that El Boccho had sent him on the thankless chore of gathering wood. He would have to remember to thank his ruthless captain . . . if he ever saw him alive again.

It was nearly dawn before the search party returned to the palace. It had been a long and sleepless night for Thera and the council, and as soon as her page came running to her chambers with word that Saxxe and his party had returned, she donned her surcoat and hurried to learn what had happened.

She found the elders collected into an anxious knot in the Great Hall, waiting for her. By dawn's light, she led them out to the arched portico in the front of the palace . . . where they stopped stock-still at the sight of Saxxe and Gasquar dragging a trussed but thrashing form from the back of a horse. Thera steeled her nerves as they wrestled the booted, mail-clad stranger forward and Saxxe forced him down on his knees before her.

"Here he is. The one who did the sheep killing," Saxxe declared, tightening his grip on the neck of the intruder's mail tunic. "We saw no others, but that does not mean there were none. This one is reluctant to talk"— he looked at Thera, then Cedric and Hubert with a flinty expression—"but we can soon remedy that."

As Thera and her elders looked on in widening shock, Saxxe seized the grizzled intruder's bound arms and wrenched them sharply higher behind his back. "Where are they . . . your comrades? Tell us now and save yourself the ordeal of having your tongue loosened." When the fellow growled and doubled over in pain, the elders covered their gasps and averted their eyes.

"Please sir!" Cedric lurched forward at Thera's side, clasping his hands.

"That will be enough!" Thera declared tautly. As Saxxe looked up, there was a stony cast to his chiseled features that added to her distress. During the long night just past, her worry over the outcome of their mission had been equaled by her worry over the fact that her people had taken this problem straight to Saxxe . . . without so much as a by-your-leave to her. It was a small but telling transfer of power, and through the night she had wrestled mightily with the conflict it generated in her.

"It is not necessary to break his arms in order to make him speak." She addressed the swarthy, bearded prisoner herself. "How did you get into our valley? Where do you come from?" But as the elders looked on expectantly, the sheep killer refused to answer, ignoring her demands with a smirk.

"He'll not tell you anything of his own will," Saxxe insisted, wrenching the thief's arm a bit higher so that the smirk disappeared with a jolt. "But a few breadless days in prison will persuade him." He looked to Hubert. "Where is your dungeon?"

"Dungeon?" Hubert said with a stricken look. "We have no dungeon."

"Imprisoned and denied bread?" Elder Audra said, stepping forward. "We could never treat a visitor in such a fashion."

"He's not a visitor, he's an enemy," Saxxe said forcefully. "Look at him . . . there's not a drop of repentance in his miserable carcass. He killed two of your sheep and would have taken more if we hadn't caught him, and he may have friends hiding in the hills, ready to take more than sheep from you." His voice dropped to an ominous rasp. "It is well-known that wolves run in packs."

A number of eyes darted anxiously toward the distant rim of the valley as Saxxe's words finally had some impact. But even the male councilors were loath to see danger in the presence of just one man.

"Is that true?" Thera demanded of the prisoner. "Are there others in the hills?" His only response was to drag his gaze insultingly over her body.

"Perhaps he was simply lost. He might have strayed from the trading road and stumbled into our valley," Audra said, edging closer to Thera. Several nods lent credence to the possibility.

"Yea—it has happened before," Elder Jeanine reminded her. "Years ago."

A murmur of agreement followed, and Saxxe watched them edging closer to the prisoner, more curious than concerned. They had no idea of the calculation and treachery that were daily facts of life for men in his old trade.

It struck him: they approached this hardened soldier with the same innocence and good faith that had led them to accept him without question. This was undoubtedly the way they would deal with the rest of the outside world as well . . . with endearing but potentially disastrous eagerness for the new and different.

"The others may not understand, but surely you do, Thera," he said with a compelling gaze, willing her to see the danger. "He is a soldier, seasoned by years of battle. Look at the blade marks on his armor." He pointed to the prisoner's battered mail tunic and the weapons Gasquar held out in evidence. "Look at the marks of use on his long blade and daggers. If he will not speak, it is because he has something to hide. And what else could it be besides his comrades . . . and their plans?"

Thera wasn't sure what she understood. She only knew that the sight of this fierce, sullen stranger in her kingdom sent a chill into the very marrow of her bones. And when she looked at Saxxe just now, she saw a tough-minded soldier . . . a man whose experience of the world had taught him to see all other men as potential adversaries. And she understood too clearly that the strength she was drawn to in him was very much a part of the volatile power that she feared.

"What I see," she said with regal deliberation, avoiding Saxxe's glare, "is that thievery has occurred. Hungry or not, this man has secreted himself in our valley and killed our sheep. Until we can be sure . . . we will keep him under lock and key, as we would any lawbreaker amongst us."

When the prisoner was locked away, Saxxe and Gasquar led Castor and Pollux back into the hills on horseback to search for other intruders. For Thera, the day seemed interminable, and when night fell and they still had not returned, the darkness of her bedchamber filled with restless whispers of recent passion, present uncertainty, and fears for the future. But when the sun rose the next day, golden and glorious, Lillith brought word that Saxxe and Gasquar had returned empty-handed, and the anxieties of the long night evaporated.

Relieved, Thera plunged into the tasks of governance . . . the ordinariness of which served to underscore her determination that nothing had changed in her kingdom.

Even as things returned to an uneasy peace in Mercia, the Spaniard Juan was making his way down out of the hills carrying word of its existence to the Duc de Verville. The duc's restless army of barbarians and mercenaries was always on the move. But to find them, Juan knew, he only need follow the trail of wrecked villages in the foothills and lowlands.

It was dusk of the second evening when he rode up a windswept knoll and through the still-smoldering wreckage of a village to reach the stone keep of the duc's latest conquest. He found the duc's captain, Scallion, near the doors to the old lord's hall, and the captain questioned him, then dragged him through the hall and into the old lord's bedchamber to repeat it all to the duc.

"One of the Spaniards with El Boccho, *mon duc*," Scallion said, thrusting him forward and onto his knees. "Tell the duc what you discovered."

"The woman in white . . . she comes from a kingdom in the highest mountains. To the north and east."

"A *kingdom* in the mountains?" De Verville rose from the bed, his eyes burning, and waved away the body servant who tried to wrap him in a robe. "All of those lands, all the way to the sea, belong to the Duc of Brittany." He came to stand over the little Spaniard with his fists clenched and his face reddening.

"But I swear, *mon duc,* I have seen it all with my own eyes!" He gestured with two fingers toward his eyes. "It is a rich valley, with a small city and marble palace. The people dress in samite and silver, and they have fat cattle and many sheep . . . and the storehouses of their grain overflow." Beads of sweat appeared on his forehead as the duc reached for Scallion's dagger and drew it with a threatening gleam in his eye. The duc's reputation for cruelty and for liberally sharing plunder were what kept his army of jackals together.

"I swear, *mon duc!*" Juan continued nervously. "El Boccho and I, we crept through their city at night to spy it out. It is rich . . . but more important, it has no walls, no ramparts"—he swallowed hard, praying his information would appease his dark master—"and no garrison."

Interest flared in de Verville's eyes as he glimpsed honest fear in the little Spaniard's face. "No garrison . . . you mean to say, no soldiers?"

"None, *mon duc.* We saw only three or four men with sword or daggers . . . the others go unarmed. They have only a small forge . . . and make no armor."

"Then how is it this rich, unprotected 'kingdom' is unknown to us?" the duc sneered, laying the dagger blade casually atop Juan's shoulder.

"It is well hidden in the mountains . . . all but impossible to reach. We stumbled across the passage in. And while there, we searched out a second entry . . . easier but farther away and still difficult."

"And just how far away is this hidden jewel of a kingdom?"

"Two days' ride," Juan said, swallowing hard. "It is not so far, but the terrain is steep and difficult. I can take you there. You can see for yourself."

De Verville slid the edge of the blade to his spy's throat and watched the growing terror in his eyes. If the wretch was telling the truth, as he seemed to be, then de Verville had found the means to implement all his plans and schemes . . . a kingdom of his own, high in the mountains, inaccessible, secure enough to exist without walls. A base from which to raid and conquer . . . a natural fortress and retreat in which to enjoy the spoils of his future campaigns.

And it came with a lovely princess to slake his passions and bear him sons.

The duc withdrew the blade, and the little spy nearly melted with relief as he turned to Scallion with a pleased expression. "Take him out and feed him well, then bring him back to me. We must pry every detail about this little kingdom from his head, so that we may develop a proper plan of attack."

That same evening, as Thera was emerging from the church after Vespers, the head stonemasons and carpenters asked her to come and see their progress on the forge's new hearths. She was surprised to hear that they had been laboring day and night and that the construction was proceeding at an astonishing rate.

Taking Cedric and a number of the other elders, she strode through the market square in the lowering light. A shout of laughter from an opening tavern startled her and she turned, expecting to see Saxxe. Instead, one of her townsmen was standing with his fists on his hips and his feet spread in a blatant imitation of Saxxe's characteristic pose. As she paused and looked around the square, it struck her that she was seeing his bold manner and unbounded vitality in the men's swaggers and energetic talk, his sensual assurance in their seductive banter with the women. And it was certainly Saxxe's beard she spotted in the lengthening stubble on a number of their chins!

She knew that aliveness of being, that grander-than-ordinary way of experiencing the world. It was exactly what she felt in his presence. And she didn't know whether to be glad they chose to emulate the extraordinary man she had brought among them, or to be terrified that they would follow his aggressive male example too closely.

By the time she reached the forge, she scarcely heard the smith's and the head mason's glowing reports. She nodded and frowned thoughtfully and feigned appreciation of the impressive size and excellent construction of the rising stone hearths. But internally, she kept seeing and hearing Saxxe as he stood beside the half-destroyed hearths, declaring that they needed bigger, better, and more ironwork. And before she knew it, she was agreeing to allow Randall to take on several more apprentices.

"A thousand prayers of gratitude for you, Highness!" He beamed. "I cannot tell you how hard it is to keep up with the work with only two lads." He turned to share the news with his current apprentices and found them missing. "Where's Gaston . . . an' that sluggard Robert? Robert!" he roared, loud enough to awaken even the laziest apprentice.

"Ain't here, Randall," said the head stonemason, nearby. "They're off with the others . . . trainin', remember?"

"Training?" Thera asked with a frown. "Training for what?"

Randall gave the head mason a silencing look, flushed, and lowered his eyes to his boots. "Just . . . trainin', Yer Grace."

They were keeping something from her, and their dread of her disapproval sent a rush of alarm through her.

"Where?" she demanded.

In mere heartbeats, she was bound for the fields at the heart of the valley. Halfway there, she met Lillith hurrying up the road, on her way back to the palace.

"I was just coming to get you!" Lillith called, running to join her. "It's Saxxe and Gasquar. They have a number of the young men and they're—"

"Training," Thera finished for her, without breaking stride. "They're teaching them some sort of wretched mayhem, you can depend on it." Lillith nodded breathlessly and fell in beside her. "Why is it every time I yield him an inch," Thera said with a groan, "he takes a blessed mile?"

A wild clamor of voices and sounds of wood striking wood drew them across a fallow field. There they discovered scores of Mercia's young men hidden among the trees near the stream . . . paired off and endeavoring to knock each other senseless with stout wooden poles.

In the thick of that chaos Saxxe and Gasquar were striding back and forth . . . fairly vibrating with unspent physical tension. Both had stripped off their tunics and wore only hose, boots, and daggers as they shouted advice and snatched staffs from the men's hands to demonstrate hand placement, footwork, or thrusts.

"Watch your opponent's eyes to anticipate his swing, and begin yours an instant later . . . catching him on the back side of his swing," Saxxe declared, demonstrating a vicious-looking blow that stopped a hairbreadth from its wide-eyed target. "Go for the knees, the groin, and the face. On an armored soldier, those spots are most vulnerable to a staff. Once he's down"—he demonstrated by tripping a fellow and jabbing the end of the staff toward his shocked face—"use the end of your staff in his face . . . and he's out of the battle."

He was teaching them to hurt and even kill . . . preparing them for battle. And after she had forbidden it! Fury rose like black bile up her throat. She charged in, ordering the combatants to halt and calling Saxxe's name above the roar of the fighting. He whirled with the staff in his hands and she saw him brace at the sight of her.

"Thera!" he said, flicking a look around him as he lowered the staff in his hands and turned to meet her. "What are you doing here?"

"Seeing for myself your latest outrage," she declared, planting herself several feet away with her back rigid and her hands clenched. His heated male presence crowded her senses as he came to her, but she refused to retreat.

"I warned you, Rouen—no more fighting."

"No more *blade* fighting, you mean," he corrected.

"One and the same," she insisted, growing steadily more furious with him.

"Nay—it is not. You forbade me to take up a blade, and that is an entirely different thing. It takes years of training to wield a proper blade, and your lads have neither the steel nor the years required to learn to use it. Gasquar and I are teaching them the rudiments of the staff instead." One corner of his mouth crooked up. "And they're taking to it like ducks to water. Want to see?"

She nearly choked. "I didn't come to watch—I came to *stop* it! You will halt this madness this instant and send them all back to their work and their families. And you will cease encouraging my subjects to engage in brute violence!"

In the fraught silence that followed, his half grin faded. "With all respect . . . I'll do no such thing. Whether you want to believe it or not, Mercia's days of isolation are numbered. Already you have had one intruder, and there will be others. Someday, perhaps soon, Mercia will face the greed and violence of the outside world, and I will not stand by and watch as lives and homes are destroyed. Two nights ago I took an oath pledging to defend Mercia, its ruler and its people," he said with rising heat, "and I intend to honor that vow."

"Mercia is not in danger," she said fiercely, angered by his reminder that her own acceptance of that vow had given him a place in her realm and a part of *her* authority. And just look how he had used it! "And even if we were in peril . . . these are my people and defending them is *my* task!"

"And just how do you intend to do that, Princess?" he demanded harshly, his patience stretched to its limits. "By offering your enemies half of your treasury to go away? By locking them all in your granary and feeding them a fatted calf until they grow so fat they burst?" His eyes narrowed. "Or perhaps you mean to just *talk* them to death?"

His comment was sharper than he intended. It shot straight to the vulnerable core of her doubts and fears like a steel-tipped arrow. How could she defend her people? She gasped as her long-suppressed anger, fear, and confusion exploded. She snatched the oak staff from the hands of the nearest trainee and swung it at Saxxe. He scarcely had time to bring his own staff around to intercept the blow.

"What in Seventh Hell are you doing?" he exclaimed. But she came at him again, swinging with surprising force. He fell back and countered her blow, still scarcely able to believe she had attacked him. But his disbelief evaporated as the end of her staff smacked into his upper arm, jolting his nerves to the familiar edge of battle readiness. "Thera!"

"My people are peaceable and gentle and loving," she shouted, swinging at him again and narrowly missing the side of his head as he ducked. "I'll not have you corrupting them with your lust for fighting!" Bettering her grip on the thick pole, she used the side to push him back through the gathering crowd. "I won't let you make Mercia into an armed camp . . . or drag us into battles just because you see enemies behind every rock and bush!" She swung again, and when he parried her blow, the vibrations rattled her teeth.

"We don't need weapons!" She swung again, struggling to control both the heavy staff and her own reeling emotions. "We don't need soldiers . . . or walls or city guards or garrisons. You will put down your weapons for good—all your weapons—and stop this wretched talk of fighting . . . and danger . . ."

The dazed fury in her face blunted Saxxe's own ire. He had never seen her like this, so volatile, so out of control . . . not even in the alleys of Nantes after he rescued her from the Mongol-Slavs. Her eyes were blazing, her frame trembled, and she hurled commands like javelins.

Commands. The realization struck him like a pail of icy water: she was absolutely terrified. And suddenly it all made sense.

He dropped back, dodging her next blow. Then as the backswing took her arms out of the way, he flung his staff aside and launched himself at her, ripping the staff from her hands and sending her flailing backward. He caught her by her surcoat, braced his legs, and just kept her from hitting the ground. Then in a reverse movement, he pulled her upward, ducked under her stomach, and lifted her up onto his shoulder.

The men cleared a path for him to his horse and stood in amazement as he heaved her sputtering, wriggling form across his saddle and climbed aboard with her. He had to get her away from her people and palace, he knew, to settle it once and for all. Over his shoulder, he called, "Gasquar—make them practice!" Then he gave Sultan the spur.

Chapter Nineteen

He rode straight for the high pastures tucked in the forested slopes at the far end of the valley. When he reached a placid meadow, shielded from the rest of the kingdom by tall, graceful trees, he decided it was as good a place as any and reined up. But if he had expected that the jolting ride had pounded some of the fight from her, he soon learned better. When he lifted her from the saddle, she groaned, gasped a breath, and delivered a healthy kick to his unprotected shin.

"Owww!"

"Let me go—this instant!" She wrenched and twisted so that he clamped both arms fiercely around her and caught one of her feet tightly between his knees. "Blackguard . . . barbarian," she panted furiously. "Do your worst, Rouen—you don't frighten me!"

"Something damn well does!" he roared, struggling to maintain his grip on her as she wrestled beneath him. "Stop it, Thera—you know I won't hurt you. Stop!" She seemed to slow for a moment, then resumed her struggles with even more force.

With an unexpected wrench in his arms, she managed to bring her knee up between his legs, and when he groaned, she broke free and bolted. After the flash of pain subsided, Saxxe gulped a breath and charged after her. Her panicky strides were no match for his long, powerful legs, and halfway across the meadow he caught up with her and snagged the billowing train of her surcoat. In desperation, she released the clasps at her breast . . . leaving him lurching for balance with a handful of silk and wool.

He growled in surprise and tossed the garment aside to race after her. This time when he caught up with her, he grabbed both her gown and her. She squirmed in his grip, and when he saw how she doubled up to escape him, he released her and let her topple to the ground. The next instant he had her pinned on her back beneath him.

"No—get off—get away from me!"

"Look at me, Thera," he ordered, panting as he struggled to maintain the upper hand. He released one of her arms to force her face back to his. "Damn it—look at me! What are you so afraid of?" He felt her gasp and flinch as if she'd been hit.

"I'm not afraid!" she shouted. "Not of anything, Rouen. Not you . . . or the warring that runs in your blood . . . or the blue steel that you wear like a second skin . . . or the way you spread disorder and confusion throughout my kingdom. I'm not afraid of pillaging Mongol-Slavs . . . or dark hordes burning villages in the countryside . . . or prophecies . . . or intruders lurking in the hills . . . or of watching the men of my people being turned into killers. I'm not afraid of anything, Rouen. Noth-ing"— her voice broke and emotion seeped through the cracks to clog her throat—"nothing at a-all." She strained her face away, fighting back tears. "I'm a crown princess, a ruler, a future queen. I can take care of my people. It's my duty. *Mine.* My responsibility to defend them."

He lay braced above her, watching her grapple with her fears, understanding her struggle with such intensity that it was almost physically painful to him.

Events were mounting like floodwaters around her; the fate of her kingdom was reeling further and further out of her control. And of all possible dangers, that terrified her most . . . losing control . . . being helpless when so many others depended upon her. The possibility she might not be able to protect her people was too horrifying for her to admit even to herself.

"You cannot defend them, Thera," he said with quiet urgency. "At least not by yourself. You wield a mean staff, but not all enemies come at you honorably and fairly, face-to-face. And not even the mightiest warrior can fight on all sides at once." He turned her face back to him and held it between his hands. "Your councilors are there to help . . . your people are eager to learn how to defend themselves and their lands. And I am here with you, Thera. You're not alone in this."

"I'm responsible," she said, averting her eyes. "I'm their ruler, the one they look to. It's my duty, not theirs. . . ."

And not his, either, she meant. His throat tightened. In that moment he would have given his very lifeblood to banish that fear from her heart.

He slid to the ground beside her and wrapped her in his arms, closing his eyes. He knew only one way to get past her defenses. He lowered his mouth to hers and a tremor of pleasure raced through his senses . . . part his, part hers. And that involuntary response told him exactly what he needed to know.

He poured his mouth over hers, kissing her softly, then deepening the contact, searching for her passions. His hands began to skim her body . . . moving over her shoulders and soft breasts, down the curve of her waist and across her woman's mound . . . calling forth her desires. He had to make her forget her fears and their differences for a time, and to that end he summoned every weapon in his sensual armory.

She slowly warmed to his potent touch, and her feeling of being trapped gradually transformed into feelings of being surrounded, then sheltered, by him. Her senses began to clear, and awareness of him seeped through her garments into her very skin. A responsive wave of dry heat fanned through her and she slid her arms around him, opening to his kisses, claiming the promises of his passion. Her fears receded into the past and future, leaving her only the present . . . this moment with him . . . this enveloping pleasure.

Through the deepening charge in her senses, she felt him lift his head and heard him groan. When he released her and rolled away, she opened her eyes in confusion and found him lying beside her in the fragrant grass, looking at her.

"I just recalled . . . I'm a knight now." His mouth curled ruefully. "It would be unforgivably improper of me to make love to my sovereign. Unlike barbarians, whose code of conduct permits them a great deal of latitude in choosing who to seduce and ravish, we knights are constrained by strict standards of courtesy and chivalry. Ladies of exalted rank are to be worshiped from afar, and crown princesses, I am quite sure, are completely out of the question." He swept her with a sultry, dark-eyed look that felt like a brazen caress.

"I fear that prohibits my giving you pleasure, Princess." He gave an artful sigh. "Unless, of course, I was *commanded* to do so. A knight is obliged to put the commands of his sovereign above all else."

She sat up, at a loss for how to respond to his outrageous suggestion. She couldn't tell if he was taunting or tempting her with it. Her confusion must have shown on her face, for he shoved up on one arm and gave her a small, knowing smile.

"Tell me, Princess . . . what would you have me do?" He leaned close and let his lips hover over hers, a hairbreadth away. She could feel their heat like a phantom touch. "Command me . . . I'll obey," he murmured hotly against her skin. "I'm yours, Princess."

She couldn't speak as he added the persuasion of his hands . . . spreading them over her breasts, close but not touching. Then he stroked her shoulders, caressed her waist, pleasuring her with only the warmth of his hand, a touch more sensuous than full contact might have been. She licked her lips and leaned toward his hand, but he withdrew just enough to maintain that agonizing distance. She reached for his mouth with hers, but he drew back just enough to prevent her from pressing her lips against his.

She sat upright, her face scarlet, her body burning with frustration. He meant it, she realized; he would not touch her except by her expressed command. And as she gazed into the provocative heat of his eyes, she understood that it was meant to be part of the pleasure.

"Kiss me, Saxxe Rouen," she whispered, unable to say it louder. She was used to giving commands, but this one felt different . . . strangely decadent.

"By your command, Your Highness. How does my princess wish to be kissed? Lightly, warmly, wetly? With open mouth or closed? With tongue or—"

"*Dieu*, Rouen! Just kiss me!" she choked out. He smiled and kissed her softly, sweetly, and all too briefly. She licked her bottom lip and frowned. "Again please . . . only longer." He did kiss her longer, warmer, but with his mouth closed. When her tongue darted over his lips, seeking inward passage, it found none. That, apparently, required a different command.

"Curse you, Rouen—" she muttered, feeling her face catching fire. "Give me your tongue." And instead of the tide of humiliation she might have expected, she felt a delicious flare of excitement deep in her breasts and loins as he complied. It was a lush, intoxicating kiss, but something—she realized—was still missing. She reached for his arms to draw them around her and they refused to leave his sides. She pulled back, frustrated.

"Do I have to command your caresses, too?" she said irritably.

"Yea, Princess." His eyes glinted. "But that shouldn't be hard for you. I believe you like giving orders." A knowing smile tugged at his mouth.

She narrowed her eyes, deciding to shock him into more sensible behavior. "Very well, then"—she tossed her head—"caress me." A moment later his fingers closed over her breasts and she gasped as he stroked and massaged them to exquisite sensitivity. Her body melted back onto the grass and his hands followed her down. "My nipples—they burn. Rub and caress them." And soon she looked up into his dark, seductive countenance and commanded: "Use your mouth as well." He fastened his mouth to each breast in turn, and teased and suckled her through the fabric until she writhed with pleasure. Her whole body seemed to vibrate with each flick of his tongue, and she yearned for the feel of his mouth against her bare skin.

"My clothes," she said, sitting up, then rolling up onto her knees before him. "Take them off." At her demand, a jolt of excitement went through his eyes. He sat patiently in front of her, working the laces, then peeling the fabric from her heated skin. When her top was bare, she didn't have to be coaxed to tell him what she wanted. "Kiss me . . . here," she said, lifting her breasts, offering him her tingling nipples. This time his arms slid around her without being bidden.

A shameless and exhilarating sense of power filled her as he claimed her breasts. It was a collection of feelings she had never even imagined: limitlessness, freedom, potency, and desirability . . . all a part of her new sense of control. He was indeed her servant in that moment, bent to her pleasure will by his own choice. He gave her that power over him.

Soon the rest of her garments were shoved down her hips and she stepped out of them and over him with a husky command. "Lie back, sir knight. And let us see just how obedient you can be."

Standing over him, she savored the bronzed sprawl of his body between her feet. "Give me your daggers," she ordered. He hesitated, but then obliged, handing them up to her. "And now your belt and boots." Tossing them aside, she sank onto her knees, astride his thighs, and began to untie his hose.

Naked, her skin bathed in the rosy light of sunset, she stripped him and then stretched out atop him. "Ummm . . . you have a wonderful body, my dutiful knight. Lie very still." She wriggled and rubbed provocatively until she felt his trembling and heard his half-audible moan. Then she paused and demanded with an opulent purr: "Pet me."

Somewhere in the flow of heat and hands and whispered commands, the margin of power narrowed between them. When she groaned, "Fill me, Saxxe . . .

now," it was half command and half plea.

From that moment on, no verbal commands were needed; he fluently read the language of her body's responses and complied with its every demand. Long, slow strokes lifted her on fluid waves of sensation . . . higher . . . until she held him tighter and urged him faster. Then she plunged into a wild, sweet spiral of release that bore her earthward, toward the source of all her pleasures. And she clung to him and uttered one last command.

"Come with me . . ."

They lay together for a long while, luxuriating in the steamy heat that coursed through their sated bodies. Thera looked up at the invading blue of the oncoming night and breathed deeply of the scent of the grasses, the damp earth, and the meadow flowers. Scarcely a month before, she would have been outraged at the suggestion that she would make naked, abandoned love in a wild meadow at sunset. She stretched luxuriously, then looked up to find him watching her.

"Am I still your princess?" she said with a siren's smile. He laughed softly.

"You are that, Thera of Aric. And a good bit more."

"Good," she said, sitting up, then pushing to her feet. "Then I command you to stay right there . . . don't move a muscle until I say so."

She strode out of his sight and returned a short while later, settling near his head, just out of his vision. When he tried to look, she scolded him. When he demanded to know what she was doing, she just laughed mysteriously and told him he would find out soon enough. As time dragged by and she still refused to let him look, both his skin and his curiosity began to itch.

"The grass is getting wet . . . and scratchy."

"Almost finished," she said, and he groaned. "Very well . . . you can turn around."

He was up on his knees in a single catlike movement and turned to find her sitting among the lush grass with a lapful of plucked blossoms and a plaited ring of pale flowers in her hands. Her bare body glowed and her eyes shone in the moonlight. She was breathtaking, a vision from his numerous dreams of her. He staggered to his feet and pulled her into his arms. Kissing her with all the joy and tenderness at his command, he lifted her off her feet and turned around and around with her. Somewhere in that dizzying kiss, she managed to recall the ring of flowers in her hand and pulled back enough to say: "Stop . . . put me down. I made this for you."

He set her on her feet, and when she ordered him to kneel, he went down before her. She ran her fingers through his long hair to tame it, then placed the coronet of flowers on his head and kissed each cheek with sovereign grace.

"Rise, Saxxe Rouen . . . Prince of My Heart," she proclaimed. And lest there be any confusion as to the title she was bestowing on him, she clarified it: "Prince of My Whole Heart."

He caught her hands and held them tightly, searching her features in the pale light and finding them filled with love. Her whole heart. She was making him her mate, her equal. His laugh was tinged with wonder. "I never expected to have a title of any kind in my lifetime. And now I've gone from barbarian to knight to prince in a space of days." He kissed her hands, then her lips. "Prince of Your Heart. No other title in the entire world could bring me more pleasure, Thera of Aric . . . Princess of My Dreams."

They stayed in the meadow for a while, lying on a bed of garments, kissing and caressing, sharing memories and experiences, and luxuriating in this new feeling between them. After a time, they dressed slowly and started back to the palace, holding hands as they led Sultan along the trails Thera knew by heart. Descending into the valley, they strolled along a path toward a haze of brightness. It was the orchards, still in bloom, glowing in the moonlight.

"This way," he said, tying Sultan to a tree and pulling Thera down a well-grazed path between the apple trees.

As they wound their way through the rows, the moon-brightened blossoms created a disorienting illusion of snow. Despite the wane of the blossoms and the setting on of fruit, there was a lingering sweetness on the air, and Saxxe halted and drew breath after breath, letting it seep into his blood.

"I love orchards. When I chased you through the trees that first day I could scarcely believe my eyes. I've never seen such blossoms. Do you know ... on my father's lands there was a large orchard. It was always my favorite place. But after they stole our water and the stream was gone, the land itself seemed to dry up and we couldn't save the trees. Other things became more important." He ducked under one especially full tree, leaning on one of the low, broad-reaching branches. Looking up into the boughs, he smiled bittersweetly.

"I've always wanted an orchard."

"Now you have one," she said, her eyes shining.

He wheeled to look at her with tension in his frame. "I do?" When he saw the smile on her face and realized what she was giving him, he burst into a huge grin. "So I do. Prince Saxxe. Prince of Thera's Heart ... and of one perfectly marvelous orchard."

He ducked under the limb and grabbed her hand, pulling her along as he ran from row to row, laughing, enjoying the otherworldly delight of the moonlight on the blossoms. When they both were panting, he stopped and turned to her with an enchantingly wicked grin.

"Prince Saxxe, eh? Perhaps I should try out some of my new powers." He reeled her closer and placed his hands on her shoulders. Even in the moon shadows cast by the branches, he could see the luminous glow of her eyes. She had just given him the key to the other half of the lesson she so desperately needed. He prayed it would be enough.

"Kiss me, Thera." The sensual command of his tone sent a trill along her nerves. Orders usually flowed in the opposite direction ... *from* her, not *to* her. She found the feeling of being compelled interesting and a little unsettling. After a moment, she reached up on her toes to wrap his neck with her arms and give him a full, sensuous kiss. "Ummm . . . very nice. Another please."

This time, he drew her head toward him and met her lips and body with his. He wrapped her in his arms and kissed her with such intensity that it left her breathless. The flow of passion between them resumed as if it had never been interrupted. In just a few kisses, her knees grew weak and her body pliant.

"Your clothes, Princess. Take them off for me. Now. Here."

She felt a delicious tension rising in her. He ordered her to disrobe for him . . . to please him. The thought both shocked and titillated her. After a moment, with a bit of self-consciousness, she began to obey. Her surcoat, her sleeves and top laces went, and soon she was able to pull the long, loose-fitting tunic over her head. She paused, standing in her knee-length chemise . . . and he waved a hand to it.

"That as well. And slowly. I want to watch your body move."

Ah, there was something powerful in this change of roles between them . . . something that made her hands tremble, her breasts harden, and her loins ache. And she made the odd discovery that to obey could be a very pleasurable thing as well. His voice came again, stroking her, invading her.

"Bring your clothes and spread them on the ground by my feet."

She shivered and did as she was told, each movement exaggerated, as if in a dream. And when she had spread them and raised her eyes to him, she guessed what came next.

"Now lie down on them, Princess."

Obediently, she sank onto her knees, then stretched out on the pale silken garments . . . expecting that he would join her. She lay half in moonlight, half in shadow, and when he didn't move, she wondered if she should open her arms to him. Suddenly he stepped over her and seized two of the largest branches above him and began to shake them.

A shower of petals fell like snow all over her, shimmering in the moonlight. She cried out at the sight and feel of them ... dusting her body and sliding down her sides ... blanketing her with their feathery softness ... as delicate as snowflakes but no strangers to warmth. They clung to her body and nestled in her hair, and still they came ... a shower of tenderness ... an exultation of love. And as the frantic motion of the branches stopped and the last petals floated down to caress her, he stepped into the moonlight, his eyes glowing like coals.

She watched him descend on her like a great snow cloud, dark and forbidding outside, but filled with the rarest and most delicate gifts inside.

"Soft to soft is drawn ... nature's softest satin for woman's softest skin. You are my princess, my woman ... and I'll dress you always thus, in my mind." He lowered his heated body to hers, crushing a thousand tiny petals between them. He ran his hands over her arms and shoulders and face, able to tell her skin from the blossoms only by its warmth.

The years of deprivation had finally ended for his starving heart, and now he kissed her hungrily, demanding the sustenance of her passions, craving a surfeit of her love.

"Open to me, Thera. Let me take you ... more than just your body ... your desires, your hopes, your dreams."

She arched and moaned beneath him, her body suddenly feverish and seeking.

"Give me the riches of your heart as well as your passions. I want your trust, your faith ..."

She tried to bring his lips back to hers, but he slid them to her throat, then to her breasts, and she groaned as his mouth found her.

"Give me the control you cling to like a savior ... let it go ... let me take you ..."

She was on fire. His words were burning into her mind and heart . . . while her hips undulated beneath his and her woman's heat rubbed against his swollen shaft, coaxing, imploring.

"I am your *khamsin*, Thera of Aric . . . the wind of your desires, the force of your destiny. Don't be afraid. I will sweep you up and hold you in my heart forever. Surrender to me . . . let me take you . . ."

There was no more resistance in her. What he wanted, she wanted to give . . . all of her . . . even that most vital possession, her precious self-control.

A low, desperate cry rumbled up from her depths . . . half surrender, half entreaty. And when he drew back and joined their bodies, he felt her still and shiver, and heard the whisper echoing from her very soul.

"Yours . . . yours . . . I'm yours."

And when they found release together, a breeze ruffled the trees overhead and the trees wept pearl-white petals, like tears of joy.

Lillith sat some distance away, on a boulder by the edge of the path, watching the place at the edge of the orchard where they had disappeared. She had seen their rumpled state and the way they walked hand in hand as they entered the trees, and now she heard Thera's cry. She started and pushed halfway up, but Gasquar's brawny hand captured hers from behind and restrained her.

"It is a cry of pleasure, not pain, *ma chatte*," he said, staring at the contrast of her fair skin and the thick, dark lashes that veiled her eyes from him. He had followed her out into the forest, then back to the orchard, where she kept her vigil as Thera's countess. And as the night bloomed, the distant sounds and blurred glimpses of Saxxe's and Thera's pleasure had surrounded them in the moonlight, raising a thick tension between them.

He pulled her closer, staring into her dark eyes, making her feel his desire all around her. "You have never known such a cry, eh? You have never felt the lightning in your blood . . . never felt you were dying in a man's arms."

She raised her gaze with a flash of anger. She was beyond bearing even one more insult to her marriage or her passions . . . especially now that they were so tangibly aroused.

"You think not?" she said, jerking her wrist from him. But instead of retreating, she advanced on him around the boulder. "You are so sure I have never known passion. Well, I have known my share, Gasquar LeBruit." She stalked toward him, her body taut, her eyes burning with long-suppressed fires.

"My good husband could not give me children, but he gave me much pleasure to make up for it." She shoved his chest, catching him off guard and sending him reeling back a step. "He made me groan . . . he made me pant . . . he made me purr like a kitten." She pushed him back another step and his eyes widened. "He made me writhe and shudder and howl like a vixen. We went three days once without leaving our bed . . . and when we finally did, every hound in Mercia was gathered outside our door."

"*Mon Dieu*," Gasquar breathed out. He had never seen her like this, hot, challenging, demanding. As she spoke he caught steamy glimpses of her doing exactly that . . . panting, groaning, purring . . . and his blood began to burn.

"But more important, he taught me that loving ought to be just that—*loving*. He taught me caring and consideration, and that quiet moments together can be as pleasurable as soaring cries of passion." She gave him another shove, then another, and sent him back into the trees.

"You may have tasted pleasure in every province of every far-flung land on earth—you may know all about the sixteen love knots of the Hindu Kush, and the nine flowering ecstasies of the ancient Chaldeans, and the twelve steps of forbidden delight of the Temple of the Veiled Venus—" She pushed him one last time, and his back smacked against a tree trunk so that he was trapped. "But you know nothing at all of the depth and breadth of love, Gasquar LeBruit!"

That last searing blast vented the very core of her ire. Her chest was heaving and her body was trembling . . . with both anger and long-leashed desire. Gasquar had beguiled his way past her defenses to rouse her passions and heartfelt longings a way no man ever had. But for him, their encounters were a devilish game in which her passions were the prize. She wanted and needed more from him, but even when he spoke of more, there was a wicked smile in his eyes that seemed to mock her most precious yearnings.

"What you say is true, *ma chatte*," he said with a peculiar thickness in his voice. "I have not known that sweet joining of hearts and souls found in true love." His dark eyes glistened in the shifting, dappled moonlight, and his face grew sober. "I have only known the great and terrible longing for it." He swallowed hard, feeling his heart pounding and his arms twitching with tension the way they often did before battle. And he sensed that this was indeed a battle of sorts . . . perhaps his final stand in his quest for her heart.

"I have lain at the edge of battlefields, awaiting the dawn . . . and the fears that chased away my sleep . . . they were not of pain or even of dying. They were of ending life without having tasted its sweetest pleasures . . . a woman's love, a bed of my own, and a son to rejoice in. And in the depths of those cold nights, I would pray upon the holy cross of my steel that I would not die in battle, so that I might yet find them."

He paused and the silence came alive with tension between them.

"You could help me find them, Lillith Montaigne. And if you will not, then I am lost." He steeled his nerve and raised a brawny hand to tap against his breast. "For there is no room left in my heart for another."

Lillith felt as if everything in her was melting and sliding to her knees. Every word he spoke had gone straight to her heart. He wanted her . . . truly wanted her. She looked at that big, callused hand poised above his chest and suddenly wanted to fill it and the heart beneath it with all the passion and joy and love she possessed. Tears sprang into her eyes even as she broke into a radiant smile.

"Look no further, LeBruit," she said, lifting his hand from his chest and placing it upon hers. "All you seek, and more, is here."

He blinked . . . started as the meaning of her words struck . . . then lifted his head and gave a triumphant shout of laughter. "Lillith—*coeur de mon coeur*—" His arms swooped around her and he crushed her to him, as if he could absorb her into him with the sheer force of his embrace.

His wild explosion of joy echoed through her own heart and sent her blood racing through her veins. And after so long a wait, after so much wasted heat, she was not content to let another precious moment pass without tasting the passion promised between them. She lifted her mouth to his and felt a warm, spiraling rise of excitement. Loving, this would indeed be *loving*.

They sank to their knees in the sweet spring grass beneath the trees, shedding garments in a flurry of hands and kisses and murmurs of delight and discovery. He was thick and hard and sinewy, as she knew he must be . . . but he was also ticklish in places and deliciously slow in his lovemaking. She was curvy and delectably voluptuous, exactly as he had hoped . . . but she was also surprising strong and unexpectedly adventuresome.

They loved long and well, varying the rhythms of their joining, each searching out the special sensations that most pleased the other. And when the time had come, he sent her tumbling over the brink of release first . . . into deep, engulfing pleasure. And it was only when he had fully savored her response that he took his own release.

Afterward, as they lay together in the fragrant night breeze, she ran a finger down the bridge of his nose with a sleepy smile. "I only want to know one thing, Gasquar, and I will never ask again." He nodded indulgently. "How many women did you really vanquish in the caliph's harem?" He laughed.

"I will tell you, *ma chatte*, but only after you tell me . . . I have heard of the Hindu Kush, and have sampled the Veiled Venus on occasion . . . but what in holy Heaven are these 'nine flowering ecstasies of the ancient Chaldeans' "?

She laughed from deep in her throat and snuggled against him. "I doubt mere words can do the old Chaldeans justice. But if you're very, very good . . . after our seventh night, I'll show you."

In the quiet darkness, Thera lay in the shelter of Saxxe's body, weeping softly, her senses stripped bare by the storm of their impassioned loving. She had lost all control. . . . As the turmoil in her blood quieted and a feeling of peace spread through her, she understood that she had not lost it at all . . . she had given it to Saxxe. She had surrendered irrevocably to his loving, his sensual power. Her *khamsin*, he had whispered, and it was true. He was her destiny. Now as she lay in the hard circle of his arms, she felt the rightness of it seeping through her.

He let her cry for a while, then, as her trembling stopped, he stroked her face and finally lifted it so he could look at her. "It wasn't so bad as you thought, eh? The Seventh Pleasure."

"W-what seventh pleasure?" she asked, taking a shuddering breath.

"The Sixth Pleasure is *control*. The seventh is *surrender*." The intensity of his gaze arrested her as she shivered and sat up, searching his odd expression. Her heart beat faster and her mind began to race as he fixed her with his devastating eyes. "You experienced *control* in our loving . . . an easy and enjoyable thing for you. But there is also a time and a place for surrendering control to another. And tonight you tasted how sweet, how freeing, surrender can be. Do you understand now?"

She jerked away with her eyes widening, but he pulled her back to him. "Nay—please—" She was too open, too vulnerable.

"Listen to me, Thera. Hear me out. You take it all on yourself . . . your people's lives, their welfare, and their destiny. But no one, not kings, not emperors, not even sages, can control their own fate . . . not even the Lord himself could control his destiny. You cannot face everything, do everything, manage everything for your people anymore." He touched her face. "And you don't have to. I'm here with you now . . . and I always will be."

That quiet assurance settled like oil over the troubled waters of her heart, allowing his other words to penetrate her emotions. For the first time in her life, she truly felt that she was not alone. She had Saxxe. He was her mate, her counterpart, in a way no one else could ever be.

She closed her eyes and felt again the sweet exhilaration of those last shattering moments of their loving. She had given herself up to him, ripped free of all moorings and constraints, and spread her soul on the powerful winds of his love. And when the storm of loving was past, he gently set her down in the very same place, in her kingdom, in her woman self, in her lover's arms. And she had felt whole and at peace in a way she had never known.

Surrender. The deepest dread of her princess heart, the fear of losing control, suddenly vanished like a vapor. She felt as if a huge burden she hadn't realized she carried had been lifted from her heart.

She turned to Saxxe, smiling through new tears. "I suppose it isn't fatal, after all . . . giving up control."

"Nay . . . not fatal." He grinned and his whole countenance radiated joy as he celebrated with a kiss. She had learned!

"I might not be very good at it . . . don't expect too much at first," she whispered when she dragged her mouth from his.

"Quite the contrary, my little cat," he said with lusty approval. "From what I witnessed not long ago, you show considerable promise." He laughed. "And I am more than willing to help you practice."

The citizens of Mercia were stirring from their beds that morning when Saxxe and Thera strolled through the city, headed for the palace, hand in hand. Saxxe was shirtless again and Thera's hair was down, and her gown was grass stained and littered with bits of old leaves. They looked tousled and sated and shamelessly in love.

Not long after they passed, Lillith and Gasquar appeared. Where the people had peeked discreetly through their shutters and allowed Thera and Saxxe some privacy as they walked by, they swarmed around Lillith and Gasquar, demanding to know if Lillith had counted yet another night. She lifted her chin and pressed on through the throng, refusing to satisfy their curiosity. But Gasquar's lusty grin and waggling brows hinted at the answer.

The people of Mercia didn't have to wait for word from the palace this time; they had seen for themselves the way of things. Saxxe Rouen was now *six-sevenths* king!

All over the city, men began to plan what events they would enter in the sporting contests, women dragged their embroidered finery from trunks, and victualers and merchants alike braced for the demand for banquet fare and new garments, in anticipation of a splendid celebration.

The commotion reached the palace as first one elder, then another, arrived in the council chamber, breathless and wide-eyed with the news. When they were all assembled, they sent for the countess and demanded an official report. Lillith managed a little smile as she raised six fingers.

Cedric sprang up, beaming, and clasped hands joyfully with everyone around him, Hubert and old Fenwick locked arms and did a little dance of joy, and Elder Audra had to be revived with whiffs of strong vinegar.

Chapter Twenty

The day was clear and warm, the mood of the city festive, and the urgent heat in his blood had been spent in the night just past . . . but something was not right with Saxxe. Something gnawed at the edges of his awareness as he went about the city surveying it from a military standpoint. It wasn't until he stood before one of the large stone granaries at midday, staring at Castor and the stout wooden door he guarded, that he realized what it was. He scowled and turned to Gasquar.

"There is something about our visitor that is oddly familiar. And yet, I cannot put him in a time or place."

"I have been thinking the same thing, *mon ami*," Gasquar said, nodding. "Perhaps we should question him again, eh? Without others to object."

When they dragged their prisoner onto his knees in the dim light, he squinted and growled and tried to wrestle away. "Who are you? What are you doing in Mercia?" Gasquar demanded as they applied a bit of pressure to his bound arms. The prisoner's long night in the pitch-black prison and the threat of forceful persuasion apparently made him review his loyalties.

"You are fighting men also . . . I can see as much," he said in a graveled voice that carried a familiar accent . . . that of northern Spain. "I will tell you . . . for a price."

But the first words out of his mouth were all that Saxxe and Gasquar needed to hear. The poor light and the stale air of the dusty granary reminded them sharply of another place and time, and when they caught the scent of garlic, a stubborn memory was dislodged.

Nantes. The tavern.

They turned on their heels and strode straight for the palace and Thera. They found her just arrived in the council chamber, enduring discreet questioning about her intentions now that her debt to Saxxe was officially paid. When she saw him, she rose with a look of relief and the council was obliged to take its feet as well.

"Princess, councilors, forgive the intrusion . . . but there may be no time to waste." Saxxe strode straight to Thera's side. "Something about the prisoner we captured has nagged at me. He seemed familiar . . . and now I know where I have seen him before." He engaged Thera's eyes. "Nantes. In the same tavern where I first heard you. He tried to recruit us to join the horde of barbarians and mercenaries pillaging the city. He is one of them, Thera. And he is here, now, in your kingdom."

Thera paled visibly and clasped her hands together. "How can you be sure it is the same man?"

"We are certain, Princess," Gasquar said, frowning. "When he spoke, we both recalled his voice. He is a Spaniard. And the leader of several men."

"Then what is he doing here?" Cedric said, stepping closer. He was roundly confused by Thera's and Saxxe's drastic reaction to his question. She sat down abruptly, looking ashen, and Saxxe glanced grimly at Gasquar before answering.

"He is undoubtedly a scout, sent ahead to spy out the land for the army of barbarians and hire-soldiers that invaded Nantes. If he is here, they cannot be too far behind." He looked to Thera, willing her to understand and praying that the lessons of the night would not be forgotten in the light of day. "We must make preparations to defend Mercia . . . if they come."

"They will not come," Thera said, but with less conviction than before.

"He may have already sent them word," he said in solemn tones. "They may be on the way even now. We must prepare for the worst . . . and hope for the best."

She understood the message in his eyes, then took a

deep breath, reaching past her fears, giving over some of her responsibility. "What must we do?"

"We must post sentries at every entrance to the valley. Several men at each, with fast horses, to warn of a possible attack." At his last word, there were several gasps. He turned and looked to Mattias. "We will need your fastest mounts."

Mattias looked to Thera, and when she nodded, his chest swelled. "You shall have them within the hour, sir," he answered proudly. In several quick exchanges, plans were under way for a number of other defensive measures and several of the elders were assigned tasks. Soon Saxxe was striding from the palace with most of the male elders, leaving Thera in a silent chamber, under the eyes of a number of gray-faced women.

"It has begun," Audra said, swaying forward, her eyes dark and fearful. " 'This hour of darkness . . . this hour of travail . . .' " she repeated in ominous cadence. " 'A dark prince . . . a man of steel, a man of blood . . . will work schemes and treachery amongst us . . . spread conflict and chaos throughout the land.' It has begun, Princess. . . ."

Thera strode out of the chamber with her shoulders straight and her head high. But when she reached the colonnade leading to her chambers, a chill shuddered through her and she sagged against a pillar.

A dark prince. Heaven help her, she had made Saxxe a prince of sorts only last night . . . crowned him with her own hands. The conflict within her was joined once more. Was her beloved Saxxe the dark, violent prince of the prophecy? And was her heart to be his first victim?

Throughout the city preparations for battle were begun . . . amid the people's joyous anticipation of Thera's marriage. To prevent needless alarm, Hubert and Castor and Pollux took the city's best archers out into the fields to practice and calmly assigned them positions around the city from which they could shoot. Old Fenwick and Gawain set about ensuring food and water for a moving populace, and Elder Marcus and Randall, the head smith, began collecting all the weapons—however ancient or ceremonial—they could find.

Thera walked the streets, maintaining a pleasant guise while her people inquired happily after her well-being and after their knight . . . Saxxe Rouen. By sunset, when she returned to the palace, she felt a storm brewing inside her. There was only one person in the world who would truly understand her conflict, and he was the very one who caused it.

She called Lillith and started for her gardens to seek a bit of peace, when a page arrived with a message from Cedric bidding her come to the Great Hall at once. Arriving there, she discovered the hall filled with a small crowd surrounding a number of men in dusty, battered clothing and slumped on the benches and floor. The onlookers parted to let her pass and she stopped dead as she recognized the weary and disheveled figures as the traders she had sent several days before on a mission of mercy to the village of LeBeau.

"What in heaven's name has happened?" she demanded, looking to Cedric, who knelt by the leader of the group, Simon Monfort.

"They were accosted by soldiers along the way, Princess," Cedric said with a worried frown. "Tell Princess Thera what you told me, Simon."

"We left by the western pass, as always, the better to reach the trading road undetected," the battered merchant trader began. "We found Jean of Poitier's cottage at the first pass, where we always stop for water, burned to the ground . . . no sign of him or his good wife. We went on into the hills and found the shepherd Dorse's cottage and byres in cinders . . . his sheep killed or scattered. And as we descended into the foothills, we saw more wanton destruction of sheep and goats." He paused to sip from a cup of wine the servants had brought, and closed his eyes, giving thanks for it. "Then, as we approached the village of Durbin, we were set upon by a band of marauders . . ." He took another drink.

Thera could scarcely contain herself. "What of these marauders . . . who were they, what were they like?" she demanded.

"They appeared more like soldiers than just thieves and bandits. They wore armor, Princess."

She gently seized his arm. "What color, Simon? What color was their armor?"

"It was black, Princess . . . like their soulless eyes . . . that much I will never forget. They rode down on us out of the rocks in an ambush. They knocked us from our mounts, beat us, and wounded poor Henri." He pointed worriedly to a fellow stretched out on a makeshift litter. "We ran for the rocks and they gave chase, until they caught Harold Beauvier. They broke off the attack and hauled Harold and our horses and supplies away with them. We started home, carrying Henri, but had to hide several times when we spotted more soldiers in black along the trading road."

"More soldiers?" Cedric looked at Thera, trying to make sense of it. "All along the road . . . and in the hills? What do you make of it, Princess?"

Thera felt frozen from icy dread.

"The force that invaded and pillaged Nantes wore black mail," she said quietly. "Now soldiers in black mail burn and pillage the slopes leading to Mercia. Saxxe was right. That same dark horde has traveled north and east, into Brittany, toward Mercia." The realization struck with the force of a fist in her stomach, taking her breath for a moment. "And *into* Mercia. We have one of them in our granary even now."

Her words echoed about the Great Hall in a silence so profound it was almost deafening. Soon, every council member present made the connection and understood the peril confronting them.

"They may already know of Mercia," Cedric said. "They may be—" He couldn't say it; he didn't even want to think it.

"Coming here," Thera finished for him.

The very thing Thera had dreaded in the depths of her soul, the thing she had vowed to prevent at all costs, seemed to be happening. When she glanced up, Audra was standing nearby with her hands folded and her face filled with tacit reminders of two prophecies.

Sinking inside under the weight of despair, she thought of Saxxe and wished he were there to advise and reassure her. She looked around her at the faces of her councilors and the others who had crowded into the hall. They waited for some word from her; they depended on her to lead them. But for the first time she had come to the absolute limit of her capacity as their sovereign. She knew virtually nothing about fighting and defenses. She had nothing to give them . . . except her faith in Saxxe.

"Saxxe must be told of this," she declared, coming to life. "I'll go for him myself." Before anyone could object, she issued a number of terse commands setting Cedric and Hubert in charge, then headed for the stables. A messenger might have sufficed, Thera knew, but with the sun setting and the day's tensions mounting, she felt a driving need for the reassurance of Saxxe's presence.

She rode along the usual paths to the east end of the valley, with its mazelike passes of rock, and discovered the sentries Saxxe had already posted along the tops of the cliffs overlooking the narrow entry into Mercia. They recognized her white gown in the lowering light and told her that Saxxe had left a while before for the western pass.

She turned back, feeling a chill in the air as the sun sank farther into the hills, dragging the last remnants of light with it. Instead of riding all the way back into the valley to reach the far end, she decided to ride along the mountain ridge instead. The trail was seldom used and somewhat overgrown, but she had ridden it often as a young girl.

The darkness gathered as she rode along, and the sounds of nighthawks swooping overhead and of her mount's hooves against rocks seemed magnified in her ears. By the light of the rising moon, she could see the whole of her kingdom laid out like a scene from a printed woodcut, and all she could think was how vulnerable it seemed. She realized she was seeing it through Saxxe's eyes . . . or through an invader's. Then she suffered a vision of a dark tide of vicious mercenaries swarming over the hills and into her valley, of plumes of smoke rising, of her people crying out . . .

She closed her eyes and shuddered, frantic to wipe those horrifying images from her mind. Searching for something good to fasten in her thoughts instead, she seized the memory of the previous night, when she and Saxxe had lain in a meadow making love and counting stars . . . learning lessons of loving that he had tried to show her were truths for the rest of living as well. Controlling and surrendering . . . needing and depending on one another . . . giving of one's self. Where had he learned such things? How had he managed to keep that core of goodness alive in him during years in the wastes and barrens of the world?

She was suddenly desperate to see him, to have a seventh night with him, now, tonight. And—please God— she would also have an eighth and a ninth . . . once they were through these present troubles.

Troubles. She shivered and glanced around her, realizing that she had entered the forest on the steep western slopes. All around her were deep shadows, shifting and moving, dark places shielded from the light of the rising moon by the aged trees. And the gloom reminded her of the dark prophecy about their future . . . of the women's doubts about Saxxe.

When Audra and the others looked at him, they saw only his physical power, his unrestrained impulses, and the desires that he made no effort to hide. They recoiled from his potential for violence. They couldn't know the extreme tenderness with which those big hands could move, the concern with which they could wipe away tears, the valor with which they could defend another. But she saw it and, in a strange way, understood it now. They were halves of the whole and she needed—

Crashing sounds suddenly rushed out of the darkness at her. Shadows took form and substance as they lunged for her, and in shock she realized they were faces and hands . . . men!

"Nooo!" she cried, beating at those dark shapes with her fists, kicking her mount and wrenching about in the saddle to free herself from their grasping hands. But they were all around her, stopping her horse and clutching at her garments. "Stop—let me go—nooo—stop!"

Her cries turned to panicky screams as they overcame her and dragged her from her saddle. She tried to strike and kick at them, but they held her securely. She couldn't get her feet free to right herself—everything was swaying and heaving—hands were pawing at her. She heard their vile laughs, smelled their filthy rancid bodies, heard their guttural speech . . . and suddenly it was the same as that night in Nantes, in the alley. Terror rose inside her like a wave of sickness, twice potent for having claimed her in the security of her home.

Her attackers stuffed something in her mouth to stop her screams and pushed her onto the ground to tie her hands and feet. Then they hoisted her over their shoulders and flung her back across her saddle, face down. Through a swirl of flashing shadow and light and the roaring of blood in her ears, she managed to orient herself and realized they were taking her upward, to the pass. Her panic swelled. She had no means of escape, no way of calling out for help—no way to warn Mercia!

They plodded upward, across roughening terrain . . . toward the pass. Saxxe and Gasquar—the sentries! They would be watching—they would rescue her! But the moments dragged by and there was only the scraping of hooves and feet on the rocky slopes and the groan of harness leather. When they reached the sheer walls of rock that lined the pass and continued through unopposed, her hope dissolved in a sea of new terror. There were no sentries—they hadn't reached the pass yet!

Scallion and several of his men waited on the leeward slope of the mountain, scanning the pale rock above for a sign of the barbarians the captain had sent in to scout the area and bring back confirmation of the Spaniard's story. For all their sakes, he hoped the wretch had spoken the truth. He didn't want to think about how the duc's wrath would flare and scorch them all if the promise of his rich prize was not genuine. As they waited, he began to worry that he should have gone himself instead.

Then he saw them emerging from the pass, outlined against the pale rock. They had gone in on foot, but they now had a horse with them. And draped over the back of that horse was a luminous slash of white . . . a body . . . a woman!

A woman in white—the duc's princess? He dug his heels and waved his men up the slope. The barbarians saw them riding hard up the mountainside and pulled their weapons, fearing they would lose their prize before they claimed a reward. There was scuffling and a few exchanges of blades before Scallion and his men were able to make the barbarians understand that the reward would be theirs . . . and took charge of the horse.

Thera heard the grunts and shouts. Her hopes roused again as her horse was pulled into a run and she sensed that she had been freed from her foul-smelling captors. But she soon realized something was wrong . . . they weren't going back through the pass but downward instead . . . away from Mercia—downward, through several narrow passes, picking their way along the well-disguised trail that connected Mercia and the outside world.

How long they rode, she could not say, but somehow through the blur of pain and jolting motion, she recognized that they had come to more level ground and were slowing. Noise increased around her . . . the smell of wood fires . . . the sound of men's voices. Suddenly she was being hauled from the horse and carried . . .

It was late and the Duc de Verville was just ready to retire to the fur-strewn bed in his luxurious quarters when Scallion burst into the tent and saluted him with a hard twist of a smile.

"*Mon duc* . . . you will forgive the intrusion when you see what I have brought."

The duc turned with a hard glint in his eyes, about to disabuse his captain of that notion, when Scallion held back the tent flap and waved his soldiers inside. They carried in a bound prisoner . . . a woman clothed in white . . . deposited her on the carpet at the duke's feet, then withdrew.

"Your princess, I believe, *mon duc*," Scallion said with a bow to his dark lord.

The goblet of wine in the duc's hand shook as his eyes slid over Thera's body, curled vulnerably at his feet. She looked up at him and blinked as if trying to right her vision, and suddenly all he could see was her sky-blue eyes. He came to his senses, flung the goblet aside, and sank to his knees beside her to pull the rag from her mouth.

"It *is* her. And . . . God's blood, she's breathtaking!" he said. "More beautiful than I imagined."

Enraptured, he traced her face and shoulders, the curves of her breasts and hips with hands held away from her . . . as if she were too precious to touch. His eyes glowed, his perfectly chiseled features bronzed with emotion as he scrutinized the delicacy of her face, the lush bow of her lips, and the voluptuous curves of her silk-clad body. Then he turned his gaze back to her eyes and he caught a flicker of fear in their depths. The sight sent an exultant surge of lust through his loins.

"Forgive me, my lady," he said in a voice filled with emotion as he fell to freeing her hands and feet. "But the sight of you has quite undone me."

Thera sat up, rubbing her chafed wrists and staring at the man bent over her bonds. He seemed tall, though he was kneeling over her, and had dark hair. He wore a black silk robe over a rich-looking tunic trimmed in gold, and when he turned slightly, she glimpsed clean, striking features . . . the promise of handsomeness.

She transferred her gaze to her surroundings and found herself in a spacious tent hung with heavy samite and exotic silk weavings from the Orient. She sat on a thick multicolored carpet amid elegantly carved furnishings more suited to a palace than a tent. Nearby was a table laden with silver bowls and goblets, and there was an elegantly carved wooden bed erected to one side and covered with furs and huge silken pillows. Light came from a candle stand bearing beeswax tapers, and a potent perfume from a censer atop the brazier filled the air.

Her host helped her to her feet, then continued to hold her hand, too tightly, as he stared at her with ill-disguised hunger. "Who are you, sir?" she demanded, drawing herself up straight and trying, unsuccessfully, to remove her hand from his. "Where am I?" Her eyes flickered around the sumptuous tent.

"Ah, permit me to introduce myself, my lady." Her host smiled, reaching for her other hand and capturing it, despite her obvious reluctance. "I am Drustane Reynard, Duc de Verville." As she looked up, directly into his face, she felt a strange chill. He was a stunningly handsome man, with strong aquiline features, large deep-set eyes, and a broad sensual mouth. But there was something about his eyes . . . a mirrorlike quality to their darkness that she found unnerving.

"And this," he gestured to the tent and beyond, "is my camp. This is my captain, Scallion." He waved a hand to the tall, whey-skinned soldier by the door. "He rescued you and brought you to me. A most fortunate happening, my lady . . . or should I say *Princess*?"

She stiffened. "You know who I am?"

"But of course, Princess. Though I do not know your proper name. I have only heard your traders refer to you as 'princess,'" he said smoothly. He had indeed asked one of her traders her name . . . that afternoon, in fact, and with the aid of a red-hot iron to ensure he received the truth. But the wretch was unable to answer satisfactorily for his miserable screams. "Indeed, the chance of meeting you is one of the very reasons I have made this journey." He waited for her to speak. When she didn't he squeezed her hands to encourage her.

"Thera of Aric," she answered, stiffening and suppressing her rising anxiety. Her traders would never speak of her outside Mercia, she was sure of it. And he was squeezing her hands much too hard, stopping just short of pain. Her heart began to pound. Something was very wrong here.

"Thera." He breathed it out as if it were a sigh, and the tension in his hands and countenance eased. "Princess Thera, I welcome you and make you my guest. You must be fatigued . . . perhaps thirsty after your ordeal?"

"I would prefer, Duc, that you allow me to take my horse and leave. I'm sure my family will be most worried."

"Nay, Princess, I could never let you go out into the night alone. It is much too late. I will send a message on the morrow. Nay—I have a better plan. My men and I will escort you home. I am most anxious to see your lovely kingdom.

"Come and sit, my beautiful Thera of Aric." He pulled her toward a wooden chair and squeezed her hands until she complied and sat down. "And tell me all about your home. . . ."

Saxxe and Gasquar had ridden from one end of the valley to the other, posting sentries and arranging for signals. When they left the east passage, they swung back through the city itself, to see how things were progressing, and were unexpectedly detained at the forge. Randall requested they look over the surprising cache of weapons he had managed to collect, to judge their battle worthiness.

Thus, it was well past Compline, several hours past dusk, when they finally reached the western pass. It was dark and quiet as they surveyed the stone formations and positioned their sentries. By the time they returned again to the city and palace, it was deep night and all but an occasional torch had been extinguished in the halls. Saxxe washed and took a little wine, thinking of Thera, wondering if she would come to his chambers and worrying that his bold action might have driven a new wedge between them. He had hoped to make this night their seventh, and the sweetest yet.

He waited and paced, feeling in his marrow that this last night had to be given freely on her part. He needed to know that if she came to him again and they were thus wedded, it was because she truly wanted him and trusted that he was right for both her and Mercia. He wanted no mistaken intentions, nothing that would later cause her to regret her choice or the way it was made.

Tension and fatigue gradually claimed him, and he lay down on the bed with his arms propped behind his head, staring up into the darkness. He must have slept, for he wakened to the sight of dawn light streaming in the garden doors. He rose, feeling little refreshed by his oblivion, and paced again. Perhaps she had simply fallen asleep. Perhaps she was waiting for him to come to her. Or perhaps she was furious with him.

Another hour went by, then two. It was well past Prime when he left his chambers and strode along the corridor, through the Great Hall, and down the colonnade to Thera's apartments. His fine resolve of the night before had worn thin and now he intended to ask her straight out to marry him . . . and put an end to his misery. He tried the door. It was latched, and he banged on it, calling her name. There was no answer, and he banged harder.

"Thera, open your door! I need to talk with you. Thera . . ." He waited and banged again. "Thera, don't be stubborn!"

"What is it? What's happened?" Lillith's voice startled him and he whirled to find her standing behind him with her eyes heavy with sleep, her lips love-swollen, and her hair hastily plaited into a rope over one shoulder. Behind her he glimpsed the reason for her exceptional dishabille . . . Gasquar, wearing only hose, boots, and an indecently satisfied smile. Saxxe gave him a wry nod of surprise.

"She won't open the door," he said, taking a deep breath.

"Did you quarrel?" Lillith demanded, scowling at him.

"We did not cross words," he protested. "Is she angry I was so late last night?"

"I don't know," Lillith said, her eyes widening. "I was busy myself last ni—Wait—you mean she was not with you?"

"Nay, I have not seen her since yesterday mid-afternoon. I waited for her—"

"Lord help us," Lillith said, reddening at this unforgivable lapse of duty. She had very nearly counted a night that hadn't counted! "After last night, I just assumed she would . . . you would . . ." She stiffened and drew herself up straight. "Wait here. I'll go through the garden doors."

Moments later, the doors to Thera's apartments were flung open and Lillith greeted them with a frantic expression. In the background they could see old Esme, Thera's servant, wringing her hands. "She hasn't slept in her bed, and Esme said she hasn't seen her since she went to look for you . . . to tell you about the traders."

"The traders?" Saxxe looked at Gasquar and frowned.

"Yea, the traders . . . yesterday evening when she rode out to the pass to tell you about the ambush and the black-clad soldiers in the foothills."

"She rode out after us? But we never saw her—" Saxxe grabbed Lillith's shoulders. "Black-clad soldiers in the hills? *Bon Dieu*—what news is this? Tell me!"

Lillith repeated the traders' story of the ambush and recounted Thera's fear that the black-clad soldiers in the hills might know about Mercia, since one of their number had been camped in Mercia's hills, and they might be headed for the valley.

It was exactly what he had feared, but the confirmation still slammed through Saxxe like a battering ram. And the fact that Thera had gone riding off into the night after him pushed his concern to towering proportions.

Saxxe set Lillith to questioning the palace staff for word of Thera's whereabouts, and sent Thera's page for Cedric and Elder Hubert to help her. He and Gasquar rushed back to their quarters for their cross braces, daggers, and swords, then exploded from the palace to search the city. They found no trace of her and so mounted horses and rode up and down the entire valley, rousing plowmen and shepherds to ask after her.

When they reached the sentries at the eastern pass, they learned Thera had been there at sunset, looking for them. They had sent her to the western pass . . . and had seen her take the high path along the rim of the valley. They pointed out the barely visible path, and Saxxe and Gasquar struck off along it. When they reached the softer ground of the great trees on the far western slopes, they spotted fresh hoofprints, then followed until they came to a place where there were a number of tracks and a few flattened bushes.

That alarming trail led straight toward the western pass itself. But when they reached it, they found their sentries, alert and vigilant.

"Where could she be?" Saxxe worried aloud as they raced back through the valley toward the city. They had just reached the palace and dismounted when a sentry on horseback came hurtling through the streets, calling for them.

The rider reined up beside Saxxe and handed him a rolled bit of parchment, panting out an explanation. Hearing the commotion, Cedric and the other elders who had been waiting for word of Thera came pouring out of the palace onto the portico.

"Not long after you left . . . a rider came and threw this down . . . at the entry to the pass. Then he wheeled and rode off before we could challenge him."

Saxxe swallowed hard and ripped open the wax seal on the parchment. As he scanned the words, his face seemed to drain of color beneath his sun-browned skin.

"What is it?" Cedric asked anxiously. "Read it, sir!"

"It is from one who calls himself Drustane Reynard, Duc de Verville. He claims Thera is his guest . . . and that he will personally escort her home in two days' time. And he expects Mercia to prepare a proper welcome and—" Saxxe halted, his face like stone and his fists clenched. Cedric lifted his widened eyes and finished it for them.

"And a *wedding feast* for Princess Thera and her new husband, the Duc de Verville." He halted and held out the parchment with a look of horror. "A wedding feast? But that cannot be—Princess Thera is six-sevenths married to you!"

A hush fell over the elders as Saxxe turned to the sentry and grabbed his shoulders. "What color was his armor—the one who delivered this?"

When the fellow answered, there wasn't a person present who didn't understand the significance of his reply.

"Black . . . it was black, sir."

Saxxe turned on them with the new fire of certainty in his eyes. "They have her. This 'dark horde' . . . they got into the valley somehow and secreted her out."

As anguished confusion broke out among the elders, Saxxe signaled Gasquar and turned to go. Cedric caught Saxxe's arm.

"Prithee, sir, where are you going?"

"Where else?" Saxxe said with flinty determination. "To get her back."

Chapter Twenty-One

"**Y**ou are not drinking your wine, Princess," the duc said, standing above Thera in the heavily perfumed warmth of his tent, watching her toy with her goblet.

"I am not thirsty," Thera said, setting the cup down and trying to control both her anxiety and anger.

"Then perhaps you are hungry," he said, making it sound like a command. He clapped his hands and issued a terse order to a harried-looking servant. Within moments, a tray of food appeared . . . figs and raisins, almonds, sweet wafers, and a pitcher of warm spiced wine. The sight of them made her stomach quiver.

"I am not hungry."

"Not hungry?" he said, a bit too sharply, then softened his tone and added a smile that was utterly charming but still managed to make her skin prickle. "You wound me, Princess. I have searched for you everywhere. One sweet glimpse of you was all that was required to set my heart aflame." He fastened his dark eyes on her and she saw them slipping to her breasts. "Sweet God . . . how I have burned for you."

Thera felt his heated maleness crowding her like the cloying and oppressive scent of incense in the air. She stiffened and suppressed a shudder.

"When did you see me, Your Grace?" she said in the same carefully modulated tones she would use to pacify a snarling hound.

He sank gracefully onto one knee by her chair, so that his chest leaned across the arm. His face was darkening and his eyes now had an odd luster about them. But it was his words that pushed her anxiety a notch higher.

"In Nantes. I saw you in the street one night . . . facing a vile pack of barbarians. I sent my men to rescue you, but you had disappeared. I tore the city apart searching for you. Since that moment, I have devoted my life to finding you, Princess. I have followed you halfway across France and Brittany." His voice was smooth and cultured, his words courtly . . . so much so that it took her a moment to collect the full meaning in his words.

Nantes? He had seen her in the market square that hideous night?

"And now I present myself before you on bended knee . . . here to woo and win you for my own, fair Princess."

And he abruptly leaned into her, trapping her against the far side of the chair and pressing a hot kiss on her mouth. She reacted belatedly, jerking her head away. "Nay!" He grabbed her wrists and held them, panting a laugh as he raked her with his eyes.

"Nay?" He seemed amused. "You would deny me a gallant suitor's reward for your rescue this night?" He lapsed once more into courtly poetry, only this time it seemed a mockery. "One sweet kiss . . . I'll drink the dew of your lips and thirst nevermore. One kiss, one caress of your sweet breast to see me through the long night?" He released her wrist, only to clasp her breast before she could push his hand away.

Her expression spoke a royal fury she had little experience at hiding. It might have proved disastrous for her, but the duc was too intent on savoring the sight of her body so near to take umbrage.

"I see you will require wooing," he said, withdrawing and rising to his feet. "Fair enough . . . there is royal pride to consider. I shall pay you court, Princess . . . as long as you do not make me wait too long. You will come around. I can be a most generous and persuasive man. I will make you a noble and attentive husband." He swept a hand around him with an expansive gesture. "Tonight, I shall give you my tent, my very bed . . . as well as my adoration."

He smiled as if recalling something pleasant, then strode to the far side of the tent and dragged a modest-sized trunk to the middle of the floor. "You will need something to wear . . . a change of clothing, perhaps."

Thera's eyes widened as he threw the lid open and she glimpsed white inside it. Her breath stopped as he pulled out a whisper-thin silk chemise and dangled it between him and the candles, leering through it.

"I have dreamt of you in this," he said, mostly to himself. "And you are even more beautiful than I imagined." Then he dropped it across the chair and seized her hand, kissing it with exaggerated courtesy. "A good night to you, Princess."

When he was gone, she took two steps toward the trunk and her knees buckled, bringing her down onto the carpet beside it. It was a moment before she could bring herself to touch the garments inside. They were hers. She dug into the chest, pulling up one familiar garment after another, seeking some grounding in their tangibility as her mind raced.

He had seen her in Nantes, that night in the market square, as the barbarians and black-clad mercenaries were invading the city. And he had in his possession the clothes the dark horde had taken from her. He wore black . . . his captain wore black . . . The separate elements finally came together in her mind.

He was their leader. The dark horde was his army! The thought sent a violent shudder through her, and her first impulse was to flee. She ran to the tent opening, listened, then slipped outside . . . straight into the restraining arms of two black-clad soldiers. She struggled, but when it was apparent she was outmatched, she went still.

She did manage to get a glimpse of the camp to which she'd been carried before they put her back inside with a snarled, "Stay there." There were several large tents, carts, and makeshift corrals for horses . . . and a field full of campfires glowing vile yellow in the night. There were men milling about in reflected firelight . . . dark, savage-looking men, some in armor, some in furs and skins . . . barbarians! The barbarians who had abducted her were obviously part of his force.

She stumbled back across the tent and wrapped her arms around her waist, staring at the beautiful furnishings, realizing they were probably the plunder of dozens of castles, houses, and villages. She suddenly understood her odd reaction to him. Beneath his handsome face and smooth manner lay a venomous spirit that burst through that veneer of nobility at the slightest provocation. He was the dark lord of a hideous, destructive force that had swept across the countryside . . . a force that was molded in his image . . . capricious, cruel, and dangerous.

The blood stilled in her veins.

A dark lord. *A dark prince of destruction.*

In one blinding moment of insight, she saw it all clearly. Events and prophecy were joined link by link to forge a chain of understanding. The second prophecy *was* being fulfilled . . . had been fulfilled since that first night in Nantes! Her abduction by the barbarians . . . the soldiers searching the city afterward . . . they had been searching for *her.* And when they found her, they would have taken her to the duc if it hadn't been for Saxxe.

I tore the city apart, searching for you. . . . I have followed you halfway across France and Brittany. She heard again that vile boast meant to flatter her. He had combed the countryside for her, leaving in his wake a trail of terror and destruction. Then he had followed her home; she had unwittingly led him to Mercia's door. The thought weakened her knees and she collapsed onto a chair. What had she done?

Through the next few hours she wrestled with the devastating knowledge that she, who was charged with defending and upholding Mercia, was now responsible—however innocently—for the danger Mercia now faced. Her personal peril paled by comparison. But as the candles guttered out and she sat in darkness, she began to understand that for all the danger she had faced, she had come through unscathed. And Saxxe

Rouen was responsible. He had been there to rescue her again and again . . . with no reason but the goodness of his heart and no reward but unending suspicion and aggravation.

Saxxe wasn't the destroyer of Mercia; the knowledge both relieved and embarrassed her. The fact that she had ever suspected him now humiliated her. And she could only pray that he would prove Mercia's rescuer . . . even as he had been hers.

Saxxe lay pressed against a huge boulder on a craggy hillside far below Mercia, peering through the early dawn light into the invaders' camp. He had been there for more than an hour, waiting for the sun and watching for some hint of where Thera was being held. He stretched his limbs, trying to stay alert and prepared. A great deal rested upon this rescue mission . . . the fate of the woman he loved and of the people who had claimed him as their own.

He had come alone. Gasquar was in Mercia, marshaling the people's resources and implementing their joint plan to defend against what was sure to be a savage attack, once Thera was free and back within Mercia. And he would have to plan his entry carefully and strike swiftly to carry off her rescue by himself.

He shifted to get a better view of the large tent near the edge of the camp. As he watched, there was growing activity around it. The huge black tent had a number of black and crimson banners hanging from its walls, a gold-encrusted pennon flying overhead . . . this Duc de Verville campaigned in luxury. He hoped the duc would see fit to hold Thera within that luxury as well.

His patience was soon rewarded, though in an unsettling way. A sudden flurry around the tent—the sound of alarm, soldiers scrambling, and a blur of white— caught his eye. He watched in complete helplessness as Thera was seized bodily and carried back inside that dark pavilion. The sight of her captive in their sinewy clutches made bile rise up his throat. But at least now he knew where she was . . . and how many guards were posted around her prison.

Planning quickly, he worked his way through the rocks toward the camp, intending to mix with the soldiers and move about as one of them. He had worn his fighting clothes—his skin garments, fur-lined boots, and cross braces—and there was a beard stubble on his face. He stopped along the way to rub dirt over his shoulders and hair; nothing would arouse suspicion faster than a clean barbarian.

Reaching the edge of the camp, he straightened from his crouch, settled a hand on a dagger, and strode casually toward the black tent that loomed over the camp. Slouching to disguise his height, he made it past sentries and around a number of tents and campsites without incident, and turned part of his mind toward how he would contact Thera once he reached the tent.

He might have made it all the way . . . except for one watchful pair of eyes that had seen him stride through Mercia's city and countryside, and had seen him fight by firelight in Mercia's hills. Juan the Spaniard's voice rang out, "Spy! There—" And in a camp of men whose survival depended on quick reactions, the response was to act first and question later.

They came at Saxxe from every direction. He just had time to draw his dagger before he was encircled. He whirled and spun to keep them off guard, but they, too, knew that strategy. Four lunged at once, all from different directions, and he found himself on the ground, fighting with everything in him . . . and losing.

Thera heard the shouting and commotion outside the rear of the tent and ran to lift the edge of the heavy canvas. She got only a glimpse before a guard shoved the tent wall down, sealing her inside again. But that brief glimpse—Saxxe struggling in the grip of half a dozen soldiers—was enough to stop her heart.

She wobbled to the chair and sank into it as that awful image lingered. He had come for her, and they had captured him! The impact of it slowly broadened in her mind. If Saxxe was captured . . . there was no one to rescue her. Worse . . . there was no one to rescue Mercia!

The duc found her there half an hour later, her eyes red-rimmed but her manner controlled. He swooped down on her and pulled her to her feet, insisting that she looked pale and needed fresh air. He seized her wrist in an iron grip and escorted her outside. He walked her around his camp, parading her before his hungry, hard-bitten men and making a point of stroking her hand, her shoulder, her waist possessively . . . in full view of their burning stares. Whenever she resisted, the pressure of his hand increased dangerously. She learned to keep pace, and after a while, she walked unresisting at his side.

They stopped near some tents where large posts had been pounded into the ground. She'd had time to prepare herself, but couldn't help the gasp that escaped her. Saxxe was bound tightly to one of those posts, his head drooping onto his chest, blood coming from his lip and swollen eye. She could see no other damage, but the sight of his big, handsome body, now bleeding and powerless, sent her into a panic.

"It seems we have had a visitor this morning," the duc said, watching her reaction keenly. "Perhaps he is familiar to you, Princess?"

There was no point in lying. He knew Saxxe had come for her, else he wouldn't have made a point of showing him to her. "He is a mercenary I hired to escort me home," she said. "An insolent, uncouth fellow . . . but a valiant fighter." It was agonizing to tear her eyes from Saxxe, but she made herself do it and managed to add a shiver of disgust. "Must you beat him so?"

With an instinct as old as Eve, she looked directly into the duc's dark, hollow eyes and gave him a stroking, feminine look. "He certainly is no threat to you now." When the duc reacted to that evidence of her feminine warming with a handsome smile, her instinct became intention. And without quite realizing it, she began to develop a plan.

He escorted her back, growing ever more enamored of the sway in her walk and the way she looked up at him through her lashes. By the time they reached his tent, he was quivering with anticipation. He pulled her into his arms and pressed a kiss on her lips . . . which she could not refuse, though she whimpered and pushed to put distance between their bodies. He apparently took her distress as she intended . . . a sign of royal and maidenly sensibilities. He ended the kiss, seeming pleased with their progress.

"I am not used to such things, sir. Mercians are taught . . . quite differently," she said tightly, turning partway in his arms and swallowing her disgust. Her eyes fell on a pair of blue steel daggers and a heart-breakingly familiar sword which had been placed on the table in their absence. They were Saxxe's weapons, undoubtedly brought to the duc's tent because of their renowned Damascus steel. Her stomach slid.

The duc laughed with a mocking edge, pulling her closer. "There are but few ways to take pleasure, Princess, and I can show you all of them in the matter of an hour."

"I speak not just of passion, Duc. If you would have the union you seek, you must give me time to . . . adjust to you," she said desperately. "And for my people to accept the marriage, you must fulfill our law . . . including our unusual marriage customs." She made an artful pause. "We are required to spend seven nights of pleasure together before a true marriage is decreed. Because the heir to the throne will place another on the throne with her or him, it is required that the seven nights be confirmed."

"Confirmed?" he said with a smirk, guessing what sort of proof was required. In many provinces the first bedding had to be observed to be considered official and proof a true marriage had occurred.

She steeled her nerve and launched into her first lie. "A princess's seven nights of passion must occur in the palace, where they may be observed by her advisers."

She lowered her eyes as if embarrassed to speak of it, but in reality because she could not bear the ugly joy dawning in his face. "A terrible burden to one born outside Mercia, I know . . . but it must be endured if you would wed me and be king of Mercia."

"Seven nights of pleasure," he said with a leer, already savoring it in his mind, "before a hall full of people. . . ." He loosed his hold and led her to a chair. "Tell me more of your lusty little kingdom."

She thought he would never leave. She talked on and on in an effort to distract him, telling such a web of lies and half-truths that she nearly lost track of them. The tent began to tremble, and when the duc threw back the opening and looked out, the wind was rising and the sky was lowering . . . a storm approached. Scallion came to ask him to secure the camp and review the preparations for the next day's march into Mercia. And when he left, the weapons still lay on the table, unnoticed among the parchments, pitchers, and goblets.

She seized the blades, looked about for a place to hide them, and carried them to the trunk. She knelt with the daggers and sword in her hands and paused, sensing she had just taken her fate into her own hands the moment she picked them up. A strange calm possessed her, a power like none she had ever known as a royal. This was personal and it came from her blood, her sinew, and her own determination. She hid the blades and sat down to wait for night.

When supper was brought and the tapers were lighted, the duc's captain brought word that the duc would be delayed. Shortly, the rains began. The duc arrived late and she pretended to be sleeping. When he awakened her, she pleaded that illness peculiar to women . . . and could see him coldly weighing her future value against this present inconvenience. In a sullen, dangerous temper, he withdrew, leaving her to her supposed miseries.

The rains continued, whipped by the wind into a stinging lash that drove the duc's men into huddles inside tents and beneath skins and blankets. Even the guards outside the duc's tent were driven to seek shelter, leaving only two stalwart soldiers guarding the entrance. When the night was fully dark and the rain hard and steady, Thera donned the duc's black cloak, secured Saxxe's weapons within a girdle around her waist, and lifted the back edge of the tent.

It was dark and the raindrops splashed mud in her face as she lay close to the ground with only her head sticking out of the bottom of the tent. The rear guards were gone; this was her chance. She crawled out into the mud as quickly as she could, gathered the voluminous cloak about her, and darted for a nearby tent. She stood with her heart pounding . . . blinking against the huge drops and thanking the heavens for that dark, concealing rain.

On their walk about the camp, she had committed as much of the place to memory as she could. Now she slipped from tent to cart to wagon, flattening against them at the slightest sound, making herself small and hiding her face whenever she spotted movement. The rain was disorienting, and it took longer than she had imagined to reach the poles where Saxxe was tied. His guards, like hers, had sought what shelter they could; all but one. She waited, praying that he too would value comfort more than his wretched duty. And moments later, as if in response to her heavenly supplication, he let out a low string of curses and lurched toward the nearest tent. She nearly wept with relief.

Gathering herself for the effort, she waited for a heavy gust of rain and dashed across the open to Saxxe. Mercifully, he was slumped enough against his bonds so that she could get near his ear to speak to him.

"Saxxe! Saxxe—it's me. Are you all right?"

Saxxe thought he must be hearing things. When he opened his eyes, he saw her face and wondered if he was dreaming . . . or dead. "Thera?"

"I'm here to get you out. Can you move?" she called near his ear. "Do you think you can walk?" When he nodded, she sagged with relief. "I'm going to cut you free. Can you stand straighter?"

He nodded and shifted more of his weight to his feet to relieve the pressure on his bonds. She disappeared and he could feel her sawing frantically at the ropes that held him. Twice they heard someone coming and twice she darted to the side of a nearby wagon as forms materialized briefly out of the dark, then disappeared back into it. Her third effort managed to free his arms, and he seized the dagger to make short work of the ropes on his legs and feet. She helped him to the shelter of the wagon, where she threw her arms around him before giving him back his blades and helping him rub some of the feeling back into his constricted limbs.

"Are you all right?" she whispered against his battered mouth, feeling his face with her fingers.

"This is nothing," he said, going for a kiss and groaning at the pain it caused. "Why, once in Damascus, when the Turks overran our garrison—"

She kissed him fully on the mouth, despite his wincing. It was the quickest way to shut him up. "Now quiet," she ordered, taking his hand. "Horses are this way."

The next part of the journey was just as difficult: finding the horses and getting away without being detected. But with Saxxe's big hand in hers, she felt more confident. She knew the general direction of the tie lines and corrals, and soon they were slogging through deepening mud and dodging tents and pole structures and carts that loomed up in their path.

It seemed to take forever to reach the horses. They selected two near the end of one long line and stealthily untied them. "Can you ride without a saddle?" Saxxe whispered as they led the horses away from the others. He saw her nod and realized he was seeing all of her much better; the rain had slackened. And if visibility was better for them, it was also better for the sentries around the perimeter of the camp. "Once you're up, dig in and ride—don't wait for me," Saxxe whispered forcefully.

"See here, Rouen, who's rescuing whom?" she hissed, scowling at him.

He flashed a grin with the uninjured side of his mouth, gave her a quick hard kiss, and boosted her onto the horse's back. "Ride—dammit!" She dug her heels in and when she shot off along the trail up the mountain, he wasn't far behind.

At the sound of the hoofbeats two soldiers emerged from a makeshift tent. It took them a moment to locate the riders. Their figures were blurred and not visible for long in the rain; the guards weren't sure whether to sound an alarm or not. But it truly didn't matter. In the main part of camp, the Duc de Verville had just returned to his tent, steeped in strong wine and determined to have some pleasure of his captive bride. And he had found her missing.

"Damn her treacherous soul to Hell!" he raged, wild-eyed with humiliation at having been cozened by a mere female. He lashed out with boots and fists, overturning the chair and table, sending silver clattering. "I'll make her rue the day she was born!" he roared. "Scallion—go after her! I want that little bitch!"

Thera and Saxxe heard the low drum of hoofbeats behind them and rode as fast as the steepening, rocky trail would allow. Thera's knowledge of the trail bought them some time, but the others were still too close for comfort. As they rode higher, above the narrow breaks in the rock, they could hear more than see the soldiers beginning to gain on them.

Hearts pounding amid the crash of hooves, they pushed their mounts, scanning the darkness for the rock cliff high above. And suddenly, the pale stone appeared and the slope became loose gravel everywhere but on one path. Thera found the solid footing, called to Saxxe to follow her, and raced for the pass.

An odd whirring sound came from the darkness to her left and then another on her right. Confused, she looked up and heard another low, singing vibration . . . something shooting past her. Saxxe shouted from behind:

"They're firing at us—your cloak . . . take it off! Show them your white gown!"

Ducking close to her mount, she pried one hand from its mane and jerked the ties of the cloak, shoving it frantically from her shoulders. The whirring stopped and they dug their heels in and rode hard for that dark slash in the rocks that meant safety. Once inside, Saxxe pulled up and shouted to the archers poised above them to fire at will.

The duc's men came charging up the slope into a hail of arrows pelting them unexpectedly out of the darkness. Two men and one horse fell, and the others reined up in confusion, then wheeled and rode back out of range. A sudden, eerie stillness settled over the pass. All that could be heard were the echo of hooves against the narrow stone passage and the quiet patter of the rain.

They continued through the pass and emerged onto the slope. Thera slid from her horse and staggered, weak with afterfright, and Saxxe joined her on the ground an instant later, engulfing her with all his strength and warmth. Tears mingled with the rain on her face as she hugged him with all her might.

"They're going! We turned them back!" came a call from above, and a chorus of cheers rolled down on them. They looked up to make out arms waving in the dimness. Saxxe called "Well done!" then turned back to hold her as if he'd never let her go.

When her heartbeat had slowed to a bearable pace, Thera pushed back in his arms and ran her hands anxiously over him, searching every part of him. "Are you all right?"

"Never better. And I can prove it." He kissed her with a force that spoke of a great release. She laughed and wrapped her hands around the cross braces on his back and pulled him tighter against her.

"You owe me, Rouen," she said with a triumphant grin. "I saved your blessed hide tonight . . . and I don't do anything without a reward." Her eyes glinted in the dimness. "Now what do you have that's worth your handsome skin?"

"Naught but the clothes on my back, Princess," he said, relishing this reversal of their roles. She looked him over with a critical eye and made a *tsk* sound.

"Not to my taste," she said with a sniff. "There is *one* thing I might accept . . ." She gave him a look sultry enough to dry his skin breeches. "Give me a night of pleasure with you and we'll call your debt even."

He threw back his head and laughed, sweeping her against him and swinging her back and forth with his cheek pressed against her hair.

"It's yours, Princess. Whenever you say."

That was where Gasquar, Lillith, Cedric, and half of the council found them . . . on the slope beneath the pass, wrapped in each other's arms, standing in the gentle rain. With whoops and hugs and shouts of joy, they escorted them back to the city, where the people turned out of their houses with sputtering torches to greet them.

On the way to the palace Saxxe recounted for Gasquar, Lillith, and the councilors a rather colorful version of Thera's rescue of him . . . dramatizing it, embroidering her deeds until Thera sounded like warrior queen Boadicea, of the Old Ones. And when he informed them that she'd had the gall to demand payment for her noble deed, they were deliciously scandalized . . . especially when the nature of the payment she demanded was revealed. Another night. This would make seven. Thera was declaring her intention to wed Saxxe Rouen as soon as another night could be arranged.

By the time Thera and Saxxe were ushered to their quarters to bathe and rest, there were precious few hours left in that night. And the people of Mercia, too excited to sleep, continued the vigil they had kept outside the palace . . . adding prayers for blessings on Thera and Saxxe's marriage to their prayers for Mercia's safety.

Just after dawn the next morning, second and third waves of mounted horsemen attacked the western pass of Mercia and were driven back by a storm of arrows from Mercia's expert marksmen. When they limped back to their camp, they reported yet another development guaranteed to befoul the dark duc's temper: the Mercians had begun to fill in the pass with boulders and rocks.

The news sent the duc into paroxysms of fury. He strode through camp with a studded whip in his hand, lashing everyone and everything that got in his path. When he saw several men being tended for arrow wounds, he struck out in senseless fury. His men went silent and taut and fingered their weapons as he raged.

"They're supposed to be soldiers, bladesmen—battle-hardened warriors. And they're laid low by mere sticks of wood!" he roared. "Three assaults and all I have to show for it is a score of bleeding cowards. I won't stand for this—there has to be another way into that rat hole!" He wheeled in a crouch and glared, wild-eyed, around him. "Scallion!"

When the captain came running, the duc ordered, "Bring me that little Spanish worm—that scout." He made a show of coiling the whip into one hand and stroking its metal-studded leather appreciatively. "Perhaps I can help him recall something more about that festering hole she calls a kingdom!"

Less than half an hour later, Juan the Spaniard was on his knees in a circle of men before the duc's tent, wishing with all his heart that El Boccho had been the one to carry news of Mercia to the duc and claim this wretched "reward." He trembled visibly as the duc's long fingers caressed that lethal braid of leather. Juan the Spaniard was frantic, trying to recall something—anything that would pacify his employer. He rambled, tracing aloud their movements and discoveries from the time they reached the valley, most of which the duc had heard at least twice before. He could see the ominous twitch of the whip and knew that the duc was losing patience. Then he recalled their trek outside the valley, along the ridge of the hills, and remembered the cave they had stumbled across. And it came to him . . . *a cave.*

"It was not much outside. I was smaller . . . El Boccho made me go in with a rope. I crawled at first, but then was able to stand. Some parts were only large enough for one man to go on hands and knees. Some places it was big as a cottage."

The duc was clearly interested. "And how far into the mountain did this cave go?" he demanded, searching Juan's frightened eyes, obviously pleased by what he saw.

"I do not know, *mon duc*," Juan pleaded. "It seemed to go beyond . . . but I ran out of rope and had to turn back." De Verville straightened and, for the first time that morning, calmed.

"Well . . . this time, Spaniard, we shall see you do not run out of rope."

With a score of his personal guard, the duc himself took Juan the Spaniard up onto the mountain to search for the entrance of the cave he had explored so briefly. They provided him with tapers, tied a rope around his waist, and lowered him into the small opening. He called back information and the duc had two men follow him down and wait in the first large chamber they came to . . . to relay messages.

Juan crawled and stumbled and flinched as he burrowed deeper into the damp cave. Only once did he have to choose a path. After a prayer, he crossed himself and chose the larger of the two passages. Again and again, he tugged on the rope to demand more slack, fearing each time that it would be snagged or cut by the rock and he would be abandoned there. But each time, after an agonizing delay, he was able to pull more rope. Some of the passages were small, some as big as rooms or even whole cottages. But finally the cave floor sloped up and he thought he glimpsed a dim light ahead.

In fear and trembling he approached it, wondering if he had found the valley or the gates of Hell itself. To his surprise, the light became a steady glow and its source became a torch in a large, hewn-stone room. When he stepped out of the passage, he found himself in an alcove of a massive underground chamber, lighted by a ceremonial torch and filled with shelves and rolled-up parchments and chamois-covered scrolls—hundreds of them! It was an astonishing sight. And on the far side of the large chamber was a set of steps leading to a massive door.

He made his way across the chamber and would have thrown the door latch, but at that moment there came a sonorous ringing . . . and a moment later a second, higher-pitched, tone joined in. Suddenly he knew where he was: under the church in the city. The caves led to the church in the heart of the city! He had indeed found a way into Mercia, and he knelt and said a prayer of thanks for the discovery that had just bought him his life.

Saxxe and Thera stood on the ridge overlooking the western pass later that afternoon, staring down at a force of at least three hundred mounted and foot soldiers. Gasquar, Lillith, and Cedric were not far away, speaking with the archers who guarded the pass and encouraging them to stay vigilant. Though they worked in shifts, the strain of the waiting and the ritual taunts of the soldiers below were wearing on them.

Saxxe saw the troubled expression on Thera's face and sensed she was recalling her time with the dark duc. He took her by the hand and led her away from the sight. When they joined the others, Lillith observed that the soldiers seemed to be waiting for something.

"Are they laying siege, do you think?" Thera asked Saxxe.

"It is always possible," Saxxe said, rubbing his nonexistent beard from habit, then catching himself and smiling. "But not likely here."

"A siege only works when you can deprive a city of something it needs to survive . . . water, food, fuel," Gasquar put in. "We have all we need of that, and they must know it. Nay, they wait for something else. They have large numbers. . . ." He glanced at Saxxe. "Perhaps they are building scaling ladders for a run at the cliffs."

"Also possible, though they would lose a great many lives. Scaling makes high casualties, and the men I saw were not overeager to die in the duc's employ."

"Then it would appear," Cedric contributed, "that we will just have to wait and see what they do."

They rode back to the city in the brilliant, sun-warmed afternoon. It was hard for Thera to believe that only yesterday she had been held prisoner in a dirty, smelly camp of soldiers by a madman bent on taking her body, her people, and her throne. She shuddered and looked at Saxxe. It was even harder to believe that bloodshed and violence were literally at Mercia's door, and being kept at bay only by slim wooden shafts tipped with metal.

It made her think of all the things she had vowed in the depths of despair, sitting in the duc's suffocating tent . . . sick with anxiety over Saxxe and what might be happening to him. By the time they got back to the city, she was resolved on a course to seize royal prerogative and use it to make at least one of her dreams happen before it was too late.

As soon as they reached the palace, she turned to Cedric and asked him to assemble the council straightaway. Then she led Saxxe and Lillith and Gasquar into the Great Hall, to the steps of the great double throne. When the councilors appeared, some out of breath, Thera mounted the steps and sat on the throne that was rightfully hers.

"This day marks a turning point for Mercia . . . a time of change and uncertainty. And I propose to make at least one of those changes in a positive direction. I wish to marry Saxxe Rouen, this day, before my seventh night with him. I have declared my intention to spend a seventh night . . . why must I sleep with him again before I can speak the words of confirmation with him?" When old Fenwick made to offer one possible reason, she glared him into silence and went on. "Mercia needs a king and queen, the sooner the better. I believe Elder Audra will tell you it could only benefit Mercia. One prophecy is being fulfilled in these events; perhaps we can avert the consequences of another if we act quickly and in good faith."

"Well, I see no objection," Hubert offered, "as long as she promises to spend the seventh night with him as soon as possible."

She glanced at Saxxe with a smile. "I am certainly willing to promise that." And she could have sworn that he blushed.

There were murmurs and puzzled head shakes here and there, but there was no objection raised, not even from Audra. Then Cedric asked for consensus and the elders raised their voices in a chorus of ayes. He turned to Thera with a beaming smile. "We are agreed . . . marry your barbarian, Princess. With all good speed."

"And the coronation as well . . ." Thera insisted. Cedric glanced at the other elders. Most seemed anxious at first, then, one by one, their faces lighted with wistful smiles.

"Good enough. Then while the vestments and robes are out, we shall have the coronation as well!" Cedric proclaimed proudly.

When Thera looked at Saxxe, there was an odd expression on his face, and she descended the throne to stand before him. "One thing remains." She took a deep breath and knelt before him, taking his hand. "Will you do me the honor, Saxxe Rouen, of becoming my husband this day?"

His face nearly split with a grin, and he lifted her up into his arms and hugged her with all his might. "Yea, I'll marry you, demoiselle . . . Princess . . . Thera. I'll marry all three of you."

Late that afternoon, the Mercian service of marriage, which was more the blessing than the binding of a union, was performed for Thera and Saxxe on the steps of the palace. All of Mercia looked on as Thera was escorted under the garlanded portico to join her life and the lives of her people to Saxxe Rouen. She glittered in the sunlight, resplendent in her white gown, coronet, and royal surcoat embroidered in gold. Saxxe stood handsomely beside her in a crimson tunic and matching hose . . . a gift prepared earlier by Lucian and the other tailors in anticipation of the royal nuptials. Lillith attended Thera, and Gasquar attended Saxxe, both dressed in their finest . . . though Gasquar caused something of a stir by refusing to leave off his weapons, even for so peaceful and dignified a ceremony.

The couple knelt to exchange the promises of loving and honoring, and to receive the words of blessing. And when they exchanged the kiss of peace and were declared husband and wife the cheering went on for a quarter of an hour. Then Cedric called for quiet and the couple knelt once more, to pledge their joined hearts and hands to Mercia's service. And when they rose again, it was, as Cedric proclaimed: "Queen Thera and King Saxxe, by the grace of Almighty God, rulers of Mercia."

With full hearts, Thera and Saxxe embraced, treasuring the warmth and power of the feeling between them and praying it would always be so. The cheering went on and on . . . until Cedric seized control and decreed the feasting begin.

It was a most unusual feast . . . held, as the wedding and coronation had been, outdoors and virtually on the spot. With no real time to prepare, the people had been asked to bring whatever food they had on hand . . . and the broad garden terraces were filled with hampers and people on blankets and the music of merchants turned jongleurs. Thera's cellars provided wine, and Genvieve and her kitchen legions emptied their shelves and ovens to provide a surfeit of food for the rest of the throng.

Thera and Saxxe were provided chairs and a makeshift table for the meal, but spurned them to take their food on a blanket just like everyone else. For a time the peril that lay just outside Mercia's hills was forgotten, and Thera's joy and her hopes for their future flowed down the terraces and into their people like a clear, sweet river.

Chapter Twenty-Two

As the people celebrated in the sun and warmth, a ripple of darkness was winding its way into Mercia's very heart, beneath their feet. In the core of the city, in Mercia's beautiful church, the jewellike light that poured through the colored glass windows was being captured and held by the sullen black garments of the forms moving stealthily about the floor of the nave, far below.

"Look at this place," de Verville said, brushing the dust of the tunnel from his sleeves and staring up at the domed ceiling and brilliant windows overhead. "It's a bloody cathedral . . . in all but size." Shoving his way past a number of his men, he strode to the chancel, swung his spurless boots over the altar railing, and snatched up the sacramental goblets. "Look at this. Gold, encrusted with jewels." He shook one in Scallion's direction. "This place is a plum just waiting to be picked. And I intend to have it."

He tossed the goblets onto the altar with a clang, demanding, "How many men are through?"

"Almost three score and ten . . . more soon. Some of the men have trouble in the small parts of the tunnel. It will be a while before we have a hundred—"

"We won't need a hundred to begin—"

"But, *seigneur*—"

"Now, Scallion!" The duc drew his sword quickly and the ringing echoed like a portent around the chamber. "I am eager to see what the rest of my new kingdom is like. Come!"

He led them to the great iron-bound doors of the church, and at his nod, two men grabbed one of the doors and swung it open. They peered out, squinting against the bright light, then stepped into the deserted street and stared in amazement at the stone-paved streets, the trees, and the immaculate shops of the broad marketplace. As they stood in the square, gawking, they heard a whistling and froze. Around the corner of the shops, two doors down, came a burly, broad-faced fellow with a tankard in his hand. When he looked up and saw them, he blinked and stopped in his tracks.

For a moment they stared at each other . . . Randall, the head smith, and the dark soldiers of the duc's personal guard. Randall dropped the tankard, pivoted, and ran back toward the waning celebration, yelling for all he was worth.

"Damnation!" the duc roared. "Don't just stand there—after him!" As a number of them ran after Randall, he turned to the others. "Spread out—find the armory and the forge and torch them! You and you—" he pointed to Scallion and a number of his personal guardsmen—"come with me. I want to find the strumpet's palace. When we take that from her, the rest of the place will fall into our laps."

"Soldiers! They've come—the soldiers—in the church!" Randall ran with all his heart. The palace was in sight when three of the duc's men caught up with him and sent him sprawling to the ground. But his cries had drawn the eyes of citizens on a crossing street, heading back to their homes as the marriage celebration ended. They spotted Randall and the black-clad soldiers, and in a heartbeat went rushing back toward the palace to sound the alarm.

Thera and Saxxe glimpsed the commotion from the terrace, and as the shock spread like ripples through the people, they charged straight toward the center of the confusion, hearing—"The soldiers, they're here! In the church!"

"Stay calm," Saxxe shouted, "and do as we planned! Women and children—this way—through the palace and up into the hills!"

"Archers to your roosts—staffmen and bladesmen to your posts! Run!" Gasquar roared, shoving some to get them started.

It took only a few of the leading women, calling to the others, to start the stream of women and children toward the doors of the palace and the safety of the hills beyond. And with Saxxe's and Gasquar's determined example, the men calmed and recalled that they had prepared for this very thing . . . they had made plans and it was time to implement them. In the midst of the confusion, a man came running from the marketplace, calling for Saxxe.

"Where are they? How many are there?" Saxxe said as he intercepted him, supporting the fellow as he gasped for breath.

"Didn't see—many—they got Randall—coming from the marketplace—the church—"

Saxxe sent a servant running for his armor and blades, and pulled Thera and the elders into the palace. "You must go with them into the hills," he said, taking her by the shoulders.

"I will not!"

"Look, I don't have time to fight both you and a dark horde!" he roared at her.

"Then don't!" she yelled back. And she grabbed his face and kissed him hard. "Go and fight—I'm queen here and I have a right to defend my own palace!"

He wanted to carry her off and lock her in a cellar somewhere, but there was no time to spare. The page was shoving his weapons at him and she was already gone— issuing orders of her own to barricade the doors and windows once the women and children were through, and to gather the palace servants into the Great Hall. He strapped on his cross braces and blade and sank his daggers into his belt. With a last glance at her, he bolted for the door and the streets of his city . . . to defend his home.

The young men grabbed their wooden staffs and the older men took up whatever tools of their trades might make for weapons . . . pruning hooks and pitchforks, hammers and cleavers. They snatched up barrel lids for shields and fire irons for clubs, and they assembled in small knots at the junctures of their streets, shoulder to shoulder.

Where they found the invaders, they engaged them, using their odds of four-and-five-on-one, and harrying tactics Gasquar had shown them, to wear the intruders down, then to rush them all at once. Where they found no enemy in their own streets, they began sweeping toward the center of the city . . . the marketplace and the church.

The sound of fighting filled the air as Saxxe ran through the city, but the bulk of the noise came from the main market square. He arrived to find Gasquar and a group of men rushing in to engage a force of professional soldiers that teemed like huge black ants, overrunning stalls and overturning carts, bringing down awnings and signboards.

Spotting Saxxe and watching him draw his huge sword and charge in to do battle, the Mercians took heart and rushed valiantly into the fight against superior skill. Their numbers were in their favor, and their makeshift weapons were surprisingly effective. Well-sharpened scythes and sickles were as good as daggers and short swords when swung properly . . . pruning hooks kept a man out of sword's reach and worked well on an intruder's legs . . . and mallets and cleavers and even benches and planks were surprisingly serviceable when an enemy's back was turned.

It wasn't gallant combat; there was nothing knightly about it. Barrels, broken boards, and beams stopped sword blows; dodging and retreating and tripping opponents were the rule; and an invader was as likely to be felled from behind as from the front. But, as Gasquar and Saxxe had told them, attempts at chivalry in such a mismatched melee would more likely bring them death than victory.

In the thick of it all, Saxxe engaged two soldiers at a time and took them down, one by one. But it seemed as soon as he dispensed with them, two more charged in to take their place. As he finished off that second wave, he spotted two invaders in the open church door and charged after them. He battled them back inside the sanctuary and suddenly found himself facing four swordsmen. He spotted Gasquar fighting near the doors and called for help. But no sooner had they dispatched those invaders than they spotted more climbing up a set of stone steps that led downward from the sanctuary.

They fought the intruders back down into a huge underground chamber lighted with tapers and lined with shelves and scrolls. When the second intruder fell, they stood gasping for breath, staring around them. Saxxe turned and was about to trudge back up the steps when a movement caught his eye, and he turned and charged full out with his blade raised. He stopped just short of hacking a slight figure, garbed in mailless black, who was cringing in an alcove.

"Mercy!" Juan shouted, covering his head with his arms. "Don't kill me! It's them—there—in the tunnels!"

Saxxe glanced at Gasquar and lowered his blade, growling, "Who's in what tunnel?" He grasped the little wretch by the nape of the neck and gave him a shake. "What tunnel?" he roared.

"T-there—" Juan pointed. "They come through the cave . . . the tunnels . . ."

Saxxe released him and rushed to a darkened opening that was half hidden by a jutting wall. "A cave? From the outside?"

"It explains how they got in," Gasquar panted.

"How they're still getting in," Saxxe said, seizing a candle and stepping into the passage. He stilled, and above the thudding of his heart he could hear the scrape of metal against stone and the echo of distant voices. "More on the way," he said grimly, ducking back into the chamber. "We have to block this tunnel somehow!"

He looked around desperately, finding only scrolls, wooden tables, chairs . . . and tapers. He ducked into the low tunnel again and glimpsed overhead beams . . .

wooden beams . . . under strain. He lurched out and sheathed his blade. "Old beams, some split . . . if we can block the tunnel and set a blaze, it might collapse."

Gasquar knew instantly what he meant. It was a well-known tactic: firing tunnels to collapse them . . . sometimes used to bring down fortress walls. Saxxe seized the little Spaniard and pressed him into service. They hauled chairs and wooden chests, tables and piles of scrolls deep into the passage . . . packing them with combustible parchment. When they had a significant barrier, Saxxe sent the others out and used a taper to set the pile ablaze. He stayed just long enough to see the flames licking up the scrolls and catching the leg of a stool, just beneath an aged roof beam.

"Even if the tunnel doesn't collapse, the fire will keep them out of Mercia for an hour or two. That should give us time to deal with the others," he declared, heading for the steps and the sunlight once again.

Smoke was now drifting over the market square. De Verville's men had begun torching certain buildings. But there was hope in the fact that there were now more Mercians left standing in the marketplace than black-clad mercenaries. The tide of battle had finally turned in their favor. Saxxe was about to plunge into the fray once more when he looked up and spotted a plume of smoke rising from the direction of the palace.

Thera!

"The palace!" He shouted to Gasquar, pointing.

They raced through the streets, heartened by the sight of Mercians now in control of most of them. Castor and Pollux appeared, running up from the southern part of the city, their faces red and their eyes alight. They carried swords they had salvaged from fallen intruders.

"What the hell are you doing here?" Saxxe demanded, slowing but not stopping.

"Things were dull at the passes, and when we saw the smoke we thought you might need help, Your Highness," Castor said, grinning.

"They fired the forge and stable and a few sheds," Pollux added. "But Mattias got the horses out. The south part of the city is secure."

It was good news, but as they raced up the terraces they saw that the smoke was coming from the palace kitchens, and the dark duc himself was directing the firing of the main doors of the palace.

"Dammit—where are those sluggards? We should have had at least another score of men here by now!" De Verville snarled at Scallion. But the captain was staring past his lord, and when the duc turned to see what had caused the man to pale, he began to quake with fury. Shoving several of his guards toward Saxxe and Gasquar, he barked, "Finish them this time, you cowards! The next time I see you you'd better be victorious or dead! The rest of you, come with me!"

As Saxxe and Gasquar rushed in with blades raised, the duc wheeled and led a half dozen of his men toward the east side of the palace, searching for an entry. They found a walled garden and doors that yielded without much resistance. Striding through elegant bedchambers, the duc paused to feel the bedhangings, and his eyes glowed at the thought that soon all this would be his.

"Check every door, every opening . . . we find and capture the princess, and the rest will be easy," he ordered, waving his men ahead into the corridor. They formed a bristling cordon around him as they swept through the passages and chambers, anticipating resistance of some sort.

But their passage through the east wing was unopposed, and with each empty chamber they encountered the duc's confidence rose. "The Spaniard was right—they have no soldiers. We haven't seen a single armed guard!" When they came to the Great Hall and spread out to check each arch and doorway, they quickly discovered the barred doors of the council chamber.

"I think we've found where the rats have hidden," de Verville said with a cold smile. "Break it down!"

Thera and the elders and servants gathered in the council chamber watched the heavy doors shuddering under increasingly heavier blows. She had prayed that the duc's men wouldn't get this far. Her heart pounded as she glanced at Hubert and Gawain, who stood braced before them with ancient bronze swords in hand. She had to help! Casting about for something to wield in their defense, she seized a long iron candle stand and ordered the others back. Old Fenwick grabbed up another stand and shuffled grimly forward as well . . . just as the door planks began to splinter.

The doors shuddered and shook . . . the hinge bolts gave way . . . and one door went crashing down. The duc and his men swarmed into the chamber with weapons raised and began slashing and hacking at Hubert and Gawain. The screams and wails of the women elders jolted Thera into action, and she swung the candle stand with all the energy of her fear and anger.

Again and again she swung, always just a bit too slow to connect with a black-clad form, but managing to keep them at bay. Through the blood pounding in her head, she heard cries and saw Hubert crumple . . . there was a clang and suddenly Gawain lay on the floor, too. Then they came at her . . . three and four at once . . . or more. But all she could see was the duc's burning eyes and his ugly sneer as he closed in on her.

They lunged all at once and seized the candle stand . . . and after a frantic struggle, the duc's hands dug cruelly into her arms. She fought, kicked, and screamed . . . but he managed to haul her hard against him. His arms tightened fiercely around her, and when she felt an edge of steel against her throat, her struggles slowed.

"Now, my treacherous little bitch," he said with a ragged sneer, "I'm going to make you sorry I ever laid eyes upon you."

Outside the front doors, Saxxe and Gasquar were still busy with the duc's men. Castor and Pollux proved surprisingly capable bladesmen, though not quite as skillful with blades as they were with longbows. With their help, Saxxe and Gasquar were able to fight their way toward the gardens, where the duc and his men had disappeared. In desperation, Saxxe reached into his sinews for added strength and charged, hacking and slashing full out. His opponent faltered at his fierce cry and savage assault, and went down with the next stroke. Saxxe whirled on Gasquar's opponent, then together they turned to help Castor and Pollux. Within moments, the last black-clad soldier fell and all was eerily still.

They staggered for a moment, catching their breaths, listening to the muffled roar of flames at the far end of the palace and to the roar of their own blood. "This way," Saxxe said, leading them back to the east gardens and into the palace through his own chambers. In the distance they could hear thudding and shouts that sounded as if they came from the Great Hall.

But as they sped through the corridor, the pounding became splintering and cracking sounds, and the shouting became battle cries and shrieks of terror. They ran toward those chaotic sounds of fighting, but just as they reached the Great Hall, the noise abruptly stopped. They halted, searching the main hall . . . and found the doors to the council chamber hanging open, one splintered and half ripped from its iron hinges. They hurried forward, then halted just outside the chamber, listening.

"Do come in." The duc's voice floated out upon the unnatural silence.

When Saxxe and Gasquar stepped through the doorway, they saw the elders backed against the far wall by sword-wielding soldiers, old Fenwick crumpled on the steps, Hubert leaning against a chair and clutching a wounded shoulder, and Thera held captive in the duc's arms . . . with a dagger at her throat.

"I have been waiting for you," the duc crowed maliciously. "You're the one who was a guest in my camp . . . all too briefly. But I don't believe we've been introduced." He pressed the dagger a bit tighter against Thera's throat. "Introduce us, Princess."

"Saxxe," she said with desperate defiance. "King Saxxe. My husband."

The duc trembled with sudden anger. "Lying, worthless strumpet! He's a common dog of a soldier . . . a hireling . . . a mercenary!"

"Yea, I was all of that—and more," Saxxe declared, his voice borne on a current of controlled fury. The sight of Thera with a knife at her throat roused every nerve and fiber of his body to a killing rage. "But as of this day I am Thera's husband and king of this good land. If you would have my throne, you motherless bastard . . . you must come and take it from me."

He raised his blade tip, curled his huge shoulders forward into a stalking crouch, and beckoned the duc with his free hand.

The duc hesitated, his eyes darting to his captain and then to his men, who watched him even as they watched their prisoners. His lip curled and he straightened regally. "I'll not sully my hands with a piece of refuse like you," the duc snarled. "Take him, Scallion."

For a moment, there was hardly a breath taken or expelled in the chamber. Saxxe had issued a personal challenge, and the duc had passed it off to a subordinate. The captain, understanding better than his lord that rank had no part in this, hesitated and circled his sword tip, then charged . . . but at Gasquar, not at Saxxe. The other soldiers wheeled to face Castor and Pollux, and the chamber rang with the sound of steel on steel.

"You let others do your fighting for you!" Saxxe taunted with a sneer, stalking closer, beckoning, trying not to look at Thera's agonized blue eyes or be distracted by the sounds of fighting. "Perhaps you only have stomach for watching other men fight and die in your stead." He saw the duc's eyes flicker . . . saw him wet his lips . . . saw the sweat popping on his brow. And he added one last goad. The perfect taunt.

"Coward."

The duc flung Thera to the floor and roared at Saxxe with desperate fury. Saxxe's eyes fell to Thera and his heart convulsed, not knowing if the duc had cut her. But a moment later the duc's blade came crashing down on his and he was jolted back to the deadly ring of steel and the vibration of the blow up his arms.

The duc bore in on him, hacking and downcutting with deadly fury. Saxxe countered defensively at first, slinging the blows aside while retreating and gathering himself. Then, after a few exchanges, his battle-honed reflexes snapped back from the shock of seeing Thera go down. And his rage erupted, crackling through the edge of his blade, discharging in a stream of lightning-force blows that sent the duc staggering.

They lunged and swung, dodged and hacked, coming hilt to hilt again and again, then breaking apart and swinging again. The duc's blade tip edged just a bit too close, and Saxxe's fatigue-slowed response was just a bit too slow . . . the duc drew first blood.

But the pain fired Saxxe's determination, and once more he reached deep into his reserves for a last burst of power that would finish his opponent. With barbarian rage welling in his blood, he let go a cry that was half battle cry, half animal roar and charged in for the kill. The duc's blade faltered at that unearthly sound, and the fighting beast that Saxxe had become for that moment tore through his last parry and sent his blade slicing through the duc's black heart.

For a terrifying moment, the duc stood, suspended by surprise . . . then his blade toppled from his hand and he crumpled into a heap. The sense of their lord falling threw Scallion and the others into a desperate rally. But their cause was lost. The captain and his men fought recklessly, but before long they lay on the floor as well. The echoes of steel and the cries of falling men reverberated in the chamber, then died away.

Saxxe staggered about to find Thera shoving to her feet. "Thera—" he cried hoarsely. Dropping his blade with a clang, he lurched toward her. She met him with open arms and they embraced with desperate force.

A tumult of relief broke out around them . . . tears, frantic voices, and heartfelt prayers. The elders rushed to see to Hubert and Fenwick, leaving Thera and Saxxe alone for a moment.

Thera's heart seemed to be skipping beats, and tears were burning down her face. Saxxe felt so warm and solid, and she could hear the powerful and reassuring thudding of his heart. When he started to push her back to look at her, she shook her head.

"No," she said against his chest, pulling him close again. "Just hold me . . . and let me hold you."

"There is more to do, Thera," he whispered finally, setting her back. She took a deep breath, wiped away her tears, and squared her shoulders.

With weapons drawn, Saxxe and Gasquar led a sweep through the palace, looking for stray soldiers. There appeared to be little damage, and they found no evidence of more intruders until they neared the kitchens. Smoke hung in the air and strange banging and ringing noises, and what sounded like muffled screams, billowed along the corridor, halting them on the steps leading down to the kitchens. Saxxe and Gasquar waved Thera and the others to stay behind and motioned Castor and Pollux to the other side of the corridor. They crept forward, listening to the grim sounds, then at Saxxe's signal rushed through the doors with their blades raised.

Their battle cries died, mere gurgles in their throats, and they lowered their swords in astonishment at the sight that greeted them. There, in the middle of the smoky, fire-damaged kitchen, stood the sooty but still formidable Genvieve with her sleeves rolled up and a long wooden bread paddle in her hands. Around her were her half-drenched kitchen folk bearing fire irons, brooms, and buckets. On the floor, at her feet, were four of the duc's men, trussed and sitting with their backs to each other . . . large metal pots and iron kettles overturned on their heads.

"This'll teach you murderin' thievin' scum . . . try to burn my kitchen, will you," she growled, letting go with a swing that set two of the kettles ringing over the soldiers' heads so that they howled and begged for mercy.

Saxxe stared at the inventively vengeful cook, then at Gasquar, in astonishment . . . and began to laugh. Genvieve turned with fire in her eyes, but when she saw Saxxe and Gasquar and Thera, she reddened and dropped a polite bow.

"Everything's under control here, Yer Graces. This lot won't be causin' no more mischief . . . not after we get done with 'em."

"Of course they won't," Saxxe said to Thera as they headed outside, laughter purging some of their tension. "They'll be deaf as posts!"

With the palace secured, Saxxe and Thera hurried to the main doors and joined a number of the elders standing on the terrace, looking out over the city. Thera gasped at the pall of smoke that had spread over the southern section, and Saxxe drew her tight against his side.

"It looks worse than it is," he assured her. "Castor said they fired the forge and stables, but that Mattias got the horses out in time."

Thera nodded grimly, trying to focus on the fact that most of the city had escaped damage. But as the wind shifted, it became clear that a significant part of the smoke was coming from the main market square. And as they searched the rooftops, she realized what was happening even as Cedric pointed and called out: "The church—the church is on fire!"

They rushed into the city streets with the elders close behind. The closer they came to the square, the more the streets were littered with debris—broken furnishings, splintered wood, crumpled bodies of soldiers in black mail. And here and there were Mercians being tended by others . . . or helped to their feet. Thera stopped by each to see how they were and found only one dead and few seriously wounded.

With grim relief, she pressed on toward the square. Suddenly there was a great rumbling all around . . . which seemed to come from under the ground itself. They stopped just steps from the market square, staring at each other and at the vibrating houses in astonishment. There was a deafening roar, and for a terrifying instant the air filled with hot billows of smoke, dust, and ash. Saxxe grabbed Thera and pulled her against a nearby wall, shielding her with his body. But moments later, as the rumbling stopped and the air cleared, he released her, took her hand, and ran with her toward the marketplace.

One entire wall of the church had collapsed, taking the domed roof and parts of the other walls down with it. Smoke rose thinly from the middle of the collapsed roof, and as they stood, staring at it in shock, Saxxe felt a little sick inside. He couldn't have guessed that firing and collapsing the tunnel would undermine the church itself. Thera spotted the soot-stained priests and sexton sitting on an overturned cart among a number of equally grimy townspeople.

"We tried, Yer Grace," the elder priest said, coughing. "We saved the altar vessels and Holy Scriptures, but the rest . . . It was too much . . . too hot. . . ."

Thera squeezed the priest's reddened hands and touched the sexton's sooty arm, then turned away to stare at the wrecked church. Saxxe took her by the shoulders and made her look at him.

"We still have a lot to do. There's still an army camped at our gates."

A short while later, Saxxe and Gasquar led a mounted party through the valley toward the western pass. They arrived to find tensions high among the archers who defended the passage. The mood of the dark horde below had turned ugly, and here and there in the throng, Saxxe could see hastily constructed ladders meant for scaling the cliff walls. He and Gasquar and several of the elders removed the bodies of the duc and his captain from horses and started up the slope to the top of the cliff with them. Thera began to follow, but Saxxe halted her.

"Are you sure you want to see this?" he said, watching her troubled eyes. "It may not even work."

"They're my people. I want to be there, whatever happens," she replied with a determined expression. He took a deep breath and waved the others on.

When they reached the top, Saxxe called out to the leader of the force, declaring that the Duc de Verville was dead. There was some wrangling, and the burly captain left in charge there accused Saxxe of lying. The duc, he declared, was an immortal who would live forever. A roar went up from the horde and they brandished their weapons.

Then Saxxe and Gasquar flung the bodies over the cliff edge and onto the slope between the armed force and Mercia's hills. "There is your immortal duc!" Saxxe shouted. "You'll meet the same fate ... and worse ... if you try to invade Mercia!"

The soldiers sent out scouts to examine the bodies, and when their identity was confirmed there was a rumble of confusion through the battle-hardened mercenaries. "Turn away," Saxxe shouted. "Go back to your camp and divide the duc's riches as your wage. You'll find nothing among us except your death!"

The captain tried to rally the mercenaries with hot words and promises of riches. But a deepening silence fell over the assembly. After a tense interval, one soldier near the front sheathed his sword and turned his horse, picking his way back down the trail. Another followed, then another. Soon the mercenaries were moving down the mountainside in numbers.

At the sight of them leaving, Saxxe turned to Gasquar with a grin, then to Thera and the others. "They're going— we did it!" A cheer went up. He swept Thera up in his arms and hugged her, murmuring, "It's over now ... finally ... truly over."

Leaving a small force of archers at the pass, they rode back to the city with rising spirits. Everyone had stories to tell, and by the time they reached the city some of the sparkle was back in Thera's eyes.

They rode past the burned forge, and she pointed to the three hearths, newly constructed, still standing among the wreckage. Saxxe grinned and declared it proof that Mercia's stonemasons were the best anywhere. The stables were a burned-out hulk, but Mattias was overseeing a temporary arrangement for the horses . . . proud that his stablemen had conducted themselves with conspicuous valor.

Riding on through the streets, they assessed the damage and found it surprisingly light. Casualties had been remarkably few, and already the physicians and goodwives were seeing to the injured. The people had taken a number of prisoners and had already sentenced the survivors to hard labor . . . clearing their streets and setting the damage to rights.

Up and down each street they rode and were greeted with joy and relief, especially when Cedric called out the news that the dark horde had dispersed from Mercia's gates. And there were stories here, too. "The tailor Lucian's wife, Faye . . . she got two with her skillet when they broke into his shop!" and "You should've seen Rousseau, the cooper, an' me, Yer Grace! We took down three of 'em . . . ringed 'em up proper!"

"Three?" came a hoot in response. "That's nothing . . . Michael, the baker . . . he clouted three with one swing of a bread trough!"

"Well, Benelton, the weaver, and his daughters"—chimed in a third voice—"they took down seven at one time . . . and wi' just a net of yarn!"

Saxxe rolled his eyes at Thera. "They've got a whole new set of numbers to argue about now." When she laughed, looking at him with eyes brightened by prisms of tears, Saxxe felt a huge weight sliding from his heart.

They rode to the terraces of the palace and dismounted. Saxxe pulled Thera back against his chest and wrapped his arms around her, turning her so that she could look out over the city. She drew a deep, shuddering breath.

"So much destruction," she said gravely. "Look what they did to my city." Then she glanced up at him and corrected herself. "*Our* city. Our beautiful church . . . our stables, our forge . . ."

"It can be rebuilt, Thera. We can rebuild it all," he said. "Perhaps even better. And this time we'll build a few city walls and a proper garrison." He shifted to look at her. "You know, don't you, that those soldiers are carrying away with them news of Mercia's existence and location. Your little realm won't be a secret anymore."

She thought about it and scowled worriedly. "More of the world coming to our doorstep, with its greed and violence."

"Yea, there will be some of that," he agreed, then smiled. "But there will be good things as well . . . writings and new ways and inventions . . . and good people. You've seen the worst, of late. But there is a lot of good to be had in the world as well. I've seen it, Thera." He saw her eyes welling with tears again and turned her in his arms.

"But my people are so—"

"Your people—" He caught himself and laughed. "*Our* people are smart and strong and resourceful, just like their queen. They'll come through, Thera. And it will be our task to prepare them for it and to guide them as they do. *Dieu*—just look how they defended themselves today . . . and against hard-bitten mercenaries. You can depend on them, Thera, just as you can depend on me."

He held her eyes with his, smiling, then grinning until she couldn't help but catch his confidence. And as they stood in the lowering sun, watching the evening breeze carrying away the smoke and the sunset washing the city in a red-and-golden light, she felt a new joy taking hold of her heart.

Up the steps from the city came Gasquar and Lillith, buoyed along by a contingent of elders. Soon Saxxe and Thera were inundated with reports of injuries and prisoners and estimates of how long it would be before the damage was repaired. In due time, Elder Audra stepped forward to make her special report with reddened eyes and a quivering chin.

"And the church, Your Highness," she choked out, wringing her hands. "When it burned, the Sacred Scrolls went as well. Destroyed. It's a tragedy . . . an irreplaceable loss. The laws, the *prophecies* . . . whatever shall we do without them?"

All were silent for a moment as Thera bit her lip and sought Cedric's eyes. He was trying his best not to burst into a blasphemous grin. She composed herself, straightened in Saxxe's embrace, and said solemnly, "We shall have our clerks and scribes write the laws down again, that's what we'll do."

"But what about the prophecies?" Audra moaned.

Hubert, whose injured arm was wrapped against his body, answered. "Maybe it's best they're gone . . . look at the worry they caused us. Maybe it's best we don't know what the future holds."

Audra sputtered and turned to Jeanine, who looked outraged.

"Well, if it'll make ye feel any better, Audie," old Fenwick proclaimed, hobbling down from the palace on the arms of two servants, "I'll write ye some." He wheezed a laugh at Audra's reddened face and raised a gnarled finger. "Startin' with . . . Prissy here's first babe will be a boy . . . handsome as his father and stubborn as his mother. An' he'll be born nine months from their seventh night. . . ."

"Excellent prophecy!" Saxxe declared with a grand laugh. He bent and scooped Thera up into his arms. "Fenwick . . . I appoint you head prophet." And as the old man cackled, Saxxe turned and strode with her in his arms, up the terraces and into the palace.

"Wait—what are you doing?" Thera demanded, wriggling in his grip as he carried her through the charred and wrecked doors and into the Great Hall.

"I believe I owe you a debt, Your Highness." He grinned wickedly. "And unlike *some* members of this royal family, I always pay my debts promptly."

"But we've duties and obligations . . . a thousand things to do!"

"At least that many," Saxxe said with a lusty gleam in his eye. "And I feel sure I can depend on you to count every one of them."

"Saxxe!" she groaned, looking for some way to halt him and catching a glimpse of Gasquar carrying Lillith in much the same fashion. Lillith waved with a glowing smile and held up three fingers, pointing to Gasquar. And as Saxxe turned toward Thera's quarters, she surrendered, smiling. And over his shoulder, so Lillith could see, Thera held up seven fingers.

Saxxe carried her straight to her quarters, straight through her solar, and into her bedchamber. He walked straight down the steps of the bathing pool and ducked under the water with her. When she came up sputtering, he set her on her feet with a joyful laugh and kissed her breathless.

"I'm going to give you a night you'll never forget, Thera of Aric," he said, his eyes alight and his hands flying over her laces. "And—who knows?—I may even give you a son." He stripped the wet silk from her shoulders and replaced it with his lips, murmuring, "But first this barbarian is going to give his princess a bath."

BETINA KRAHN

Winner of the *Romantic Times* Lifetime
Achievement Award for Love and Laughter

CAUGHT IN THE ACT
75778-8/$4.50 US/$5.50 Can

In a Tudor England teeming with intrigues and absurdities, a daring thief of hearts and an innocent, yet ingenious, young beauty will be undone by rapturous, irresistible love.

BEHIND CLOSED DOORS
75779-6/$4.99 US/$5.99 Can

A sheltered English rose and virile "Viking" nobleman are drawn together by reckless passion—surrendering to the forbidden ecstasy of soul-searing love.

MY WARRIOR'S HEART
76771-6/$4.99 US/$5.99 Can

Only by conquering the spirited woman whose breathtaking beauty haunts his dreams can Jorund win the respect of his people...and quench the searing flames of his desire.

And Coming Soon

THE PRINCESS AND THE BARBARIAN
76772-4/$4.99 US/$5.99 Can